HEY, GOOD LUCK
OUT THERE

HEY, GOOD LUCK OUT THERE

GEORGIA TOEWS

DOUBLEDAY CANADA

Doubleday Canada and colophon are registered trademarks of Penguin Random House Canada Limited

Library and Archives Canada Cataloguing in Publication

Title: Hey, good luck out there / Georgia Toews.
Names: Toews, Georgia, author.
Identifiers: Canadiana (print) 20210380586 | Canadiana (ebook) 20210380594 |
    ISBN 9780385696715 (hardcover) | ISBN 9780385696722 (EPUB)
Classification: LCC PS8639.O386 H49 2022 | DDC C813/.6—dc23

This book is a work of fiction. Names, characters, places and incidents are products of the author's imagination or are used fictitiously. Any resemblance to actual events or locales or persons, living or dead, is entirely coincidental.

Jacket design by Emma Dolan
Jacket illustration based on a photo by Cordelia Molloy/Science Photo Library/Getty Images

Printed and bound in Canada

Published in Canada by Doubleday Canada,
a division of Penguin Random House Canada Limited

www.penguinrandomhouse.ca

10 9 8 7 6 5 4 3 2 1

Penguin
Random House
DOUBLEDAY CANADA

For my mom.

Part I

"Will she run?" asked the counsellor.

The question startled my mother. She looked at me. I shook my head.

"Don't run," said the counsellor. "You're going to be happy you didn't."

We all smiled at each other, politely. A silent agreement: nobody runs, everyone gets out of here alive.

But after that? What happens then?

The counsellor, whose name was Barb, according to the name tag on the lanyard that hung around her neck, asked me to take a seat in the hall. I listened to Barb and my mother sort out my future.

"It works if she works the program," said Barb.

They came into the hall. My mother was obviously trying to think of something encouraging to say, but fell short.

"I love you so much."

She leaned over and hugged me, then quickly straightened and walked towards the door. I looked at her at the end of the beige hall, she was trying not to cry, smiling at me.

"It's like you're going off to war."

"You think they allow guns in here?"

"You're gonna be okay."

I wanted to finish the stupid joke, I was gonna say, "'Cause I'm packing two!" But she was crying now, and then I was crying. I stood and she came back and hugged me again and told me my father would drop off some books. And then she was gone.

Barb took me to a small room. There was a circular table with a few chairs, a microwave and a pale green couch with pink flowers. Two large plants were dying in the corner, which I found a bit ominous, especially since they were leaning against a poster for "Living Well! A Woman's Guide to Taking Back Her Power!" I couldn't read the fine print on how a woman was supposed to do that, maybe I would learn later on in my stay.

Barb brought out a large stack of paperwork and started ticking boxes.

"You're here for alcohol, any other substances?"

"Not like, consistently."

"Do you use other substances?"

"I've tried um, other stuff. I guess mostly cocaine, I used to smoke weed—"

"Opiates?"

I had only tried heroin once. At first I thought it was great, then I puked all over the floor of a popular Irish pub. I stood outside the bar for a while trying to see straight, and I remember a young, attractive man complimenting my boots. I looked up and saw he was with a girl I went to high school with. She was drunk and laughing, they were mocking me, they didn't like my boots.

"My dad gave me Percocets when I got gum surgery."

"They weren't prescribed?"

"No. But I was in a lot of pain."

"We hear that a lot."

I watched her tick more boxes.

"Um, is there a place to exercise? Or work out if we have free time and we're bored?"

"No, we can't encourage that. It's not fair to offer activities that can't be inclusive."

"But aren't endorphins good for you?"

"You can go for short walks."

"I just thought it would be nice to do sit-ups or lunges, or . . . something."

"Do you have an eating disorder?"

I felt the waistband of my jean shorts digging into my stomach. They'd been given to me by a friend in high school shortly before she tried, unsuccessfully, to kill herself. It occurred to me that maybe these shorts were cursed and I should get rid of them.

"No, I don't have an eating disorder."

"Are you sure?"

I had tried to have an eating disorder. In junior high and high school I would hold out as long as I could through the days, just drinking water. Then I would get home and feel guilty about not eating dinner. I didn't want my father to feel as though I didn't value his cooking, or my mother to worry that my abstention from family dinners was somehow her fault.

"I'm very sure."

"You're going to be very busy. You won't have time to exercise."

"My dad's gonna drop off books."

"As long as they're appropriate. I have an eating disorder, bulimia," said Barb. "I can tell when it's a problem."

I'd never been able to throw up soberly. I'd tried, I'd spent a terrifying few hours scrolling through pro-ana websites when I was fifteen. I'd kind of hoped I'd just fall into some sort of disordered thinking and come out of it a week or two later thinner, more beautiful, happier. I didn't like the idea of joining an online forum in hopes of instigating it though. They seemed militant in what they expected: total starvation and/or constant purging.

I watched as Barb rifled through the things my father had packed for me, which included, for some reason, all of my fanciest underwear. I could've been more embarrassed, but I just watched, numb, as she pulled out lacy blue and green thongs. I worried for a moment when she went through my wallet. I was quite certain I still had a flap of cocaine hidden in one of the compartments, but she found nothing.

"And when was the last time you used?"

"Um, shit—shoot, sorry. I did one line last night. It was like, cheap though. It didn't do anything."

She stared at me, snapping her gum. It was the first time I had done cocaine sober, and it hadn't had much of an effect. Maybe it blurred my judgment a little? My older brother had flown in from New York a week ago, under the guise of attending a work conference that never seemed to materialize. Last night, before my surprise intervention, organized on the sly and attended by my entire family, my brother had said he just wanted to hang out, so we went to a movie, but it was sold out and we ended up watching this arthouse film, *Enter the Void*. I didn't really get it and found the ending to be especially awkward. My brother cried the whole time. I probably should have picked up on his sadness and made light of the film, but . . . I apparently *was* high off one shitty line of cocaine.

I tried to make a joke. "Shoulda had a Red Bull instead."

"Should we be sending you to detox?" said Barb. "When was your last drink?"

"Detox? I think I'm good? I don't feel physically like . . . My last drink was, I think, three days ago?"

It was a bit of a lie, but three days ago I was tremendously drunk, and I'd had to sober up in a hospital room with a big camera pointed at the bed I was told to stay in, so the doctors could watch to make sure I wasn't dead or self-harming after my mother had begged them to put me on a twenty-four-hour psych hold. They only kept me for twelve, they were short on beds. When I got out, my mother let me back into my apartment one last time, alone, to grab a few things before sweeping me off to her home in Peterborough. She must have thought she'd removed all the alcohol and drugs (I had kept my cocaine hidden in my wallet), but I remembered I had a half-drunk orange soda spiked with vodka sitting in the bottom of my garbage in a McDonald's cup. Most of it had leaked out and been watered down by the day-old melted ice, so . . . the amount I managed to drink seemed negligible.

"Any withdrawal symptoms—hot flashes, nausea, seizures?"

I had been terrified of my mother smelling the booze on me, either driving me right back to the hospital or, even worse, just driving away. After the McDonald's cup, I pried the little plastic stopper off a small bottle of oregano oil and drank that. I had diarrhea for the next twenty-four hours, which was awful but also made the other hangover symptoms seem, again, negligible.

"No. Guess I'm not that bad, right?"

"Why do you think you're here then?"

I shrugged, trying to appear brave, like I truly wasn't "bad."

"Your life has become unmanageable because of your addiction to alcohol and substances."

I felt compelled to nod, hoping my compliance would expedite this one on one. The room was starting to feel even smaller.

"Here is our schedule, and your welcome package."

In the package there was a new toothbrush, toothpaste, a few stickers, along with an agenda like the kind I had in elementary school.

"Routine is important."

"I have an appointment booked—"

"Your mother told us on the phone; you can't cancel?

"No . . . I can't like, I can't cancel it."

"Well, we can't keep you from going to medical appointments if they are absolutely necessary."

She looked at me, waiting for confirmation it *was* absolutely necessary, in response I burst into tears, realizing I was the villain here, not the victim, not that I wanted to be either. I was so hungry and tired and pissed off and sorry for myself and I hated the shitty breakroom and Barb's bulimia. Her bulimia had nothing to do with it actually. I just wanted to attack her and that was the only thing I really knew about her other than she was from Sweden or Switzerland or maybe Montreal, I wasn't listening well.

"You won't have chores until Monday, and technically your program doesn't start until then, so tonight you don't have to go to a meeting, but tomorrow you will have to."

"But tomorrow doesn't count."

"Right. It's good timing though. Dinner is about to start, I can introduce you."

I nodded and in a terrible moment reached for her hand, to hold, to guide me. She looked at my outstretched palm. I swiftly jerked it towards the door, hoping it came across as an "after you" gesture.

I was loudly snorting up snot and wiping away my self-pitying tears as she led me into the dining area. There were six round tables, and then a larger rectangular one where the counsellors, all wearing lanyards, sat. There was also a couch, a TV, and a few bookcases with games I recognized from dentists' waiting rooms.

"This is the dining area, and you can have your free time here. That's one of two payphones—you're all set with a calling card?"

I nodded.

"Hi, ladies, just wanted to take a quick sec, we have a new intake with us—"

The rest of her words were a blur. Some women stared back at me as I looked around the room; some into their food, bored; a few smiled politely; one smirked and bared her teeth at me, laughing as she gurgled her water. I followed the counsellor, who sat me down at a table and placed a plate of macaroni and ham casserole, with a small side of deflated green beans, in front of me.

"We do plate checks. I would eat. After dinner, come on back to the office and we'll get you into a room."

I nodded at her, and she went to get her own dinner and then joined the counsellors at the far table. I watched her as she tentatively picked at her food, maybe she wanted me to have an eating disorder so we could talk about it together. Maybe she'd go home later to eat a better meal. The rest of the counsellors seemed to pick at their food as well, but when the chef came out from the kitchen they all thanked her for another great meal and she bowed in gratitude, smiling at all of us women, proud of her work.

"I'm Steph. It sucks here, but it's better than some programs."

Steph had a deep, raspy voice for someone who looked barely five feet tall. Her dark hair was badly bleached into a patchy orange, and wild curls were pulled back tightly to a ponytail at the top of her head, which gave her an extra couple of inches. She resembled a pineapple I used to learn French from in elementary school. She had smudged mascara around her wide-set large brown eyes. When she smiled at me, I noticed her two front teeth crossed over on another, and her face was scabbed and slightly picked at. She was so young, you could almost chalk it up to a rough day on the playground. She must have been just eighteen, but just.

"Least you can smoke here."

That was Madison. I recognized her but couldn't remember from where. She had glossy blond hair extensions that clung to dark roots, and small blue eyes that, opposite to Steph's, crowded her large pointed nose and thick puffy lips that looked manufactured. She stared into a compact and plucked her eyebrows instead of eating. She was probably only in her mid-twenties. Despite the deep lines around her eyes and her gaunt cheeks, a swath of baby fat still clung to her jaw.

"Where couldn't you smoke?" Steph asked, pulling her fraying sweater down over her palms.

"Up in Uxbridge, I was there last year."

"This is Mad's fourth time," Steph said to me.

I gathered that Steph and Madison were friends, despite Madison being older and much more glamorous. She put down her tweezers dramatically and cocked her head to look at me.

"Some people are sicker than others."

I didn't know how to respond. She made it seem like she had a cancer that kept coming back despite aggressive treatment. I nodded and turned back to Steph. Madison turned back to the tweezers.

"Is it your first time?"

I saw Madison roll her eyes, but Steph smiled warmly at me again.

"I'm what you call a frequent flyer," Steph said. If she felt any shame, she covered it up with a shrug, pulling at her sleeves again.

"Is that normal?"

It was the wrong thing to ask. What was normal? I looked at the cast of women sitting around me, some making small talk, some picking at their shitty food, and they all looked like normal fucking women in some bleak cafeteria, even the gurgler who intimidated me. I didn't know what I'd expected, more physical cues of suffering, track marks and missing teeth, women shivering and screaming in corners, bloodshot eyes.

Steph was scratching her forearms under the table, still smiling at me. "You hope not, right? Least you got a family that loves you, or you're rich."

"I'm not rich," I said.

"You're coming in on a Saturday, which means you paid or came from jail."

Madison looked offended. "I didn't come from jail."

"'Cause you came in on Monday, bitch."

"I came in on Tuesday 'cause detox was a bitch, bitch."

Steph looked at me. "You didn't do detox, right?"

"No, they said—"

"Alcoholics like, never have to detox, it's a fucking joke." Madison clicked her teeth at me.

"It's like, a thing," Steph intervened, I could tell she was trying to diffuse the situation. "Like, alcoholics get McDonald's and addicts get methadone. We're both here for heroin."

"I'm just an addict, period." Madison said defiantly. She seemed angry with me.

I started sweating. "Sometimes I do drugs," I said, trying to impress her.

Madison snapped her compact mirror shut and cocked her head at me once more.

"Like I said, some people are sicker than others."

"Do you wanna smoke with us?"

Steph was so kind, and I felt embarrassed not to be as far gone as the beautifully mean Madison. I just wanted to find somewhere to cry again. Plus I didn't smoke. Another failed addiction. I imagined trying to light a cigarette, fumbling with the lighter, promising Madison that "sometimes I smoke too!" I shook my head and they promptly left without me. I thought about calling my mother, asking her if maybe we could just bank this whole rehab experience. I'd come back when I was an industry professional like Steph and Madison, a full-blown addict on whatever they're pumping out on the streets. She would have to believe I wasn't that bad. Not comparatively.

I found my counsellor and she led me to my room. It was in the corner of the third floor, there weren't many rooms that high up. She paused at a chalkboard and told me if I felt inspired I could write a nice message. I looked at the chalkboard: someone had drawn a flower and the anarchy sign, which the counsellor erased before showing me a boardroom across the hall from my new abode.

"We rarely have meetings here, and you're not to be in here alone, touching the TV or anything."

"Do a lot of women touch the TV?"

"They'll push it. Any way they can."

I had a very strong urge to touch the TV.

The door to my room was closed, which upset my counsellor, she rapped on it impatiently. She told me my roommate's name was Helena. A very tall tattooed and tan woman, maybe in her early twenties, answered the door wearing two towels, one on her head and one across her body. The counsellor left us, me standing in the doorway smiling, the tall woman dripping and staring.

"You gonna bring your stuff in?"

"Yup."

I placed my suitcase and purse on the bed, not sure of how to introduce myself, wondering if she'd already seen me crying in the common area.

"Do you mind?"

"Sorry?"

"I have to change."

"Right."

I turned away from her, pretending to study the wall.

"No, you have to leave. When the door is shut, that means I'm changing."

"Okay."

"Take your purse. I won't steal anything, but just get used to having it on you."

"Okay."

I left the room and she closed the door loudly behind me. I wasn't sure where to go but felt very odd waiting right outside the door. I stared at the chalkboard. I could eat the chalk, I did that as a child, my first-grade teacher caught me and humiliated me in front of the class. But this was coloured chalk and as a connoisseur I knew it wasn't as good as the white stuff.

I was hoping I'd have a roommate I could be friends with. Like in an '80s teen movie, we'd get ready for meetings together. We'd be okay changing in front of each other. We'd both have our impossibly perky breasts exposed as we danced and laughed because we were both confident in our bodies and understood our nudity together was not sexual but a defining moment of sisterhood. I did not have impossibly perky breasts, however, and she did not seem like the type to dance to "Gloria" by Laura Branigan while applying frosted blue eyeshadow and teasing her hair. She finally opened the door.

"Jesus, there's benches and like, magazines."

"Oh, sorry, I didn't know. I didn't mind though."

I'd never pissed so many people off by being polite before.

She had already walked away, inside our room. She continued getting ready in a small mirror over the sink.

"Are you coming tonight?"

"No, she said I didn't have to. Think I'm gonna sleep."

"Well, you're fucking lucky. I'm sorry I'm just like, PMSing and like, not in the mood to go to fucking church."

"Even when I'm not PMSing, I don't want to go to church."

She turned to me and smiled. She had absolutely perfect teeth. "Right. Fuck you're gonna hate it here. No, fuck, I shouldn't say that. It's nice like, not feeling fucked up or like, hungover right?"

"Yeah."

"But it fucking sucks. Like, what am I never gonna go out on a Thursday again with my ladies? Like, I don't wanna be that nerd but I know if I'm going out like, I'm gonna be on one.

That's the thing—they're very like, one way about things here."

"You could say you're the DD. Generally you get free unlimited pop, so . . . pretty sweet silver lining."

She laughed, I was grateful she knew I was joking.

"Fuck off with that, I need to get in shape. I feel like all I do here is eat and like, I don't eat when I drink, so I'm getting fucking fat."

She didn't look fat, she was just a very large woman, her shoulders were broad and she must have been almost six feet tall. While she swore at me, she was blow-drying her dyed jet-black hair into a very straight but full-bodied asymmetrical bob, which just added to the space she took up.

"Okay, well, I might wake you up later like, coming in."

"That's okay."

"Everything will wake you up. There's no fucking AC."

"Oh, I'm fine."

"Yeah well, I'm not, do you know about these things?" She pointed to what looked like a very old radiator.

"I think that's where hot air comes out, doesn't it?"

"Oh my god, seriously? I've been turning it on wondering where the AC is. Fuck, you think I'm an idiot."

"No, it makes sense 'cause types of air come from it."

"But not cold air! Are we both just stupid? I can't, I can't live like this. I'm not stupid, right? Don't be offended if I move rooms, okay? Don't. 'Cause I can't. See if you can figure that thing out to make the cold air come out."

Then she stormed off, briefly stomping back in to grab her purse. I hadn't moved.

"My purse, fuck. Also it's just Lenny, Len. Helena makes me sound like an old fucking woman."

"Lenny Bruce."

"Mm. Just Len."

She left. She probably hated that I was her roommate. I wondered what else she couldn't live with. What could her bottom be, if lack of cool air set her off?

It was hot in the room but I still wanted to close the door, something the counsellor had reminded me we couldn't do unless changing. I kept peeking out, wondering if someone was watching me, looking for cameras, a sign that I was under twenty-four-hour supervision. I moved to the corner of the room, where someone walking down the hallway wouldn't be able to see me, and searched through my wallet. No cocaine. I would've thrown it out if I had found it . . . or traded it? My knowledge of prison versus rehab was skewed, mostly informed by movies and *Oz*, but I had entertained the idea that I could trade a crumb of coke for something of value, protection from Madison maybe.

I thought about unpacking, looking through my clothes that the counsellor had already sorted through, but that made this all seem too permanent. The first and only time I went to a day camp, I'd lasted two days and then broke down crying to my mother, telling her how awkward I felt. My only friend was in a different group and the other kids were already close. She said I never had to go back and could spend the rest of the summer hanging out with her, or the friends I had already made in the neighbourhood, when they were around. She didn't care that I had wasted her money and quit, she just wanted me to be happy.

In my suitcase there was a neon-pink journal with gold embossed letters on the front—"Let Them Eat Cake!"—and a note from my grandmother on the inside. "For you to write your thoughts and feelings and feel better!" The edges of the paper were also gold, it was feminine and beautiful, and not deserving of my thoughts and feelings.

It felt like a cruel joke. I had willingly moved with my divorced parents to Toronto right after high school, to study creative writing. My parents both felt they needed to leave Winnipeg with its landmarks of stinging trauma and loss, so my father drove a U-Haul with all their possessions across the country, and it was here that I watched them divvy up their belongings, the remnants of our home in Winnipeg. My mother moved to Peterborough, my father was downtown, and I lived in a small dorm room in Etobicoke to attend a college that I had no real interest in attending, but, like rehab, my parents needed to put me somewhere.

During their breakdowns, and the emptying of our childhood home, I had promised I would take off when they did, maybe travel, get some life experience or something. They told me to apply to school in Toronto, just in case; they didn't want me to go so far away. Maybe I didn't want to be far away from them either, trying to hold on to some semblance of family. My brother had left a couple of years earlier, before our parents' big breakup, and was living in a makeshift room in a dance studio in Brooklyn. He hadn't had to witness the utter destruction of our nuclear family. He attended the odd family dinner, remaining stoic and unbothered. I hated him for his ability to come and go, to safely observe from a distance while I was caught on the frontlines of both our parents' mental and physical breakdowns.

At one point in my intervention, seconds before I broke down and agreed to get in the car and come here, to rehab, my brother put his hand on my shoulder and told me he loved me. I wanted to believe him, more than anyone. I wanted him back in my world, to be a more reliable witness to what we'd had when we were kids, and to what we had now. That we'd had unconditional love and safety and support and that he'd felt the fallout too. I wanted to share the weight of the loss of it all. I could forgive him for having left home if only he would protect me moving forward, not from the shitty people that came into my life, but from the pain of feeling what was lost. I wanted to talk about it, joke about it one day, instead of just crying and telling each other we fucking loved each other in times of duress.

It was really hot in that room. I kept checking the small clock radio next to my bed, listening for signs of counsellors. I didn't hear anything. I wanted time to slow down so I could continue to be alone, away from the other women. I also wanted time to speed up, to get to the end of my sentence. I looked at the journal, it was almost throbbing, it was so bright and neon and hopeful. My thoughts and feelings. I got through college, barely, not because I was genuinely talented but because I was good at slightly altering stories about people I knew, conversations I'd overheard. My teachers called my work rough but honest. I didn't like to write deep shit, stuff about *my* specific feelings, because I'd learned it could be used against you. If you take a slab of yourself and put it on a page, there's no one guaranteeing your slab is protected.

In high school, I had this teacher, Mr. Raymond. He taught AP English and we thought he was cool because he treated us like we were university students. He wore tweed blazers, had one ear pierced and never forced us to write essays. Many times he said, "Read the book, and then just record yourselves, two or three of you, having a conversation about it." I thought that was really fucking cool. He never really noticed me, and I didn't stand out academically. My mother, though sick at the time, was starting to gain recognition. She was a photographer, in a journalistic type of way. She took ugly pictures of rock stars, and beautiful pictures of regular people, and there's more to it, but it was becoming a thing. Interviews with her—talking about the humanness of her subjects, the realness—were all over the paper, the breakfast TV shows. At the end of the year, we had to write a provincial exam, it would be anonymous, we were assigned a number. The last question (which we were allowed to prepare for ahead of time because it was worth fifty percent of the overall exam) was to write anything, an essay, a short story, monologue, whatever, about anything. Just a piece of creative writing.

I trusted it was anonymous, and I trusted Mr. Raymond when he told me, despite not being academically gifted, that I was a good writer. I wrote a short story about a girl watching her parents futilely fighting for each other. The girl watched as her father drank himself almost to death on many occasions, as her mother blacked out the windows for fear of being watched, and chain-smoked in her bedroom, asking who the girl was, was she really her daughter, time and time again. The girl watched as, in moments of clarity or sobriety or just plain fucking desperation, the mother and father clung to each other on the couch, spewing half promises to save each other and half apologies for their impending divorce, a divorce they said was necessary because of how much they'd changed and, as a result, hated a large percentage of the new version of each other. The girl, invisible, watched as love fucking failed, best intentions unravelled, simple brain function gave out. The girl didn't ask to be held or for promises from her parents to stay together; they wouldn't have heard her anyway. She watched the parents lying to each other . . . night after night . . . and they didn't get better. Not for a long time.

Two weeks after writing the exam, we got our results back. I looked at the series of numbers that protected my anonymity and drew the line from that to my score. I got ninety-eight percent. I looked down the line at the other scores; there were none that came close. I kept drawing my finger from number to number to make sure that my sad little story had really garnered me ninety-eight freaking percent.

Mr. Raymond came up to me, smiling. I silently drew my finger from the list of numbers to the percentages so he could see, so he could be proud of me. He nodded. "I know."

How did he know?

"I saw it and thought I should look it over," he said. "It's good work. You got the highest mark on the provincial exam."

For a moment, I felt okay with the breach of privacy because it came with him telling me it was good.

"Did your mom help you write it?"

I didn't know if it was a joke, but I laughed, breathlessly. My mother was on a psychiatric hold after attempting suicide and I hadn't seen her for a week because she refused visitors at the hospital. I wanted to say something, to defend myself, of course she hadn't helped me; what an asshole, he'd broken the rules by reading my story, it was supposed to have been anonymous.

But instead I just smiled stupidly, and he nodded smugly, like I had confirmed that I wasn't capable of greatness.

After school, a bunch of us went and got drunk at a bush party. I met a boy who, I guess, I flirted with, because two months later, at another field at some music festival campsite, and after getting drunk again, he had sex with me while I pretended to be asleep. When I staggered back to my tent in the morning after passing out in his, everyone acted like I had "got what I wanted."

Some friends lovingly called me a slut while others shook their heads . . . and then we just went on with our day.

It was so fucking hot in this room. The meeting would be over any minute now. The journal was still empty. My thoughts and feelings. You want my thoughts and feelings? I felt like Robert De Niro in *Taxi Driver*, threatening this bright pink journal: *You talking to me? You want these fucking thoughts and feelings, you precious pink piece of shit?* My hands were sweating and the pads of my fingers left marks on the linen cover. I repeated Len's statement: I can't live like this. As though this fucking hot room was my rock bottom. Not even fucking close.

Dear Journal.

No, that was dumb, my journal wasn't a sentient being. I couldn't write quickly enough, my hand smudging my illegible handwriting.

I am not at my fucking rock bottom. I am not supposed to be here. But I go everywhere, everywhere I'm fucking supposed to. You wanted me in Toronto. I moved here. You wanted me to go to school, to go to college, and I fucking did because that's what I was supposed to do. You wanted me to lie in a fucking field and close my fucking eyes until it was over and I did. And then you put me here as if I didn't do everything I was fucking supposed to do? Like I, me, had finally reached my breaking point? Because YOU decide??? You have no idea what my fucking breaking point is, my fucking rock bottom. You just put me where you want me, but I'm not doing it this time. You don't think I can go three more rounds? I've taken bigger hits, I've taken bigger hits than anyone can fucking imagine. This isn't it. This is supposed to fix me? Talk fucking therapy and sad women supporting each other? I have fucking bled and cried and . . . it's not enough here. It's not out there. Because I'm not at fucking rock bottom.

I thought about signing my name. Almost as if it was a love letter to my family, friends, my first but not final rapist. I looked at the smudged writing like a dog owner looks at the carnage an untrained puppy leaves in their absence. I thought maybe I should tear out the pages, make the book pristine again. Where would I put the pages?

I tucked the journal at the bottom of my suitcase, but not before wrapping it in a bulky sweater, hopefully making it harder for . . . someone to find. I wasn't crazy, I just needed to put the part of me that I couldn't quiet somewhere else. I used to write down shit like that before going on a trip. *What if this plane crashes?* Almost as if by thinking and writing it down, putting it away somewhere, it couldn't happen. Sometimes it's hard to keep up with the bad thoughts. When you're driving and want to steer into oncoming traffic, you can't stop to write down what will happen. When you want to hurt someone before they hurt you, you can't ask them to pause so you can grab a pen. So your brain is filled with what ifs that become promises of revenge and anger and it's a fucking . . . it's just a defence mechanism. Like humour, I guess. But I didn't think the counsellors would get any of that if they read the journal. The monster I had left in the bottom of my bag.

I was exhausted but calm. The heat was still unbearable, I needed to leave the room, despite my paranoia that someone would enter while I was away and find the journal. I tiptoed out into the empty hallway and, after getting a bit turned around, found the payphone in the stairwell, and called my father.

"I need to leave."

I heard him sigh.

"Seriously, there's like, meth heads and criminals here like, did you know that? It's not just alcohol. It's like, bath salts and shit! What are you gonna do if someone eats my face?"

"Do you really feel that unsafe?"

"I don't belong here. You left—you left rehab because you *knew*! You knew that we don't belong here."

"That was a different situation."

"I need to go home."

"When you get out, you'll figure out a new apartment situation, you'll get a job, and you'll be fine."

"This place is a nuthouse."

"We looked at other facilities, they were far away or for, those who may be mentally ill, medicated. Your mom wanted you at least close to me—"

"Why? It's way easier to escape here! You put me in the woods and where am I gonna go? I can't camp!"

"Try to get some sleep, please, you will be okay, and—"

"Dad, I wasn't that bad."

"Well . . . you were."

"So were you!" I only half hissed it at him, immediately losing my breath and shutting my eyes tight. I didn't want to hear some bullshit excuse about why he still gets to drink while I'm in a sober sauna.

"We're not going to do this." His words were sharp. I'd hit a nerve. I wanted to undo it, put the mean part of me in the pink journal and be soft on the phone, be his little girl again. I started to cry for the millionth time.

"I feel like you hate me."

"No one hates you."

He was never good at saying "I love you." I knew that would be the closest I got.

"Everyone hates me."

"We just want you to sleep now, okay? It's one month. Remember Belize?"

When I was sixteen, I had gone to volunteer for a month in Belize, building a small community centre with other middle- and upper-class white kids looking to bolster our college applications. We were surprised by the amount of actual manual labour we were expected to do, though I ended up loving it for the most part, embracing the disgusting amount of sweat pouring down my face while I hauled cement in a broken wheelbarrow. The other girls sat in the shade, trying to avoid the one-eyed man across the dirt road who blasted two Akon songs over and over and just sat smoking weed, watching us. I was thrilled at my adaptability and small teenage muscles, until on one of the last days I was robbed and had a panic attack. Up until then I'd felt like I could actually accomplish something.

"I can't be here."

"Get through the week. Okay?"

I went back to my room. A young, thin, and oddly fashionably dressed counsellor was in there. Len must have told her about the rad on her way out. I glanced at my suitcase, it didn't look as if anyone had opened it, and she seemed very focused on the radiator, which was leaking water all over the floor. I saw her crouch awkwardly in tight designer jeans to put baking sheets under the radiator in an attempt to catch the water. She just kept spilling more water onto the floor. She kicked the baking sheet under the radiator and finally noticed me, once again looming, once again tear-streaked, waiting in the doorway.

"I'll make a note that they should fix this, or change your rooms tomorrow. I can't make that call."

"Okay."

"I can try and get some towels."

"Sure."

"But you're supposed to bring your own."

"For showers?"

She sighed. "Keep your shoes on. I'll see if I can find something."

I stayed standing in the doorway, afraid if I tried to help, the counsellor would leave me to fix it all by myself. It was easier to pretend to be interested in the redrawn anarchy symbol on the chalkboard.

She came back with two rolls of thin brown paper towel. She stared at the radiator again.

"These never work."

"This happens a lot?"

I watched her sop up the water.

"I was in here a few times. Obviously got sober, just trying to get my hours for social work."

"At least it finally took."

"Yet I'm still back here. Dry enough?"

"Yeah, it's perfect."

"If it overflows in the middle of the night, can you use your towel?"

"Sure."

She took the soaked brown towels and left. Eventually Len came home. I pretended to wake up long enough to be sure to blame the water on the counsellor, and then went back to pretending to sleep while she muttered curse words under her breath at the radiator. I hoped she believed me.

I woke up before the alarm. Len was still asleep so I lay very still until a counsellor came by and yelled, "Feet on the floor." No one had told me you needed to fill out your breakfast sheet the evening before, so I was left with toast. There was also assigned seating. Steph was about to switch her cards to sit next to Madison when a counsellor gave her a look. So it was just me, Madison, and a lithe middle-aged woman who talked incredibly fast about her pet rabbits and her training regime and her mother who she didn't trust to treat the rabbits with enough compassion. Madison was mugging to Steph how obviously insane this woman was from across the room, but the lithe woman gave me her yogurt, a trade for nodding at her as she talked about her rabbits. I wanted to quote *Of Mice and Men* but thought better of it and continued nodding.

"She'll probably pet them," I said.

"She won't! She calls them rodents, which they obviously are, but you don't say that! You can't say that to them!"

"Rabbits aren't rodents. Rodents have different bones and like, more teeth. They're a different species."

"Exactly, every animal deserves love!"

"Yes. She will probably pet them."

"But she won't hold them!"

"Maybe not, she probably wouldn't want to lose them."

"I would die."

Most of the women in rehab seemed to immediately leap to the most dire conclusion—death or murder—in hypothetical situations. Addicts don't talk about the pain, the loss, the moments of deep sorrow that anchor us to the underbelly of society. It's always good or bad. High or low. Dead or not dead. The lithe woman would not die if she lost her rabbits, but she may not survive the pain of their absence.

I had to go to that day's meeting. I was told Sunday afternoon meetings rotate locations, both within an easy walking distance. I tried to hang around Len, but she stuck close to Steph and Madison, so I made small talk with two older women as the fourteen of us walked down Dundas. I wondered if the shop-keepers—the whole community really—knew what they were witnessing. Every second Sunday the march of the addicts. There they go, off to find salvation. Did anyone make it a game, point-ing us out from windows overlooking the street, making fake bets—"That one is definitely going back to the streets"? Because I'd have done exactly that, guess that's karma.

There were other women, besides our group, at the meeting. Some looked happy to be there, conversing with their neigh-bour as if they were ladies who lunch. A few women sat rest-lessly, waiting for the meeting to begin so they could focus on something other than the itch at the back of their neck, the cal-lous on the palm of their hand. We were in a preschool class-room in a community centre, the walls held colourful alphabet letters, along with finger-painted artwork, and a poster with the names of children followed by what they wanted to be when they grew up. I didn't read it. Pangs of jealousy, of innocent chil-dren possessing hope, even more than hope, opportunity, gave me a sudden stomach ache. I looked at the floor and focused on not throwing up.

I saw a woman hand out laminated sheets, or try to, a lot of women shooed her away, and finally she went to the front of the room, clearing her throat.

"Hi there, welcome to Second Chances this sunny Sunday, my name is Haley and I'm an alcoholic."

The women spoke in an unenthusiastic chorus, "Hi, Haley."

I didn't know it was call and response. The chosen women read from the laminated cards the rules, the steps, and a few mantras; some of the other women mouthed along with them. Then Haley spoke, telling us about her own journey into and out of addiction. I tried very hard to stay focused, to be inspired, to pull anything out of her story that could springboard me onto my own path to recovery. I couldn't. Like the first and only time I attended a Sunday evening mass at the giant Roman Catholic church across the street from my house in Winnipeg. I was ten years old and my neighbours and friends were members and I thought I would become closer to them if I too trusted in the same, or any, God. Before that service, my only connection to God had been my great aunt Amity calling repeatedly to tell my brother and me that if we didn't accept him into our hearts he would damn us to hell. That's about as far as she got before my father would pick up the phone and tell her to stop calling. My parents were young and too liberal for fundamental religious prophecies. I always likened God to Santa, a nice thing to believe in for a while, but once reality hits it's like, Okay, there's no dude bringing presents or holy miracles. Just like when I was ten in church, I didn't understand the chanting in this morning's meeting, the call and response of "Hi, Haleys" and "Amens," and as much as I wanted to want to believe that this God could make me feel loved and protected, I couldn't. I couldn't believe that

Haley or Jesus would save me from myself, nor would their congregation of lost souls. After going to church that one evening, I went home and stole my brother's Notorious B.I.G. CD, which was the furthest thing from Christlike hymns I could think of. Why would a ten-year-old white girl need Jesus when she had New York's finest gangsta rap, telling it like it really was.

At the end of the meeting, we had to hold hands and say the Serenity Prayer, something that everyone seemed to have already memorized. The holding hands was tough. I ended up between Len and another woman who was not a part of the Centre. Len seemed embarrassed and we just kind of brushed the backs of our hands together, while the woman next to me held tightly onto mine, squeezing and shaking it as the prayer ended with the exhortation, "keep coming back."

"Are all the meetings like that?" I asked Len as we shuffled out, back towards the Centre, before she could zip in front of me to smoke and chat with Madison and Steph.

"Nah, this one sucks. Some are okay. We go to a real fancy place on Thursdays and they always have snacks and shit. And don't say anything, I know I gotta stop eating those fucking little cookies."

I noticed Len's arms had tattoos of cherubs and biblical references, and she wore a delicate cross necklace.

"They're all pretty religious though?" I asked. "It's not a bad thing, I just didn't know it was such a factor."

"Ha, all the counsellors say like, it's whatever works for you and your higher power, but it's always Jesus. And for me, I'm like, Well, Jesus that hates gays or like, chill Jesus? And then they talk about stone-cold fucking killers getting sober and finding God and it's like, God's not forgiving you."

"It's a bit tough to navigate."

"What do you mean?"

"Just that it's confusing, the plan I guess, it's vague."

"Whatever keeps you sober and shit, I guess. Just gotta tell them something when they talk about your higher power."

"I'll probably say it's Biggie Smalls."

She burst out laughing—it wasn't a joke I thought warranted such an enthusiastic response—and ran up to grab the girls.

"Yo, tell them what you just said, that's so jokes."

Steph and Madison looked at me, waiting for the punchline.

"Oh, I was just like, kidding around, saying that like Biggie Smalls was my higher power."

They stared at me blankly.

"Notorious B.I.G."

Madison took a drag of her cigarette and let it cling to her lip gloss. "You should really try and find God. It's the only way out of this life."

I nodded, trying to appease her. "True that."

Then I went silent.

I stayed silent on the walk home and throughout the rest of the day, watching women preach and cry and share and bond from the bubble I had created for myself. By politely answering questions but offering none in return, I was soon ignored, my line drawn in the sand, and I wondered if I didn't speak at all in the twenty-eight days, if maybe that could be some type of meditative experience for me. It wasn't until bedtime that Len forced me into conversation again. We had moved our things to a room on the opposite side of the hall that stared into the small smoking area, in silence.

"What does this mean?"

"Yield."

"And this?"

"No right turns on a red."

"A red light?"

"Yeah."

She was flipping through a driver's ed book, making notes. She kept covering up her work with her hand like I was trying to cheat off her test.

"You studying for your learner's?"

"Yeah, I never got it 'cause I'm always too fucked up to drive, but like, maybe it'll be some sort of fucking motivation or something."

"I can help you."

"You don't have to."

"I know. I like flash cards though."

"Kay, 'cause like, fuck. I can read, right? But some of these words are like stuff I don't know. Like a lot of them. I'm not book-smart but I'm not fucking dumb."

"Okay, I'll help."

"Can we start tomorrow night? My brain's done."

"Yeah, of course."

We said goodnight, and I fell asleep dreaming of winning the lottery and buying Len a big Ford truck because we'd both stayed sober and I'd helped her get her licence and despite the odds we were friends and I was a hero.

The next morning was the start of my first official day. Our chores were posted up on the corkboard in the dining room next to the suggested community events to participate in after our departure. It reminded me of the posting of cast lists when I was a kid, excitedly huddling around a bulletin board to see how talented a part-time Winnipeg theatre teacher thought we were. I was the lead a lot. That's not bragging, or is it because I was proud of it? I don't know if I was actually ever a good actor or, like with writing, just a talented mimic. Someone would tell me to do something, and generally I could replicate their movements, their inflections and subtle facial gestures in a realistic manner. It helped me make friends when I was younger. Everyone loved to see themselves mirrored back. I knew my impersonations were good enough but never great, and receiving applause for them eventually made me angry, as if the audience was pandering to me. It wasn't *real* acting. By age twelve I felt dumb being on stage, so I quit, something I still tell myself was a great indicator of self-awareness and not, as some therapist put it in my teenage years, self-sabotage.

I got toilets. Before heading off, I quickly scribbled into my pink journal:

Dear beautiful and lovely loving journal!

Sobriety begins with cleaning everyone ELSE'S shit up! Glory be! And yes I mean that literally AND metaphorically, my lovely journal. What the fuck is this? Is this because addiction is the great equalizer? That's the point, right? The life lesson? Addiction doesn't discriminate, EVERYONE eventually ends up in shit. Because that's bullshit, but you know that. Addiction may not discriminate, but recovery . . . Cleaning toilets for a week won't change a thing.

I pushed my bed slightly away from the wall and tugged very hard at the broken drawer beneath my bed, then pushed the journal inside, all the way to the back. I felt like I had gotten away with something, like I had this dark secret that separated me from the other women, and that made me feel better.

It turned out all I had to do was restock the paper towels and toilet paper. I didn't have to touch the bathroom garbage, and any serious damage was to be reported for the actual cleaners to address. Most of our chores seemed arbitrary like that, because cleaners did come while we were at meetings. Chores were solely to get us in the habit of creating "healthy, productive routines." Routines were very key in recovery. There was a daunting print-out framed in plastic that read "No Routine or Responsibility = Relapse!!" over the sink in the kitchen. Sometimes girls assigned dish duty would purposely splash it when they weren't being watched by counsellors.

I was learning my state-of-the-art rehab centre was a glorified dormitory with two (only one in use) boardrooms, a small eating and recreational area, two offices, a waiting area, and two pay-phones. I wondered what, other than the terrible food and constant surveillance, my mother was actually paying for.

I'd been told to meet in the front foyer of the Centre after I restocked the bathrooms. Every new intake was required to have a blood test and see a doctor off-site to make sure we were physically fit to withstand our newfound routine and responsibilities. There were six of us gathered in total: myself; two older women; a pissed-off woman about my age named Ellen with a long face and a high, dark, severe bun secured on top of her head; a Stevie Nicks look-alike; and a chipper twenty-something named Kate. Kate's fingernails were long and incredibly packed with dirt, her hair was unwashed, and her thick bottle-cap glasses were smudged. When she cheerfully smiled at me, she revealed thick layers of yellow plaque on otherwise straight teeth.

The two older women were allowed to take a cab to the doctor's office on account of their limited mobility. The rest of us took public transit. A counsellor doled out bus fare from a Ziploc bag filled with tokens. I watched as Kate's encrusted fingers grabbed three or four while the counsellor was distracted watching the older women get into the cab.

"Go straight to the lab, then walk over to the doctor's office, then back here. No other stops. Did you ladies need a map?" This was yet another counsellor, and apart from the night counsellor who had tried to fix our radiator, they all seemed so far to be blond and mid-fifties, though this one was much sterner than the others.

"I know where we're going," Kate said. The counsellor sighed. She pulled me aside to hand me a map, "just in case." We never used the map because Kate was another one of the Centre's frequent flyers and promised us she knew many shortcuts that would buy us some extra time to smoke.

By the time we had reached the lab we were late, something the receptionist made clear she would be reporting back to the Centre. Kate started to cry, she hated giving blood. I looked at her badly done tattoos and various scars. I wanted to feel more empathy, but she was causing a scene amongst the general public, the elderly men and women getting blood drawn, the few do-gooders donating. Ellen looked at me and rolled her eyes. She had befriended me on the journey, enough to feel comfortable complaining about Kate after every so-called shortcut had proved useless.

"Fucking lunacy."

"I wonder if it's very obvious we all came from prison."

She smiled, then frowned at me. "You came from prison?"

"No, I was kidding, it just kinda feels like it. I just got a shitty early afternoon pizza party with my family telling me I was fucked up and . . . off I went."

She seemed unimpressed. Rightly so, it was an unimpressive intervention. My father sighing sympathetically, my brother's hand on my shoulder, my mother gently telling me this was the only option, no more bailouts for rent or bills. A lot of pizza went untouched as I robotically hugged each silent family member and got in the car, too stunned to say much of anything, and here I was. Picked up and placed, and now about to be poked by a weary-looking nurse.

"I just mean it's kinda like a prison sentence. Or like we're inmates on a day pass."

"That's funny. Humiliating in its truth, but funny."

"Thanks."

"What are you in for? Don't they say that in prison?"

"Ha, yeah, see? But, uh, just alcohol and drugs, mostly just the party stuff. Not really into psychedelics or like, meth. Not into meth at all, I mean not that there's anything wrong with meth like, using it. I mean you shouldn't use any drug I guess. But . . . meth is fine, heard you get super strong, which has its perks."

She seemed to take a while to digest what I had just rambled off at her before we were called to numbered chairs, side by side separated by short dividers. We silently watched our blood drain. Only once we were done did she speak to me again.

"I'm not in for meth. Strictly alcohol. I thought this program was exclusively for alcohol. Imagine my surprise . . ."

Kate had told us on the way that she was in for opiates, and she didn't really care which ones, just any type of pills really, benzos, uppers, downers, whatever she could get.

"Yeah, I guess sick is sick."

"I guess it is."

I longed for Ellen to like me, she seemed to command respect somehow. I wished I hadn't told her meth had perks, but she made me nervous, as did the whole losing blood situation, as did just about everything.

After the blood bank, we reconvened with the older, less mobile women at the doctor's office. The receptionist there also pointed out that we were late. Ellen's eyes seemed glued to the ceiling, stuck in a permanent roll; if we hadn't spoken, I would've been concerned she was subtly seizing. Kate was telling Stevie Nicks the names of the tattooed animals on her unwashed arms. Nelson Mandelephant was a crudely done stick-and-poke piece that wrapped around her wrist.

The waiting room was the foyer of an old Victorian house. When it was my turn to see the doctor, I was taken into the basement. The shelves, instead of being adorned with medical books and doctorates, held at least thirty mason jars of what looked like urine, and thirty ashtrays filled, exclusively, with cashew nuts.

"Blood results." He held up a file ominously, fitting for a man with an apparent urine/cashew fetish. Should I ask to eat one? Why else would they be displayed in such specific and overbearing quantities? But then I'd be stuck eating his piss nuts . . .

"Am I dying?"

"Do you believe you are dying?"

"Like, in a sense."

"Why do you believe you're dying?"

"I just meant, like, we're all dying, like, death is inevitable, yolo."

"Yolo?"

"Like, ironically."

"Recent STI tests, negative across the board. Of course, you're pregnant. Did you know that?"

"I didn't know about the STIs, so that's . . . a win. Um, but yeah, yes, I knew about the other thing."

"Eight weeks."

"Right."

"Have you thought about it?"

"The fact that I'm pregnant?"

"What your options are."

"I have an appointment next Thursday."

"With an OB?"

"No. I'm only twenty-two, um, it wasn't . . ." I shrugged, hoping that small, simple movement was a clear enough plea for the conversation to end. I didn't really think it appropriate to share the memory of finding out I was pregnant; of my ex-boyfriend Chris threatening to kill me, the embryo, and himself, in various orders depending on his mood; of how I had told Chris it was funny because if he hadn't raped me, we wouldn't be in this situation; and of how that made him madder, crueller.

"Well, other than that, you're healthy."

I wanted him to tell me it was okay, that whatever choice I made was okay.

"Still dying though, right?"

"Do you often think about suicide?"

"No."

"You seem to talk about dying a lot."

"You have a lot of cashews."

"Would you like one?"

"No, thank you."

That night was movie night. We watched *Days of Wine and Roses*, starring Jack Lemmon. A few of the girls who had cycled through the Centre complained it was boring.

I don't know why I expected movie night to be anything other than movies about alcoholism. I guess I'd figured if we watched something like Disney movies, no one would be triggered and we all might have a good time. Not to spoil the movie, but in the end, lo and behold, good ol' Jack Lemmon got sober and turned out to be a caring father. He watched his wife walk away to drink, and while, because he was a good man he wished he could help her, he knew he couldn't because she would lead him to drink again and he had to be a good father to the child she'd abandoned. It felt like a cruel joke to show a group of women in rehab. Look how much damage you can do to a man and his child if you continue to fuck up. Look how sad but very, very heroic Jack Lemmon is because his wife is a drunk and he's now a brave single father.

I'd never been one to watch movies alone. They always, no matter the genre, had a way of making me sad. Where's my inspiring-yet-generic montage of self-improvement? As Madison made clear on Sunday, I was nowhere near redemption, so I got nothing out of the movie. I preferred TV shows with laugh tracks, the tinned sound of fabricated joy was comforting white noise when I drank alone. I didn't have to guess what was funny, I didn't have to question anything, because every thirty seconds, along came the live studio audience, reminding me we were all having a good time.

———

Later that night, while Len was in the bathroom, I quickly pulled out my pink book, hoping to offload the vitriol inside of me before it kept me up all night, restless and picturing scenes where I explained to the producers of *Wine and Roses* everything that was wrong with their film.

My god you pink piece of shit journal, I got a story for you!

Fucking Jack Lemmon! I bet he's some misogynistic old man with a pill habit married to some foreign child bride—

I heard Len's footsteps and shoved the book back into the drawer, then pretended to fuss with my sheets.

"They always ride up," I told her defensively.

"I didn't sleep for the first week."

"Plus that room was so hot."

"Fuuuck. Can you imagine if we were still in there? I'd fucking leave. Like, I like waking up sober and not all fucked up but that shit . . . like, torture."

She had said that when we first met too, that it's nice to wake up sober. It was the most helpful thing anyone had said yet, because it was simple and true. It was nice not fearing waking up, knowing what lay in store for the day. Not that I ever let myself feel too hungover for too long. I was excellent at waking up early, pretending to feel fine while drinking the half-finished warm beers left behind by "friends." A learned practice from my father, who called it a "stabilizer," something I took to heart. I didn't know if waking up sober was enough, but it was something.

"Did you like the movie?" I asked.

"Fuck no," she said, turning her small lamp off, signifying our conversation was over for the evening.

I wanted to ask her more, but I knew better. I turned off my light and turned away from her, we never fell asleep facing each other.

"Hey. Hope you get some sleep." She said it quietly, towards her wall.

"Thank you."

By Tuesday morning my newness was wearing off. When I went down to breakfast, the counsellor on shift handed me a stack of books my dad had dropped off during movie night, along with letters from him and from my mother and my grandmas and my brother and my cousin. My grandmothers both wished me well on my "journey," and my cousin wrote (in printed-out text from an email), "Tell her I can't wait to catch up!" The books were mostly what I had asked for: mysteries, pulp fiction written by men. I didn't want anything I could relate to. I preferred to picture myself as a retired detective haunted by the memory of the last case he couldn't close, the last dame he let slip through his fingers, wondering, as he smoked Cubans and thumbed the barrel of his dusty .45, if he could even the score, would he have the courage to?

I should've been focused on sharing during the morning's group. Every morning we had to start by identifying ourselves by our names and addictions and then "checking in" by saying how we were feeling. Some women really got into it. No one was allowed to say they felt "okay." This morning I said I was tired, but that wasn't allowed either, so I said I was tired because "it's tough but necessary to change my sleep habits from staying up all night to a healthier routine." That pleased the counsellor, and we moved on.

As one woman talked about how wonderful her husband was and how he just wanted the best version of her, the one that bakes and can entertain guests, I watched Madison braid Steph's matted mane, as Len picked bits of fruit out of her teeth, from her breakfast yogurt cup. Those girls, Madison, Steph, and Len, were starting to talk to me more. Madison still controlled much of the direction of any conversation, whether there would be any at all, but slowly I felt I was being welcomed into their fold. Maybe because I happened to be Len's roommate, and as she put it, "I'm so glad you're not like, a fucking weirdo." I made very sure to be as "normal" as possible after that. The only problem with being closer to those girls was that I was privy to their opinions of the other women, and I felt compelled to roll my eyes alongside them when people they didn't like spoke during sharing time. They didn't like Tess.

I'd never spoken to or sat with Tess before, but I'd been commanded to speak to her. Her roommate had come back after breakfast panting and crying that someone had taken fifty dollars out of her purse, which she had left on her bed while she showered. Madison, Steph, and Len told me to strike up a conversation with Tess on our walk to the meeting to see if I could solicit a confession, with the goal of getting her kicked out.

Even Steph, who was generally so kind, couldn't stand her. "I never want anyone to like, stay sick, but stealing is where I draw the line. It's like, you gotta go bitch."

Madison, who wasn't as forgiving as her God, replied, "She's a fucking skeez. She's so negative and like, she's always lying. Everything she says is a lie, like, I can't put myself out there and heal knowing there's a rat here. And she's like Ronald McDonald with that hair and fucking beer belly."

"Oh no, that's like, belly ribbons, I think she's dying. Straight up like, that's why she's yellow," Steph said.

Madison shot her a look. "Then why is she even here? Like, go to a fucking hospital and sort your shit out. It's like a favour."

"I'm finna punch her out if she tries to steal from me," Len said. She was the muscle of the crew.

"What's finna?"

The girls looked at me. I assumed it meant "gonna," but I was hoping to distract them, maybe shift the talk to society's latest slang and its origins so I wouldn't have to go on my undercover mission. But Madison was hell-bent.

"*This* is why you gotta talk to her. You're all innocent. Go like, confide in her. Say you stole some shit."

I nodded. Her directive was clear. I looked over at Tess. She was getting ready to walk to the meeting alone, she always walked alone but in a defiant way. I took a deep breath and skipped up to join her in the front of the pack.

"I like your tattoo."

I'd caught her off guard, she jumped a bit. She always looked a little scared.

"Thanks, I actually drew it all myself."

"Yeah, I heard you say that this morning, that's so cool. I wish I could get them, they're just so expensive."

"Don't you draw too?"

"What?"

"During group, you're always doodling."

I didn't know she'd been surveilling me back, a wrench in the plan.

"Oh, not like you though. I just . . . like to draw. But I'm not good."

"I almost went to art school, thought about it when I was making good money."

"Awesome. Um, doing what?"

I half hoped she would say "robbing banks" and I could call it. I didn't want to be the reason she was kicked out of the Centre, but I also didn't want to go through the next three and a half weeks friendless.

"Mostly bartending. It's the only gig that you can make money and drink. I worked down at this place in Parkdale that was a shitshow."

"Oh yeah, I worked for about a month at this place, the Lionhead—"

"No way, that was my place too. That's funny that we're so similar."

Except we weren't. It stung that she would say we were the same, as if soon my skin would be tinted yellow too, a flashing advertisement for the destruction of my liver. We were not the same. She was hopeless, and I . . . at least I could still pretend I had hope, most days.

"You know that dude Guy?" she said, snapping me out of my thoughts before I could spiral into real anger.

"Yeah, he was another bartender?"

"That's my ex."

Guy had to be about twenty years older than both of us, at least. He was always sweating profusely. He wore rockabilly shirts that clung to his own beer belly, and his receding hairline and lack of a chin made his head look impossibly long, extremely equine, which I think is why he wore non-prescription, white-framed glasses. Add some dimension to his head. She shouldn't have dated him. He was mean to the servers and mocked the customers.

I knew why he bothered me so much—because he reminded me of Chris. The father of my unborn child. For a moment, I was afraid her belly was swollen from Guy's last violent attempt at sleeping with her. I shuddered imagining us as broke young moms together, drinking boxed wine while our children rolled around on a thin blanket in some co-op housing. Later, I would defend myself to myself in my pretty pink book—*We are not the fucking same because she's FUCKED UP and I know I am too but I'm not*—but in this moment, I realized I hadn't spoken in a while, and said, "Guy was kinda weird, huh?"

She nodded. "Yeah, so gross."

"So, who do you think would rob your roommate? Crazy. Right?"

She looked disappointed in me, the jig was up.

"No idea. I'm gonna grab a slushie before this."

"Oh, I don't think that's allowed."

"You don't have to come."

She ducked into a 7-Eleven. I returned to the girls, having failed my mission.

"She wouldn't say anything but was like, so shady. Like she's fucked."

Madison smiled. It was never about getting a confession, it was about proving my loyalty. I had passed my initiation into the rehab's most coveted and extremely temporary gang.

A spritely young Indigenous woman spoke at the meeting, telling us how it wasn't easy, but she was sober a year now and hoped to see her kids soon. She told us how the cops had shown up in the middle of the day and broken down her door and grabbed her kids, bruising their arms, while she hurled plates at them, only to be punched in the face and detained for three months. I realized the girls beside me weren't listening, only a few of the older women from the Centre were, nodding their heads in solidarity.

It was easy to blur the meetings together, we had at least three versions of meetings a day. Big Blue Book discussions, check-ins, guided meditations followed by more discussions, and out-of-Centre meetings. I had only been in rehab for four full days and already I was beginning to forget which woman had suffered what, which woman was attacked when, who ran from the cops or whose boyfriend found her seizing in the doorway. That must be the point. Inundate you with horror stories and trauma until you realize how serious your addiction is and finally give in to the program, your only saving grace. But at this point, I didn't feel shockable, I just felt that all that bullshit was a given.

I also wanted a better answer. Why couldn't *I* drink? Because the speaker was telling me how bad it could get? How I shouldn't wait until I hit "rock bottom"? I think all addicts crave that rock bottom. It's a comfort. If we survive an OD, if we lose everything we love and still manage to survive, adapt, then have we hit bottom? I always thought my bottom would be obvious, but it just adapted. I had new standards, lower lows. And the lows justified the highs—the more hurt, the more need for healing. An addict's way of healing. It's true I wanted to heal, but not like this, not here. Bad wasn't enough, bad was relative, and bad could be manipulated to support any narrative of why I could or couldn't drink. So unless this speaker had some sort of answer that made sense to *me*, I would just continue to run the clock, waiting for some sober epiphany.

———

"Steph's father raped her."

Len told me that before bed, after the evening meeting, then she shrugged and said maybe that was why Steph was so fucked so young. She told me Steph was only seventeen, but the Centre took her anyway because of her situation.

"That's also why she's going to court, don't bring it up, she goes nuts. That's my girl, but she goes loco."

"I think anyone would."

"My father would never fucking do that."

"Does she get actual help?"

"She doesn't get kicked out. That's a miracle."

I wasn't sure if Steph's youth meant she would have a fighting chance in this world, time to heal before being plunged into adulthood, or if it meant her life was over before it could begin.

On Wednesday morning, Barb, the thin counsellor from intake, pulled me aside after breakfast.

"I have a task for you today. You're gonna go with Tess to get her cheque. Can I trust you?"

"Yeah."

"You want to take this seriously?"

"I do."

"Because we don't trust her."

"Okay."

I didn't know why everyone was so adamant I keep tailing Tess. I also didn't know why anyone thought I was trustworthy. More rhetorical questions to save for my pink journal, where I tried to solve the riddle of myself:

Aren't I still an alcoholic? Isn't that the whole fucking point of me being here? Either I'm some doe-eyed salvageable case or I'm in deep

*shit like the rest of the girls. If I'm the former, then why can't I just go
to therapy twice a week like every other privileged white girl with a
mild coke habit? Don't say I'm fucking trustworthy but then check
my purse and toss my fucking room.*

I wondered if my journal would ever be looked at as my man-
ifesto, that terrible massacre of scribbling. If caught, I would have
to explain to the counsellors that it was a manifes*tation*. Of violence already done and lived. A way to expel adrenaline after
every fresh new hellish experience.

"You'll leave now. There and back, no stops. You hear me?"

"Yes. I'm like Kevin Costner."

"That is the attitude I'm talking about, this is serious."

I nodded my head sombrely, but I wasn't joking. I was like
Kevin Costner, and belly-ribbons Tess was my Whitney. I was
really starting to worry that being sober meant no one had any
fun at all. That we had to air out our collective baggage so frequently, and the rooms we inhabited were so thick with dark
memories, that everyone could only move in slow motion,
humourless, working to simply breathe.

Tess and I were less recognizably broken women when it was
just the two of us and not our larger group. We could actually
pass for two friends out for a stroll downtown, until we got to
the building where Tess was supposed to pick up her cheque.
She got to go to the head of the line because she held her belly
like she was pregnant. I watched her rub her hardened torso and
briefly felt mine. It was very soft, it felt safe. Maybe Chris was
right: I would be a terrible mother, and the only reason I would
ever have this child would be to spite him. No, Chris was wrong.
I looked into the sun and squinted so the tears that had flooded
my eyes would evaporate. Tess didn't notice either way, she was

just proud her trick had worked. The line was already snaking down the block, mostly young people, many in torn clothing, grown-out beards and body hair, with bad dye jobs and matted dreads. A few older people with swollen red noses and pock-marked skin.

Tess looked at me looking at them. "You have to come pick it up if you don't have a mailing address, they won't send it to shelters or halfway homes either."

"I thought you said in the morning meeting that you had an apartment?"

"No, I didn't say that."

"With your cats?"

"They're not mine, I just love them."

I was confused, but the line was moving and I was told by a security guard that if I didn't have a cheque to pick up, I had to wait outside. I tried to whisper to the guard that I was Tess' bodyguard, but he didn't care, I couldn't accompany her. I was left standing next to him in silence while I waited.

After she came down, Tess said she had to go to the bank. There, she gave the teller a different name and asked her to turn the cheque into a money order made out to yet *another* name. I noticed she already had two twenties in her wallet. She didn't acknowledge the strangeness of the situation, and I was tired of playing detective, so I stayed silent.

"Did you know after seven years your debt is just forgiven and you don't have it anymore?" she said when we were back outside.

"Really? Why seven years?"

"It's the law. That's why I'm saving money. I'm gonna move to Britain with a friend after this and wait till my debt's cleared, then I'll come back and start over."

"Britain sounds nice."

"Yeah. My friend is like, super rich too, so I probably won't have to pay for anything."

"Why save money then?"

"I want to get another tattoo."

"Yeah, they're pretty cool."

"I could design one for you. You'd have to pay me but I could have it done before I leave."

"Oh, thanks. I dunno though, I really have to save up for first and last."

"I thought you lived on Queen."

"I did, but . . . you know how that goes. Plus like, the roof was kinda leaky. Um, one time I thought I heard squirrels in the walls, it was just . . . bad."

In reality I had stopped paying the rent long ago so my landlord was forced to charge my mother, my co-signer, for the last few months' rent. She had told me at the intervention that she would no longer pay for the apartment, and with no one willing to take me in I really had no choice but to come here. A convenient solution. I had some money tucked away that logically I should've offered to my mother as repayment, but I justified keeping it. I would need to find somewhere else to live.

"Least it's not a shelter. You should just stay till you find a new place. I slept in a Coffee Time before coming here."

Two days ago she'd said she was living with a new boyfriend, Stu, and her cats, then they weren't her cats, and he wasn't her boyfriend and now she was living in a Coffee Time. I couldn't believe anything she said, but at least I felt better for having told the girls she was shady—it turned out to be true.

"Well, I gotta find something new."

"Don't end up like Steph," she said quietly.

"I don't think Steph was trying to end up homeless."

"She's just such a victim."

"Least she's not a thief." I didn't know why I'd said that.

Tess turned to me, outraged.

"I meant like . . . Aladdin. Like, he's homeless and steals bread and shit. Steph doesn't do that."

She rolled her eyes at me pityingly, almost like she was embarrassed that I couldn't stand up to her. I wanted to take it back, tell her I wasn't talking about Aladdin, I was talking about her, Tess, if that was her real name.

She walked ahead of me but not before saying under her breath, "He had to steal to feed his monkey. Bitch."

The girls flocked to me with questions about my day with Tess, the pariah of rehab. I was still angry and I was meaner than I should've been. I likened Tess to Homer Simpson, with her yellowing skin and protruding belly, only dumber. I said she used a fake name to get a money order, and how she was a liar and had said shit about Steph. I shouldn't have been so vicious. As soon as I told the girls, I regretted it. They swarmed on her before we sat down to watch the evening movie. Madison attacked first.

"Bitch, we know you stole from Fatima."

Tess widened her eyes, she looked cherubic when she was scared, she turned to me for assistance, clarity—what had I told them?

Steph, kind Steph, went in next. "Also what the fuck? You were making fun of me for being homeless? You were fucking some dude just for an apartment?"

I hadn't said that. I said it was confusing because she said she was staying with a guy but then that turned out to be false. I was breathing heavily, trying to gasp out some sort of mediation. Tess started to cry, it weakened her defence.

"What the fuck, I never said that, and I never fucking stole. I have my own money. I don't talk to fucking junkies."

Madison really lost it then. Len stood up behind her, always the muscle.

"Who's a fucking junkie, bitch? You're yellow! You're already fucking dead, you look like a fucking zombie!"

Tess put her hood up, shrunk into her shoulders and began aggressively drawing in her sketchpad. "I'm sick."

"Yeah, you're fucking sick."

The girls stood over her, waiting for her to challenge them again, and then the counsellor walked in and they dispersed as if nothing had happened.

Maybe I was more like Tess than I wanted to admit, because once the lights were dimmed I too put my head down to doodle in my workbook, quietly crying. If she were to leave because of this incident and die in the booth of some Coffee Time, it would be on me.

We watched *28 Days*. The women liked Sandra Bullock, especially in this movie: she was beautiful and damaged but at the same time easily fixable, because somehow, only twenty-eight days later, she was cured. We went to bed with the humbled Sandra fresh in our minds, our inspiration for the night. An hour later I heard one of the girls vomiting in the toilet down the hall, then the sound of sirens outside the building, and a woman screaming. Len slept through the whole thing.

Steph didn't come to breakfast or the morning meeting. Madison said she had picked at her face so much she bled and lost her mind screaming because she was supposed to go to court today to testify against her father. I asked Madison, while she was smoking with Len and discussing how to better tan her underarms, if Steph was coming back.

"Of course she is. Why wouldn't she come back?" she said, hands above her head and armpits faced towards the sun.

"I don't know, if she needed like, medical help or . . . I don't know how court works."

"You think she's going to jail?"

"No. I mean, why would she? I thought like, she was a witness or something."

Len gave me a look, she had told me about Steph in confidence, I wasn't supposed to know anything about her situation. I'd promised Len I wouldn't gossip about it. Madison let an arm fall to take a drag of her cigarette and stared at me, blowing out a large cloud before she spoke to me again.

"Her dad's saying she stole some money from him. He's tryna attack her character. And that's fucked. 'Cause like, all she has is her fucking character. She's a sweetie, but she's not smart."

I was surprised to hear Madison say that about Steph. I thought her to be smart enough, it took smarts to be kind the way she was and to survive as long as she had on the street.

"She seems smart."

Madison ignored my comment, staring at me again and smoking, one arm still above her head.

"Why do you look tanned?"

"Oh, it's a moisturizer that tans you the more you put it on. I can't reach my back though so . . . I'm kinda tie-dyed."

"I need to borrow some for my pits."

"For sure."

Steph showed up at our next meeting with Band-Aids all over her face and her hair washed and in a tight bun. She didn't speak, which didn't matter because we were focusing on art therapy. Ellen was being cruel to the counsellor, telling her there was no scientific evidence that art therapy was helpful in healing long-term trauma. This counsellor, Zoey, was the youngest we had, she talked like a SoCal surfer chick and wanted to be liked more than she wanted to guide us on our journey to sobriety, so for the most part she agreed with Ellen but said we had to do the assignment anyway, it was part of the program and that's what she needed us to do.

"So we're doing you a favour with our recovery?" Ellen said.

"Well . . . couldn't hurt. It's art. Just let the colours soothe you."

Ellen grimaced.

"Picture freedom man, draw what frees you."

"Are you kidding me?"

"Dude, I didn't make the curriculum."

"My point exactly."

"You gotta draw."

"I don't find my artistic shortcomings healing."

"Dude, doodle then, just put pen to paper, please."

Ellen sighed deeply and loudly. I felt stupid for being excited about art therapy. I'd figured if I couldn't talk, at least I could draw something that would resemble vulnerability, or hope. I looked at my piece of paper, I had tried to draw myself as a child on stage, performing for a crowd. I remembered what it was like to be validated for being a tiny clown. I hadn't had to be silent then, or cruel to be liked, just silly, simple.

"It's bullshit," Ellen continued.

"Okay, stop, everyone, let's . . . man, let's all draw ourselves as a bird. Whatever bird you wanna be. Caged . . . or free . . . birds," Zoey said.

I watched as everyone at the table crumpled their pages and started to sketch variations of birds. "Free Bird" by Lynyrd Skynyrd ran through my head. I remembered my parents torturing my brother and me during one of our summer road trips with that song, singing it loudly when it was their turn to play a CD, after I had exhausted my only copy of the Spice Girls' *Spice*. I crumpled up my semi-artistic rendering of my childhood performance and tried to draw a minivan with wings.

Len looked over. "That's a fat bird, yo."

"Oh, yeah."

"You're not even fat."

"I will be soon after eating here for a month."

"*Such* jokes, girl. I fucking hear that."

Zoey should've reprimanded us for talking during what was supposed to be quiet art time, but she was looking at her phone. Ellen put her head down to nap, and I continued to shade feathers onto my fat bird.

Steph was missing at lunch and a new girl was welcomed into the fold. She was excessively glamorous, short neon-blue hair coiffed into a sort of faux-hawk, heavily drawn-on eyebrows, lips lined in pale pink, and fake eyelashes so long and thick she was constantly blinking under the weight of them. The counsellors didn't bother to show her around, they just offered her lunch. The glamorous blue rooster sat down at my table. Madison didn't seem to appreciate another woman as kept up as herself and made it her business to come over and chat with her. She was a much more direct interrogator than I was.

"This your second time?"

"Third here, I had to come back after prison."

"My third too."

"I love your lips."

"I bought 'em."

"I can't wait to buy a big ass."

"Yeah."

"Last time I was here though, I gained like thirty pounds."

"Me too."

"Least it went to your ass."

Troubled Steph felt far away as the two beautiful recurring rehab tenants bonded over fat asses. Glam rooster, whose name I learned was Maci Ann, had paid for her extravagant spending habits through her pimp/heroin dealer's credit card fraud business, which Madison seemed quite curious about. Tess looked on wide-eyed, and Ellen rolled her eyes at every illogical thing they said. Madison insisted you could whiten your teeth with regular bleach, Maci Ann said you could use Krazy Glue on lashes for a night out.

I felt more tired. When I'd first arrived, I was always awake and alert, even curious about what each day might hold. Now I felt like a driver of an airport shuttle bus. Listening to tales of adventure or anticipation of what the next destination may hold. I just had to stay the course, driving round and round, nodding my cap and feigning interest at the newest traveller's story. I felt I'd already learned everything I needed to, the social dynamics of the women and arbitrary rules of the counsellors, and each day was more tedious than the last.

I almost fell asleep on the streetcar on the way to the evening meeting. I sat beside Steph, still dressed in her courtroom attire, who sat beside Len, who was next to Maci Ann, who was beside Madison. Already a new pecking order. The girls were excited for this meeting, it was the fancy one for well-to-do alcoholics from Forest Hill. Maci Ann kept saying that was where Drake was from, she knew because she had been in one of his music videos. Madison replied that she'd been in a video for Swollen Members and Madchild was just as sexy. Ellen, who was standing, leaned in and whispered to me that they were the two dumbest women she'd ever seen together, and that that was a lot coming from someone who'd worked in the service industry for eight years. I didn't tell her I'd been a server before this. Maybe I was dumb too. A part of me envied Madison and Maci Ann: they wanted admiration and validation and they got it, by any means. I'm sure their reasons for needing it so badly, enough to lie, would be heartbreaking, but on this streetcar, they were so committed to their stories of turning down the opportunity to suck a Canadian celebrity's dick that we all listened in awe. True or not, it was kind of cool to think about a heroin addict with daddy issues having the courage to tell sweaty Drake that his moist Forest Hill dick was gross.

At the meeting, the speaker told us, in essence, that despite having an alcohol- and Vicodin-induced mental breakdown at an international conference, she was too rich and powerful for it to affect the company that she had single-handedly built. She told us how a friend took her to his lake house and let her sober up there before she flew to a rehab far away where nobody would know her. Steph watched her with such longing, this successful braggart of a woman. She whispered to me, "She's one of the biggest donors the Centre has, sometimes she comes to visit, she said she loves us." Then she grabbed my hand and squeezed it so tightly that I could feel the empty divots around her fingernails where she'd nervously chewed off her skin.

By Friday, I realized I was not a fat bird but a chameleon. I thought of how just a week earlier I'd been terrified and crying. I had played the new girl, the kind girl, the detective, and the cruel girl, and now, as I watched Madison shave Steph's legs for a secret rendezvous with two gentlemen that evening before our meeting, I was just an ornament. I could be in the room and not really bother anyone. I wasn't some phoenix rising from the ashes, I was a fucking googly-eyed lizard skittering around from one meeting to the next, blending in when necessary, surviving and sustaining.

My favourite moments were right before bed, when Len and I would talk like friends at a sleepover. I liked her when we were alone, she was goofier than she'd ever let Madison or Maci Ann see, she trusted me with secrets and silliness, and I loved her for that. Tonight she told me there were ants everywhere in Kate's room. She acted out the ants hitting the jackpot finding a chocolate bar in Kate's room, and I clapped at her performance. I didn't know how Len found out all the information she did, but I always felt excited coming back to our room in the evening knowing she would be there to tell me new stories.

Whenever I brought up studying for her driving test, she would shake her head. She said she was dealing with a lot and maybe it wasn't the best time. So we would gossip until it was lights out, and laugh, and sometimes she'd even share with me a bit about her family dying, her fear of going down that same path and her resignation that she probably couldn't change her fate either way. She said she had wanted to come here just to see if it would work, then at least she'd have tried, which is better than her parents, best friends, etc., could say. So far she wasn't sold.

Saturday was Family Day, and there was a different type of energy in the facility, nervousness from those who knew family was coming and for those who knew no one was. Soon, it would be made clear who was wanted.

Neither Madison nor Steph was at the morning meeting. I had heard yelling the night before but hadn't been sure which room it was coming from, it happened sometimes and I tuned a lot of it out, mostly pretending to myself I had left the TV on, that the faraway voices were actors playing pretend. It turned out it had been Madison yelling at Tess. Apparently, Tess had told a counsellor that Madison's boyfriend made her uncomfortable when he took the streetcar back with us after last night's meeting. He and Madison had been engaged in some sort of foreplay on the ride home. I had tried not to watch while Madison screamed with delight. Steph and her appointed boyfriend had sat next to each other and hadn't spoken. I saw Steph rigidly accept his hand and tense up when she had to lean into him to avoid getting kicked by Madison's heel at one point.

And now Madison was gone. Kicked out. Maci Ann, Len, and Steph were fuming. I worried Tess was going to get beat up. Did people shank people in rehab? Did people still shank people in jail? The word *shank* had lost all meaning to me by the time I made it down to the dining area. Was it *shiv* or *shank*? I hoped I would never know.

I was surprised to find that on some level I was relieved. Tess had removed Madison from the equation, the mean girl I had to pacify in order to have some semblance of friendship in rehab. She also, by snitching, made me feel less guilty about what I'd done to her. I didn't need to worry anymore about making it right with Tess, standing up for her—it was too late for that now.

Kate with the ants ended up having a Family Day visitor, it was shocking. He was a varsity-football-playing, Tommy-Hilfiger-polo-wearing, father-is-probably-a-lawyer looking dude. Tall, broad, and with impeccably styled blond hair. He hugged her for a long time.

"Girl must have some wild pussy game."

I don't know why Maci Ann whispered this to me, and I had no idea how I could ever respond to an observation like that. I widened my eyes in sheer terror and thankfully Maci Ann left to smoke.

I watched as Tess invited her not-boyfriend-man-she-lived-with into our eating area. He was much older but looked much worse off than her, incredibly thin with a bloated belly to match hers, dull grey skin, and jeans worn threadbare at the heel. I was just happy that for these next two hours she had protection.

"Waddup player?"

I turned around; it was my father. My stomach dropped and I had to catch my breath so I wouldn't cry. I'd been so mean to him on the phone, and because we could never offer apologies or sincere words without cutting them with sarcasm or self-deprecation, I knew his dorky salutation meant he had, on some level, forgiven me. I was all at once so grateful and so guilt-ridden that I wished he hadn't come.

"Heeey," I said.

"Nice digs."

"Honestly I was hoping for the Ritz, but this is an incredibly close second."

"It's temporary."

"I know."

"You're settling in then?"

"Mmhmm. My roommate's out there, but don't look."

He looked anyway at Len and Maci Ann smoking in the four-square-foot courtyard.

"The tall one."

"She looks nice."

"I like her."

We made small talk, he gave me more books, complained about the counsellors checking his bag and taking the snacks he had brought for me.

"I don't understand what's contraband about almond butter. There's no peanuts."

"It's like elementary school, if you bring it in you have to share it."

"They said they'd think about it."

"Thanks anyway. I wrote a few letters back if you wanna give them to Grandma and stuff. I don't think I'll call."

I handed him small folded pieces of paper I had quickly jotted down niceties on. *Thanks Grandma! Miss you! Can't wait to see you soon, hope the Blue Jays are kicking ass!*

"Don't read 'em though."

"I wouldn't . . . Are you feeling better?"

I tried not to let my few tears snowball into more, wiping them away quickly. He sighed, flexing his hand into a fist as if he was unsure of whether to put it on my shoulder. He looked younger than he actually was, and I didn't want any of the women thinking he was a boyfriend or something so I made sure to speak a little louder once I had stopped my incoming tears.

"Yeah, *Dad*. Yeah, it's good here."

"All your stuff is safe, so when you decide what you wanna do after, the storage locker is not too far from downtown, three months paid for. Should I give you the key or should they hold onto it at the office?"

"I'll take it, I'll put it in my purse."

"Have you called your mother yet?"

I shook my head. It was a lie. I had tried once, a few days ago, between lunch and afternoon chores. I was terrified that I would have to lie to her, the person who probably loved me the absolute most, I would have to say that she was right for putting me here, that it *would* work. I didn't want to set her up for disappointment, give her false hope. At the same time, I didn't want to give her the satisfaction of thinking she'd been right, that she *did* know what was best for me. I'd gotten her voicemail, which I should've expected because she always had her phone on silent, and I knew she was travelling for work, in a different time zone with various obligations, but it made me so mad that I was there, on the other side of the phone, ready, despite all that fear, to lie to her, for her, and she hadn't picked up. I hung up without leaving a message and hadn't tried again.

"Well, you should do that. You may want to stay with her for a bit, of course your bro said you could visit him for a few days but . . ." He trailed off.

"What about your place?"

"It's just so small, and we get up early."

It was a stupid excuse. I got that it was small, every new condo in Toronto was. I knew the real reason was that they'd filled their one bedroom plus den with two separate well-stocked bar carts, and they didn't trust me alone with either of them. I wanted to call him out but he, like all men, seemed so much more delicate than the women in my life. I could talk so much more shit to my mother than him, and he looked so weary and beaten down just being here, seeing his daughter in this place.

"So it's New York or Peterborough. The age-old question. I thought Mom didn't want me living with her."

"I don't know kiddo. Maybe for a week or two until you find a spot to land. That's why you should call her. Or if you have any . . . safe friends to stay with."

"What's a 'safe friend'?"

"A sober friend."

"How do you think adults make friends?"

He leaned back in his chair and sighed. I knew he wanted my mom to take me in so she could keep an eye on me. But she lived with her boyfriend and his three adult kids in the middle of nowhere in Peterborough. I couldn't go back to Winnipeg, all my old friends were kind but straight-laced and probably terrified of me, and they all still lived with their parents while they finished school and worked towards their collectively bright futures.

"Well. We just want what's best."

"Yeah."

"For you to be happy."

"Okay."

"And to get you your almond butter."

I cried harder than before. I wanted to talk to him like we were close, like we used to be when we would drink together, when I was not just his daughter but his friend. I felt like we couldn't bridge the gap now between caring father and partner in crime, and it was my fault because I couldn't be like him. I couldn't drink like him and not fuck everything up. I didn't want to move around conversations with him, have that be all that was left in our relationship, skirting topics that might elicit any sort of real feeling. I felt so far away from him.

"It'll get easier," he said.

I nodded, trying to wipe away the snot and salty dew on my face.

"I need some money."

He gave me forty dollars. We had a quick one-armed hug, and he jokingly tried to give me a noogie.

"Don't let the man get you down."

"Thanks, Daddio."

Then he left, and I was tasked with cleaning up our dining area before dinner and the next meeting.

On our way to that evening's meeting, Hannah, the lithe trainer with the rabbits, darted off the subway two stops before we were supposed to. Ellen told her it was the wrong stop, thinking she was incompetent, but I saw that her purse was stuffed with clothes, and she yelled back at us that she just had to see her rabbits. Then she was gone. Ellen rolled her eyes and said she wasn't going to be held responsible for her. I caught some of the other girls motioning that she was actually going to snort coke, and overheard Len say she'd already failed one drug test. Steph looked uncomfortable and Maci Ann poked at her, smiling.

By the time we got to our stop, the lithe trainer had fallen from our minds. As we reached another foreboding church, the girls around me got a bit giddy. A large group of men stood outside, almost all of them smoking. They were from the men's centre. This was my first time running into them. One of the men explained that because they were men, and therefore either less vulnerable or more trusted or both, they were allowed to go to whichever meetings they pleased, solo or in a group. They didn't even have to go to meetings, they joked about going off to see movies or walking around town because there was no accountability. The men's facility was a sprawling house in the Annex that had a beautiful large backyard. In our backyard, we were made to come back inside as soon as our smokes were out because unwanted visitors hung out in the alley behind and leered at us.

Another older man made sure to point out that we women had to walk in a group for our own protection, that he knew what boys were thinking when they saw a pretty lady on the street by herself. A few of the girls tittered at this, taking in only the "pretty" part. I just stared at him. He had a heat rash across his face that encroached past his fading hairline and a skin tag that took up valuable real estate on his left eyelid. His lips were chapped, and he continued to suck them in and out while he looked at us. The rest of the men stood behind him. I realized he was their chosen leader, the one who was supposed to mesmerize us with false pleasantries until we split off and his minions could corner us one by one. All of us women slowly shuffled behind the men into the church after the speaker apologized for the delay in setting up. We huddled in a group behind the rows of chairs, unsure of where to take a seat. Break off and sit alongside the men, or stay together in our group, for our own protection.

"Oh, girls, here's the real steak to your potatoes." The leader scrunched his nose into a sneer, which caused tiny orbs of oil to secrete from his pores. He cocked his head towards a man who had just entered the church and was wearing a leather jacket despite the heat, his hands in the pockets of his incredibly tight designer blue jeans. I recognized him but was unsure from where. The leader must have greatly overestimated how much addicts and alcoholics keep up with Canadian pop culture. Most of us had been busy trying to survive attacks from men a lot like him, not scouting the latest issue of *TeenBop*.

Maci Ann spoke when the provincially semi-well-known man went to get coffee. "I've modelled with that guy, he's such a pill head."

"I think he's in a band," I said. I was remembering now, I thought it was a pop-punk-rap hybrid, maybe?

She looked at me angrily for daring to question her. "Whatever, still a douchebag, I wouldn't touch him."

"Why don't you say hi?"

"No fucking way. He's like . . . I'm over it."

"Whippets," a tall, alarmingly tall, man in his early twenties whispered at me.

"Sorry?"

"Nitrous. We're both in for nitrous."

"Oh, no, I'm in for like, alcohol and other . . . Sorry, what's nitrous?"

"I meant *he* and I. Gavin. He's Gavin, I'm Dave."

"Dave-on-nitrous."

"Not for the past seventeen days."

"Can't you guys go to NA?"

"Yeah, but then we wouldn't run into you ladies."

"I mean a lot of us do drugs too so . . . it's a melting pot."

"Yeah, everybody's got a past."

The other girls were watching us. The attention they were giving me for being singled out by a man was making my cheeks burn. I was worried the meeting was starting soon and he'd ask to sit next to me, which would mean I'd have to hold his hand, and though I didn't mind holding a stranger's hand so much anymore, now that I knew his name was Dave-on-nitrous it felt like hand-holding could have some weird new significance to it, like it was a stolen moment between two addicts in the throes of recovery.

"I'm gonna get a coffee before this whole . . . show, so good luck with the whippets. Or avoiding them in future," I said and made finger guns at him, a clear sign, I hoped, that I was not sexually attracted to him.

"Yeah, could you grab me one? Milk and sugar?"

"Oh, ha, I'd just mess it up. I shouldn't . . . so you're welcome to join me, I also want to grab cookies, so . . ."

"Probably too late for coffee anyways, but hey, if you girls have to run out after the meeting, can I grab your number, for when we're actually out of here and need real support? You don't seem like those other girls, you're pretty real."

"I am that."

I looked over at Len, who was making kissy faces at me and at Kate grinning and nodding and mouthing, "Get some."

"I got a pen and paper, hold up."

He produced a small gold notebook and pen from a fancy hotel. I thought of my own journal and was briefly amused at the stark difference between what was likely to be inside our books. I quickly scribbled down my number, resenting myself for being too polite to give him a fake, though I wouldn't have my phone until I was out, and even then there was little to no chance I'd run into Dave-on-nitrous unless I found myself newly addicted to nitrous or hitting up NA meetings on a whim. I handed him back his pen and shook his hand and felt my face redden even further as I went to get my cheap coffee. I let the bitter water burn my throat as I chugged the first cup, before getting a second one and taking my seat beside Len.

When we returned to the Centre from the meeting, Ellen told the counsellor on duty that the lithe woman was gone. The counsellor looked unsurprised. She sighed and yelled behind her, "Shari, Hannah left. Did she leave anyone to call?"

Another counsellor joined her, both blocking the door to get in, so we were all stuck waiting on the stairs, purses and bags ready and open for inspection. Shari looked us over.

"No, just bag her stuff in case she tries to come back. We'll hold it for a day or two. And check them thoroughly."

Then she yelled out to us, "Did anyone talk to her before she left?"

We all shook our heads. It was a hot night and we just wanted to get in for our evening snack, we were like children, cranky, ready for bed.

Later, Len and I continued our nightly routine of gossiping before lights out. I was sure she had more information on Hannah, from what she'd said on the subway.

"Did she really fail a drug test?"

"Yup, I think that's why she was all hyped up."

"But how would she get drugs?"

"How anyone gets them. Man, I bet you every time she was calling her mom about those fucking rabbits it was really her dealer. Like, code names."

"She seemed to really love them."

"As much as she loves coke? *Fuck*, it makes sense too because rabbits are white, right?"

"Mmhmm."

"That's why she ran off like, Gotta go feed my rabbits. It's like she was feeding herself. Feeding the fucking beast." Len was so pleased with herself for making this connection, I didn't want to disagree.

"So they're just gonna trash her stuff?"

"Oh yeah, one hundred. She ain't comin back."

"It's just like, we have to pee in a cup like, she knew she was gonna get caught, right?"

"Some people are sicker than others."

I nodded. I hated that mantra, because I was still waiting to somehow be sicker, or realize I was just as sick as everyone else, so that I could finally start healing. Why not wait? Or if other people absolutely couldn't wait to use again, why could I? Because some people are just fucking sicker than others?

Len turned to her wall. After we'd been silent for a while, I began scribbling in my journal in the darkness.

How could you be so fucking stupid and make it look so fucking easy to leave, and I bet you'll be so fine I bet you'll be forgiven and keep your fucking rabbits. I can't leave. I have no one to call that will take me in and get me high. Not without paying the fucking piper. But you made it look so easy. Because you're so sick, you're so so sick. You poor unfortunate soul.

I didn't have coke dealers that I could call with hypothetical code names for shady pick-ups, but I did have male contacts in my phone who could. Coke made it easy to keep drinking, and I called these men because I wanted to keep drinking to keep feeling normal, but . . . that's not how it works. I was so naive, every time, thinking, Okay, you'll party with this guy, yeah you might end up doing a little blow, but he'll drink with you and make you feel like you're funny and smart and normal, and when the night's over, you'll go to bed.

But that's not how men, these men, wanted to end the night, even if I was crying or passing out. I dunno, maybe that was just some silent agreement I made at the beginning of every one of those fucked-up nights. Maybe it was all my fault because I continued seeing them, it wasn't just a one-off, each time wanting to believe we would party and then go home, alone, like normal friends.

I couldn't risk waking Len by cramming my journal away in the drawer beneath my bed so I tucked it under my pillow, imagining the ink lifting from the pages and snaking its way back into my veins and up to my brain so that I'd wake up spitting black and cursing out the world in tongues. I gently stroked the pink linen under my pillow, asking for it to be kind to me. To stay put, and let me sleep.

My second Sunday in rehab. Another morning meeting, this one in a ridiculously large open circle, where any drug talk or mention of any substance other than booze was met with loud protest from some of the lifers. Len told me a lot of AA meetings were like this: the attendees were puritans of their disease. It was *alcoholics* anonymous, not ambiguously addicted anonymous.

There didn't seem to be an all-encompassing group in the world of addiction, you had to major in at least one substance. AA, NA (narcotics), MA (marijuana), the list goes on. There was a very obvious hierarchy when it came to addiction. Alcohol was at the top of the pyramid, an everyman's addiction, if you were just an alcoholic, sure you were still a piece of shit but you'd maintained some wherewithal not to fall into hard drugs, and that was what put you at the top of the piece of shit food chain. Next were pills and cocaine, but cocaine in powder form, not crack cocaine. Uppers and downers were an elite addiction, though still for pieces of shit, and because of the variety of options available they weren't as pure an addiction as alcohol, but a close second tier. You could be fancy sick on pills and cocaine, or at least feel fancy sick, suburban-mothers-chasing-Xannies-with-white-wine-spritzers type of fancy. Then came the real hard opioids, not to be confused with your PG-13 narcotics. Oxy, heroin, crack, and fentanyl all fell into this third tier. The real fucked-up, the stab-your-mom-and-rob-your-grandma fucked-up. The lower the tier, the less likely any type of prolonged recovery was. Your dopamine and serotonin levels so irrevocably fucked that even, even if you had managed to escape drug-induced or related trauma, you'd still maybe never feel happiness in the ways you had in the past. The fourth and final tiers were meth and gas and glue and basically anything cheap that could be homemade and that lead to you digging holes in your face and letting the puss and blood from your inner mouth abscesses leak out while you ground what few teeth you had left. Fourth tier almost never made it back. Almost no one came out of smoking meth for ten years to say they'd finally hit bottom and were sick of that shit. They're dead, or as close to it as you could be.

Being third tier or lower was a curse but also a badge of honour. A fuck-you to those basic alcoholics who thought they'd suffered. They made me want to share much less. How do you follow a story by a meth user who said they didn't sleep for five days and then, in a psychotic state, tried to stab three people in broad daylight because the devil told them to? I'm supposed to follow that with "I got drunk and made my mom cry"?

"That's why we have separate meetings," Kate said knowingly to me after another audible outburst at the mention of drugs. "You bitches can't relate."

"That's the fucking dream though, isn't it?" Len said, as we were getting ready for bed.

We'd been forced to sit through an evening meeting run by two very attractive women who talked about how bottle service and the club scene wore heavily on them, and how lucky they were to have made it out sober and now be running a lifestyle blog for young women in recovery. Ellen had rolled her eyes every time the women talked about being "blessed" and mentioned "vibes and tribes."

"Running a blog?" I asked.

"Like, working for yourself, just like, being a businesswoman like that rich chick on Thursday too."

"You should do that when you get out, start a business."

"I'm not fucking good at anything. Maybe like, dog walking."

"Yeah, that'd be awesome, just hang out with like, a hundred dogs a day and no people."

"Fuck yeah, right? Fuck, I should do that."

"Just like, put up flyers and stuff, it seems pretty easy actually."

"Just gotta deal with so much dog shit. I have three dogs already, man, fuck, that'd be a lot of dog shit, right? Like a hundred dogs? How much is that in like, a day?"

"Oh, I was exaggerating, you wouldn't walk a hundred dogs a day, maybe seven or eight."

"How much you think you make per dog?"

"Maybe thirty bucks for like, two, two and a half hours, if you think about pick-up times and drop-offs and park time."

"So how much money is that for, say, seven dogs."

"That's two hundred and ten dollars."

"And that's like, every day?"

"I think you'd make your own hours."

"Fuck that's a lot of dog shit still."

"Yeah."

"We gotta think of something else."

"Something with less dog shit?"

"Yessir."

"Mmm. I'll keep thinking."

She threw a piece of paper at me and then a pen.

"You can make a list if you want, I'm going to bed."

"Okay, maybe I'll start tomorrow."

"Whatever."

I looked at the empty sheet of paper. Maybe Len and I could start a dog-walking business together, so long as I picked up the shit. It seemed like quite the fall from grace. Get sober just to pick up shit all day. Maybe I could be a garbage man when I got out. I remembered hearing they actually have great benefits. Instead of padding my breasts like I would normally do for a serving job, I could pad my arms, be a very appealing muscular candidate. I should write that down. Once I taught Len to drive, we could branch off and start a private garbage collection company for the rich recovering alcoholics of Forest Hill, maybe one day stumble upon something revealing in some wealthy politician's trash, use it to blackmail them, and be richer than the people we once cleaned up after. It was a cracked-up fantasy, but the prospect of getting out with nothing, no hope that picking up shit would lead anywhere other than more shit, was too much to think about. I'd get out, get a job, apartment, and get happy. It would be as easy as creating a private trash-collecting empire.

Monday was a busy day. A number of women were graduating, some I'd sort of become friends with but was confident I'd never speak to again, some who I honestly thought didn't stand a chance. I wasn't used to the revolving door yet, even though Madison and Hannah had already disappeared. I foolishly thought the women I had started with would, in a sense, be my women. A constant sisterhood moving through our thirty days together. It was more like a fucked-up summer camp. Whatever fair-weather friendships we created here weren't real, we came and left alone.

Replacements came in. A small, plucky, wide-shouldered young woman named Hilary excitedly told me her father was an addict and had gone to the men's centre years ago. She was very excited to be here. Of course, we all asked her what she was in for, and she replied, pluckily, "Weed." There was a noticeable pause as we all tried to think of what to say next.

"So how much did you smoke?" Maci Ann asked her.

"Oh, yikes, gosh, a whole lot. Every day, and, um, yeah, gosh, it was just getting harder to plan fun things, travel, 'cause you gotta get your fix, right? Plus I want to get back to the gym, I'm a gymnast, this whole thing started after an injury, I wanted to treat it naturally, take some time off, I hated gymnastics by the end of it, I'd been practising at least five hours a day, and smoking weed and watching TV is a lot more fun, I'll tell ya. I'd really like to hike more, I only go, gosh, twice a week. I work in retail, so the hours are nuts, you guys have no idea. Unless you work in retail."

She started laughing and moved on to introduce herself—"Hilary, drug addict"—to the other women.

"I can't fucking do this," said Ellen, who was already in a bad mood because she had received a write-up for cutting her own hair in the wee hours of the night. She said she had only cut it because the amount of times she was stuck waiting for the shower and then running to meetings with her long hair sopping down her back was driving her crazy, plus she joked that it was the first step to her complete mental breakdown, which she was sure to have while staying here. I had overheard her arguing with a counsellor that girls were allowed to dye their hair, so why was this any different, and the counsellor replied it was because she procured a weapon to do so.

"The fucking scissors were in the craft box! I cleaned them and put them back!" she'd said.

"Those scissors are for crafts."

"Which we have access to because we are encouraged to do banal art therapy."

"Please don't question the program, you brought a weapon back to your room."

"I brought it to the bathroom, I never brought the scissors back to my room. What is the legitimate difference between using the scissors in one public place versus another, especially since I managed not to harm myself or others?"

"The scissors need to stay with the craft supplies."

"I understand the scissors need to stay with the craft supplies, that's why I borrowed them during a time when no crafts were being done."

"But you did move them from the craft station. What if you had hurt yourself?"

"If, by some miracle, the very dull scissors used specifically for crafts that no one enjoys somehow slipped and caused a deep laceration, I would welcome the hospital visit, as it would be a beautiful break from this hellhole."

"Do you want to hurt yourself? Is the hair a cry for help?"

"Please just write me up. I'd like to leave."

The other new intake, Aruna, a shy Indian woman, was shaking everyone's hands politely. She was in for alcohol and drugs, mostly just ground-up back pain medication, she laughed that she had never "scored" and would not know how to do so.

"Oh, Steph can help you with that," Tess told her, but I was the only one who heard it. Tess knew she would be eviscerated, possibly physically, if any of the other girls had heard her. I admired that she was still taking shots at the other women, despite being outnumbered. I wouldn't tell her that, having fully distanced myself from her, but it was good to hear she had a bit of fight left. And it was true that Steph said she was very proud of her ability to score whatever she needed at any given time. She said she may be seventeen but she'd never had any trouble getting into bars or buying cigarettes.

I had to do my first in-house urine test. I'd never peed into a cup, and I was nervous about peeing on myself because the girls told me there was a woman in the room who watched us and I thought it would look suspicious if I peed all over myself. I wanted to impress this strange woman allocated by whatever company it was to watch women urinate. Impress her with my aim, like I'd been around the block, I'd peed in a cup or two, lady, not my first rodeo! Plus I wondered if there was any scientific bearing to nerves affecting the quality of one's body waste. Surely that's how prostates got inflamed. I made a mental note to write in my pink journal to look up how prostates got inflamed once I got out and finally had access to internet again.

While we waited, a glamorous older counsellor told us about the dangers of replacing one addiction with the other, only she told it by relaying the time she drank tequila instead of doing cocaine and ended up ruining her daughter's wedding by fucking not one but two of the groomsmen. "Young men," she said, laughing. "I swore off sex and tequila the next morning, not that night, of course, because I'd already dug my hole. Why not sit in the mud for a little longer." Maci Ann and Hilary loved her. She winked at me and I didn't know what to do with my face or body because I was still thinking about prostates, I didn't actually know if I could identify one if I saw it, and was that the organ women didn't have? I just gave her a double thumbs-up and said, "Yeah, you gotta keep on keeping on."

While the experts analyzed our urine we shifted to the main floor boardroom for another meeting, another groupthink on steps to take to make the road to recovery a smooth transition once we were left to our own devices and free to pee when and where we pleased. Aruna took up a lot of the meeting with her questions.

"But how, without medication, can you feel happy?" she asked. Her soft-spoken way of talking sounded like a song.

The glamorous counsellor seemed to be trying her best to be sincere after just regaling us with her sex stories.

"I think certain medications, if prescribed and monitored, for something like depression, are fine. It's more about creating a new happy, a sober happy."

"Or even not happy, how can you feel different? All I think about is . . . I can't take the subway to work anymore, I just want to jump in front of it. I try not to think of my children, but they don't want an unhappy mom either."

"I think you should be grateful every time you don't jump. It means you want to fight."

"No, I worry I will be a burden in my final moments. Most people get angry when their commutes are slowed. I just want to know if this, the program, if it is supposed to change your mind, the way you think."

"It will if you let it, if you give in to your higher power."

"And if I am still unhappy?"

"You could think about medication."

"But on my own, I cannot change the way I think?"

"Not without a higher power."

"Ahh."

Then we watched a Meg Ryan movie with Andy Garcia. Meg Ryan slapped her daughter and went to rehab and got better. I spent half of it worrying that Len would demand the list of possible career options I was writing for her and be angry when she saw garbage man.

Len never confronted me. We were distracted gossiping about Kate being kicked out, once and for all, for failing her drug test.

Kate had tried to argue that if they made her leave, she would probably have to go back to jail.

Who got kicked out and who could stay all seemed pretty arbitrary to me. Hannah had returned—she'd been allowed to stay because her mother had agreed to pay for an outpatient program run by the Centre, something you could attend after your time here was up. I'm sure Steph was consistently using, the way the girls joked about it, the way she tore herself apart every other night. But the counsellors liked her. They didn't like Kate, or her mess. So she was gone.

Later in the night there was a scream, then the thumping of footsteps up and down the stairs, then, a few minutes later, the sound of an ambulance. The next morning, we found out Aruna had been taken to the hospital. Her roommate was a large woman with FAS. We didn't get many answers from her as to what had happened. She didn't like the attention on her, she just bowed her head and said, "I think she's probably dead, fuck."

Steph said she was triggered and felt a panic attack coming, and she missed the rest of the day. The counsellors let her stay in her room, one sitting with her the whole time. Everyone wanted Steph to do better, including me, like she was our collective higher power—if she could get sober, we all could. But she kept letting us down. I knew she was scared of the jury in her upcoming trial against her father, because they probably wouldn't believe her, even though we all thought it was true. Why should they believe her? She had stolen from her father, been kicked out and cut off. She was an addict and lying's what we do. What the jury wouldn't see is that whatever the outcome of the trial, the stress of it all in the first place would probably kill her, it was already killing her.

I don't think she was triggered by the idea of Aruna being dead, she was jealous that she was free.

The day was heavy until the latest intake showed up. In all her five-one, eighty-pound glory, there stood Tammy. She had wiry grey hair that stood up à la Phil Spector, and she insisted on wearing large sunglasses emblazoned with rhinestones, on account of "a fucking eye thing, okay?" Her jowls hung low like a bulldog's, her nose was swollen, and her stick-figure legs were covered by skin-tight grey leggings with what looked like a large diaper made from toilet paper or paper towel poking out underneath. Throughout that afternoon, I noticed Tammy often put one hand on her hip and the other one palm up, a lit or unlit cigarette in it. She mouthed words, silently, and shook her frail body as if she was still talking and had forgotten to turn up the volume.

She was mean and sarcastic and hilarious, and smelled terrible. When asked by the plucky pothead Hilary what she was in for, she looked at her and said, "Well, obviously I have a bit of a fucking problem, okay?" Then asked where she could smoke. A counsellor intervened.

"Free time is designated in your welcome package."

"I was too blinded by the fucking glitter stickers."

"And if we can watch our language."

"Sweetheart, I have never been told when I get to smoke. One vice at a time, okay? It's like a goddamn concentration camp."

Hilary had issues with this. "I'm Jewish!"

"So was Jesus."

"I just think it's a little bit rude to compare the two."

"Well, Jewish Jesus Christ, I wasn't trying to be fucking rude, I was trying to smoke, okay?"

Then Tammy stuck her tongue out at the now less plucky Hilary, and somehow the argument was over. I don't know why I liked Tammy, maybe because although she was angry and petulant, she didn't seem to want to hurt anyone's feelings, she just was loud and brash and kind of oblivious. She farted during our mindful meditation time and completely owned it, saying in her annoyed drawl, "Well, what are you gonna do about it, okay?" I watched her as she continued mouthing silently, but then the counsellor gave me a look to close my eyes and continue to be mindful.

While we waited outside for our evening meeting at a church nearby, Madison pulled up in a Benz and stepped out onto the curb newly Botoxed and filled, and smiling at everyone as if to say, "I'm fine bitches, better than you." Steph gave her a huge hug and Madison told her to stop fucking with her face. Maci Ann whined that life had been so boring without her, and Tammy took one look at Madison and said to me, "Who's the freaky Barbie chick?"

"Her name's Madison, she left a few days ago."

"She doesn't look sober."

"Uh, I think she left early."

"So is it just a crock of shit then?"

I wanted to tell her yes, but I didn't want to say it out loud. We could joke that rehab sucked and failed us daily, but I didn't want to say definitively that it wouldn't work. As if I could some-how put what miniscule seeds of hope I had in the program into Tammy and let her, with her armour of cynicism and take-no-bullshit attitude, protect it and save us both. I wanted to tell her that the truth was it was so fucking scary. And that she had no fucking idea. It was all so stupid, but stupid was all we fucking had, and if we gave up on this . . . man, we would have fucking nothing. We'd be toast. Yeah, it was a crock of shit mostly, but I guessed we deserved it, didn't we?

"I think if you're here, at least you're not out there."

"Well, I don't wanna smoke next to her, she looks too flammable."

Then she stalked off to stand next to a tree. Madison didn't say anything to me, just took Steph around the church to talk privately, maybe to do more drugs, as one does before a sobriety meeting. I didn't actually know, I'd never asked Len where or when the girls that secretly used did so. I was afraid of harder drugs and of getting kicked out, and afraid too that I might just happen to show up to the spot where the girls were using, if I knew.

The first time I got drunk I was twelve. I'd followed some older girls, at one of my last cast parties, into a Branigan's bathroom. I knew they were drinking and that they'd find it so fun to get the foolish younger cast member drunk. I went in after them, wide-eyed, "Wow, you're doing shots?"

I did the same thing the first time I knew a friend had cocaine. I followed her to the bathroom at a house party and then acted surprised there were drugs out, but, of course, I deigned, seeing as I was there, to do some. I was a desperate loomer, wanting to partake but never able to ask, so I played the fool, and the fool could not be held culpable for her actions.

Real ignorance was my only saving grace at this point, because I wasn't a fool. Plus Tammy was watching me closely, miming silently in my direction. I couldn't let that strange woman down today, not when she was protecting my hope. It may have been the most responsible thing I had done in months, forcing myself to go inside and sit next to Plucky Hilary, who became very serious and moved by everything the speaker had to say while I counted the number of times she put her hand over her heart and nodded, eyes closed. Sixteen. I wanted to like Hilary but her sincerity bugged me and I found myself comparing her to Tammy and, for the next twenty-five minutes of AA talk, tried to picture them living together in a sitcom dream world. It made the time go by faster, and I wasn't thinking about whether Aruna was dead or alive, wondering if she'd finally found a way to feel different. I kept looking over my shoulder for Steph and Madison, hoping they were only making out with more boys. I felt nauseous.

Tammy came down to Wednesday's breakfast still wearing the same clothes and oblivious to her toilet-paper diaper sticking out the back. She had forgotten to order any eggs, so she stuck her tongue out at the chef and went to the courtyard to smoke, somehow pilfering a vanilla yogurt along the way, which she ate angrily while staring at us through the glass. We had art therapy, which she was very annoyed at, until she started drawing dicks like a young schoolboy and laughing at them, despite the counsellor's obvious dismay.

At lunch, Tess graduated. Maci Ann and Len rolled their eyes, but since all the counsellors were standing by, it ended there. No snarky remarks.

"I just wanna say thanks, I really hope this is the ticket."

She clutched her thirty-day token. Her other hand rested on her bloated stomach, and I tried to push away any thoughts of what was growing in mine. I made more mental notes of the terrible thoughts I'd write out later, pointing out how contradictory it was that I could be happy for Tess making it out of rehab alive, for having completed the program, and at the same time know that it was the outside that would probably eat her up, and that she'd probably be dead soon. And I thought, Am I just like Tess? And in that moment, I hated her. But I was also happy for her, truly, and it confused me.

"Glad to be going home though."

I wondered if she even knew where home was—most of us didn't. The remnants of my former life were tucked away in an overpriced storage locker with a hard deadline. When I had first pictured leaving the Centre, I thought it would feel like coming up for air, I'd breathe again, I'd see the city with new eyes, but now it felt like a tunnel that was getting smaller and smaller as I moved forward. I had nothing out there. I had no real friends, no job, and no home. I watched Tess shake the hands of the counsellors, and when she was done, I excused myself to go cry in the washroom quietly, and so very briefly.

I didn't want to stay here, and I couldn't leave. I needed a quiet place of my own to heal, a self-imposed quarantine, except I guessed I would need to work and maybe even socialize. A life, a life and an apartment and things to bounce off so I wouldn't be alone too much, but could be alone when I needed it. I felt guilty about wanting things. I listened to women moan and cry and tell tales of such terrifying abuse and I was upset because I was twenty-two with no plan. I washed my face. I wouldn't be homeless, I told myself. I'd think of a plan. I'd take the first job I could get. I'd take the first basement bachelor that was available. I would grind it out and move up quickly and move on and I wouldn't even remember this brief breakdown. I'd just keep my mind filled with motivational quotes and I'd laugh again and be fine. If not, I'd just kill myself. But I'd hold off on that for a little while. Maybe move back to Winnipeg first, and I didn't want to kill myself in Winnipeg because it just seemed excessively bleak, overkill really. I probably wouldn't actually kill myself, but telling myself that I could, just in case, made me feel better.

When I came back from the bathroom, most of the women were waiting for official lunchtime to be over so they could smoke or leave for the allotted twenty minutes to buy more smokes.

"You wanna go get a coffee?"

I turned to see Maci Ann and Len standing behind me. Generally, they didn't invite me out, I just latched onto whoever was going out and walked behind them, chugging my extra-large double-double as the women spoke to each other. Once a loomer, always a loomer.

"Yeah, that'd be great."

I followed them as they hurried out, barely signing the exit sheet, you had to write down your name, where you were going, and the exact time you had left. Upon re-entry the counsellor checked the sheet, making sure you hadn't wasted a moment buying smokes at the Lucky Moose, otherwise you had to answer a thousand more questions. It made anyone sneaking drugs inside much more impressive.

"Do you want like, a latte?" Maci Ann asked me.

"Oh anything's fine, just caffeine."

She rolled her eyes.

"I want a latte."

Then the two girls sped up in front of me, ducking into some tacky internet café I hadn't noticed before, just half a block down from the Centre.

"They have coffee here?"

"It's an emergency."

I watched as Maci Ann and Len scurried to a computer near the back and pulled out a bunch of credit cards to buy time. The man behind the counter squinted at them, I realized they weren't buying coffee, but I ordered one anyway.

"Could I just get a large coffee, any blend, um, do you have cream?"

"Where are you girls coming from?"

"Um, school, the art school."

"You're artists?"

"Yeah. Trying to be."

"Three seventy-five. If your friend wants internet she has to buy it here."

"Awesome, how much is . . . the internet?"

"You can buy time."

"How much is time?"

"How much time do you need?"

"Uh, just like ten minutes? Actually, for two computers."

"Fourteen seventy-five."

I slid next to Len and Maci Ann with my expensive and terrible coffee, and two slips of paper with our internet time code. I passed one to Maci Ann.

"Hey, you actually have to buy the internet up there, so I got you ten minutes. That guy's kinda cranky."

"We're not supposed to be here, the guy knows it. Did he ask if we were from rehab?"

"He asked where we're from, I told him art school."

Len sneered, "Yeah right."

"Fuck, I hope he doesn't fucking rat. I just need to check like, one fucking thing."

Maci Ann and Len were glued to their computer so I fired up my own, trying not to look at the man behind the counter. Could he really rat on us and get us kicked out? Couldn't I prove I bought a coffee from here? My hands were shaking as I tried to quickly skim through Craigslist, looking for apartments, no idea what I would say if I found one. Can I come see it in two and a half weeks when I'm out of rehab?

"You should try Facebook. Unless you wanna get raped and murdered."

"Huh?"

I saw Len looking at my screen.

"If you're looking for roomies like, reach out on Facebook, 'cause then it's like someone knows someone, not just some rando who wants to wear your skin."

Len seemed very sure of herself, not that I thought she was speaking from experience, but I went to Facebook anyways. I quickly typed into my status that I was in need of an apartment or roommate at the end of the month. I ended by saying I promised I wasn't some creep trying to wear anyone's skin. I immediately regretted posting it, but before I could edit it I saw a message, just one, an angry little red flag blinking atop a blue envelope. I opened it.

"You've got some fucking nerve calling me out like you did. I am just trying to help you, I love you but you're so fucking crazy. Sweetheart I want to be there for you, but you can't cause another fucking scene. I have too many people counting on me for you to try and fuck up my life. I'll see you soon. I love you."

It was from Chris. I hadn't spoken to him since right before my pretty shoddy suicide attempt. My already rapidly beating heart was climbing up my throat, I looked over at Maci Ann and

Len, they were having an artistic discourse about nude photos Maci Ann was sending to an admirer. I didn't know what to say. Fuck you? That wasn't enough. Tell him I'm in rehab? The blood was draining from my face. I shouldn't have told him about the appointment. He wouldn't remember, I told myself, he'd said see you soon . . . as a threat?

"Cheap-ass cunty motherfucker!" Maci Ann exclaimed, furiously turning off her computer. She stormed off and Len followed her, motioning for me to go too. I deleted the message from Chris.

I tried to nod at the cashier as I ran after the girls. Please don't rat on us, I thought. Instead of writing them in my pink journal, I pictured spray-painting the words on the side of the café: "Snitches get stitches, motherfucker." No, I'd write something more terrible than that. The threats were jumbled up in my volcanic head. *Fuck you fuck you fuck you.* But there was no reason for him to say anything. Why would he?

"Throw that shit out!" Maci Ann yelled at me in between drags of her cigarette. Len pointed at my take-out coffee cup, which was stamped with the forbidden café's logo. I sprinted to a trash can halfway down the block and back again. I was out of breath by the time I reached the girls.

"That shit woulda gotten us caught."

"I'M SORRY!" I hadn't meant to yell, or start to cry, as I grabbed the bus-stop pole and keeled over, breathing heavily.

Maci Ann looked at me in disgust. "Can you chill?"

Len didn't say a word to me. I gathered my composure before we went inside. Len and Maci Ann disappeared back into the courtyard for another smoke. A counsellor approached me before I could sneak back into my room to wash my face, slit my wrists, I wasn't sure.

"I need a word."

If that cashier had ratted, I swore I really would kill him, I wasn't even supposed to be there.

"Why don't you come in here?"

Most of the counsellors were white, blond, mid-thirties to fifties, and indistinguishable between their backstories and self-identification of also being alcoholics. But this one always wore an oversized army jacket and combat boots. Our sober drill sergeant. She took me to the room where they administer medication before breakfast and bedtime. We're not allowed to keep our own prescriptions on us, so anyone who needs daily medication has to wake up early and wait in line for it to be given back to them.

"So how are you finding the program?"

"It's fine."

I felt like she was about to threaten me with being kicked out, the hammer was about to drop, I shouldn't have gone to that café, followed Len and Maci Ann, but then I shouldn't have done a lot of things that had led to this moment. My heart was still in my throat, I just needed to breathe.

"You don't seem to be talking much in group."

"I do."

"You don't. It's come up a few times with the other counsellors. You don't seem very open to sharing at all."

So I had gotten away with the café but was being punished for being shy? Bullshit.

"I just feel like if the other women want to share more, I shouldn't like, step on their toes. Like, listening is good for me, I think."

"But how are you going to get better if you're not honest and open with the group? I don't know anything about you. I don't think you know how to be very open."

"I do . . . What do you want to know?"

"How'd you think you got here?"

"I drank too much, I did drugs, um, ha, I don't know, just a shitty human being I guess."

I had a habit of nervously laughing when confronted with, well, most social situations, really. Laughing let a bit more air in. She squinted her eyes at me, I laughed again.

"That's funny? That's funny that you're a shitty human being? Or is everyone here just shitty?"

"No, it's not actually funny. I just, I don't know how to answer that."

"Have you been through a lot of trauma?"

"I guess . . . Like, it's relative, right? But I don't know."

I felt like the counsellor was trying to intimidate me into some sort of cathartic confession. I didn't feel the need to hide my past, I just didn't like being forced into labelling myself as some kind of victim. She kept spreading her legs wider under the table and leaning towards me, head cocked to one side.

"What would you say is the most traumatic thing that's happened to you?"

"I don't know, I don't know . . . how to compare like, bad shit, it's all kinda . . . just one thing after a while. Like, it doesn't get worse or better, it's just what it is."

"Have you been assaulted?"

"Yeah."

"In what way?"

I couldn't help but laugh again. "In every way? It's just . . . it's all the same."

"And that's funny? Also, emotional abuse is not the same as rape and physical abuse. Have you experienced that?"

"Yeah." I shrugged and she mimicked me, like a schoolyard bully.

"And you're okay with that?"

"I'm not like, happy about it but like, it's done. I'm here. I just . . . like, it's not . . ."

I couldn't find the words to articulate it. I wanted to say something about the details—how would the details of the first time I was raped or the details of the last time I was beaten help me heal? How could I possibly use them or compare them to get some sort of answer? How would it make me a lighter person to sift through and relegate each detail of every separate event into neat stacks according to how much they fucking sucked? What the first man smelled like in this pile. What it felt like to feel my skin breaking under the skin of a man's hand in this one. So I could look at the little well-organized piles of hurt and think, Glad that's sorted, now that my lowest moments have been coded in terms of relative damage to my soul, I think I'm ready to be a healthy, well-adjusted person.

"But you can laugh about it now?" she said.

I would have done anything to get out of that room. I understood coerced confessions. If she just gave me the pen and paper, I'd sign my name to whatever she wanted me to sign: *Yes, I am a rape victim, physical assault VICTIM, trauma VICTIM, and I'm an ALCOHOLIC and ADDICT and I LAUGH WHEN THESE THINGS ARE BROUGHT TO MY ATTENTION IN THE FORM OF THREATS.*

Or maybe I wouldn't sign. I'd pretend to, but I'd replace her words with my own, then turn the paper back to her, waiting for her reaction: *I'll rip open my fucking chest right now so I can just fucking breathe. You'll go to jail for murder lady, I'll bleed out all over your fucking combat boots.*

I looked at her, confused for a moment, I couldn't remember her question. I answered vaguely, "No . . . I mean, sometimes? It's just like . . . fuck—"

"*Language.* I don't think you fully feel the weight of your past."

"Okay."

"And I'm not a therapist, but I think you should see one. Would you be open to that? Or would you just laugh through it?"

"I'm laughing because I'm uncomfortable."

"Not because you think you're tough shit? Because you're not. And that attitude, young lady, that'll get you killed out there."

"I don't think I'm tough shit, I just don't like talking."

"Well, you need to talk to someone. And in group. None of this is funny."

"Okay."

"I hope you let it help you. I do. I'd be disappointed to see you in the obituaries."

"Me too. Like, seeing it in theory, not like . . . as a ghost. Sorry."

"I'll see you in there."

Len and I didn't address my minor freak-out while we got ready for bed. She told me Maci Ann had been trying to sell some dude nude pictures and "maybe more," but she'd wanted payment up front. When he'd refused, she'd run out of the internet café, and that was all that we discussed, I was edited out. Then we joked about how bad we would both be at sex work, even just taking sexy photos. She started imitating all the ridiculous poses she had seen of Maci Ann in the photos, making outrageous faces and contorting her large frame on the narrow bed. God I hoped she would be this silly when she got out. I hoped alcohol didn't make her a bad bitch like she said it did. I didn't realistically think she would stay sober for long, but if she could still be playful, still laugh like we did, that was good enough for me.

"Nah, fuck that, I gotta get a real job. Did you ever make a list?" Len said.

"Oh yeah, I actually thought maybe like, a garbage man."

"What?"

"No, no, I mean like, a job like a garbage man. Like a city job, part of a union, benefits, protection. That sorta thing. Good salaries too."

"What do you mean by protection? Like, am I walking around with a bodyguard picking up litter?"

"No, just rights. Like they can't fire you for calling in sick or like, discriminate against you—"

"Like, for being gay?"

"Yeah."

"Shit, I gotta get me a city job. I could use some protection."

"Yeah."

"I'm so fucking happy you are my roommate. I mean, you still got me for like, four days."

"Mmhmm."

Before she said goodnight, I told her I was gonna sneak off to the washroom. We had a sink in our room, but I wanted to be alone as I cupped cold water below my eyes, trying to shock myself into not crying. I wanted to tell her how scared I was for her to leave, I didn't want to lose her, and for tomorrow and the appointment. I wanted to ask Len to be my protection, not just because I was scared Chris would show up, but because then it would be me and Len experiencing it together. I would do it, I would get the abortion, but I wanted to share it with Len. If rehab had done anything for me in these two weeks, it was her. It was the fact that despite failing to share, failing to give myself to God and the program, I had found someone who pretended to be ants hitting the jackpot and who liked to gossip and talk about dog shit. We never said the word *friends*, but we were. We were friends. But tomorrow I would be alone, and after Monday's graduation, she would leave.

I stayed up all night fantasizing about seeing Chris and a drive-by shooting happening as we approached the clinic. He would, of course, perish (not instantly), I would take just one bullet to the gut, and after hours of surgery they would save my life but confirm I'd lost the baby. People would think I had tried to help Chris, that I was a hero, and because of my traumatic loss, the men who shot me would be forced to pay me fifty thousand dollars. I would take the money and move somewhere warm, warm enough that I could wear bikini tops all year that showed off my bullet-wound scar, but I would never talk about it.

I asked the counsellor on duty if I could skip that morning's meeting to get ready, and she asked what I had to do to get ready that couldn't be done between breakfast and the meeting. I didn't really have an answer, because I didn't know how one got ready for an abortion.

We started our group the same way, having to identify and check in. When we got to me, I identified and paused before my check-in. I was supposed to be sharing more, another counsellor was poised with her pen, ready to write down my response, evidence of my participation.

"Today I am feeling . . . like . . . what's that, what's that song?"

The group stared at me blankly, crosstalk was not allowed.

"A change is gonna come. And I dunno, I mean I guess, for better or worse, um, we'll just . . . see where we land."

I was shaking, it was the most I'd ever said in front of the whole group, I was good at small talk with one or two women, three at most.

The counsellor pressed for more. "So it's a good change? Has anything changed specifically?"

"Well . . . that's the million dollar question, isn't it?"

She didn't smile, no one smiled, everyone looked confused, rightly so. I didn't know how to conclude.

"I guess like, TBD. Stay tuned. Um, that's it. Is that okay?" I turned to Hilary. "You're up."

I saw the counsellor jot something down, hopefully something along the lines of "Why did we ask her to share again???" Hilary started saying how today she too felt like she was changing, and that gave her hope and renewed energy. I was happy she ran with my nonsense, validating it. But she rambled long enough that halfway through her speech I had to get up and excuse myself, I had to leave for my appointment, which just further confused the group as a whole.

They allowed me to go unchaperoned. Again, the rules of who could leave alone and for what were all arbitrary, and the counsellor made it very clear that I was not to make any extra stops and that you never knew when they would randomly drug-test.

"What if they give me like, painkillers?"

"Tell them just Tylenol."

"Is that safe?"

"Ask them. I don't see why not."

"I don't wanna fail a drug test if they give me something weird."

"Make sure you write down what they give you so if you are tested and it gets flagged, we can compare."

"Okay."

It felt odd being in the city with no phone, no lifeline, only my Ziploc bag full of change and tokens. The city felt foreign to me, and I felt anxious about leaving rehab. I felt like a tourist, rereading the subway map, making sure I didn't go the wrong way. I had lived here for years but always with the armour of earphones and access to the internet, to people. I tried to focus on the positive, the time to breathe, to be alone, without my group of girls, just sitting and watching people unburdened by addiction and vindictive ex-boyfriends showing up to their abortion appointments.

Even from a few blocks away I recognized him. My stomach dropped. His hair tied back in a small bun, despite it thinning terribly at the hairline. His big belly, seizing after every cough. I watched him as he took another drag off his cheap cigarette. He was staring into his phone, I wondered if he'd seen me and was waiting until I got closer. Chris, the father of my unborn child.

It had happened after we had broken up for the fourth or fifth time. I went to his house in a drunken rage, sorrow, whatever you wanted to call it. He had been lying to our friends, saying I was prostituting myself, telling the girlfriends of my male co-workers that I was sleeping with their men, that they should show up at my work to confront me, solve the problem. I went ready to defend myself, or to beg for him to stop and tell the truth. Instead he raped me. Then he threw me out, where I vomited outside a Thai restaurant until someone called the cops to bring me home. I was grateful they didn't arrest me, but they didn't arrest him either, my accusations chalked up to drunken ramblings.

I couldn't stop myself from walking towards him now, even though I knew I needed a plan of what to say, what to do. I knew I could fill my pink journal with braver and more hurtful words after the fact, but what about right now, when he was here—and suddenly staring at me. With every step I could feel the blood draining from my face, hands, down my legs, onto the street. *You need to replace the fluid, fill yourself with enough vodka and cocaine to be able to fucking strangle him to death. Burn his shit to the ground.*

He spoke first.

"Hey."

Fuck him.

"Hi."

"I thought I should be here."

I didn't answer, staring at the sinews of my shaking white knuckles.

"I'd like to be here."

I'd like to fucking kill him.

"No . . . I don't think so. I don't want this."

"Jesus Christ, come on. Sweetheart."

". . . I'm sorry."

Punch your own fucking lights out, you coward. You're not fuck-ing sorry.

"I'm trying to be the better man and be here for you. You . . ." He got very close to me, he always got close to my face to whisper threats. I couldn't breathe, I needed quiet and for Chris to put his fucking smoke out. "You're not making it fucking easy. You stir up all this shit and then just disappear, and everyone's looking at me like I fucking killed you. What am I supposed to say?"

How could I give him words when mine were failing me?

Do something then. Tar and fucking feather him and put his head on a stake so everyone can bear witness to the fat fucker's crimes.

I couldn't breathe, both monsters, the one in my mind and Chris, waiting. Clearly I needed to abort this baby because Mom was crazy and Dad was a rapist. Mom. Not Mom. Just me, I was crazy, I was an alcoholic, addict . . . that's what he wanted to hear.

"I'm in rehab, they don't allow phones."

He backed off, lit another smoke. I watched him cough, hoping he'd choke.

"That's the first bit of fucking logical thinking you've done. Maybe would've appreciated a heads-up. I really don't think you fully understand the stress, and the, the fucking nightmare. I don't even wanna see my friends, you did that. I can't go back to normal life and now . . . now you're getting help and I'm just left out to dry? Tell me how that's fair. How is that fair to me?"

"I said I was sorry."

I watched him take a drag.

"I don't wanna speak to you ever again, you understand me? I don't want you speaking to the guys or calling your fucking mom on me, I'm done. Let's just get this done."

"There's not really much more for you to do."

He sighed and rubbed his hairless temples, like I was putting him through an immense amount of pain. I constantly victimized him: he reminded everyone of that whenever he could.

"I'm so fucking done with your shit."

Me too.

I was drunk when I found out I was pregnant and I made the mistake of telling him. We weren't speaking at the time but I thought it would be such sweet revenge, for him to have to feel some sort of consequence for raping me, something he couldn't ignore or talk his way out of. Any time he assaulted me I covered for him. I took the fall, apologizing, Sorry I pushed you to bruise my ribs, I should've been more careful with my words, to not upset you so. But this baby was its own thing, new, it could live and breathe and learn to say fuck you all on its own. Which is what I texted Chris, my way of telling him I was pregnant.

He started showing up at my work, right as my shift was ending, with friends, our friends, urging me to drink, knowing I wouldn't publicly humiliate him at the risk of coming off as hysterical or alienating the only people left who I thought might like me. He would bring me a glass of water which was vodka, or rally our friends to cheer me on to drink with them, knowing I wouldn't have the courage to spoil the fun by sharing our "happy news," while he would get close and whisper promises of murder-suicide if I kept the baby, telling me I was ruining both our lives anyway. He would tell me he could arrange for me to have an accident if I wanted to do it the hard way, and when I would vomit from nausea and stress, he would mock me to our friends saying I was a drunk and no wonder a real relationship had never worked out. Then he'd send me home in a cab, just to show how kind he was, a couple times coming with me, forcing himself on me as a trade-off for not punching my stomach in.

One night I had had enough, enough of him forcing drinks on me in public and sex on me in private. I screamed at him in front of the entire bar (where up until then I had managed to keep a job), telling everyone he raped me and beat me and all I wanted was for him to leave me alone, to leave the child alone, we didn't want anything from him, just peace. He told me to go home, but I didn't. I ended up going missing long enough for my brother to fly out from New York and for my mom to have me committed to the psych ward for twenty-four hours.

I wasn't really missing though. I'd merely taken a bus to Kensington Market, chatted up some random dude outside a bar, and convinced him to come to an afterhours with me. The bar had been thick with smoke, cheap Christmas lights hung on one side, an old pool table on the other. I was so cold, it was summer but the nights were still very cold. The men there kept pulling at my shirt to try to see my breasts, and I laughed while trying to reason with myself that this was enough, this was too much, I needed to go home. Instead I drank more, took more cocaine and ecstasy, a voice told me to stay, *This is the happiest you'll ever be.*

And look at you, I was fucking right.

The next thing I remember, I was waking up and it was a full twenty-four hours later, I was in a strange apartment, and a man was yelling at me that while he was fucking me from behind, I had shit all over him. Then I remember him carrying me to the shower, handing me a bottle of cheap rum, and making my hand masturbate him while the water poured down on me. He threw my clothes on the bathroom floor, and by the time I got dressed he was gone, and so was my watch and the remaining cash in my wallet. I remember smiling, a real moment of euphoria because I knew I had only taken eighty dollars with me, so he hadn't gotten much.

Then I heard my brother yelling my name, the cops had tracked my phone after my mother had reported me missing, begged them to find me. Apparently I had texted her sometime within the last day telling her "goodbye, I'm dying now." I slipped out of the apartment, bleeding and mostly incoherent, to meet my brother in the stairwell of the complex. He asked me what I'd been doing, who I'd been with, but I just shrugged. I protected the man in the apartment for reasons unknown to me still. My father was on the ground floor, waiting with two cops, assuring them he had "got this" and thanking them for their help. What more could they do?

My mom was waiting with her boyfriend's car and took me to the hospital. I was still drunk. She and I were sitting in the waiting room, I told her that I was bleeding but not from my period. She told me she couldn't do it anymore. I replied by showing her the deep cuts on my legs that I'd made in a shoddy attempt at killing myself at some point in the night. I'd seen a *Grey's Anatomy* episode where they'd said you can bleed out quickly from a large artery located in the thigh. Then I told her to go fuck herself.

A nurse gave me the proper paperwork to schedule my abortion and I stupidly texted Chris about it. I was out of my mind. And drunk. And terrified. I thought it would be the thing that would convince him to leave me alone. Now here he was.

I looked over the form as I waited in line for reception. Chris stood a foot behind me.

"I'd like to go with her," he said over my shoulder to the receptionist.

"That's *her* choice, sir."

He stared at me, pleading pathetically at me with his eyes.

"Can I say no?" I asked her.

"Of course, ma'am."

He rubbed his eyes.

"Do you want him removed, ma'am?"

"Jesus, okay, look lady, I'm the father, get it?"

The nurse stared at him blankly and I started to laugh. I couldn't help it. His final tactic, his last stand, was to identify as the vodka-soaked fetus father. It was so tragic and horrible and great.

"Fuck, be alone then. Fucking nutcase."

The security guy looked over.

"I'm leaving! You text me to lemme know it's done."

"No phone."

He looked at the nurse like she should help him, like the world had gone mad.

"So, okay, what am *I* supposed to do then?"

"Sir, do you need to be escorted out?"

He stormed off without saying another word, I could tell it was killing him, not to utter one more threat, but I also knew that he was a coward and wouldn't risk being roughed up by the large security guard with a taser gun.

The procedure itself was less painful than a pap smear. The doctor tried to be very friendly and asked me lots of questions, she smiled at me, a nurse held my hand, and then it was over. The longest part of the whole thing was waiting afterwards, until I was cleared to go. I kept wondering if any slight pain or strange nerve twitch was the beginning of a bloody emergency. Twenty minutes came and went, and I was sent on my way. I held my breath for a moment before going back out into the street, but I knew Chris better than that: he would already be home, getting high and yelling for justice after being killed by an eight-year-old boy in some shooter video game.

As I stood on the sidewalk, shaking my head at cabs that offered to pick me up, I realized I was kind of free. Did the counsellors know how long an abortion took? What if I said there was a line? Like, a busy day at the clinic, extra paperwork. I looked at the bar across the way, opening up for the lunch crowd, just past 11 a.m., legal to serve.

Maybe *this* was the change I'd felt was gonna come, the change I'd mentioned in the meeting. Because I didn't feel angry, I didn't feel the need to spit vitriol into my bargain-bin positive-affirmations journal. I had left everything back in that office, literally, which was a terrible abortion joke but, man, maybe I should write that down. Turn my journal into a whole joke jam, start a stand-up comedy career.

What's the deal with men anyways? Like, sure I know "not all men." But honestly some of you are really fucking shitty! A lot of men say they're trying, and we can't fault them for how they were raised. They grew up on John Hughes films where consent was kinda . . . well, it wasn't the requirement it is today. But that argument doesn't hold up! I was raised on Harry Potter novels but when I didn't get my letter from Hogwarts you know what I did? I accepted that magic isn't real. I didn't try to play devil's advocate and find some loophole to explain why I may still be a wizard. And I certainly don't go around creeping people out by trying to cast spells and shit just because it was an integral part of my formative years.

My body was on autopilot as I walked away from the bar, my brain workshopping bad comedy bits I'd jot down later. The mesh underwear they'd given me at the clinic kept slipping down below my waistband. I didn't know if I was supposed to keep it on. But I didn't care. I didn't mind having to stop every twenty metres to yank up my temporary underwear. I felt good.

I finally found what I was looking for. Internet café and bar. I'd use this time to check my emails. Check my desperate creepy Facebook post. And definitely not drink. I sat by one of the computers and someone came over with a menu.

"Oh I just need like ten minutes."

The server looked at me and then at the menu. I realized that at this café you didn't buy time, it was a minimum drink spend.

"Could I have just like a coffee, um, and . . . the pilsner. Please."

The server nodded and flipped over the menu to show me the wifi code before she walked away. My heart began to race and my cheeks burned. I somehow expected my father, an old friend, someone to come running through the door, to find me, a failure. My stomach was cramping, I was worried I had internal bleeding and would slowly die here and they would find my body with the pilsner next to it, such a fucking shame.

You're good. You're so good. You put Chris in his place, you are no longer pregnant with his kid, you're free! You're better. You have a clear career path. You're not sick, you're whole again.

While I waited for my drinks I went onto Facebook, an old friend that I had lost touch with had messaged me. We hadn't lost touch because of my drinking, she had left to travel for a year with her boyfriend and for a while we would chat online and I would say how jealous I was, but over time we just stopped. She said she had a friend who was looking for a roommate at the end of the month. Shanti, she lived in Parkdale, had two cats, and was a pastry chef. I told her to please virtually introduce us, that

I was backpacking at the moment and had limited service, and I would be happy to be her friend's roommate.

The server arrived with my drinks.

"I'll pay for it now."

"Thirteen."

I put down a twenty, my heart still racing, staring at the bubbles evaporating from the top of the glass. I could see the condensation already pooling on the table. I went back to Chris' profile on Facebook, the message was deleted but I hadn't blocked him, an oversight. I decided to draft him one final thought, but not before I took a large gulp of the beer. It was colder than expected and burned as it went down.

"I will never forgive you."

I sent it, then blocked him, then looked back at the beer, the residue from my Chapstick on the lip of the glass. I chugged the hot coffee, black, trying to drown out the taste. The server was bringing me my change as I leapt up and ran out of the café. I popped about a thousand pieces of minty gum into my mouth, mashing my teeth together as fast as my jaw would allow.

You could still go back.

I was violently chewing, going over my story. I'd just been testing the waters. Proving I could be in control. Proving I wasn't sick. Yes, I could go back and finish the beer but I wouldn't. Maybe after rehab.

Now that's comedy.

My heart had stopped racing by the time I got to the subway. I watched a TV screen display the latest news, a stabbing, a good Samaritan found a lost dog, the train would be here in two minutes. I wondered if this was how Aruna had felt when she waited for the train.

When I got on the subway, I was limping. I wasn't sure why, I wasn't injured. I wonder if it was the only way my subconscious could think of to convey its larger pain. I should've corrected myself right away except there was another older gentleman with a limp, and I didn't want it to seem like I was mocking him, first by limping and then seconds later not limping, so we both continued to limp around other commuters to the handicapped seats that I had no reason to use.

I limped beyond the subway station, just in case someone was taking the exact same route as me and thought, Hey, that girl was faking it just for the seat. I knew that wasn't realistic but it gave me something to focus on. I was still limping half a block away from the Centre, where I saw an ambulance taking Steph away.

Steph didn't come back till late Friday afternoon, slipping into the back of the group discussion. Her wrists were bandaged and her face was swollen. She must have gone to court from the hospital and then back, because her massive mane was pulled back and she was dressed in a scoop-neck yellow dress that was too big for her, with a white turtleneck underneath. Her large eyes looked extinguished, the irises floated untethered inside the muddy whites of her eyeballs, like an old Windows computer screensaver where the logo bounces around the screen but never touches the edges.

We were supposed to be writing a letter to someone in our lives that we wanted to apologize to. It shouldn't have been that hard for me to choose, I needed to apologize to everyone, to my mom, dad, brother, strangers, everyone I'd ever offended with my drunken antics. To my maternal grandmother. When her daughter, my aunt, killed herself, I got drunk before the funeral and crawled into my grandmother's bed, crying that I barely knew my aunt, how was I supposed to mourn when all I knew was her sickness, her deep depression. My family shared memories of my aunt playing with me as a child, buying me big frilly dresses because she loved French fashion magazines, but I couldn't remember any of it. I had no idea who we were losing, and I'd been so fucking selfish making my grandmother console me because *I* was sad that *I* couldn't feel the loss as deeply as everyone else. But my grandmother tells that story now with such love, disregarding or maybe even unaware that I'd been so drunk. She says that it was just so sad I'd never gotten to know my aunt, and it had been a beautiful moment when she could hug me and tell me stories about her, as I started to pass out in her arms. I couldn't write about that, make it real, so I chose another shitty memory instead.

Tammy was ahead of me in the circle, to read her letter aloud. "So I tried to do this, what is this, an exercise? Jesus—"

"Language," the counsellor warned her.

"I just don't have one person. My mother left me a hoarder's house of god knows what, I have to clean it but every day I seem to busy myself with a bottle of gin. And it's heavy shit."

"Tammy."

"I'm getting to my point. Can I get to my point? The only person I want to apologize to is myself. Because I'm old, and I'm here with"—she motioned to all of us at the table, I couldn't help but smile—"so I've obviously wasted a lot of my own time, it's . . . it's like, What the fuck?"

"Last warning."

"But really, I deserve an apology, and so I guess I'll decide when I'm going to forgive myself, move the fuck on."

"I think the forgiveness needs to start today."

Tammy did her best to lift her jowls into a sarcastic smile for the counsellor. "Guess I'll ask the manager."

The counsellor sighed, but not without thanking Tammy for her share, and motioned to me to read my own apology letter.

"My turn? Um, okay, uh . . . I like the self-apology, I do."

Tammy shrugged at me in lieu of accepting the compliment. I rambled on as quickly as I could.

"But I wrote that I would apologize, uh, to my grandma. My dad's mom. I have two, like most people, or whatever. Mmhmm, so I just said I would apologize for getting super drunk last Christmas and kinda ruining things or like, we were all playing that game Cards Against Humanity and just like, we were all having fun and I don't see her really except at Christmas because she's in Winnipeg so it's like, a big deal when she comes out and we, I, like Christmas and playing games with my family, like, it's silly but—yeah, I just drank too much and ruined it, I guess. I don't really remember obviously so—"

"Do you think your grandmother would forgive you?" the counsellor asked me.

I was shaking, the paper was shaking, and I could feel my cheeks getting redder the longer I was in the spotlight.

"Yeah, I mean it might not have even been that bad? I dunno and like, most of her sons are alcoholics and she like, deals with their shit, sorry, like they have outbursts and she deals with that so I dunno—maybe I wasn't that bad like . . . on a scale?"

"Do you think that's fair to your grandmother, having her sons struggle with alcohol and then her granddaughter, that she wouldn't actually be used to it, but recognize the disease, that that might upset her?"

I looked at her, and at what I'd written. I should've written something else.

Jesus fucking Christ, lady, you don't know shit. You don't know my fucking family—you don't know anything! If the abortion didn't work, this fucking stomach ulcer will kill everything. Got me shaking like a fucking chihuahua, I just gotta fucking slit my fucking throat.

"I don't know . . ." I could barely speak, trying to force words out breathlessly. "I mean that's why I wrote the letter."

"I really appreciate you sharing, thank you."

Then the women all said thank you, in unison, the way we'd been instructed to, and I slid further down my chair, and as Ellen began to read her apology to her husband, I started playing Christmas songs in my head.

"You wanna hit up Shoppers?"

It was Family Day, and my father was out of town, my mom still travelling for work, my brother was back home in New York, and I had no one coming to visit. It was kind of Len to invite me out again after my last freak-out. I would have preferred to go back to the internet café, to check if that room in Parkdale was a go, but I assumed the Shoppers plan had been set by Maci Ann and that I had no real say in the matter.

"Yeah, I wanna get out of here."

We got extra time if we were family-less on Saturdays, and I was happy to have something to do other than try to read and risk falling asleep. We were allowed to smoke constantly on breaks, but for some reason naps were prohibited.

Len never asked me about my appointment, which I appreciated because I didn't want to lie, or tell the truth. Even though I knew she didn't want children, I didn't know how deep her vague religious affiliations went, and if it would taint our friendship. Since she didn't ask, and it wasn't something to share at group, I was able to kind of ignore it.

I thought I would be more affected by the abortion, either with guilt or a feeling of freedom, but I felt neither. It was like a video game, where a character is running over a bridge that is crumbling into turbulent water below. Unlike every other trauma that rehab had forced me to look back on and unpack, no one forced me to look back at that day, so it just kind of fell away from me. I didn't look back, and it was swept away by the water.

We wouldn't be tested until Monday, and I kept telling myself it took twenty-four to forty-eight hours for alcohol to clear your system, that it was such a negligible amount, that surely they wouldn't catch me. And it worked, I convinced myself, because I had to.

I had been to this Shoppers Drug Mart many times, sober or drunk, buying tampons or cheap lip gloss. I hadn't been categorized then as an addict, I'd been just another shopper in Shoppers, unburdened. I looked at magazines now, realizing I had no idea what was actually happening in the outside world, and considered buying a newspaper, plus I'd have a crossword then.

"Do you think they'd tell us if like . . . something big happened?" I asked Len, who seemed irritated by the question, she furrowed her eyebrows and walked around me.

"What do you mean?"

"Like if a 9/11 happened, do you think they'd inform us?"

"I dunno."

I was basically talking to myself and to the smouldering men in the cologne advertisements.

"Yeah, I get that news is not really helpful to the journey, but it's kinda weird, we're in a little bubble. Like, Newfoundland could sink or something and we'd just be like, chilling and chain-smoking."

"Who gives a fuck about Newfoundland?" Maci Ann piped in as she looked at hair dyes with Steph.

Len yelled from a few rows over, "What is Newfoundland?"

"Newfoundland and Labrador, it's a province," I said.

"But why would we care if it sank?"

"People live there."

Maci Ann shook her head. "I read, like, half of Canada is just snow like, all year and polar bears. Like, people don't actually live everywhere in Canada."

Steph nodded. "Like Russia."

Maci Ann knowingly tilted her head at me like, "See, idiot." Then she got distracted by hair dye. "Do you think this is like, a purple toner or like, purple dye?"

I didn't know why she was asking me, I looked down at my dirty-blond hair, the split ends like bell-bottoms spilling over the slight ridge where my breasts barely existed.

"Does it say?" I asked.

"I thought you wanted gum."

"Oh, right, okay, I'll meet you up there."

I went to buy my gum, then saw the three girls run outside and around the corner. I just hoped if they were caught for stealing, I wouldn't be implicated. I made sure to neatly fold my receipt for my gum and placed it safely in my wallet, for evidence later.

I returned to the Centre, the girls just ahead of me, where a counsellor barely checked our bags. She was too busy giving a tour to one of the visitors for Family Day. Up the stairs and into the mostly unused boardroom on the second floor the girls scurried, and I followed. There we found Tammy, wearing her giant sunglasses and watching the forbidden TV.

"You're not supposed to have that on." Maci Ann was really just trying to get her to leave.

"No one has told me to turn it off."

She was watching some dating show, I assumed, there were a lot of sexy young women and men frolicking on the beach and then a few other sexy people side-eyeing them and gossiping. Maci Ann seemed to relent, pulling out her stolen dye, and the girls began setting up their various stations, grabbing towels and coconut oil for their hairlines. I sat beside Tammy. I was antsy to talk to this woman in Parkdale about her apartment, but didn't think any of the girls would risk going to the internet café with me. I should've dyed my hair, convinced them to go back now that we had disguises.

"Is this how you talk to each other when you want to fuck?" Tammy kept her sunglasses on as she pointed to the TV.

"No, I think it's all scripted."

"It's not!" Maci Ann yelled at us from her station.

"Why don't you throw some of that shit on my hair?"

"Because your hair is fried, Tammy!"

"Reason two I don't shower here. Hard water."

I didn't get a chance to ask what reason one was because Maci Ann stomped over with her jar of coconut oil and Saran Wrap. "Put this on your head and wait till the evening, then wash it out. Once a week. It'll help."

Tammy made it clear I was going to be applying her hair mask, and the girls snickered as I spooned out tablespoons of half-melted oil onto her head and wrapped her up in plastic.

"Good to go."

"Can you do me next?"

Steph was having a hard time with her massive mane, so I waved her into the chair beside Tammy (she wasn't going to move unless forced to) like an old-timey barber. Maci Ann and Len were already on their way to wash their dye out. Steph took her seat.

"I hate Family Day."

I nodded behind her, trying to ration out the one box of dye for all her hair.

"It's like cats in heat."

Steph ignored Tammy and continued to talk to me. "Do you like your parents?"

"Yeah. Yeah, I do. Like, I was mad they made me come here, but I get it's cause, like—"

"They love you."

"Mmhmm."

I felt bad saying that I was loved. I wondered if I should tell Steph I loved her, as a friend, if that would make her happy and absolve me of my guilt.

"I actually kinda like my mom, kinda. She doesn't go to court anymore to support my dad, so, that's like, cool of her. She's like, neutral."

"I don't trust the court system," Tammy said.

Steph turned, I was trying to squeeze as much dye out of the bottle as possible.

"Why's that?"

"Because it's just *those* guys, but in suits and ties." She pointed at the TV. It showed the men leering at the girls frolicking on the beach, then it cut to a confessional.

"I know I'm here for the right reasons, and I know I can make her understand that I'm the good guy. I'm the guy you're gonna marry."

We were standing on the sidewalk outside a community centre not far from the rehab, waiting for our Sunday morning meeting to start. We watched a woman, either coming down or still high off something, trying feverishly to collect her belongings strewn all over the sidewalk while she smoked a half-finished cigarette Steph had given her moments before.

"They came while I was sleeping! They raped me and took everything!"

The woman's dress blew up around her waist revealing her bare vagina. She didn't seem to notice and continued smoking. The woman walked back and forth between small piles of soiled clothes, a few tapes and file folders, then squatted and rubbed her eyes frantically.

"They pissed on fucking everything. This is my shit!"

The woman who ran the community centre meetings looked at us from the doorway, she said we could wait in the park next door but couldn't come in until the cops had shown up to take the woman away. She told us the woman had pissed on half her clothing, that she was insane on meth. Like I said, there's a hierarchy to addiction. The woman started crying. Tammy stood by, smoking, and said to the woman, "It's not a big deal babe, it's all shit anyways." The woman seemed comforted by that and calmed down for a moment, until the cops showed up. Then she started screaming at them that she was a victim, but they accused her of trespassing and holding.

"Don't you think if I had fucking drugs I'd of smoked 'em by now?"

Then she lifted up her dress to show them her naked body, at which point one of the officers reached for his gun, and Tammy started to laugh. The woman running the meeting ushered us to come inside, so we never saw who won the standoff, vagina versus gun, but when the meeting was over the woman was gone, and her urine-soaked belongings were stuffed in a nearby garbage bin.

The girls didn't seem that upset by the woman—neither was I, really. She was one of us, just a week prior to detox, or a few years after another failed attempt at sobriety. Her mania, outrage, it wasn't specific to her. Active in addiction, or active in recovery, the war was the same, only the ammunition was different. And we all knew it. A few of them joked about it, about times they'd been arrested, out of their minds like the naked woman.

The speaker at the evening meeting was the same as the others, bragging more than speaking ruefully about her prior misdemeanours. She was pulled over for a DUI and had her licence suspended, she was caught streaking on public property, and the real cherry on top, she was once put in the drunk tank for a few hours after excessively tailgating at a CFL game. Hilary liked her and said, "I like how she puts it in perspective that things can be serious but not have to be *so* bad."

Ellen and I caught each other's eyes. Of course we should be happy for plucky Hilary, that her life wasn't so damaged beyond repair because of her addiction. Of course we should accept that everyone's journey is valid and you don't need to experience great trauma in order to seek a better way of being. But I had spent an hour that morning figuring out how to secretly throw away my abortion-issued mesh underwear so that the other girls wouldn't see me doing it. Which had reminded me of the last time I'd thrown underwear away. Like the woman outside the community centre, I had pissed all over them, drunk out of my mind and too terrified to move, rolled up in a bathmat. The man who raped me had roughly tried to put my clothes back on and rolled me up, maybe to keep me warm or to dump my body in later.

When I have memories like the bathmat, I try to flip the page in my mind. Go somewhere else, some fantasy. Change the song, make a new soundtrack, set a new scene, anything else.

That night, I doodled in my journal while Len was in the shower. I couldn't stop sketching violent images, like when I was in sixth grade and kept drawing what I thought the D.C. sniper looked like. I drew them in the hope someone would find them and see how scared I was of violence and death, and tell me it was okay.

You are okay.

I didn't write that sentence down, it just appeared, like a shadow. I could draw terrible things but I couldn't write down that I was okay. Like writing down I was "strong," I was "brave," or, worst of all, I was "worthy." Of fucking what?

No, this was a private test, and I would pass. I forced myself to write *I am okay.*

A semi-positive affirmation. Except writing it under the screaming faces and bloody bodies I had drawn just moments earlier kind of made the words look psychotic. I closed the book and hid it back inside the broken drawer, asking it to please stay put till morning.

"I feel like I'm not gonna be able to sleep tonight, I'm so excited. It's like Christmas," Len said.

"Do you have plans for tomorrow?"

"My girl's gonna pick me up—wait, maybe my girl, we'll see how it is, you know, being sober. It's so weird though, 'cause like, I wanna celebrate but like, how?"

I was watching Len happily pack her bags, trying to be happy for her, hiding how much I would miss her.

"You could get ice cream."

She turned around to give me a mocking smile. "Might get my eyebrow re-pierced. I really don't think I wanna beer though. Like, I do, obviously, but I also kinda don't. Like, I really kinda wanna try."

"I think you'll be great."

"We will see."

"Get your licence?"

"Fuck, I totally forgot. Did you make me cue cards?"

"Shoot."

"All good, fuck, I feel like I'm missing clothes. I just washed everything."

She stomped out of the room, and I'm sure she spent the rest of her night before lights out saying goodbye to Maci Ann and Steph, she only came back in once the hallway lights had shut off.

Monday brought more women. A middle-aged woman who looked like a TV sitcom mom, she had a perfectly coiffed and tastefully highlighted blond bob and wore pressed white capri pants and a conservative dark pink blouse. The woman coming in behind her was the exact opposite: wild and unbrushed stringy blond hair; extremely tight, stained jean shorts with a rhinestone-emblazoned crop top that exposed her bloated stomach mottled with eczema. The sitcom mom stood when she was being introduced, giving a stately wave and humbly thanking us all for letting her be a part of our healing. The second woman leaned back in her chair, legs splayed, picking her teeth, and said, "I'm here for it." And then laughed as though everyone was in on some joke. Tammy nodded her approval in the second woman's direction and then again to the invisible audience she was always communing with. I found it hard to focus on them knowing that both Len and Steph were leaving.

"We have two very special graduates today, first Helena, please come up and get your thirty-day chip."

Len grinned self-consciously, tugging at her tank top to cover her belly button ring, adjusting her bra straps and fixing the ball of hair styled on top of her head.

"Do I have to speak?"

"Just a few words."

"Fuck—sorry! I am sorry. Shoot, this is so tough. I'm happy, I am. Definitely happy to go home and see my dogs. Um, it's cool, it's nice, like I said it every day but it's really nice not waking up like . . . ugh, like a real piece of poo. I feel . . . frig, I know I'm not but I feel like I'm in better shape. Um, thanks though, can that be it?"

"Thank you, Helena."

She covered her eyes, still grinning, and sat next to me, showing off her thirty-day chip to Maci Ann.

"And we also have Stephanie, we're so proud of the work you've done. Would you please come up and get your thirty-day chip."

Steph sighed and heaved herself out of her chair.

"Would you like to say anything, Stephanie?"

Steph looked at her chip, smiling, at that moment she looked like she was twelve years old. Most of the time it was easy to forget she was only seventeen, her face was so scarred and she always looked tired.

"Yeah, I—I'm so embarrassed, hold on. I just wanted to say thank you. To everyone, to the counsellors . . . ha, I didn't make it easy on you. I'm sorry. Um, but I really want this to be the one. I really hope it works, um, I know if I can do the work, I mean . . . sorry, I mean I hope I can do the work. It's scary, it's not, but you get what I mean. I just hope I don't let you guys down . . . 'cause I want to be better, don't wanna die. So thank you for your help and, yeah, for this, and the hope of it all."

A few of the counsellors cried. I wondered if they were crying because they would miss her, or because they knew they couldn't protect her anymore. She wouldn't be able to come back for at least six months if she relapsed, and she'd already been living on the streets beforehand, so basically it had to work. Even if she could stay clean, no one could keep her safe. Steph often said it wasn't fair that it all got so bad so quickly. She said she wished she could've at least made it to her twenties, being able to drink and use (just a little, she said) before it got this bad. She'd had so little time to be young, truly young. She said nothing had been the same after she turned twelve, and that if she could, she would give up every adult pleasure to be eleven forever.

I wrote my number in Steph's AA guidebook, my email, and my full name to find me on Facebook. I wondered if I'd ever see her again, if we'd be friends, outside of the politics of the Centre and the girl clique. My mother always told me there was a fire in me, but it wasn't a light like Steph had. If I had a fire it was fuelled solely by my mother's love, I could not have created or stoked anything in myself like my mom did. I thought of writing that in Steph's book: that she had a light in her, that if she let it, the world would love her, that she would be okay if she could let the light guide her, instead of the darkness. It all sounded too hokey though when I thought of it in print, so instead I wrote beside my contact info, "Girl! You're the best! Good luck, you got this! Thank you so much for being awesome!" It was generic but she loved it and gave me a big hug, then left.

While Len searched for her missing clothes, I wrote and drew her a big letter, trying to make it fun and using cartoon imagery to make it easier to read. I wrote how I couldn't wait for her to pull up in her whip to pick me up for coffee. How I was so excited for her to start hiking with her dogs (and maybe other dogs to make money?), and good luck with her maybe girl, and to remember she deserved to be loved properly. My dad always told me, "Everyone deserves to be loved properly," though I never heeded it. I hoped Len would though. I sheepishly gave her the letter, realizing that the fact I had put so much work into it might embarrass her, as if I was dedicated to her much more than she was to me. She looked over it and told me to read it, so she could hear it in my voice. I was a bit disappointed, I'd been excited to see if my cartoons worked, but I read it to her quickly and she grinned uncomfortably.

"Girl, you're jokes."

"I just thought, I was just happy you were my roommate, and not like . . . Tammy."

"Fuck," she said, stretching out the word. "I'd leave, ha ha."

I smiled, she was all packed up, waiting for the right time to make her exit.

"I put my contact info on it—"

"Oh fuck, yeah, I'll take it with me, I didn't know if it was like, a *letter* letter."

"Oh no, it's nothing, you can just, if you want, when you get your phone back you can put that stuff in it and throw the letter out."

"No, no, I'll keep it."

"Yeah okay, whatever, don't want Dee to think I'm writing you love letters."

"It's kinda like a love letter."

"I didn't even use cursive!"

"What's cursive?"

"Like, handwriting, to make it look romantic."

"True, it's more like, kiddie."

"Yeah."

"Okay well, I'll call ya in like, what, two weeks? Shit, you know what, let me put my number in your book 'cause I don't know when you're getting out."

She scribbled it down quickly, passing it back to me, then stuffed my letter into her large purse. I wondered if she actually wanted me to call. We were friends, but we were addicts first. That's not something you can forget. It's why I didn't trust sponsors, volunteers willing to take on another person's pain, so close to their own.

I thought of a childhood friend of mine who died of an overdose, alone and hurting. It happened just a few months before I came to rehab, I'd been ignoring his calls because I knew I couldn't carry the weight of his pain even by telephone. He called and called. Instead of feeling guilty I imagined putting him on an airplane, sending him to Amsterdam, the last place, he'd told me, he was happy. The last place he felt free to be himself, a gay man. I left him there in my mind, dancing, laughing infectiously, telling myself he would never call again because he was too busy having fun. I looked at Len's suitcase, wondering, If I couldn't be her friend, where could I put her in my imagination?

I gave her a half hug, we had discussed before how we both didn't like touching, but I thought she would laugh at me if I tried to shake her hand. She kind of hugged me back, but she was holding on tight to her luggage.

"Hey, good luck out there."

"Girl, I'm gonna get my motherfucking eyebrow pierced." She stepped towards the door. "Sorry you won't have another roommate as cool as me!"

It was nice waking up alone, without the immediate presence of another woman, but also a sad reminder that one of my closest friends was gone, and that my knowledge of the inner happenings of the Centre would be greatly diminished. Ellen didn't gossip, she was too annoyed by the women to spend any time dissecting exactly what annoyed her. Maci Ann was all right, but we had little in common, and I found it tiring to pretend to be impressed by all her falsehoods.

I was allowed to miss Tuesday morning group because of my appointment with the therapist. Most of the girls were jealous, a few were impressed that I was messed up enough to warrant therapy. Like I was hiding some deep inner turmoil that could only be professionally evaluated. The counsellor told me beforehand to jot down a few talking points, things I could use help opening up on. I opened my neon-pink journal once again, wondering how to put trauma into bullet points. I couldn't bring myself to print the words clearly onto the page. It was like a film playing on an old projector, with the lights on. The images were blurry and it was hard to make out the details. If I were to write the words down, to turn off the lights and see the film clearly, with the colours saturated and faces defined, I think I would fall back into the story. I needed a kind of smoky haze, a mental buffer, between me and the words. So instead I wrote down clues, happy words tied to terrible memories: *field, Christmas lights, beach . . .*

I was nervous before the meeting, despite having seen many therapists in the past. The first when I was thirteen—I had fainted when getting blood drawn and lied and said I hadn't eaten for a week. I had, my parents had been fighting and I just wanted the attention. The second time I was eighteen and dating my first boyfriend, Evan . . . or was there another therapist in between those two, to try to deal with the fact that two of my family members had killed themselves? But, anyway, the second/third time was because I kept having panic attacks after getting date-raped at a bar. The therapist had asked why I'd been drinking alone and I said because I was about to see my boyfriend and I hated him so it helped to be drunk. She then suggested that I break up with him but I didn't want to hear that so I never went back. Then the third (or fourth) time, the therapist was an older man who seemed overwhelmed when I told him about the first time I was assaulted, so for the next few sessions I just told him banal details about my week so he would feel like maybe he could help me, but soon I was too broke to afford to lie to him anymore so I cut that off pretty quick.

This therapist was an older woman with long, curly grey hair. I recognized her from the posters by the stairway payphone. She offered healing seminars and retreats for former addicts to ascend to a higher state of mind. I thought that word choice was poor.

"So why don't we start from the beginning," she said.

I looked at my small collection of words. "Just like, everything?"

"Yes, where you think you first noticed addictive behaviour."

"I ate chalk as a kid."

"Did you get high?"

"No, it was like . . . school chalk."

"Interesting."

"Is that a sign?"

"Could be, do you think it is?"

"I think I always just expected to be sick, at least like, mentally ill, from as early as I could remember. My grandpa killed himself, and my aunt said we had to protect our minds, like as a warning, but then she killed herself too, so I mean yeah, I guess it was a warning of some sort. My dad's side has the addiction, but mainly my dad was just depressed. My mom got pretty sick too for a bit like, in the head, she was in the hospital, so I just kept kinda waiting for my . . . like, my wave of insanity to hit."

"How did it feel to have so many family members passing? Was it all at once—"

"No, no, my grandpa . . . I was young like, eight maybe. I didn't get it, what had happened, but then with my aunt, I just saw her getting worse and worse and like . . . I guess I got it. I'm not saying that makes it, like, okay, I'm just saying I understood why."

"So when your mom got sick, and your dad? That must have been pretty scary knowing how it could end up."

"Yeah, I guess. But like, you can't get mad. Like, I can't be mad at them 'cause it's not fair and like, you can't even be sad about it because then you're gonna make them feel guilty, and that's gonna make it worse, so you just, you gotta be happy. You just gotta stay happy, right?"

"Did that actually work for you?"

"I wasn't walking around like, laughing. But you gotta be happy. Like, I got raped the summer before grade twelve but it's like . . . I don't wanna be that person with the fucked-up family and the baggage or whatever. Like, you have to at least pretend to be happy and normal. And then everyone got healthy so it worked so . . . yeah, it did work."

"Who got healthy?"

"Like my parents, my family, my dad got better, um, my parents got divorced but that was a good thing, they were happier after they stopped trying to save each other from themselves. My brother was doing good, he never seemed to get sick though, like, he always had his shit together, but he was gone, moved out, so . . . he didn't really watch the madness unfold, which . . . I'm happy for him."

"But you weren't healthy."

"I was fine. Like, we all moved from Winnipeg, my dad moved, he's not far from here actually, um, and my mom's in Peterborough, so I stayed in my college dorm in Etobicoke and like, it was normal."

"But it didn't stay normal, did it?"

"Well, then I started dating someone, Evan, he was a very rich drug addict, well, his parents were rich and clueless and gave him a million dollars a day or something, and then after him like, another bozo, Chris, that was his name, is his name . . . and just copy and paste 'abusive relationships' and being hospitalized, then more assaults like, all types of kinds or whatever, and I guess I was drunk or high for most of it but like, also living normally? If that makes sense. And last week I had an abortion, 'cause . . . I was kinda, I just kinda had to."

"It sounds like you've been through a lot. None of it sounds very normal."

"Is what it is, I guess."

"When you say that, you seem to have put it all in one box, all the bad stuff, and it seems very peripheral."

"Oh, I just thought like, in the spirit of time or like, just the relevant stuff to like, the being here type of thing . . . I feel like I'm not making much sense."

"What about the good times?"

"Like, before or during?"

"Just good times."

"I mean I have those—my family, somehow, still loves me, pretty sure, most days, um . . . and I still have a few friends who'd probably like, get coffee with me, they're in Winnipeg, so that's probably why."

"That's nice to hear you have good things in your life now, but what about the past?"

"I don't know, I have a lot. Like, I didn't have a traumatic childhood . . . all that shit like, yes, people died, but I also got to play tag all the time. What's the time frame?"

"Do you think it's harder to articulate the good times because it's actually more difficult to process the loss of that, than processing the troubling memories?"

"Um, maybe? I guess it makes me sad like, that I'm not still a kid on a bike with purple tassels. Now I'm drinking cheap coffee in rehab, it's, uh, quite the fall."

"How would you feel now if you saw that bike?"

"I never learned to ride it, I was too scared of hurting myself, but I walked it a lot of places 'cause it was pretty."

"You were too scared of hurting yourself?"

"Or like, looking dumb 'cause I can't ride a fricken bike. But my friends didn't really like bike-riding 'cause then you gotta lock 'em up, so it was better just to walk. So it wasn't really an issue."

"You seem very protective of your narrative."

"I just like, it makes me feel shitty my parents were broke and bought me a nice bike but I didn't ride it. And they probably don't care now, but I don't like thinking about it."

"That if you were braver, you would have ridden the bike, and you wouldn't feel this guilt?"

"I just don't think the fact that I can't ride a bike, like, correlates to me being . . . this."

"I think all of our experiences, good and bad, lead us exactly to where we are today, wouldn't you say?"

I stared at her for a moment. And down at my journal with my list of words, trying to read what was on the page versus what I saw.

That's what fucking life is, good and bad experiences, and then the result of said experiences being your present situation, you fucking cunt.

"Yeah. I was just told to make a list, so—"

"You put 'bad things' on the list, but you seem resistant, from the way you fire them off, to explore these 'bad things,' and even more resistant to speak on the 'good things.'"

"I don't know."

"I think you do."

"I don't deserve good memories like, if it's tit for tat. Like, that's the price, if you don't wanna remember the bad, you don't get to take the good."

"Even though in your 'bad things,' most of the time you're the victim? Why are you punishing yourself?"

"I'm not a victim, I just . . . It's like the good is a reminder of how far I've fallen. And everyone wants to remind you of the good, to relive the good, to get back to good, but it's like no one sees how much space is in between. And like, yeah, shit happened to me, I guess, in that space, but I also like, fucking filled that space with my own shit and I don't . . . I don't wanna wade through shit to get back to something. Like, I can't go back to what good was, it's not there anymore."

I hate her. I've never hated anyone more.

"Do you think there's a lot of pressure on you to be happy?"

"Who doesn't want to be happy?"

"Do you ever get flashbacks or anxiety?"

"Kinda but not . . . debilitating, is that a word? I just don't think about it too much, so it doesn't keep me up at night. I just think about something else."

"Do you think you've fully processed it all?"

"I think so. I think people hear all that shit and expect me to be, like, more fucked up, but like, I'm fine."

"Even though you're here."

"I'm here because I drink too much."

"But why do you think you drink? Maybe you're afraid of feeling everything if you unpack all your trauma?"

"No, I've like, unpacked it, that's the thing, I unpacked shit, I did, and it's not better. Like, I don't care, I don't feel anything, and that's why I drink, I'm not happy, I'm not sad, I'm not funny, I'm not . . . Nothing moves me unless I'm like . . . I just wanna feel normal. Un-self-aware. Like people walking around, laughing at stupid shit, and making friends and eating ice cream and being fine."

"I think it will get better, but I don't think you're ready to fully unpack everything right now. I think it's okay, for now, to leave it all in your little box. You can take it out when you're truly ready to heal."

"I just, I have to believe it's more than trauma. That I'd be like this without all that. Like, it's inevitable, so it's not anyone's fault, it's just shitty wiring that I just need to . . ." I tried to mime untangling the wires in my head.

She just looked at me sadly. "I can't answer that—if things would be the way they were if you had a different journey—but I do know you *can* control your new journey."

"Do I have to take a seminar?"

"It might help."

"I have no money."

"There are government-assisted outpatient programs for when you get out, there's sober living."

"I think I have a roommate situation happening."

"That sounds good in theory, but will you be safe? It says in your file you self-harm."

"Yeah, but that was . . . What's that word for like, a random, not real thing?"

"You need to continue to work the program."

"Yeah."

"And do the steps."

"We do the first couple here like, one I think is just acknowledging it, so that's covered."

"I appreciate that you use humour as a way to protect yourself."

"That's showbiz, baby."

"Okay, well, thank you for speaking with me."

She gestured to the door, I didn't want to thank her but I did anyway.

She replied, "Of course, I'm happy to have helped." Maybe she helped by telling me to put everything in a box and file it away, or maybe she didn't.

The same counsellor in combat boots who arranged the meeting was waiting in the hall when I got out. Probably trying to listen, make sure I was sharing.

"How was it?"

"Good."

"Just good?"

"I'm never gonna say the right thing."

"I'm not asking you to be right. I'm asking you to be honest."

"She told me not to talk so much about the . . . bad stuff. Like, she said to wait."

"I doubt she said that."

"What? She's right there—"

"Sometimes it's braver to be vulnerable."

"I'm not lying. Why would I lie?"

The sitcom mom had come down the stairs, either lost or waiting to talk to the useless counsellor.

"I'll be with you in a moment." The counsellor looked back at me. She would've been a terrific cop, just fantastic at eliciting false confessions.

Fuck you fuck you fuck you. I squeezed the journal tightly, trying to calm it down. I was sure I felt it shaking.

"I really tried. I did, and I told her shit and she said I wasn't ready to fully explore—"

"Because you're not brave?"

"I guess! I am trying. You're just like . . . busting my balls."

I saw the sitcom mom smile, I was glad I hadn't offended her.

"Language. I can see you now, Darlene."

"No, wait, I'm sorry. I don't want to get kicked out."

"No one's threatening you. We all want the best for you."

"Could I use the office computer? It's not for like, bad stuff. I just have this roommate lined up and I need to just, like, solidify—"

"I can't allow that."

"But it's a place to stay after, you arrange aftercare—"

"Do you want to arrange aftercare?"

"No, but this apartment—"

"It would be irresponsible to let you arrange some apartment, especially in your state."

I wasn't in a state, but her accusing me of being in one caused my body to start shaking. Tears began to run uncontrollably down my face. I was exhausted and empty.

"But I'm not doing anything wrong."

"Why don't you have a snack? Darlene, if you want to come into the office."

I stood there, letting the tears blur my vision, and saw a blond coiffed bob approach me. The sitcom mom, Darlene, hugged me, a real hug, and I started to cry harder and held on to her, despite my flaming skin, itching to push her off. She let me go and I went downstairs to eat the only available snack, bread. I sat by the new intake with the sparkly crop top.

She looked at my puffy red face. "They really fucking break you down, huh?" Then she gave me a fist-bump.

Later in the evening, I discovered she was kicked out for having an undisclosed disease, and despite it being pretty improbable I would catch shingles from a fist-bump, I refused to use my right hand for anything other than vigorous handwashing. I got stuck in my sweater before bed and started to laugh for the first time in days, thinking of how fucking stupid it would look if someone came in and found me suffocating in cheap cotton because I was an anxious freak.

I wanted to pay Darlene the sitcom mom back with kindness somehow. I watched her from afar during breakfast, wondering how such a put-together woman had ended up here. I learned the answer at that afternoon's meeting. She was braver than me, so she shared.

"I guess, well, I was up to drinking about one litre of vodka a day, maybe a few glasses of white wine, Sauvignon Blanc, if, well . . . No need for specifics." She was still trying to remain remarkably composed, but I could see the levees buckling, I wondered if she'd actually let herself break.

"See, I had this backpack, oh it's just . . . the things we do. Anyway I'm sorry, this backpack, it was the same as my youngest, Kevin's, beautiful boy, he's seven now, um . . . just four days ago, and . . . *whoo-wee*, okay. I was always very careful, I would store the vodka in my backpack. My husband, um, he, for a while the wine was fine to be out because it was social, having a glass of wine with friends at dinner, um, though, after some time, that went in the backpack too. I was, yes, careful that the backpacks stayed separate, it was merely an illusion because my husband, bless him, he works so hard and the children . . ."

She wadded up Kleenex and pushed it against the bottoms of her eyes, a proactive move to catch any tears that might build.

"The children are and always have been my responsibility, I am a stay-at-home mom, and I love it, I truly do. You see, he wouldn't check the backpack because he would assume it was Kev's, and Kevin, he's my, I'm so sorry, one moment. Sorry, okay, so one day, Kevin, no . . ."

She held up a finger, composing herself, and we waited.

"I mixed up the bags. He went to school with my backpack. Of course there were phone calls, and we were all so humiliated, my husband, and Kev . . . I couldn't go back. I just, so Kevin stayed home with me after that. Just to put some space in between . . . and I was so angry with him, I kept him home and I was so angry that if he was home, I couldn't drink, because he's so smart and sensitive and I couldn't let him see *that* because I'm, I'm his mom. So, I tried, as moms do, to make it better, I took him to the mall and gave him all the cash I had and said go to a movie, go, spend it, go, buy anything, and I didn't go with him, I went to the Cheesecake Factory. All by myself, and I let him go to the mall alone, and I promised him just one hour, I just needed one hour alone. Maybe have *one* glass of wine."

She was crying but her makeup didn't run, she skillfully caught every tear before it passed the contours of her subtly blushed cheekbones.

"And it wasn't an hour, or one glass, and I get security calling me after who knows how long, and Kevin was so upset and it, it was just like the school, so I took him and we went home. No, I drove home, with my beautiful boy in the back, the last thing I remember is screaming at him for not buying toys, where were his toys? Then I woke up and the car was halfway through the, um, closed garage door, Kevin was crying and, oh lord, he had peed himself and my husband thought I was dead and was banging on the window . . ."

She finally dropped her wadded-up Kleenex and sobbed into her manicured hands.

"I'm the mom, and Kevin, physically he's fine, but how could I do that? I didn't believe it controlled me, but what mother does that? He's just seven. He won't forgive me."

We had already been given a warning about crosstalk so we watched as she sobbed and I tried to catch her eye to somehow telepathically tell her it was okay. She still looked beautiful, I hoped her son forgave her. I wished later on in life he could see this, and see she was trying, and not have the Cheesecake Factory ruined for him forever. I should've returned the hug after the meeting was over, while we all shuffled out to the dining area, but she had already moved on.

Before dinner I tried to call my own mother. I smiled at the women passing me in the stairwell as I slid my quarters into the payphone. Of the two payphones, the one in the second-floor stairwell and the one in the dining area, the stairwell was much more private.

"I'm not here to take your call, leave a message and I'll call you back!"

I wondered if she would suffer, seeing another missed call from an unknown number. If she would feel badly. Before I was in the Centre, despite her travelling, her schedule, she would always call me back, or text multiple times, multiple exclamation marks, about how she couldn't wait to talk.

"Hey Mom, just . . . Dad said you wanted me to call so . . . this is the call! Uh, yeah. Alive and, well, um, we're doing it . . . so, yeah, haven't run, remember they asked if I would run? No guarantees though, kidding . . . I will—"

The loud beep of her answering machine cut me off, and the terse voice on the other end asked if I wanted to listen, delete or rerecord my message. I hung up.

She wanted you to call, you fucking called! Two fucking quarters for a shit-ass message. Why the fuck should you call if she won't answer?

I lightly punched the wall, in slow motion, pressing my knuckles against the peeling beige paint. I kept repeating the motion until I heard Tammy's drawl descending from the third floor, usually she snuck onto the staff elevators, maybe they'd caught her.

"It's not a fair fight."

I looked up, her freshly washed hair made her look like a spring chick, all soft and downy. She wore a towel across her shoulders like it was an expensive pashmina and dollar-store sunglasses that eclipsed her face, a rehab movie star.

"Sorry, did you need the phone?"

She slowly came down the stairs, holding the railing, her thighs were about a foot apart from each other and didn't seem to hinge at her hips, so she twisted her body from either side to lower herself onto each step.

"And listen to more people's problems?"

She twisted past me, continuing a silent conversation with the ghosts in her entourage. She looked ready for tonight's meeting at the fancy Forest Hill location. We would listen to another high-powered exec tell us how they almost lost it all, but then they found God and got to hold on to all their millions.

Wednesday nights, today was Wednesday. I had taken a urine test Monday, and nothing . . . which meant I had got away with it. My single gulp of beer. Nothing bad had happened, I didn't lose everything. What would've happened if I drank the whole thing?

Maybe everyone's just a goddamn liar.

Just be grateful, just forget it. Part of me wanted to admit it, the gulp, and start over, do this thing right, but I knew that wasn't how the world worked, so I repeated to myself, Just fucking forget it.

Based on the stories the speakers told in meetings, it seemed to me there were only a few ways to recover:

1. Recover in shit. Like, halfway houses on the same block where you probably pissed yourself and vomited in your neighbours' yard because you don't have the financial means to remove your-self from your toxic environment. So, ignore the pressure of poverty and hope the program is enough to help you navigate through the past trauma you've experienced all while facing the same routine and obstacles as ever but without the crutch of alco-hol/drugs. And stay sober, don't slip, because you don't have the money for therapy to deal with the guilt of failing, and the group will seem more and more intimidating the more you slip and have to start again.

2. Be privileged. Spend disposable money on "healing" pro-grams for the tax write-off and the feeling that you're making amends to some karmic god. Buy yourself a new life, you have the dough, why not take up spinning or crystals and devote your free time to the capitalist model of self-care, take baths in rose petals and see chiropractors weekly. If you slip, call your therapist immediately to book an emergency session and lie on their leather couch and figure out what the trigger was, then pay for it to go away. Publicly talk about your struggles, be praised, get a spray tan.

3. Be somewhere in the middle. Lower-middle-class, able to scrape enough together to move from one small apartment to another. At the very least, buy something to remind you that this apartment will feel different, a throw pillow. Hold on to that throw pillow, that is now your most prized possession. Go to meetings, find a sponsor, repent, find faith, or at least pretend enough to keep you sober for another day. Stop going to meetings, tell yourself you're too busy creating a new, better life, that it's all in the past anyway. Be vague about why you don't drink at boring company parties. Slip, hate yourself, cry, call your sponsor, they've moved on but convince you to go to a meeting, you hate it but feel like you've got it now. You'll be better. Stay sober for a bit longer, or forever, maybe you're the lucky one. Maybe you learn how to manage long spats of sobriety followed by binges and blackouts and meet someone who puts up with you crying in the tub with the shower running over you every couple of months. Maybe you die. Maybe you live.

I knew I was being bitter, pessimistic about recovery. I was just tired of being open, trying to be open and vulnerable without any sense of real direction. I wasn't myself anymore, just a lump of guilt hoping to be moulded into a healthy woman. I had stopped reading, stopped trying to pass the time more quickly, I just sat with the girls as they smoked and listened to them lie to each other about their past lives, lying about what they would do after, how well everything would go. I was doing math in my head and statistically we couldn't all succeed.

Friday morning brought Grace, the newest intake, and since it was an off day, she'd either come from the courts or paid. Her face was so reptilian, her age was tough to pinpoint. She had thin lips that spread from cheek to cheek, a pert nose, and almost black upturned eyes. She was seated next to me at lunch and started talking.

"I am so happy there are other pretty girls here, I thought it was gonna be a bunch of like, retards."

"Please don't use that term, it's offensive." Plucky Hilary was also sitting at our table, separating the hard-boiled eggs she'd saved from breakfast into chalky yolks and rubbery whites to eat one by one.

"Okay, well, I wasn't talking about actual retarded people. I was talking about how I was happy there were normal people here."

"You can't call them *retarded*, it's not polite."

"Oh my god, are there any here right now?"

"No, but I feel offended."

"Well, that's retarded."

Hilary stopped talking, she wasn't good at confrontation. Earlier, at this morning's meeting, she said she'd had an epiphany. She realized that the two times she'd ever drank in her life, then just a teenager, she had drunk too much and, in her words, "lost control." When the counsellor asked what that meant to her, she said, "I think I was twerking, and I know that the first time it happened I made out with a guy who was not my boyfriend." After that she reintroduced herself as Hilary, the addict *and* alcoholic. It bugged me that I was bugged by this, like it was about rank or something, as though she had no right to claim a type of status she hadn't earned, like we were in some kind of perverse Boy Scout camp where our merits came from having worse and worse addictions.

Grace turned her attention back to me. "How many days do you have left?"

"About ten, maybe nine, maybe I'll get lucky and get kicked out for something dumb."

"Oh my god, you are too funny, this place is shit, right?"

"It's not the worst I guess, I've heard it's better than jail."

"Oh fuck yeah, I hate jail, you just get fat and the drugs suck. I'm so fucking happy they sent me here, you can wear your own clothes. No boys though, that's the biggest issue, or it's not, I get very competitive."

"Well, you can have all the men at the meetings."

"There's guys there? Are you a lesbian?"

"No, just—"

"They're all trash and you're just being a bitch, giving me the rejects?"

"I'm just not looking."

"Oh my god, I was kidding, you looked so sad. I am always looking, the last time I was arrested it was 'cause my fucking aunt called the cops on me for dealing out of her house, because I slept with her husband. But, like, I can't help it, he wanted me. Like, she sent me to fucking jail, and I got babies at home, all because she couldn't keep a man happy."

"Was it a recent marriage?"

"Yeah like, five years or some shit."

"And you have kids?"

"Yeah, they're not my aunt's husband's, all trash dads though, but I like being a young mom like, I don't look like it though, right? Like, I have three kids, when I get out I'll get 'em back 'cause they're with my mom now. Do you have kids?"

"No, I can't even keep houseplants alive."

"You are too funny. Kids are little shits, but I love 'em. Do you live in the city?"

"Yeah, I gotta find a new place after this though."

"Oh my god, we should be roommates, I think I wanna move to the city, like serve or bartend or something. I've like, never had a real job but it's like, bringing food, a fucking donkey could do it—I didn't say *retard*, all right? Like, it's just a job for hot girls."

"Yeah, bartending's tougher 'cause you have to remember how to make a lot of drinks."

"Fuck that, I'm not making martinis, that shit's for douche-bags. Just like, drink your beer, eat your burger, and tip me. Plus I wanna get my boobs done."

"I think your boobs are fine for serving."

"Oh my god, you are such a lesbian, yeah they're fine, and God blessed me with an ass, so we'll see."

"I gotta get my chores done."

"Can I come with you? I don't wanna sit here alone like a loser."

Hilary was still eating her eggs silently, but it was clear she and Grace were not going to converse if I left the two of them together. So I let Grace shadow me as I swept the common areas, she talked the whole time about how gross it was and if she got that chore, she just wouldn't do it because she wasn't "some foreign cleaning lady." I was pretty sure I was her best friend, she linked arms with me as we walked to that evening's meeting, and made me share my lip balm, which I later threw out and thought up an elaborate story of how I lost it, in case she ever asked for it again.

After my lunch chores, Grace and I went to get coffee, and she brought up the idea of being roommates again, promising me she'd put a sock on her door if she was getting lucky. I tried to brush it off without being rude. She told me all about being a low-level coke dealer in Port Perry, how her father got her into it, how her dad's friend tried to pimp her out, but she ended up getting pregnant with his kid, so that really fucked him over. She told me her family was close and loved bonfires and drinking Canadian beer. She didn't ask me any questions about my life, my family, and I was grateful. I wondered if it would actually be possible to live with her, to just listen as she prattled on, sometimes telling me how funny I was, throwing arbitrary compliments my way, then going back to her main story. She was incredibly offensive but not uninteresting, I could just exist in her space and nod every now and then and vaguely comment back at her so she was confident I was listening. Then she got to the part of her story, which had somehow started with dirt bikes, about the cops raiding her home while her children were in it and arresting her for intent to sell. She'd said, yeah, she was gonna sell it, but if they actually knew how much coke she was snorting, they might've just charged her with possession. I decided we shouldn't be roommates, I wasn't ready to be an accomplice to drug trafficking charges.

As we walked back from our coffee, I saw a beautiful young woman waiting beside a tiny car, one of those smart cars, in front of the Centre. She was thin with well-placed tattoos, olive skin, and bright blue eyes. She was the addict everyone wanted to be, tortured but still salvageable. Her arms were crossed and she looked annoyed, but I was overjoyed, she looked so normal, a new intake I could bond with, I could cast Grace over to Maci Ann, or leave her to duke it out with Hilary. I felt the urge to hug the young woman as she smiled, wearily, at Grace and me. We waved at her. A counsellor was waiting at the top of the stairs to check her bags.

"Are you a new intake?" Grace asked her.

The beautiful normal girl closed her eyes for a second. "No, my mom."

I looked inside the car: there was a scared-looking woman, her face so small she could've been mistaken for a child. The daughter sighed and waved to the counsellor for help. I watched as the two of them hoisted the woman out of the car. Her arms were incredibly brittle-looking, and her gaping chest, sternum, and nipples were exposed, in spite of her daughter's best efforts to cover them. The woman's stomach was bloated, as if full-term with child, and every time she heaved to take a breath the loose fabric of her thin dress stretched out a little more. She was wearing paper sandals below swollen, purple, and scabby calves.

Grace smoked and looked away while the scared woman was slowly helped inside.

"Did her daughter look Black to you?" she asked me.

"Um, I dunno, she had nice eyes."

"Mixed babies are so fucking cute. I would love to fuck a Black dude just to see if those big dick rumours are true. I honestly am sick of white men. You ever fucked a Black dude?"

"Yup."

"And?"

"I dunno, I was super high on MDMA and blacked out."

"Fuck, those are the best times sometimes, right?"

"Um, I think . . . Well, I guess it depends on what the other times are that you're comparing them to?"

"Fuck, you kill me, you're really not a lesbian? JK."

At the afternoon meeting the scared woman took up both the good chairs because her swollen legs had to be elevated to ease her pain. Grace and Maci Ann were not pleased about this. I didn't like getting the good chairs anyway. The counsellor was trying to get us sharing about what we would say to our younger selves, but the scared woman kept sobbing and interrupting.

"I'm so, so sorry, I'm just so happy to be here. I didn't want my daughter to see me like that, living in a storage container, but she found me and now I'm here and . . . I'm so grateful, I'm sorry." She let tears and snot drip down her face until the counsellor brought her a box of tissues, which made her cry more.

Later that night an ambulance came to pick the woman up, and the next morning Grace told me she was off to palliative care. I didn't know what that was, so Grace said, "It's where you go to die. I'm surprised they even let her in here, dead woman walking."

Another Family Day, and the nice sitcom mom's blond children arrived. Her youngest, Kevin, didn't hug her, he just clung to his father's legs as she kissed the top of his head. Grace demanded Maci Ann and I sit with her since her mother hadn't brought her children. I was confused about whether Grace wanted to move to Toronto, away from her children and in search of crazy obliterating sex, or if she wanted her kids back. I don't know if she knew.

"How come your family didn't show up?" Grace asked me.

"They both work a ton, my mom lives like, out of the city." I tried to be as vague with personal facts as possible with Grace, worried that once we were out she'd show up at my door or at my parents' door, demanding we be roommates.

"You're better off that way."

"My mom said I was better off in jail. Like, who says that to their daughter?" Maci Ann said. "Like, 'cause she was an addict too, right? So it's like, okay, Mom, but it's your fault."

Grace pursed her reptilian mouth into a thin line. "Yeah, my mom and dad are drinkers, probably alcoholics but fuck, isn't everyone? The way they describe alcoholics here like, honestly I only love coke, I don't have an issue with alcohol, but that fucking counsellor this morning was like, 'Oh, maybe you do.' Like fuck off."

"Everything's an addiction. Even sex," Maci Ann said.

"Oh, *hell* no, I am not giving up sex. I will give up coke if I have to, but that's a no. And coffee and cigarettes—"

I sometimes (often) forgot to isolate stupid thoughts in my head and I blurted out, "And good times."

"What?"

"Oh, I said you're not gonna give up good times."

"Um, no."

"The way you were talking just made me think of country songs, all about like, cigarettes and cold beer and good times."

"Fuck, I look good in a cowboy hat."

Maci Ann piped in, "Me too, girl, when I had my extensions, sexy."

That was the nice thing about these two, even if I interrupted with non sequiturs, they enjoyed talking about themselves so much they would just take it and run with it. I could yell out "Pizza pie!" and it would start a conversation about how they could each eat a large pizza and not gain any weight, or only in their asses. Or "Drywall patchwork!" and they'd spin that into a story about sexy men doing manual labour. Since I had figured this out, it was a lot easier to hang out with them, I didn't have to keep up entirely with every conversation and could dip into my own thoughts without seeming weird.

They barely noticed when I slipped out of the room, I was forcing myself to call my mom again. I apologized to the wall I'd punched previously before I dialed her.

"Hello?"

"Hey Mom, it's your favourite daughter in rehab."

"Oh my god, sweetheart! I was so upset I missed your calls, I was doing this stupid—whatever! I'm so glad you called back, I've missed your voice, how are you?" She sounded genuinely happy, as if I was on a fabulous trip.

"I'm good, just . . . have some free time, so figured I'd call."

"I'm so glad you did. How is it there, how are you feeling? I know your dad said it was a little rough at first."

"Yeah no, it's, uh, it's getting better for sure. Definitely helping like, some of the stuff, I think like . . . You take what you can get from it type of thing. They set me up with a therapist too so . . . like, we're on it. Just getting fixed up in the shop."

"You saw a therapist? How was that?"

"Okay, yeah, it was okay. She told me maybe don't talk about stuff till like, I'm ready, which feels like a first from someone who makes their living off people talking . . . Maybe that means I'm a real special case."

"Oh, why would she say that? You don't have to listen to that, you can talk and cry, you know, to anyone. To me. Anyone. Who is this woman?"

"No, it's like, a good thing. I think like, I have my shit together enough that, like, no need to unbox it all here, it's like my brain is sustainable for now."

"Well, for now? But what about after, what about six months from now?"

"I feel good. I don't feel . . . like, I feel sad sometimes, I'm not sad but it's all . . . I feel like it's manageable."

"So it is helping?"

"Fer sure. Even if only as a scare tactic to never come back here."

"Sweetheart."

"I'm kidding. It's *all* good. In the hood."

"Are you making friends, is there a community?"

"Yeah like, all types of characters. But yeah, it's like a weird summer camp in a way. But helpful, really. Um, but, hey, speaking of people and things, uh, so I was talking to this girl, do you remember when I worked at Starbucks, I had some friends, anyways one of the girls, her friend Shanti is looking for a roommate in Parkdale and it's actually pretty cheap so . . ."

"That sounds promising. Is she sober?"

"I don't know, she doesn't seem like a party girl, but like"—I had to whisper this part—"I wouldn't want to live with someone from rehab, right? Like, a lot of women get out and get right back to it."

"Not you."

"Right."

"Right?"

"Yes. I just mean like, she seems like a normal nice girl and it's cheap, so I think it could be good."

"Mmhmm."

"I just can't really get a hold of her 'cause like, I don't have access to the internet, and I didn't realize we're not supposed to go to the internet café the girls took me to—"

"Why were you there?"

"I just followed them, it's fine, I'm not going back, but anyway I started to arrange the apartment but I can't go back to the café, so I was wondering if you could, like, go onto my Facebook. I can give you the password and you can message her to set it up. I could even pay you back if she wants like, a deposit."

"Mmhmm."

"Do you want my password?"

"Sweetie, I just don't know if it's a good idea. Do you really know this girl?"

"Kinda, but it's better than like, Craigslist right?"

"Won't they help you set up some sort of a transition house?"

"That's just like rehab, continued, with all these rules—"

"Maybe that's not so bad—"

"You said twenty-eight days! And it's actually thirty, and how am I supposed to be like, back on my feet if I'm stuck in a friggen, like . . . no. No! That's not what we talked about."

I was sure she could hear that I was crying, I probably sounded more like an addict than ever, trying to make deals, trying to get her to front money I promised I would pay back, I knew how it sounded and I hated her for making me sound like that.

"Why don't we just see how everything looks when you get out? We can talk about it then, I'll be back from my trip before you get out, so I could pick you up, and we could look at a few options—"

"This is an option!"

"I know, sweetheart, I know."

"Okay, well, I gotta go."

"No, honey, we can talk about this."

"No, seriously there's a time limit and other people are waiting, so—"

"But are you okay?"

"Never been better."

"I love you."

"Yup." I hung up on her.

You need to let the blood out. I can't fucking breathe. No one wants to fucking help you because you're a fucking mess. I hate you I hate you I hate you I hate you.

I had to get out of the stairwell and back to my room, to put the words on paper, instead of letting them scream at me by the payphone.

Go to your room, you fucking child. Kill yourself.

I didn't want to kill myself, also I had no way to achieve killing myself, I shouldn't have to explain that to myself, I just had to get to the book in the broken drawer and sort this mess out—but there was a woman sitting on my window sill. My new roommate.

She looked maternal, she wore a flowy peasant blouse and her blond-grey hair was curled into a tight bob. She was probably six foot two, with shoulders like a linebacker. She told me she was a former nurse with an opiate addiction. She injured her back six years ago, and was on disability and oxycodone, then Tylenol 3s, then back to oxycodone. She returned to work only to access more medication, and when her bosses found out, instead of pressing charges they asked her to resign and strongly suggested she come here. So she and her husband paid out from their vacation fund.

"Too many goddamn nice people in this world and you still wanna say fuck 'em all."

She said this while straightening out her bed, then she offered me a chocolate mint. I declined and she gave me a look like, "Fuck you, it's a mint," and went back to the window, humming

"Moon River." We weren't going to be friends, but she wasn't going to steal from me, I was very sure, and she wasn't going to threaten me, though she'd win in a fight if she did (unless her back was still out), and in rehab, feeling that you and your stuff was physically secure at night was not the bare minimum but the best you could ask for.

At Sunday meeting I found it hard, yet again, to focus on the speaker. Her bottom had been on the streets of East Vancouver, prostituting herself out for what she called "her vice," as this was the meeting where drug talk was strictly prohibited. I watched the men watching her speak, I wondered if they pictured her at her bottom, half naked, willing to give herself to them for a single hit.

When the men spoke at meetings, it was in much more physical terms: "My body was this thin, this fat, this sick. Missing teeth, black eyes, etc., etc." Men didn't talk about things getting so bad that they had to offer sex, or pay another man most of their meagre income to be promised safety in return. Women had other criteria. We had to ask ourselves, clarify, was it bad enough that I was *raped*? We tried, meeting after meeting, to step around the words *rape* and *prostitution*, and we all knew these experiences represented a kind of border between us, and within us. Men didn't have that line, maybe because AA was founded on religious beliefs that still had homophobic undertones, or they didn't feel comfortable sharing, because we knew it could get that bad for men, but not once, in any meeting, did a man talk about losing autonomy over his body, or his family. They would get "in fights," but never "beaten" like women. They would be asked to stay away from children, but not stripped of their right to see them.

I kept catching myself thinking of children, of childhood, of babies, and becoming sad, so, like changing the song on the radio, I forced my brain to switch topics.

Fuck everyone.

No, I pivoted, focusing on the alarming number of matching rubber sandals on the feet of those in attendance today. I wondered if they were issued by hospitals and detox centres. I had seen them on the streets many times. Thin blue plastic slides. Often worn down to almost nothing on the pad below the big toe.

I found my mind wandering back to children again, wondering if this child I had recently eradicated might have saved me. Given me new hope or, at the very least, if I died in a storage container somewhere down the line, my mother and father could have the child as a sort of peace offering, and raising my orphan would force them, in grief, to keep their wits about them.

I was seventeen when I left a shitty high school party early and snuck open the drawer that held my mother's medication. I had no idea what any of it was, but after her last suicide attempt and stint in the psych ward, she had kept coming home with little orange bottles, so I took a few from each, hoping to go undetected. I wasn't trying to kill myself, I was just trying to come close, to see if that otherworldly feeling, that brief moment before death, was an utterly euphoric thing, and if it was, then maybe I could understand and forgive my mother for chasing it. Then I could believe she didn't actually want to die, she just needed to feel that rush of happiness to get her through the next few days, so she could come back to me and love me again.

No one fucking loves you now.

I felt closer to my parents that night than I had since I was a child. It's not logical, but I was a teenager and didn't understand chemical imbalances or deep-rooted sadness or loss. I just knew that the people I loved were hurting, and if I could take what they took and drink what they drank, then I could understand them better. They wouldn't be alone and neither would I, and that would make us better. We'd all be fucked up together. But my mom and dad got better without me. Because children don't save you, even if you want them to, and even if they want to.

No one's getting saved here.

It was my last week in rehab. One more week and then what would I do? Hang out in Peterborough with my mother and her rent-a-family until I found an apartment? Force my father to let me crash on his couch, listen to his wife sigh every time I slept past 7 a.m. and was startled by her grinding coffee? I was anxious about my potential roommate not holding my place for me. I wanted to explain to her that, despite being a little messed up, I was extremely easy to get along with, and tidy, and quiet. I fantasized about breaking out in the middle of the night to message her, scaling the walls and sneaking back in. It made me less patient in group, I was sharing more but only going through the motions, trying to get to the end.

"Today I feel a little apprehensive about the future, but hopeful, maybe even excited."

The counsellors would nod approvingly, I was doing so well. Then on breaks I stood on the sidewalk and stared at the internet café while Grace talked at me, calculating how I could get in there when the rat wasn't working.

My last week brought more intakes, one woman whom I regrettably but immediately nicknamed the Heroin Witch. She *was* addicted to heroin and had a large crooked nose and a protruding mole on her cheek. Her two front teeth were rotting, and her fingers looked like they'd been broken and put back together again by an impatient surgeon who hated his job. She pointed at people during group if she liked what they said, and it looked like she was cursing them. I overheard her on the phone screaming at her husband (ex or present, hard to tell) that if he didn't put money on her horse at the tracks, she'd kill him, and she went into great detail explaining the glee she would get from it and exactly how she would do it. By Monday evening, she had zeroed in on me and showed up in my doorway at lights out, pointing a crooked finger at the pile of paperbacks at the end of my bed.

"I want those."

"Oh, sure, I brought them from home."

"Uh huh."

She smiled at me when I gave them to her. "You'll get them back when I'm done."

I doubted it. I watched as her hands curled around the carefully curated books my family had picked out for me, already trying to fashion an apology as to why they were no longer in my possession. I wondered if I just straight up told them a heroin witch took them, if that would suffice. I made a mental note to check the newspapers in the next few weeks for a grisly murder with an ice pick by a scorned horse-race-loving wife, or ex-wife.

Tuesday, having completed her court-ordered rehabilitation, Maci Ann left, and Grace cried and said we had to stick together now more than ever, I was her only friend. My roommate was kind of my friend though, despite my not remembering her name, she'd said it once but then I forgot and found it much too rude to ask. She would sometimes say funny things before bed about the other women, and she was utterly pleased when I would agree that, yes, most of the women in here were . . . eccentric. Then she laughed and said, "Well, we aren't exactly a pair of fucking Marys either, are we?" I didn't know what that meant, but she had started leaving those tiny chocolate mints on my pillow, like in a hotel, so I laughed at her jokes and ended every evening cheersing her from my bed with a mint.

Wednesday, I was biting my nails. I wanted to call my mother to scream at her, but I knew that would only exacerbate the situation. Grace told me I was disgusting for putting my fingers in my mouth all the time. Then told me she was fucking kidding and that I should relax.

I was beginning to feel at home in rehab. The arrivals and departures of women didn't faze me, I had been there now longer than anyone, save for Ellen. I had talked to a man at a meeting who had just got out of jail, and he said he missed it. I wondered if I would feel the same. Here, with my seniority, I was finally a part of something, not the most ideal fellowship, but I was safe, for the most part.

Before the Thursday night meeting, I spun in the good chair until I was dizzy then chased Grace by using one leg to push myself along, rolling wildly towards her, yelling that I was gonna run her down. She played along and laughed as I scooted after her all down the hallway.

I didn't have any friends left in Toronto, I hadn't really had any to begin with, not close ones, and Grace wouldn't be one when I got out, but it was still nice to laugh with someone. I thought about how I would approach my remaining friends in Winnipeg when I got out. They were so patient and forgiving but had kept me at a distance when I'd started to unravel. Saying they couldn't help, but they loved me and wanted the best for me. I could tell them life was great again, to come visit. And Shanti would become my friend, and introduce me to her friends, and we would all be so happy. We would be real friends, not like the ones I made through drunken adventures and lost to subsequent drunken misadventures. Rehab would be a blip, and each day that I was at the Centre would fall off the side of the world with all my troubles. The counsellors called this feeling "pink clouding," but I called it hope, so fuck them, I *was* the exception.

With both my parents still out of town, this was my last Family Day without a date. My last Family Day in general. Grace was busy, an older man came to visit her, though I couldn't tell if it was a lover or a family member and was afraid it could possibly be both, so I made myself scarce. My roommate's husband had come to visit her so I had the room to myself. I tried to reread passages in my journal, but it was like looking at a foreign text. It wasn't me, these terrible things. This was a stranger, some shadowy figure that snuck in and bled all over my golden pages. Just like the first night, I wrapped the journal gently in a large sweater and placed it back in the bottom of my suitcase. The stranger wouldn't visit again, I told myself. I would dispose of the journal come Monday. I'd even find an exact replica if my grandmother ever asked about it, and I would fill it with hope.

I wondered if I had actually changed, if, in all my time trying to be so acutely self-aware, some of the group therapy or speakers' messages had slid into the back of my mind and was reshaping my brain from within. I didn't feel different or look different. I still wanted to be able to drink, to get high, but not more than I wanted to succeed and prove to my family I could. I was going to be the special one, the girl that seamlessly went through rehab and transitioned into city living and never looked back. I wanted to separate myself from the other women, and maybe that competitiveness would be my saviour.

I thought about the families embracing each other when they arrived. My family would hug me like that if I stayed sober. I would stay sober, it'd be easy, just don't drink, don't get high. I'd watch bad TV with Shanti until she went to bed, and then I would go into my beautifully decorated room and just think and think and think and eventually time would pass. The drug dealers would be asleep and the bars all closed. And day by day and night by night, as long as I could think and think, I'd be fine. That's all I needed, a place to think, without interruption or judgment. A place to pass the time dreaming of funny situations in which I was much stronger and more beautiful and richer than I was now, and that would be enough. I just needed to think around those things and through them until I blurred the lines between truth and fiction. It would be my own type of high, a self-imposed brainwashing. I was excited about this plan, about next steps, and then a counsellor came up to my door and told me, flatly, that she had a message to pass on, that my father's mother, my grandmother, had died.

"That's ironic on Family Day," I said. My grandmother was dead, it didn't mean anything, it didn't sound right, the sentence didn't make sense. She handed me a letter, I recognized my dad's writing.

"We still need you to come for dinner and evening meeting."

"Can I go for a walk?"

"Not alone, we're all so sorry, I think there's a few girls in the courtyard."

I watched her go, trying to will my feet to follow her but I was glued to the bed. When I finally exhaled, the air rushed from my lungs in wheezes and I began to cough, doubling over on the bed to catch my breath. My roommate appeared at the door with her husband.

"Oh, sorry, I wanted to show him the room."

"I'm—just—leaving!" I managed to huff at her and catapulted out of the room into the foyer, as if I could run away from it all.

She died while you were in fucking rehab, you asshole.

Tammy was arguing with the counsellor about going to buy smokes, she wasn't allowed to go alone. The counsellor lit up as she saw me.

"You two, you can go together."

Tammy looked at me and shrugged. I nodded and off we went. She insisted on going to the convenience store at the shitty mall further away from the Lucky Moose where most girls bought their smokes. I didn't speak. Tammy talked to the ghosts on the sidewalks for a while before turning to me.

"It's so hot. Why are you quiet?"

"I just found out my grandma died."

"Well, shit."

"Yeah."

"I don't really hug, so I guess *shit*'s all I got."

"That's fine."

"So you're gonna be terrible company."

"Yeah."

"So is this the woman you ruined Christmas for?"

"What?"

"Those fucking letters."

I was too shocked that she remembered to be angry, to be sad really. Tammy fucking Rain Man.

"Yeah, that was the one."

"Well, she probably wasn't thinking about that when she died."

"Yeah."

"Just saying, people tend to be all rainbows and sunshine when they kick it. Like, if you have happy thoughts, you're going to meet fucking *God*." She smiled at her ghosts. "Or maybe she was thinking about you and was thrilled she didn't have to put up with any more of your shit."

I burst out laughing, it was the worst thing you could say and it made me so happy. "That's it."

"People don't die because of other people, except murder and that shit. Heartbreak and all that sappy shit won't kill ya."

"Still feel kinda like an asshole."

She shrugged and we stepped inside the store. I watched as she haggled with the man behind the counter for her smokes, eventually swearing at him and mocking him to her invisible friends. We then stood outside the McDonald's next door so she could smoke. I thought about the hope I had given her, on her first day, and wondered if she still had it.

I wanted to drink. Not here outside the McDonald's, or at the internet café, or sneakily after lights out in my room. I wanted to be in Winnipeg, with my family, where she died, and I wanted to drink with them. That's how they would be mourning her, drinking and laughing and crying, telling stories and singing songs. But I couldn't, because I was the alcoholic granddaughter that ruined Christmas. And this wasn't a fucking wake-up call, not some moment where I realized this is how I must honour her memory, by staying sober, or whatever bullshit. It was fucking ruthless.

The next morning, I told myself I wouldn't cry anymore. I felt angry, but I didn't know where to direct it. At the versions of myself I saw sitting in meetings? The versions that scared me the most? The lowest, most degraded versions of myself? The ones reminding me that I was where I belonged, this was the club, and this was the uniform?

She had died on Wednesday, the letter from my dad said. I guess my family thought it best to wait for three days and tell me at the very last minute, protecting their expensive investment and making sure I didn't leave early to fly home and lie down beside the tin of her ashes, sobbing and justifying my inevitable relapse. Then I remembered that I hadn't signed the sheet my mother had asked me to, the one that allowed the Centre to pass on phone messages. My family could only send letters, and if my father had sent it Thursday morning, early, after learning the news, it made sense that it would only arrive Friday, and be opened and screened that evening or the next day. So I wasn't angry anymore, once again I felt nothing, I had to feel nothing. This was my biggest takeaway from rehab.

I thought maybe I should try to feel gratitude, that I was here and far away from the chaos that would follow my grandmother's death. Death was better at a distance—I received only the facts, in timely fashion. She had entered the hospital two weeks ago, thinking she had a stomach bug, which turned out to be stomach cancer. Somewhere in that timeline she went septic, and before she could be sent to palliative (a word I now knew) care, she died.

She had enough wherewithal, even on morphine, to tell her sons no funeral, it was a capitalistic endeavour that made money off the grieving. Just throw her ashes to the wind and eat a waffle or two. Waffles were very popular on the paternal side of my family.

While everyone was eating waffles and grieving, I walked with Grace, before the afternoon meeting, to Tim Hortons and listened to her talk about why we shouldn't tip servers (a week ago she had wanted to be a server) because they're just doing the bare minimum and usually not well. I nodded absent-mindedly, wondering when the best time to contact my father would be, to send my condolences. I told Zoey, the friendliest of the counsellors, that I had to email my family right away, to let them know about funeral arrangements and other excuses death provides. She let me use the office computer which I used quickly to send Shanti a message confirming I would be her roommate, before Zoey noticed and I told her it was force of habit to open Facebook. I opted to wait until the next day so I could call him and hear his voice when I was out, when my rehab stint was officially over, when I could be on the phone for more than ten minutes.

At the meeting that afternoon, Grace pulled my hand up when the speaker asked if anyone had thirty days. Technically I didn't, because of that sip of beer I'd had a week and a half ago, and I felt like shit. All I'd had to do was be sober for thirty days. But I was forced to stand in front of all the women and graciously accept the chip. The speaker shook my hand and told me, "It's a good start, huh?"

I stood and stared at all the women sitting in the neat rows of chairs behind the pulpit. I understood why my grandmother hadn't wanted a funeral. I felt like I was about to eulogize myself.

The death of an alcoholic, followed by the purgatory of recovery, and, if deemed deserving, the paradise of successful sobriety. Other than the money grab of it all, my grandmother hadn't wanted a service simply because she had died; she wanted to be remembered by the ways she had lived. In waffle parties, in garage-sale hunts on a Saturday, in protests for women's rights, and in rum and Cokes and Blue Jays games.

I knew in that moment, staring at Grace's self-satisfied smirk, the Heroin Witch wildly nodding and smiling, and Tammy bored and miming at her invisible friends, that once I got out of here, I'd never go to another meeting. I'd recover as my grandmother had lived, fearless with the world and tender with the ones she loved. She used to tell me not to stay with anyone or in any situation that didn't make me happy, that I could do it on my own like all the women in the family could. I don't think I believed her.

I didn't deserve this chip, or the love of my grandmother, and despite telling myself just that morning that I wouldn't cry, I stood there in front of the women sobbing until the speaker rubbed my back for a moment and told me to sit down.

I didn't sleep well on my last night. My roommate talked in her sleep and I tried to distract myself by silently answering her random musings through the night.

"These couches are crooked," she groaned, and I mouthed, "Happens every time those neighbours come over." As if we were on a bad sitcom.

After a bit of snoring, she said, "I'd like a birdhouse, where's the birdhouse?"

"Raccoons took it, it's war out there."

I stayed up listening to her snore and counting the seconds of silence between each breath.

There was no fanfare the day of my departure. A counsellor came up to me during breakfast looking angry.

"Your mother is here."

"Really? I told her I was going to call her when I was out."

"She said she was here to pick you up."

"Okay, so can I go?"

"What about the graduation ceremony?"

"Well, then she's gotta wait all morning. I finished all my laundry."

"We still have to have your last interview. Are you done breakfast?"

"Yup."

Grace saw me get up and raised her eyebrows, silently asking where I was going. I shrugged, knowing that I was never going to see her again. The counsellor led me to the office where they dole out the pills.

"Plans for aftercare?"

"Just like, the meetings and finding a sponsor."

"You know about our outpatient programs?"

I nodded. I wouldn't qualify for any halfway houses or sober living facilities because I had just showed up and paid, I hadn't gone through the system and applied, and wasn't about to ask my mother for another couple grand so I could skip the line again.

"And you have your agenda? Good to stay busy."

"Yeah, I'm gonna go back to work, so that'll help. Get to the gym."

"We talked about that. Is that an okay idea for you?"

"Work and the gym?"

"Both. It says prior to this you were a server, is that a healthy environment? And the gym, is that something that could trigger addictive behaviour?"

"Um, I don't think so, like, I'm not bartending, so just bringing food and drinks to people, most managers prefer you don't drink on the job so . . . and like, I just run, not for very long, sometimes I just walk, listen to music."

"Okay, just take it easy."

"Mmhmm."

"Do you feel confident in your recovery?"

I tried to play rehab back in my mind like a montage: Did it work? Was I cured? "I mean, I don't wanna come back here, I don't wanna die or . . . like, be homeless, so yeah."

"But do you want to be sober?"

"Yeah like, I just want to be, I dunno, even-keeled, just happy and doing . . . my thing."

"And what does that mean to you, even-keeled?"

"Like, just . . . chill. Like, sleep, eat, work, I dunno, not . . . party, sleep, cry, repeat."

"Uh huh. And how do you plan on dealing with cravings?"

"Um, I dunno about the physical craving thing, like my body doesn't feel weird or shake, and I don't drool if I see a cocktail."

"Well, how do cravings feel mentally for you?"

"It's just like this . . . it's not a craving to drink, it's like, to stop this . . . unstoppable force, like there's someone outside your house, and you don't wanna let them in, but the pressure of knowing they're there is just like, just open the door, let them in, deal with the mess they make afterwards. Like, they're gonna get in somehow, just let 'em in."

"Is it a certain person or memory that's haunting you?"

"No, more like . . . a thing, a creature, it's like . . . Frankenstein, not the monster with the bolts and green and shit, sorry, but like . . . I'm the doctor and I've created this thing and it's in my head, I see it, but I can't explain it."

"Try."

"It's just this thing, it's terrorizing the townfolk, who are also kinda me, but I guess that's not . . . So if I just . . . if I can control this creature thing, then I won't have cravings. I just . . . I haven't read the book since high school."

"So what if you put this creature somewhere outside your house? The house in your mind."

This was one of the trippiest conversations I'd had, on drugs or sober.

"Like, sic it on someone else?"

"Well, just take this creature, whenever they're trying to get in, and try to picture them far away from your house, somewhere so by the time they get to you, it's the next morning, and you can start again."

"Okay. It's still coming for me though, huh?"

"Always."

"Well, that's a bummer."

"Yeah. Do you have any other questions before lunch?"

"No, just stay sober, right?"

"It works if you work it." She handed me another chip with the rehab's logo imprinted on it. "Right. Is there anything you want to say to the group? In lieu of a speech?"

"Um, what's that saying? Like, it's not goodbye, it's see you later? But like, the opposite. Like, hope I don't see you guys again!"

"That's not very nice."

"No but like, in rehab. Like, hope we all make it, go team."

"Would you like me to take you to your mother?"

"Yeah."

It felt like I was stepping off an airplane after a very long trip, walking down the runway, my mother waiting with open arms to welcome me back to the world I knew. She hugged me as the counsellor smiled at me.

"You got everything?"

I nodded and she profusely thanked the staff as I double-checked to make sure they'd returned my laptop, phone, and other belongings. They all said nice things about me, I ignored it. Then I followed her out to her boyfriend's car, a free, sober woman. I felt nervous, suddenly, to be alone with her. How does one act like a free, sober, fixed-up woman? What did a free, sober, fixed-up woman talk like? Sit like? I realized I was smiling like a fat frog, lips pressed together, which pushed out either side of my cheeks.

"You seem happier."

"I am. I got that apartment, uh, a counsellor let me use the computer, and I told Shanti I don't drink or party, so she's cool. She said she works a ton and stays at her boyfriend's most of the time anyways so . . . it's good."

"Okay, that sounds okay."

We finished packing my stuff into the trunk, I was unsure whether I should hug her again or to just get in, a long car ride ahead of us. If I didn't want to run thirty days ago, I wanted to run now.

"Yeah and it's available on the first, so just like, two nights up in sunny Peterborough for me."

We got in the car, I knew it would be rude to turn on some music, plus she hadn't started the engine.

"Sweetheart, I'm so sorry about your grandmother. I am."

"Yeah."

"But I'm so proud of you, and it's good you were there where you were safe."

"Yeah, I think it was easier."

"It was, right?"

I fidgeted with the seatbelt, without the AC on the car was so hot, and I was beginning to feel sick.

"I'm just so proud of you, everyone is, we just all love you so much."

"I know, I mean . . . I love everyone."

She squeezed my knee and finally started the car, I watched as Grace walked out the front door lighting a smoke, she didn't wave goodbye as we pulled away.

Part II

I tried to tell Mom jokes about the women I'd met, but she kept responding that we were all there together and it was all so sad, and that she was proud of me. I could never tell her my doubts about the program, or my fears that I hadn't taken what I was supposed to from it. Instead we talked about my brother, his life in New York, she didn't bring up my grandmother any more than confirming that the waffle party had been yesterday. She said I should wait to call my dad until tomorrow since he'd probably be hungover. She didn't hate him, I don't think. I think you say things like that about people you loved, when they go out of their way to make themselves impossible to love. You feel so stupid, holding all this tenderness, and then all you can do is throw it away, pack up, and move on.

"I don't like, blame him for my alcoholism."

It was a bad time to say that, she was pulling into the driveway of the home she shared with Devin, her boyfriend of two years, and his two youngest children.

She sighed heavily. "Maybe you should. Maybe you should blame both of us."

"I'm not gonna *blame* anyone. It's like, a disease, right?"

"You would tell me if you were still angry with me?"

It made me think of all the cheesy romantic movies I used to watch as a teen, where the woman would scream, "I want to be able to tell you I'm mad at you!" The understanding hunky male lead would respond sincerely, "So be mad, I deserve it." And the woman would say she can't, because as mad as she is, she god-damn loves him too much!

"I'd get around to it . . . Are you still angry with me?"

"Oh my god, no!" Then she dove towards me and squeezed my head as we sat side by side facing Devin, who was waiting for us on the porch.

"I love you so so so *so* much. Maybe I get angry but only *because* I love you so much. Okay? I'm not angry at all, this is not your fault, okay? You're gonna be so great."

"*All right.*"

She released me and allowed me to exit the car.

I gave Devin a salute. "Howdy."

He was an incredibly thin man who wore incredibly wide-legged jeans, when the wind picked up he must get nervous. He parachuted down the stairs to assist with my bags.

"Hey, hi, hello there! In the flesh! You're looking like a woman with aplomb, world is your oyster!"

"What's ah-blom?"

He grabbed my bags, ignoring my question and giving my mother a quick kiss on the cheek. I thought for a moment he was going to click his heels, he was so sprightly for a guy his age.

"The kids are all inside, we've got food, we've got clean sheets, and per your mother's request, we have the cinematic classic *Cats Don't Dance*."

It was a gut punch. Yeah, it had been my favourite movie as a child, but I didn't want to share it with this new family. I felt humiliated. Fresh out of rehab and I'd be forced to sit through my beloved obscure cartoon musical of a tabby cat trying to make it in Hollywood. Plus, his kids hated me. I had hoped they'd be away travelling or, I don't know, just not there. His eldest daughter had an apartment in the Annex. When my mother and Devin first started dating, they wanted us to try to be friends since we were the same age, so we went out one night. At first we bonded over how weird it was for us to try to be friends, but then, apparently, I drunkenly made out with some dude she liked, and she started crying and screaming at me in the middle of the bar, and I gave her the finger and left. We had not spoken since.

His two younger children were twins, nineteen years old, a boy and a girl, and they were very close to their father. They were all close, which made them untrustworthy. I kept wondering if my mother was inserting herself into this happy, well-adjusted family as a defence mechanism. Did she *really* like Devin all that much, or was he just so vanilla and safe compared to what she'd had before? It sucked being with her *and* them, watching her play the role of sparkles and sunshine when I'd grown up with a mom who blasted Nirvana to wake us up for school.

During dinner I tried to pretend I was still at rehab, that everyone else at the table was just as sick as I was, and that we were all bonded by our terminal human condition. It didn't exactly make it easier, but I enjoyed picturing Devin and his children high on meth, giddy and as close as ever, committing some ill-advised caper, like robbing a Best Buy in the middle of the day. We all watched *Cats Don't Dance* afterwards, and I pretended to laugh while Devin commented on each scene.

Will he just shut the fuck up and let the fucking cat sing?

I glanced at my suitcase in the corner of the living room.

The following day, the happy family wanted to run errands together, a smiley perfect unit, but I excused myself to walk around the block. I sat outside a gas station for a while, savouring the dollar coffee I bought and didn't have to chug because free time was over, and then I called my father. He sighed before he even said hello.

"Hey, kid."

"Hey, Dad."

"Got your phone back."

"Mmhmm, Mom sprang me from the pen."

"That's good."

"Uh, I got the letter Saturday so . . . I'm sorry. I should've been there—"

"No, no, it's good you weren't. I just can't handle any more drama or . . . She wouldn't want that."

I cleared my throat, trying to ignore his confirmation that, yes, the alcoholic granddaughter would not have been welcome. "I meant just to be there."

"She didn't want anything big, or—it's good you're with your mother. We had our waffles and said goodbye, and . . . like that."

"Mmhmm."

"It was quick—Fuck—sorry. It's all a bit much."

I could tell he was trying not to cry, or was crying, I could hear him sucking in air as if he'd just had a large sip of something that took his breath away. I waited for him to breathe again, it reminded me of when I was child and would stay up all night listening to him drunkenly snore, choking on his own mucus. The house would go quiet for a minute or two and I'd hold my breath hoping he was still alive, then the cacophony of phlegm would erupt from his throat and I swear the house shook.

"But it's good you're not here. Just keep doing you, kid. You don't need to be sad or . . . make it a thing. We're okay, I'll be okay, you just keep doing you."

The tears welling up in my eyes blurred out the taillights of the cars pulling out of the gas station. I didn't want to blink and make everything clear again. The picnic table I was sitting at, covered in shitty tags, the gas station attendant smoking outside and doing lunges around the ice machine, I hated it all.

"I sure will. Uh, I guess lemme know when you're back, we can do dinner or something."

"Yeah, yeah, I don't know exactly when that'll be, have to sort so much shiiit out. Pack everything, and logistics. But! You have a phone now, so I'll be in touch."

It was worse that he was trying to sound chipper—if he could just tell me he was heartbroken, I could say it too. What a shitty stalemate.

"Kay. Say hi to those guys from me."

"Yeah."

"See yuuuuuh."

He hung up without saying goodbye. I went to Devin's couch and lay there until dinner. I kept repeating to myself, Tomorrow

I would go to my new apartment, tomorrow I would "keep doing me," tomorrow I would make a new friend and be happy and be healthy—

You're so fucking lame, you sound like a terrified kid on her first day of school.

Tomorrow I'd be less lame! I promised that to my suitcase in the corner, it looked like it was glowing from the inside, a faint neon-pink light, blinking on and off. "I'll be less lame tomorrow," I whispered towards it.

I found it hard to sleep, the light from the suitcase was keeping me up, flickering and creating menacing shadows on the ceiling. I thought about going over, unzipping it, sneaking out to the yard, and burying the journal. It would be tough to explain if I was caught. I turned my face towards the back of the couch, pleading in my head for the light to burn out.

"I'll only be gone for a week this time, and then I'll have a few more very short trips, beginning of next month, but really not that much! After September I'm back and not going anywhere."

My mother talked at me from the front seat while Devin drove. He filled the silence between her positive affirmations by humming one of the songs from *Cats Don't Dance*.

"And if you need anything, of course Devin is here, you can always stay with us even if I'm not there, if something happens or whatever!"

I could see him nodding while he hummed, I wondered if that meant, "Yes, I am obligated to let you stay at my house but please, don't."

"Was that all my stuff?"

I was referring to the stuffed black garbage bags that filled the trunk and backseat and lay on top of me. I wanted to be angrier at my mom for not packing my things in clearly labelled boxes, but today was not the day to fight.

"We didn't think you wanted that old mattress, and the desk belonged to Devin so we put it back in his house . . ."

My mother trailed off and Devin finally stopped humming.

"Is this apartment not furnished?" Devin asked.

"I don't know."

"You didn't ask?"

"I didn't really have the luxury of time."

"There's always IKEA," he said.

He can go fuck himself.

I shook the suitcase on my lap a little, it was a long car ride.

Luckily Shanti was up early. She was more beautiful in person, tall, slim, and dressed in very hip thrift store (or made to look like thrift store) finds. She was a year younger than me but she carried herself like a real adult.

"I'm so sorry I can't help unpack. But it's really nice to meet your mom and dad!" she said, handing me a key.

Devin put his hand on my mom's shoulder and waved at Shanti as she jetted off to work, shutting the door quickly so her cats wouldn't get out. My mother sneezed, she was allergic. Devin threw the last of my black garbage bags into the empty unfurnished bedroom.

"We should probably get you out of here so you're not too stuffed up for the flight."

"Yeah, I'm sorry, sweetheart, it's the cats—"

"It's all good, I gotta unpack, find a bed."

"Maybe you can order online?"

"Yup, really it's fine. I haven't been alone for a month, I'm gonna put on some bad music and just get settled."

"And you're okay alone?"

"Mom, I'm good. Really. This is good, I can see the lake if I lean out of my window. That's like, high class. I'm happy."

"I love you so much, honey. You are strong and inspiring and I love you." She went in for another hug and Devin came in around my back to sandwich me in.

"I love you too," I said into her chest, I hoped Devin knew it was just for her.

She sneezed into my neck, and then they were off, I held the cats back with my foot as I closed the door. The cats were not pleased that I'd thwarted their escape. I wondered why they hated it here.

"Do you guys dance?"

They both ran off under the couch at the sound of my voice. Aside from my empty bedroom, the apartment was full of Shanti's things. I felt like a guest. She had asked me, as she was running out the door, to not touch the TV before she could show me how to use the remotes and to not let the cats in her room. There were dishes in the sink and cold coffee in the pot.

I looked in the refrigerator. Some condiments, an old Tupperware container of pasta, and two craft beers, half hidden by a jug of pomegranate juice.

You can replace those. Celebrate your freedom. You did it. You landed on your fucking feet. Screw those kittens, you've got nine fucking lives, baby.

I closed the door. It was 8:30 a.m. I was better than this.

I peeked into Shanti's bedroom. It was messy but cute in a young womanly way. She had cheesy French posters up that she probably overpaid for at some place on Queen. A few vintage photos in Value Village frames of people she probably didn't know but whose aesthetic she enjoyed. On her desk was a photo collage in the works, mostly made up of photos of her and her boyfriend, I was guessing, or just a very beloved young man. I noticed a vibrator on the floor, then I saw one of the cats lunge for it.

"Shit!"

I grabbed the cat and nearly flung it into the living room. But the other one darted under the bed. I trapped us in Shanti's bedroom, trying to call the cat out from below her bed, also trying not to mess anything up or touch the vibrator. The beast was hissing at me from behind a leg of the bed, and I finally managed to bear-hug it close. It cut my arm up in protest and wriggled wildly while I opened the door just enough for us to escape but not enough to let the other cat back in.

"You fucking asshole!"

As soon as I dropped the cat onto the couch, it rolled onto its back, licking its paw nonchalantly as I surveyed the damage to my right forearm. There were a few minor scratches and one deep one that was already reddening. I went into the bathroom, the water ran super hot immediately.

"Fuck off!"

I wrapped hot wet toilet paper around my arm and went back into the living room, staring at the cats.

"This is not a good start!"

I had to go buy Band-Aids and a bed, a dresser, probably a desk. Fuck. I hated this apartment and these ridiculous cats.

Fuck Shanti! You're already going out, just replace the beer.

No, I wasn't going to cry in front of these stupid cats, and I wasn't going to drink Shanti's beer. I imagined drunkenly phoning my mother right before she got on the plane, telling her that her perfect plan hadn't worked out. I'd ruined everything again. I needed to find a bed.

Shanti came home around 6 p.m. with the man from the photo collage. I was sitting on her couch scrolling through IKEA's website. I had failed in my mission to buy both furniture and Band-Aids that would appropriately hide my war wounds, mostly because I didn't trust myself to move from the couch. I had no one to tell that I was scared of fucking it all up on my first day alone, that even going to the kitchen was stressful, knowing the beer was there, that it was immobilizing. So I told myself that I couldn't move, I had to monitor the cats, they were planning a coup. I really had to pee.

"Hey."

"Hey, how was the move?"

"Oh good, thought I could find some cool vintage furniture on Queen, but it's all pretty expensive."

"You didn't bring furniture?"

She gave me the same disappointed look she'd given me in the morning when I was chucking my garbage bags into my room.

"No, but it's fine like, I can go to IKEA tomorrow."

"Do you have a car?"

"Uh, nooooo, but! I do have a lot of quarters for the bus, so I'm set."

"You're gonna take a bed on the bus?"

"Oh, they come all rolled up, and then I could just order the bed frame and stuff afterwards."

"Well, we were gonna watch a movie out here, like, we need the PS3 so, but, like, you can sleep on the couch I guess when we're done."

"Oh cool, yeah, yeah, I'll get out of your way."

Shanti noticed my arm as I was packing up my computer charger.

"Did Greyson do that?"

"Is that the grey one?"

"Yeah."

"Yeah, it was my fault, I tried to pick him up."

"He doesn't like being picked up."

"Oh, I got that pretty quick."

"They just need time to get used to people in their space, so just be respectful of their boundaries."

"I do, I will, sorry. I'm gonna use the washroom."

"Okay."

She'd seemed so excited to have me as a roommate when we chatted online, but now I felt like an intruder. She had a very carefully curated home, and I did not belong.

I sat in the corner of my empty room, I could hear them watching some sort of action movie, they made fun of it a lot, sometimes I thought they were kissing, I tried not to listen too hard. After the movie ended, they put on *The Office*, it was clear they weren't going to bed anytime soon, and I couldn't continue to stay up looking at Malms and other Swedish beds. As quietly as I could, I lay down on the garbage bags filled with clothes I hadn't worn since high school, trying to get comfortable and to not make any rustling sounds that might alert Shanti and her boyfriend to the embarrassing fact that I was making a bed for myself on trash bags.

When I woke up in the morning, there were deeply embedded marks from the plastic all over the left side of my body and face.

I had made it to IKEA just fine but I'd underestimated how difficult it would be to carry a heavy rolled-up mattress all the way back. I declined in embarrassment every time someone offered me help, cursing internally, telling them, "I got it." By the time I made it back to Parkdale, I was sweating and dangerously thirsty.

This is what normal people do. They sweat and curse at moving and then they cheers with friends once the moving is done. A well-deserved imbibing.

But the two craft beers were gone from the fridge, and the small bit of disappointment I felt was soon overtaken by a sense of relief, I was safe. Besides, I had no friends to cheers with, only two cats who would rather eat my body. I cut open the packaging on my mattress and watched it slowly expand. Should this be an important moment? Watching this cheap piece of furniture take its first few breaths of stale apartment air? A new beginning in my sober journey. It reminded me of the way dead bodies bloat when they're left in a river.

Shanti had told me she wasn't coming home that night, "the place is all yours." I wanted her to come home. I wanted to show her my bed, and actually talk to her, make up for the weirdness of last night. She left instructions on how to feed the cats and how to turn on the TV "if you have to." I didn't know what to watch so I put on old episodes of *Friends*.

It was nearing dinner time, the cats made sure I was aware of it. I didn't want to leave the apartment after my epic journey, but I needed food, I needed something.

You are alone in your own apartment.

But in rehab they told us we shouldn't be alone too much. Community! Support! I looked through my phone at the few unanswered text messages I had collected in my thirty-day absence from technology. There weren't many. Most of my recent friendships began and ended on a bar stool, out of sight, out of mind. And my old friendships from the Peg didn't need to be continuously stoked. Every few weeks, months, a "Hey, miss you!" or a friendly comment on a "candid" Facebook photo. In my texts, there was only a weak acquaintance from my serving days asking to go for drinks, a high school peer from Winnipeg wondering if they'd seen me at the airport, and Matt, a dude I slept with over three years ago on the shore of Lake Ontario one drunken night at a party, telling me he was just curious what it would be like "to hook up sober." He had also texted me a month ago, when I'd been in the car on my way to rehab. My pizza-party intervention had just ended, and when I texted back telling him where I was going, he hadn't seemed fazed. He wished me luck.

Later, as I waited for two slices of pizza at a nearby take-out place, I texted Matt that I was out and would "be down" to meet up. I didn't actually want to hook up, I just wanted him to come over and make fun of the cats with me, make fun of each other, me for rehab and him for . . . I'd think of something. Instead he told me to come by his work sometime and "we'd go from there."

The girl handed me my pizza, she smiled warmly at me, and I thanked her much too effusively. I thought I should try texting Len, ask her to come over, to hang out again, but to have her alone in *my* space seemed so . . . intimate. If we weren't assigned to share a room, I doubted we'd find ourselves in the same place at the same time ever again. We may have had a good thing going, but it was only meant for a short time. That's just how good things go.

I didn't have any other "safe" friends, as my dad would call them, and I didn't know if I was safe either. I stood alone on Queen Street, not much further west than where I used to live before everything fell apart. I knew where the liquor stores were, I knew what bars were offering drink deals until ten. I told myself that I couldn't bring pizza into a bar. Just get home and eat it and if you still want to go out again, you can always go back out. That's what they called relapsing in rehab. "Going back out." I had to stay in, I had to go home, but I wasn't moving. I was stuck outside the tiny pizzeria.

Are we gonna do this every fucking day? Every time you step foot outside, are you gonna try and act all damaged and philosophical until I fucking shut you up? You're not some princess with a happy ending, you're still just a junkie slut who wants Mom and Dad to be proud.

It felt like the words were coming from outside me, I wanted to yell back, out towards the space they were attacking me from, if I could figure out where that was. Instead I ran home as fast as I could, stuffing pizza into my mouth and trying to swallow between laboured breaths. I ran up the stairs to the apartment and slammed the door behind me, soaked in sweat and shaking.

I tried to do a DIY face mask, but I used too much apple cider vinegar and my skin started to burn and turned bright red. I put foundation on to cover it. I looked through Shanti's kitchen cupboards and drawers, making sure there was nothing else to tempt me, and double-checked the fridge as well. I scrolled the Facebook of the girls who insisted I follow them outside of rehab, Maci Ann, Steph, Madison. Ellen had given me a fake last name, I thought that was funny, very on brand for her. I sat and watched more *Friends*, all the while imagining that somehow, in the cupboards, there was a hidden bottle of booze, a mound of cocaine, and either a thick wad of money or a gun, depending on the fantasy. It was 10 p.m., the liquor stores had closed.

I wanted to text someone. I wanted to stay busy. I wished I lived in the age of chat rooms. The beer and wine stores would still be open, you just couldn't buy hard liquor after ten. I looked through one of my garbage bags, it was full of terrible clothing I couldn't remember wearing. Was this even my stuff? I tossed it aside and jumped when it landed with an uncharacteristically loud thump. Nothing in any of the bags should have thumped that loud . . . Unless it wasn't the bag. Unless it was a very stealthy intruder. Could someone come in through the window? Were they hiding in my closet?

If you kill someone in self-defence, most likely someone will offer you a drink after all is said and done.

I sighed, it was another bad fantasy. Someone breaks in, I defend myself, the first officer on the scene says how amazing I am. He says his shift is ending and offers to take me out. Afterwards he asks if I have somewhere else to go but I say no, so he lets me stay at his place. I can drink there because he loves me and has a steady job and will take care of me. All because I killed a man trying to break into my apartment.

It was 11 p.m., and now I really couldn't buy booze anywhere.

Can't go to sleep though, can you?

I looked at my opened suitcase, knowing the journal was still sitting at the bottom, loosely wrapped in my sweater. I zipped it up, I would unpack tomorrow. I turned the lights out, *Go to sleep, suitcase goblin.*

There was another loud thump. But I was brave. I needed to figure out where the sound was coming from. The lights went back on. If someone had snuck into my closet, by this point they would've come out, right? Wouldn't it be odd to sneak in somewhere, find it empty, and just . . . wait it out to see if someone or something came along? Plus, ghosts weren't real. Although any time I entered a dark room, a basement especially, I still felt there was, like, a seventy percent chance of encountering a ghost, so maybe ghosts were on the table . . . I stared at the darkness in the gap below my closet door.

There were no intruders. The thumps had been caused by a pair of red cowboy boots falling out of the bag. I had thought those boots were so cool when I first moved to Toronto. They had hand-embroidered flames and stars stitched into the leather, and were outrageously expensive, my mother had bought them for me impulsively in celebration of our new big city lives.

I held them close to my chest and lay down on the naked mattress, not daring to turn off the light again. I kicked the suitcase, hoping that it would shut up for the night, and then I lay there, motionless. I closed my eyes, forcing myself somewhere else, to a desert oasis surrounded by sand, or something like that, where I was beautiful, calm, and unbothered by the noises I could hear coming up from the street below. I lay there until I was sure it was past last call, and I could finally move, just to turn over, and go to sleep.

I woke up to a quiet knock on my bedroom door.

"Shit, sorry, one sec!"

Who the fuck was knocking on my door this early? Except it was 11 a.m. I had managed to sleep through the sun beating down on me through my uncurtained windows. I had sweated half my makeup off onto my no-longer-crisp white mattress.

"It's Shanti, I just wanted to have a quick chat."

I wondered if I had offended her cats in some way. I checked my appearance in my phone camera. Yesterday's foundation was barely covering the new pimples that had colonized my chin and left cheek. I finally opened the door, she was standing in the kitchen waiting for me,

"Sorry, I stayed up kinda late."

"Did they get breakfast?"

"No, not yet."

"Yeah, they're angry."

"I'll feed 'em—"

"It's fine, I'm here now."

"Sorry. I didn't know it was like, a rigid schedule."

"They're living things. I don't actually want to talk about the cats though. There's, um, a serious issue. I feel really bad 'cause you literally just got here, but the landlord reached out to say there's been more bed bugs."

"Here?"

"I haven't seen any in this apartment, but you should still just, be cautious, especially since your bed is kinda vulnerable, 'cause it's on the floor, right? No protection."

"Yeah, I couldn't carry the frame."

"It's just that there's three months left in the whole lease of it all, and this is the third time this building has had issues so I'm just over stressing about it. It's gross, right?"

"Yeah, they won't kill you but definitely gross."

"They bite you."

"True."

"Have you been bitten?"

"I don't think so."

"So I'm actually gonna try and get out by the fifteenth, but I'll give you the full deposit back. I'm gonna start moving all my stuff tomorrow morning though."

"Wow, that's so quick. So it was an actual issue for a while or . . . ?"

She sighed, as if I was wasting her time.

"You know Parkdale. It's always an issue. I thought it would be fine but . . . it's a shithole, right?"

"Yeah."

"Do you think you could be gone by tomorrow too though? It might help if I tell the landlord that."

"I guess, yeah. I don't wanna stay if it's a big deal."

"I *really* think it is."

"I will make like a tree and leaf."

She didn't laugh.

"Hey, you're pretty lucky though, huh?"

"Why's that?"

"Well, all your stuff's already in bags."

"It's not garbage."

"I just meant it's ready to move."

"Oh . . . yeah. Don't gotta get ready if you stay ready."

"You should still wash it though."

"Mm."

It was the first time in my life, really, that I had no place to go, and more than that, no one to tell me where to go. So often I had blindly followed family, men, "friends" to new cities and dark alleys. But not now . . . New York seemed too far, honestly so did Peterborough, and what would I say? "Guess you guys weren't expecting this first setback quite so soon?" My father's place was empty, but also too tempting. Maybe it was karma, finally biting me for instigating that fight against Tess in rehab—I would now be forced to sleep in a Coffee Time.

Shanti and I never spoke again after that. The next day, I handed her the key, and then she helped me pile garbage bags into my arms, which I noticed she tried to touch with only the tips of her fingers. I left my mattress in the apartment. She could deal with it or leave it to the bugs. It really was like a dead body, slowly it would decompose, maybe eventually someone would call to check in on it because of the smell. The landlord would find a half-decayed cheap Swedish mattress with the imprint of my face on it, but they'd have no idea who I was or where the mattress had come from, another cold case in Parkdale.

I took a cab to a laundromat that would wash, dry, and fold everything for me.

"You want it all washed?"

"Yeah, is there like a super hot option? Like, to make sure it kills everything?"

"Deep clean?"

"Yeah."

"You want it back in the bags?"

"Please yeah, but folded, right? You guys do that?"

"Yes, but then back in the bags?"

I looked at the stretched-out, ripped black garbage bags in front of the cashier.

"I'll bring new bags."

"Yeah good. See you tomorrow."

I had texted Matt to see what he was up to and he told me again to come by his work. I was hoping I could find some way to get myself invited back to his place afterwards. His work was a two-and-a-half-hour trek on the TTC when all was said and done. He worked at some large industrial warehouse, about an hour away from Pearson. I still had my suitcase on me, now lined with a garbage bag and containing only a few toiletries, my journal, and laptop. The few things I thought couldn't possibly have bugs. I hoped that I looked like a young traveller heading off purposefully, on her way to the airport, on an adventure.

I stood outside a metal gate that read "Outgoing Vehicles Only." Matt buzzed me in, the gate opening very slowly. I walked across a large empty parking lot and found the door he'd told me to wait at. "Personnel Entrance Only."

"Jesus, you moving in?" Matt said, emerging finally.

I wonder if he was as disappointed as I was. I had tried to look attractive, covering up my new blemishes, putting on old dry mascara, and combing my hair into a ponytail. I was wearing my red boots, despite the fact that it was summer, and paired them with my one and only white sundress, a romantic outfit, I thought. He looked worse than I remembered, or had pictured him in my mind. His belly was round and exposed between buttonholes, but his boyish frame hadn't filled out. He had grown a thick beard and shaved his shaggy dark hair down to his skull and his teeth had yellowed. He still had nice eyes, I would just look at his eyes.

"Sorry, I don't have a backpack, just still kinda in transition."

"Okay. You wanna come in?"

I followed him up the stairs to a boardroom that overlooked the whole warehouse. There was an empty table, a few fold-out chairs, and a mustard-yellow couch at the end of the room.

"This is where you work?"

"This is it."

"It's very minimalistic."

"Sure."

He took my suitcase from me and put it in an empty corner, then lifted me onto the table.

"Oh, will it hold my weight?"

"Guess we'll find out. I'm fucking stoked you're here."

Then he reached to pull off my underwear, which was difficult because I was sitting down on my dress, and I kind of had to drape myself over his shoulders and shimmy back and forth so he could get some leverage. I had hoped for some sort of banter, or something, beforehand. A little icebreaker. I couldn't even remember the last time I'd had sex sober. I tried to remember, I was sweating, I was reciting the months of the year in my head. He pulled out his penis, presenting it to me. He was clearly proud of its length and girth, I tried to think of what a sexy porn star who wasn't drunk would say.

"Oh jeez. That's a lot of penis."

"You want to suck it?"

"Yes."

I didn't, plus I was already sitting on the table and he was standing, and I had to fold my body to reach it. It was a very unproductive two minutes of fellatio before he stopped me.

"Kay, now I'm gonna fuck you."

"Okay."

"You have to be quiet though, I'm not sure if anyone's still here."

"Okay."

Then he humped me very quietly for about six minutes. I was grateful his body was pressed firmly up against mine, I wasn't sure what type of facial expression to make, I only had to focus on squeezing his hand encouragingly to try to mime to him that he was doing a good job.

"Worth the wait?"

He was proud of himself, packing his genitals away with a satisfied smirk. I was more comfortable now that we'd gotten the sex out of the way, maybe we could be friends now.

"Hey, no grass stains."

"I think your underwear is over there."

"Oh, thanks. You bring a lot of girls up here?"

"No actually, I like it though."

"You're welcome."

"For what?"

"Introducing you to a whole new place to sleep with women fresh outta rehab."

"Fuck off."

"You could catch 'em coming off planes too, make a deal with some of the shuttle drivers."

"Jesus."

"It's a great way to make some overtime. Workin' late." I tried to wink at him in a cool, sexy way, but he was staring at his phone.

"I should actually get ready to head out."

"Oh, did you wanna get some food?"

"Nah, I gotta get home, I just wanna crash before another day in paradise."

"You're in Milton now?"

"Yup. You wanna grab your stuff?"

"Where's Milton?"

"You just keep going west, like, half an hour."

"You wanna show me?"

He gave me a look like I was crazy. I followed him back up the stairs to the boardroom, he went into his office for a second then came back out, car keys in hand. I could've texted Shanti to ask her to give me back a key, let me sleep in her bug-infested apartment one last night, but what if she didn't answer or said no? I would be alone in Parkdale with no place to stay.

"Where are you headed?"

"I thought I would go with you."

"Uh, nope. I still live with my dad."

"You've never brought girls back before?"

"Not since I've been living there with my girlfriend."

"You still have a girlfriend?"

"Always did."

I didn't want to get angry, it seemed pointless, so I nodded at him, trying to maintain some dignity as I held my suitcase.

"Don't you have an apartment?"

"Uh, no, kinda lost it in the whole rehab of it all. But I have a place lined up for tomorrow, I just like, I didn't plan for tonight 'cause I thought we were like, doing things."

"Ughhhhh. Shit."

"Yeah."

"There's hotels by the airport."

"Matt, they're like, expensive and shit, I can't do that."

I could force myself to pay for a hotel, but I doubted I could force myself to stay in the room alone without checking out whatever the Hilton Airport Inn had to offer in terms of a hotel bar.

"Could I crash here?"

"Well, fuck. I work here . . . I've got guys coming in for five thirty a.m."

"I could be gone for five?"

"Seriously?"

"Yeah, I'm an early bird. No one will ever know."

"I'll be here at five to let you out. Do not go into the warehouse, just stay in this room."

"Is there a bathroom?"

"The office. Seriously though, fuck, this is serious."

"I won't fuck it up. I promise."

"You seriously can't."

"I promise."

"Fuck . . . yeah okay."

He was about to leave before he came back and kissed me, hard. "Five a.m."

I walked to the window and looked out, facing west, or what I thought was west, out towards Milton. I was desperate for a place to sleep. I whispered to his girlfriend in his father's basement, "I'm sorry."

The couch looked better than last night's accommodations. I found a protein bar in Matt's office that I saved for dinner. There was no threat of warm craft beers hiding in the back of any of the shelves, the protein bar was miracle enough. I texted Matt for the wifi password so I could watch shows or something, but he never answered.

There was no security monitoring the warehouse. I knew the gate was locked, and that a person would have no reason to come in looking for a young woman wearing cowboy boots to murder. I was alone and bored and hungry.

———

It wasn't difficult to wake up at 4:30 a.m. I didn't want to burn my bridge with Matt. I felt like I owed him the world for allowing me to sleep in his otherwise empty boardroom.

I was at the door at 4:59, just to show my respect for his time, but he arrived at 5:10.

"Jesus, you fucking scared me, here take this."

He had brought me an extra-large coffee, it was so sweet I almost kissed him.

"Wow, thank you, I wasn't sure whether to wait in here or out there."

"Either way, I guess. I'll open the gate for you."

"Did you have a good sleep?"

"What?"

"Did you get enough sleep?"

"I need about six more of these." He didn't seem to want to talk. "Thank you so much for the coffee."

"All right, well, I'll see ya around I guess."

I didn't want to leave. For a brief moment, I wondered if Matt could love me or if I could love him, if we could love each other somehow, some way, then I remembered the girlfriend in the basement.

"Yeah, text me when you're horny and not homeless."

Then he walked past me up the stairs, leaving me to let myself out. I kept spilling hot coffee all over my hand as I tried to wheel out as gracefully as possible. I realized the buses wouldn't run for another two hours, so I walked towards the airport, trailing my suitcase along the small boulevard between the highway and industrial fencing of the neighbouring compounds. There were large open fields on the other side of the highway, and a garbage dump way off in the distance.

It was 9 a.m. by the time I made it back to the city. I wondered if I ran back to rehab if they'd take me in, give me one more night to figure it all out. I couldn't afford a hotel, but I didn't want to go to a shelter. Steph told me she was safer on the streets, she'd been raped twice in a youth shelter.

I made it to Union Station and took a cab to pick up my freshly debugged clothes, but not before I dipped into a convenience store to buy a new box of garbage bags.

"Fresh bags."

I thought the laundromat cashier would be pleased I had kept my side of the bargain, but he just rang me through without a word. From there I took another cab to the storage container my father had rented for my stuff. I kept looking over the shrinking stack of bills I had in my wallet, cabbing was killing me but there was no logistically possible way I could bus with all these bags.

There wasn't anyone attending the locker, you were just given a code to punch in to get through the gate and a key to your own site. At my locker, I unpacked some of the bags, carefully selecting a few items of clothing to put in my suitcase. Then I buried the journal at the bottom of one of the bags and threw the bags around so I would forget which one had the terrible book inside of it, my own manic shell game. It was so cold in this four-by-four cell, and I was tired. I sat on one of the bags. I thought if I set my alarm, maybe I could just close my eyes for a moment, pretend I had dozed off by mistake if anyone found me.

I must have been still for too long because the lights shut off, and suddenly I was in the dark, alone in the locker. I'd seen enough horror films to know this didn't bode well for me. I hoisted myself off the bags and tried to move as much as possible to trigger the lights to come on. My half-hearted shimmying did nothing. I walked around the bags and tried to find the door by the light of my phone.

My mom would be calling to check in soon, and if I didn't answer, or if I answered to say I was stuck in the storage container, I knew she would fly back. I knew she would. She would sigh and say she was happy I told her, but then worry if or when I would truly ever be healed enough to do anything on my own, and move me into Devin's house, where I would most likely stay under her watch until I died of boredom. When she texted, I would answer I was doing fine, I wasn't alone in the dark and never had been! And I would find my way out of here, I wouldn't let her find my body in a cold dark cell after days of searching back alleys and seedy bars, expecting me to have relapsed.

I kept jumping every few steps, hoping the automated lights would recognize there was a human being in their midst and turn on, but nada.

'Cause even the robots don't give a fuck about you.

Of course robots don't give a fuck about me, they're not human. I found the door eventually, escaped, and slammed it shut behind me.

Outside, I mimed incredulously to the air, shrugging my shoulders to the wind like, "You see that shit?" I was becoming Tammy, debating with the voices that followed me out of dark corridors.

I started crying on the bus. Not too much, just a few tears, I was exhausted, and it had been scary to be in the dark, and also funny, sort of, and I wanted to laugh, but I was alone, and crying alone on the bus seems way less obviously crazy than laughing alone on the bus.

"Hey! I'm out! Literally!" I texted from my bus seat, looking for a distraction.

The reply appeared almost immediately. "wut u mean?"

"I got stuck in my storage locker, shit's crazy on the outside, ha ha."

"da fuq?"

"I was getting my shit out of my locker and all the lights went out!"

"Jokes."

Len obviously didn't care. I knew she didn't really understand what I was saying, but she was right, it was fucking jokes, wasn't it?

I ended up not far from my old apartment, maybe a twenty-minute walk. East this time. It was a hostel I had heard one of the busboys at work talk about. He had come from Ireland and had stayed there while he was looking for an apartment. He'd told us in his thick accent that we didn't always understand that it was a "helluva time" and crowded, and something about "right with good lads to chat up."

I told myself it was temporary. I'd just be crashing there for a day or two, max. By the end of the week I would find a job and apartment, and the hostel would be only a minuscule plateau before I ascended to normalcy. In those rehab movies we watched there was often a montage of the young ingenue being lost, then quickly, to an inspirational pop track, getting her shit together.

I booked the hostel on the bus twenty-three minutes before I arrived. The website advertised a clean, safe, and, above all, good place for a good time. There were a lot of happy people in the photos provided. A lot of white men with dreadlocks and laughing women. I didn't care who actually awaited me, because it was two or three days tops, this is how it works, you find an apartment, you take it, and boom! You're a real-life living breathing sober adult.

The man at the front desk had blond stringy hair that frizzed out around him like a lion's mane. He was balding at the top, his shiny patches of skin like a razed battleground where hair had once stood and subsequently fallen, never to return. He was most likely in his late thirties, but his skin reminded me of my late grandmother's, hers worn hard from a lifetime of sun and cold in the prairies. He had braided bracelets that said "LA VIDA LOCA" and "DTF IN BELIZE." He smiled and winked as a punctuation to every sentence. He told me his name but I immediately forgot it, Hal or maybe Hyle, his nametag was blacked out and Sharpied over to say "Good Tyme Guru." He couldn't find my reservation, maybe because it had been made so recently. He rifled through his papers, smiling and winking.

"Eager little beaver you are, huh?"

"Oh yeah, or last-minute planner, just got . . . back in town and realized I needed a place to stay."

"And how long are you planning on staying for?"

"Oh, honestly I don't know . . . hopefully not long, not, I mean the place looks great. I'm trying to find an apartment though, so . . . hopefully not long."

"There's a month-long discount. You can pay week by week for now, and the fourth week, if you're still here, we'll deduct the discount from that week's total due. Little employee discount."

He winked again. I wondered if he understood that things weren't an employee discount just because the employee was the one providing the discount. It was clearly laid out on a sign

behind him that the hostel got cheaper the longer you stayed—
for a maximum of two months, as decreed by management.

"Can you only stay for two months or is the deal only good
for two months?"

"Man, it's the summer so, turnover, but hey, we can always
work something out."

"Yeah, I mean I won't be here that long, I just wanted to check."

"Some kids drink the Kool-Aid. So should we do the tour
now? You wanna nosh a bit? Or are you the type of girly who eats
like a little bird?"

"Oh, um, I'm pretty tired, so maybe just the room, and then,
is there a cafeteria or?"

"There's a common area, kitchen, dining room, couple
couches to kick it on. Dinner prep starts at five, it's not like we
can make you do it, but if you cook, you get a free meal, gotta
clean too, you know, like a . . . community."

I was pretty sure he meant commune, or cult.

"We don't have a bar in-house but I got us a nice hookup half
a block down at the Fox and Farmer, show your reso, get ten percent off rail liquor and domestics till nine." Another wink. "And
there's a super rad rooftop chill spot too, I like it up there, you'll
find me on my breaks, off days, catching rays. You a bronzer?"

"Um, no, sun safety first."

"No doubt, so food?"

"Actually just the room, I think, um, you know jet lag . . . I
should lie down."

"Where you coming from?"

"Morocco."

"Really?"

"Yes?"

"How was it?"

"Hot."

"Bet. But sun safety, right?"

"Mmhmm."

"Bring any trinkets back? Any gifts for new friends?" He winked again and tugged at his fraying wrist adornments.

"Um, tried to bring a parrot but customs wouldn't let it fly."

I don't know why I tried to make a joke. Or why I lied about going to Africa in the first place, but I was sick of being honest and open. And didn't feel like being introduced and known as the girl fresh from rehab, even if I'd only be here a few days. I was pretty good at identity fraud, I'd been practising for twenty-two years.

"Yeah, they're pretty conservative people. Probably a bit scary for a young pretty thing."

"It *was* a good-looking parrot."

"You like birds, huh?"

"I'm partial to pigeons."

"You could feed 'em on the roof if you want. Get a lot of pigeons."

"Maybe."

"You're all signed in, pay weekly charge for monthly, it'll be our secret though, you can owe me." Another wink.

I wondered how much I would have to pay him to not wink at me anymore for the duration of my stay.

He offered to show me the roof, then to show me the common area, but I declined, so up we went to my new lodgings. A large undecorated room filled with fourteen or so bunks, a few double bunk beds, but mostly singles, lined up neatly, each with a small cubby at the head. On one wall was a line of hooks for coats and bags. To the right there was a line of sinks and mirrors. There was a plastic tub beneath each bed. It looked like a prison for troubled youth rather than accommodations for young travellers.

"Extra storage space for longer-term guests, but you can always just lean it up against the wall if you feel like living out of your suitcase."

Various woven colourful hemp backpacks were strewn across three or four of the beds.

"Where is everyone?"

"Outside enjoying the day. It's pretty quiet up until dinner prep, no naps on vacay, right?"

"Napping is like a vacation to me."

"Yeah, we all gotta reset, I feel you. Bathrooms across the hall, unisex, oh, you have flip-flops, great, wear those, you know?"

He patted me on the back and I almost seized.

"Tight from travelling?"

"Just . . . really tired."

"That vacay after the vacay vibe."

He nodded and left me with one last wink, then he was gone and I was alone. At least I had wifi, so I looked up Morocco in case Hal/Hyle asked me any more questions about it, I didn't want to blow my cover. Though I doubted he'd remember, he smelled strongly of marijuana and beer.

Around 4 p.m., travellers started trickling in. A few nodded in my direction, the others just went about their business, changing without discretion in front of one another, sneaking sips of prohibited liquor. I watched two women dry-shave their legs in bunks that were not theirs, topless. I felt very uncomfortable on my thin sheets, like I could feel coarse hair poking through. Eventually the group shuffled down to make food. I pulled out the half-eaten wrap I'd bought before I checked in.

You're fucking living now, aren't you?

I shook my head, knocking the words out, and stuffed them back in the storage locker. I could hear music coming from bars close by, the city sounded busy and alive. I looked for any sign of Steph on social media, based on some fleeting idea that she and I could be friends. I couldn't find her.

"Fucking jokes."

It was weird hearing my voice, it sounded small in the cavernous room. It was all jokes though, me being here, in a hostel in a city I called home. Seriously, what the fuck? But I was looking for apartments, they were everywhere, this was temporary. Apartment, job, it was doable.

I'm lonely.

I looked over at the empty beds, filled with evidence of human beings living life much better than I was. The music was so loud I knew I wouldn't sleep until 2 a.m., when the bars finally closed. I looked at photos on my phone of all the people I once knew having so much fun.

I'm fun.

I thought about my creature. I'd told the counsellor it was like Frankenstein. Maybe that was my mistake. I'd tried to give it a real physical body, but it was hard to nail down, it encompassed so much venom. It was like a cartoon character, a bit like a gargoyle, a bit like a large Rottweiler, vomiting fire, with a human face so contorted it could pass for a drugstore mask. I imagined it in different scenarios, shot into space, weighted down by cinder blocks at the bottom of the ocean. But the creature kept coming back, unfazed and energized. Finally I provided my creature a car, not a very fancy one, an old Toyota Tercel, and set it on a course to nowhere. It wasn't an elaborate scenario, in fact it was more of a tableau. I could picture the prairies, thirty minutes from where I grew up in Winnipeg. There was an old road and an endless horizon, and the creature in the Tercel with the cracked leather, the failing AC system, and the windows slightly rolled down. It smelled like old cigarettes in the car, and a week's worth of empty McDonald's bags, the food long gone but the napkins still smeared with crusted ketchup and sweet and sour sauce. I kept telling it to go, drive away, but I had trouble getting it to move.

It was just too loud to sleep. But I could drown out music with music, so I put on my saddest playlist and prepared for the real world of tomorrow.

I had been in my apartment, before rehab, for so long, I'd forgotten how difficult it was to lock down an affordable place in Toronto. I was looking at studio basements with black mould for $1,675 a month. For a "gem," the rare place that had enough room for you to lie down horizontally and didn't make the bathroom part of the kitchen, viewing lines snaked out the doorway and around the block.

I was in line to see a place now, the woman in front of me took up the whole sidewalk with her wide-legged stance. She wore a thick pink T-shirt and high-waisted grey sweat shorts, along with a polyester fanny pack. I liked her pink shirt. I had seen a woman about her size, younger though, across the street from my house, when I was a kid home from school for lunch. That woman had also been wearing a pink shirt, she was crying and screaming at no one, sitting on the top of the stairs to an office building. Someone from the office came outside to talk to her and the woman in pink whipped off her shirt, exposing her breasts, and then ran down the stairs. It was shocking to see such large breasts and disregard for authority, and it was also confusing to see someone suffering so loudly and publicly. I hadn't known that was a possibility, that someone could go that far. I knew we cried and we hurt, but quietly, I'd thought.

Now, seeing this woman in front of me, I imagined her to be the older version of the suffering woman, the stronger, more self-assured version. She turned to me and her face was different, paler, her eyes small beneath her glasses. Her lips were chapped and her skin was dry.

"Are you wearing deodorant?"

Oh god, my sweat, *was* I wearing deodorant? I was sure I'd put it on earlier, maybe it had rubbed off. "Yes, I put it on earlier."

"Scented?"

"No, some natural thing, I think, no aluminum."

She nodded, but she didn't look convinced. "My nose is itchy."

She turned her entire body towards me and went on to show me her lanyard, which had a laminated list of everything she was allergic to, almost all scents, various foods, creams, fabrics, metals, it was a very detailed list, I understood why she'd laminated it.

"I'm Agatha, but I won't shake your hand."

"That's okay."

"Maybe that's why I never get an apartment, I never shake hands."

"Well, it's an old formality—"

"I usually do a little bow."

She had been in the lines for over a year now, she told me. She substituted as an elementary school music teacher, because she loved the recorder in its simplicity and couldn't handle the mixture of BO and cheap scented sprays that accompanied the junior and high school kids.

"I could probably do something real special with a group of sixteen-year-olds, but they love their Juicy Fruit and sparkly shit."

I thought about how much I loved sparkly shit when I was in junior high. But in high school, if you had thick black eyeliner and sparkly white eyeshadow that meant you probably slept around, kids had weird rules like that, but we abided by them, so at most I wore mascara, even though I would've loved to have worn copper eyeshadow, I thought it would make my eyes look impossibly blue.

Agatha also made macramé plant hangers, which is why her hands were especially dry, she told me. "Hands like a sailor." She seemed proud.

It was harder than I'd expected to have conversations while sober. I seemed to have lost all social skills. It was easier in rehab, when we could start with "What are you in for," follow it up with completely degrading but relatable stories, and bookend it with how grateful and happy we were for the future.

When we did finally step inside the building, the landlord yelled from the top of the stairs, "Six more to apartment 223!" Agatha and I entered first. It was small. I always hoped that there was something beyond the photos, that it had an extra room, unadvertised. There was just the one room though, and to the left a small bathroom with a low-ceilinged shower and stained white tiles on the floor, pieced together in no apparent order. It had a window, just one, a little kitchenette, a mini fridge, and a few cupboards that didn't seem to close all the way. Agatha approached the window, feeling the trim, the paint seemed to disintegrate under her calloused fingers.

"Bullshit."

She began desperately wiping her hand on her shorts and then stormed out of the building. I wondered for a moment if I should follow her. Were we friends? Was she okay? Was the disintegrating paint one of her allergies? I imagined her hand swelling up as she looked for help, and the cold disinterest of those still waiting in the line. But I didn't move to help her, she wasn't my Tammy.

I had a choice to make on the bus back. Prepare, eat, and clean up dinner with the rest of the guests of the hostel, or pay for a meal. I needed to save my cash. I had a habit of feeling the smooth bills in my wallet between my fingers before I went to sleep. I was too anxious to actually count them, so I just felt them. I was bad at saving money and very good at justifying spending it. Here I was, bleeding my first and last month's rent dry in a downtown hostel. I focused my attention instead on deciphering the text message I'd received from Len.

"hey gurl! Wats hapenin? Lez hang out sun!"

She had seemed so disinterested when I'd texted her about the locker—I was surprised to hear from her. Maybe she was drunk, or sober and incredibly bored. From the bus window I watched a group of young friends all staring at their phones. I told her yes, we should hang out soon, and almost added that I missed her, I missed all of it, especially the naive hope that we were going to be better when we got out.

I wrote, "No more counsellors!"

She responded, "No more piss tests ;)"

I felt anxious, like I was about to get on a roller coaster at a shitty carnival, where the bolts were loose and the wooden tracks were cracked and the carnies running the rides were low-level gangsters on the lam.

I ended up eating a lukewarm shawarma while I sat on the concrete stairs leading up to the entrance of the hostel. I would've preferred to have eaten in secret, further away, to create the illusion that I was an obviously well-liked person who surely had fantastic dinner plans, but I didn't want to walk any more than I had to, and I didn't want to stand awkwardly outside the shawarma shop, it smelled strongly of urine.

A few travellers passed me during my dinner, none stopped to say hi, they came in groups of two or three, joking together, often in languages I didn't understand. I finished my shawarma and braced myself before entering, knowing that once I went back to my bunk, that was my evening—bookmarking apartments and smiling politely in the dark with my blue illuminated face at the other travellers as they straggled in halfway through the night. It was good I was as lazy as I was, too tired and self-conscious to go out alone. I might be an alcoholic, but I wasn't a motivated one, and it kept me safe that night.

Around 3 a.m., the woman in the bunk beside mine arrived back in with a very small and enthusiastic man. I accidentally made eye contact with him and he smiled apologetically at me before lying down with the woman and having loud sex. Unsure of what to do, I pretended I'd instantly fallen asleep. The couple was so close to me, it just seemed aggressive, like they had involved me without my consent. I turned the other way and tried to become invisible. Did no one else mind this? Did they have a system where they would pick nights to have sex while the others pretended to sleep? I was feeling sorry for myself, angry at the woman, she should know better, she should be better.

Weren't you just whoring yourself out to Matt so you could crash on his couch? Why don't you slut-shame your own fucking self?

I saw a flash of an empty burned-out Toyota Tercel in the middle of a prairie road. I turned away from the voice, as if it were coming from the empty bunk I was facing. On my other side I saw the woman post-coitus, awake. She smiled at me and winked. Did everyone in this fucking hostel think that was an acceptable way of communicating? I didn't want her to feel as shitty as I did, so I winked back, even though it made me feel sick.

I pretended to fall asleep again. I pictured being alone in the hostel, that no one else would come and eventually they would just say, "Well, you outlasted them all, guess this is your place now." I would have a huge kitchen, and beds to make forts in, though with no friends in the city, my forts would be empty, an abandoned playhouse for a stunted adult. They would probably make a movie about me after I died, the sad woman who lived in a hostel and created forts for no one. It would be a better movie if I let people come in and stay for free, but then I'd still have the same problem, strangers, now burdened with having to be nice to me for giving them shelter, and I would never know if they actually wanted to be friends or just felt obligated to fill my forts as a thank-you for the free housing.

My umbrella was soaked through. The line outside the apartment looked like an ancient army barricading itself from slaughter, umbrellas stacked on top of one another, a shield against the rain. I put my hair up, hoping the rain would help it look sleek.

"How about this weather?" I said to the tall man ahead of me, my umbrella was wedged under his.

He smiled at me, I took a better look at him, he was about my age, almost as wide as he was tall.

"My socks are soaked!" he said.

"Yeah, I keep telling myself I need to buy rubber boots."

"It's really coming down, cats and dogs. I'm gonna start coming out in hip waders! Can you imagine?"

I laughed.

"Hip waders," he repeated.

I nodded and smiled.

His name was Thomas, not Tom, he didn't *mind* Tom, but everyone called him Thomas, or Toe Man, but he didn't like Toe Man because he thought it had less to do with the fact that it was kind of similar to his name and more to do with his big bald head and short neck, when he was naked he thought he resembled a toe.

"It's probably because of your name." I didn't want to imagine him naked or have him think that I wanted to imagine him naked.

"I hate my name, but I'm stuck with it," the young woman behind me piped up. Her name was Becky, but she preferred Becca. Her family didn't like Becca, because they didn't like the name Rebecca and had named her Becky. She wore a long wool vest, she was short and curvy, with wild dark curly hair and thin wire glasses. She had a beautiful voice, though she spoke tersely, as if she was trying to sound tougher than she was.

"I'll call you Becca," Thomas told her, I nodded in solidarity.

"Thanks, thanks a lot. I won't call you Toe Man."

"Maybe we should all make up our own nicknames?" Thomas suggested.

"I just want Becca."

"Becca the home wrecka?" Thomas joked.

She didn't laugh. "No, just Becca."

"Alright, JustBecca."

She didn't get the second joke, or didn't like it, and I didn't want to laugh and make her feel dumb, but I also didn't want to let his joke fall flat, so I smiled widely at the two of them, a compromise. I wasn't good at one-on-one small talk but I was even worse in a trio. Finally my brain kicked in.

"Are you guys from Toronto?" I asked.

They looked at each other, as if waiting for the other to talk first. JustBecca won.

"No. I went to school here three years ago and then moved home to run a gallery, but the gallery went bankrupt so I saved up and moved back, and now I frame a photographer's work, Margot Puge. They're mainly of boats in South America. Sometimes old doors. I enjoy it, I don't think photography is for me, I don't really see the artistic merit actually, but people love photos of boats."

I didn't tell her my mother was also a photographer, with artistic merit. I didn't want to argue with Becca, or have it escalate to a rainy day fist fight that Thomas refereed, in defence of my mother and her work. I'd never fought anyone, but with Becca it seemed like a natural progression when I pictured it in my head. Instead, I told her that was really cool, being surrounded by photographs of faraway places, imagining the stories.

She shrugged. "I could look at pictures on my phone if I wanted to, it's not that interesting most of the time. I prefer contemporary installations. In my old gallery, we had six thousand dildos plastered to the wall one time, all different colours, some even lit up. And we had four rabbit heads, real rabbits. That was a different installation, but you can imagine there's much more of a story there."

I didn't know how to talk to her about contemporary art. I told her if she ever opened up another gallery here, I would be interested in seeing it.

"Obviously that's the plan."

Thomas made a joke about the dildos, Becca didn't laugh, and I was caught smiling again, in limbo. I learned a bad joke didn't stop Thomas from making another, and undeterred he answered my question.

"I'm from just outside the city, Etobicoke, but my parents are moving to Barrie, so I decided to come here. I wanted to move out anyway. I can work from anywhere . . . like God."

Becca and I both smiled uncomfortably.

"I work in mysterious ways." He continued, not leaving room for us to laugh, and said that he managed automated helplines for internet returns. He had three monitors and a headset, he added.

"Do you tell a lot of jokes to the people that call in?" I asked him.

He pursed his lips. "Never, we have a script, we're not supposed to go off script. Plus they're usually very angry by the time they get to me."

"That must be tough, to talk to angry people all day."

He shrugged. "I smoke a lot of weed, usually it's pretty funny after that."

Becca chimed in. "Ugh, that's exactly what I need right now, these lines make me so antsy."

Thomas' eyes lit up. He offered to smoke a joint with her behind a convenience store not far from there, and then they could get a soda after. For a moment I forgot what to do with my face, standing between them. I tried to smile but also look as disinterested as possible. I didn't care for weed but I had nothing against it, it always made me feel like I might pee my pants, and on the off chance that actually happened, I didn't think it would help me seem like a reliable tenant.

"You want to come too? We can ask someone—"

"No, no. I'm fine. I can stay."

They didn't argue and happily exited the line, mumbling to the others around them that it was time for a bathroom break. I saw another man not too far down the line smoking a joint. They came back fifteen minutes later, each with a massive two-litre bottle of Coke in their hands, it seemed a bit overkill. Thomas told me I could have his spot, as if doing me a favour, so I made room for him to stand in the middle of us, and he moved closer to Becca.

They talked more quietly than before, giggling, I didn't know if I should try to participate because, after all, I had been talking with them before, so I stood facing the street, not facing them or ahead, trying to appear open to conversation but not so open it seemed intrusive. Every now and then, if Becca didn't giggle at one of his jokes, Thomas turned to me and repeated it, and I laughed, and tried to think of something to say to regain my place in the trio, but he would turn back to her and start off on another tangent, and I would watch the cars pass, wondering what the chances were of one of them losing traction in the rain and pummelling into the line.

After what felt like ages, we finally made it to the front of the line. Because of Thomas' "kind" gesture, I went in with the group ahead of Thomas and Becca. The rest of my group looked tired, one man audibly sighed as we climbed to the third floor, I couldn't blame him. We reached the apartment door, which was slightly ajar, a guy from my group pushed it open and we found a small, smiling woman standing on the other side. She moved aside and we all shuffled in, everyone mumbling the same apology for our wet shoes which she shrugged off.

Her name was Ophelia, she was the landlord. Her brothers had bought the building when they were very young, after their father died and left them quite a sum of money. Being a woman, she inherited nothing but was allowed to live in the building and help with the more feminine repairs. (I didn't press for details about what feminine repairs consisted of.) Her brothers all died one after another in rapid succession not too long ago, but all of normal illnesses, she assured us. So now the building was hers. I maybe should've found her story alarming, but she was so warm, this tiny guide of ours, she wore a clean floral dress that clung to her incredibly small frame, she couldn't have been more than five feet tall, and she had styled her hair with a large butterfly clip, as if we were important guests and she our loving host.

The apartment itself was exceptionally awful, maybe this was why Ophelia was being so kind. The walls and ceiling were stucco, with cracks along the corners where they met. There was one window, a small square, not a rectangle, and it was off centre, it had bars on it, despite the fact we were three floors up, and there was no trim, just cracked stucco framing it. The floors were mismatched beige and brown tiles—that the floor was tiled was the only thing preventing it from looking like a torture room in a Bond movie.

"The hot plate comes with the apartment," Ophelia said, still smiling.

I wondered if I asked her nicely to do some feminine repairs this place could be livable. But I couldn't shake the feeling that this was where someone came to die, that maybe this was the room where all of Ophelia's brothers had died, at her hands. She had had enough of their boorish behaviour, the unjust ways they spent their father's money, so one by one she asked them here to this small bachelor apartment to show off her handiwork, and then she tortured them until death.

I smiled at Ophelia, and she took my hand and shook it delicately, the tendons of her hand stretching to wrap around mine. I hoped she'd find a nice tenant, one that she wouldn't have to murder.

Near the bottom of the stairs I passed Thomas and Becca on their ascent to the angry apartment. Thomas stopped me. "How was it?"

"Well . . . there's a hot plate on the table."

"No oven? Microwave?"

I shook my head.

"Well, fuck. Not gonna bother."

He turned to Becca, waiting to see if she would follow.

"I never cook."

"I'll wait for you down here then."

She raised her eyebrows, like it wasn't a concern to her whether he waited or not, and carried on past us. We stepped out into the rain, lifting our umbrellas.

"That's pretty shitty you waited so long and didn't even see the apartment."

"Was it worth seeing?"

I shook my head, it really wasn't, but I tried not to get too down on wasting another day.

"Are you hungry?" he asked me.

"Uh, yeah. I mean kinda, I'll probably grab something on my way back."

I didn't want to cook with the other damp travellers, and on my way to the line I had passed a convenience store that was offering energy bars for a dollar. If I paired that with a bag of chips for another dollar, I'd be in pretty good shape.

"Do you like French fries?"

I nodded, I did like French fries.

"Do you like French *guys?*"

I smiled obligingly.

"Me neither, but I do like French fries, there's a restaurant, The Potato Place, they make the best potato everything. I go there a lot, it might be why I kind of look like a potato, Po-Ta-Toe, like with an *e*, get it?"

"I don't think you look like a potato."

"You are what you eat."

"I eat a lot of shawarma."

He looked me up and down, very seriously. "It all makes sense."

I liked Thomas, he liked to try to be funny but without using funny to get something. Sometimes his jokes worked, sometimes they didn't, but he kept trying. I imagined us as cartoon characters, Shawarma and Potato, we would get in fights with other foods, he would smoke a lot, it was entertaining to me to imagine a smoking potato.

Becca exited the apartment, she seemed satisfied.

"I can't believe you didn't look at it, Thomas, it was minimalistic perfection."

"Yeah, but I want an oven."

"No one cooks anymore."

"So you applied?"

"Of course, it was very much my aesthetic, and I appreciate that it's run by a woman."

I couldn't help but think, Yeah, a woman who is also a murderer, but Becca would probably be in favour of that, she was very aggressive herself. I told her I hoped she got it, and she replied that of course, that's what you're supposed to say. This caught me off guard, I began to hum and looked away, waiting for Thomas to fill the silence.

"We're gonna get potatoes, fries probably, but the world's our oyster, or potato, they don't have oysters, wanna come?"

She shook her head. "I have to get back to work."

"Alrighty, well, in case you don't get the apartment, why don't I take your number so we can meet up for the lines again? Or if you do get it, then I'll know to get you a housewarming gift."

She sighed. "Will it be a potato?"

"Most likely yes."

She reached for his phone and stamped in her number. "I don't like phone calls, only for business, no voicemails either. But texts are okay, but not long ones, and not a lot in a row, that should be obvious."

"Duly noted."

"Okay, well, bye. Nice meeting you."

I didn't think she was addressing me, but I didn't care.

"Shall we?"

I had thought for a moment that with Becca's decline, the plan would be off, but like a failed joke, a failed invitation didn't seem to deter Thomas, so I followed him through the rain towards a gleaming white-and-yellow awning emblazoned with "The Potato Place."

I ordered plain, he got a combination of sour cream, salsa, pulled pork, cheddar cheese, factory-made bacon bits, hot sauce, and vegan gravy. I wondered if he actually liked fries at all. He also got another large Coke to go with it, telling me it paired nicely with the meal.

Distracted by his fries, Thomas didn't make as many jokes. We talked about what our ideal apartment would be, our horror stories of roommates. He once had a roommate who would sleep-walk and shit in the living room, nowhere else, just the living room. One time Thomas caught him and tried to wake him up, then realized he hadn't been sleepwalking at all. He was angry with Thomas for always being in the living room playing video games and thought if he continuously made the room smell like shit, Thomas wouldn't use it as frequently. I asked Thomas how he'd managed to hang out in the living room before this discovery, with the shit stains and the awful smell.

"Well." He took a sip of Coke and leaned back. "I kept the windows open and sprayed that fresh linen stuff around. My bedroom didn't have room for a TV, so it was the shit smell or no video games at all."

"What did you say to him when you caught him?"

"I told him it was a real shitty thing to do."

On cue I groaned, and then smiled.

"No honestly I was just so confused, I went back to bed and

in the morning I packed my things and moved back to my parents', that's when I decided to save up for my own place."

I was sad that his story was over, I didn't want the questions to be directed at me.

"How come you're looking for a solo abode?" he asked.

"I dunno, I think it's easier, less stress."

"Plus you never have to wear pants."

"That's really the main factor. No, actually, I don't, like, drink or party, so I just want a chill place."

"Are you, like, religious?"

"No, I'm not. I just got outta rehab. So . . . I just liked to party, I guess, too much. Nothing bad like, happened, I think it was just, the what if like, the what if of it all. And for health too, my liver and my skin breaks out, it's a whole thing. I did cocaine sometimes."

I didn't know why I was telling him all this. Maybe because he didn't matter to me, he was just a safe, soft potato man who was impervious to angry people on the phone and no one laughing at his jokes. Maybe he did matter to me for that reason, he didn't care what people threw at him, he would try to make them laugh regardless.

"I tried cocaine once. I got the shits."

"That's a thing, yeah."

"That's what I heard! I have no idea why everyone does it. Everyone must just be secretly shitting at the discos all night long, or wherever people do it."

"It is quite a problem in the disco scene of Toronto."

"That's why they gyrate so much, just trying to clench it in."

"This is not dinner conversation."

"Yeah, I'm regretting the gravy right now."

"Ughhhhh."

I watched him decide whether or not to have another bite of poutine. He opted for a sip of Coke.

"I had a cousin that went to rehab, for pain pills or something, she was still pretty cool. Not that I'm saying you're cooler on drugs, 'cause now you can get those *X*s tattooed on you."

"For straight edge? I dunno . . . I'm not very up-to-date on the punk scene."

"Friggen square."

"Yeah, seems so."

"Better a square than a toe. Trust me."

It was a compliment, I think, one I enjoyed. He was nice, safe in a nostalgic type of way, like the friends you meet when you're a kid, no agenda, if you want to play you play, if you want to talk you talk. I thanked him for showing me The Potato Place, and he said we could come back any time after the lines, they're actually a chain so there's a lot of them. As we walked out, I asked if he was going to try to pursue Becca. He said he'd texted her his own number and "game's in her ballpark now." I didn't think he was meaning to make a joke, in the short time we'd known each other I'd realized he sometimes mixed up common sayings, but I didn't want to embarrass him by pointing it out. So we shook hands and that was it, playtime was over, and he toddled off in the rain.

I headed towards the hostel. The rain was heavy, but there was no wind, and the cool water was a nice relief from the muggy day. The weather reminded me of a stoic skater boy I'd had a massive crush on as a teen. I'd told him we should run out into the rain, trying to embody some manic pixie dream girl. He'd half-heartedly agreed, but we were too new and unfamiliar with our gangly teenage bodies to dance and skip about in the puddles, and too self-conscious to howl at the moon, to free ourselves from our built-up teenage angst, so we just sort of stood there getting soaked. We went back into my living room, our fingertips pruned and clammy, unsure if we should touch or even sit. He decided since he was already wet, he might as well try to make it home.

He got sick with the flu and I didn't talk to him for a week after that. Then we saw each other at a party, and he let me wear his hat, a stupidly large, wide-brimmed baseball hat that said "ANARCHY." It didn't look cool on me, it kept falling over my eyes, but I wore it the whole night, waiting for him to walk over and ask for it back. He ended up getting so drunk he shit himself outside in the yard. He didn't show up to school for another week after that, and since I didn't want to remind him of the night he shit himself, I just held on to his hat, waiting. He never brought it up again.

When I walked into the lobby, one of the travellers, a middle-aged woman wearing a shirt with a Swedish flag on it, openly grimaced at me, what a travesty for me to be soaking wet. I tried to give her a look like, Tell me about it, but she just turned to the window, shaking her head. It was almost dinner time, which meant I would probably have the room to myself for a little while, I could wring myself out in private. Before I could squish upstairs, Hyle called me over.

"Hey hun, just wanted a quick check-in."

"Oh yeah, okay."

"Just making sure you're having a good stay."

I nodded.

"Guess you wanna get changed and get to the kitchen?"

"Oh, a friend took me out. So, I'm okay."

He tilted back in his chair, squinting at me beneath a bronzed fold of forehead skin. "We never see you at dinners, you know?"

"Yeah, I guess, I dunno, I always get hungry when I'm out and I gotta eat like, then, so . . ."

"It's just that we really wanna foster a community environment here, you know? Working together, providing that experience, it's important for all of our guests."

"Mmhmm."

"I just think you would feel more fulfilled with your stay here if you joined in on that community, plus, you know, you're getting that subsidized rate."

"I thought the rate was for long-term guests, for a month or more."

"Yeah, yeah, but there's a certain expectation, an understanding, you know? Like, you crash on a friend's couch for a night, are you expected to help out with groceries? No, but"—he placed his dry crepe-paper hand on my wet one—"if you crashed on that friend's couch for a month, you'd probably be expected to clean up after yourself, right?"

"Yeah." I slid my hand out from under his, slowly, and pretended to check my phone.

"So you know, we're like your friends, and you're our friend, so we just expect you to . . . be a good friend. You know?"

I'd never heard friendship used as a threat, except when reading about gang initiations. I'd have to check the website, I was certain the subsidized rates weren't asterisked with a footnote that said I had to be a good friend.

"Yeah, I'm just soaked, so . . . and I ate."

"Tomorrow's another day."

He winked, a definite threat, maybe not at a cartel level but a hostile-hostel level. Join the group tomorrow or . . . or what? I was paid up till Monday and I'd never seen anyone kicked out, not even the rowdy German kid who unscrewed all the light-bulbs. I felt Hyle watching me as I walked up the stairs, lion man stalking his prey.

You could walk out of here right fucking now, slit this guy's throat, grab the cash from the register, and beat it. There are no cameras, there's no one that's gonna miss him.

I pictured all the travellers discovering the body, talking about me in various languages, how weird I'd seemed from the get-go, how lonely I must have been for far too long.

Maybe I needed to add more friends to my revenge fantasies, make-believe comrades supporting the cause, but then was that how a person became a serial killer? I turned my focus back to getting dry, thinking as many happy, positive thoughts as I could, the last thing I needed was to turn into a full-blown psychopath.

As a kid, my friends were the children around me. We screamed together, ran, gasped for air, chased each other, and fell down laughing, and that made us friends. I don't know when we stopped chasing each other, probably when it wasn't cool anymore. I think I held out for a long time, terrified of what it meant to stop running.

High school was all liminal space, I longed to be a kid for a little longer, to take more time with it, but already I was priming myself for what I thought adulthood should be. I didn't want to deal with the in-between, I didn't fit in the middle. The drinking, and the drugs that followed, they bridged the limbo, they made me an adult, I thought. They brought me closer to my friends, gave me new ones, fleeting friendships born in dive bar bathrooms and at damp bush parties. They should've prepared us better in high school, teaching us about taxes and the art of small talk. How to form a bond with another adult human being without word-vomiting all of your collective trauma upon first meeting and just hoping they don't scare easy. Without play, the only way I knew how to be friends with someone was circumstance. I looked around the shitty hostel room, my current circumstance. I didn't want my only friend to be Hyle or the grimacing Swedish woman.

I pretended to be very engaged in my National Geographic documentary about endangered macaws (if only to further pad my false Moroccan parrot backstory) while the travellers got ready for another night out. I had borrowed it from the hostel's library, it had hard drives full of movies, but most were horror movies or pornography. I stuck to the animals, they were more human to me than a man in a hockey mask killing sexy teens, or sleeping with them, depending on which movie you picked.

"Do you want to come out with us?" I heard faintly.

I looked up from the macaws to see Lotte, a Dutch girl, she had the nicest face, it was so round and shiny, and she always clipped her platinum-blond bangs tightly behind her ears. I took out my headphones.

"Do you want to come out with us, downtown?"

The other girls weren't looking at me, they probably didn't care either way, but Lotte was smiling, reclipping her hair behind her ears. I wished I had more time to think about it, it could be fun, I could meet new people, be out in the city at night. I also might see someone I used to know, that was the risk of being downtown at night. I pictured being out with them, watching as they danced and pounded sickly sweet shots, smiling and shaking my head when they offered me one, repeating and repeating that I had a big day tomorrow. Why go out then, to watch them? To watch how free they were? I would just make them feel uncomfortable, they would be embarrassed for me.

"Oh no, thank you, I just have to get up pretty early for this apartment thing."

"It's going to be fun. Come get ready with us and talk." She seemed so kind, so sincere.

I moved onto Lotte's bed, hoping my body was dry enough that it wouldn't leave an imprint. The girls moved around me in a flurry, offering me drinks, until their game of musical chairs around the mirror left one of them, Ebba, without a space and she focused in on me.

"Do you do makeup?"

"Not professionally."

"Can you do my makeup?"

She held out a large brush expectantly, so I obliged.

"You're a real Canadian?"

"Yeah, my apartment fell through so I'm here in between—"

"Cheekbones."

"Right. Sorry."

She handed me a dark pot of eyeshadow and another brush. She closed her eyes and began to yell at her friends, she made grand hand gestures that I had to dodge as I tried to apply the sparkly black pigment. She seemed much drunker than her counterparts.

"You know that Jack called me cunt. Cunt! He is just bad man."

Lotte looked back at her, nonplussed.

"And why you think?" She opened one blackened eye at me.

I shrugged, not knowing who Jack was or why he would call her a cunt.

"I tell him I feel like I need, like . . . a near-death experiment to change my life, to lose weight. My mother is heavy, if you saw her . . . she's *bum bum bum*." She rounded her shoulders and swung her arms back and forth and I had to jump back to avoid getting punched.

Lotte yelled back, "Didn't his last girlfriend just randomly die in bed next to him?"

Ebba squinted her very dark uneven eyelids angrily. "I'm not talking about her!" She paused. "But yes, some heart *fuh-fuh-fuh*, and *ahhh*. I understand the sadness, okay?" She fluttered her hands and shook her face to simulate what I guessed was supposed to be dying. "But this trip, this trip is supposed to being life-changing and what are we doing?! We're going out, gonna dance with some Canadian asshole, and come home and get chips, or something. So I tell him I wanted that moment, where you *think* you die, or dying."

Lotte looked at me and rolled her eyes. But Ebba was not done and grabbed my wrists, bringing them back up to her face to continue painting.

"Like when Mila got cancer and she changed her life and beat it! Then she have, like, this *doo doo doo*"—she was either miming typing or playing the piano—"on YouTube and people love it. Love it! So why not if I'm worry I'm gonna die and then I get all *rah rah rah* and go and lose weight. That's the only way I see it going to happen."

The girls were trying to stifle their laughter, I was trying to keep up, the black pigment was spreading high up to her eyebrows because she was moving so much.

I wondered if I should tell her fear was a terrible motivator. Fear, if prolonged, only makes you complacent to more and more things, the shittiest things a human can do to another human. And death, death isn't a catalyst or force that demands change. Death demands nothing, it just happens. It doesn't quicken or slow your pace, it's just a crack in the sidewalk.

"But a *cunt*? Really?"

Ebba was rubbing her eyes and it was turning into quite a horrific sight. I looked over at Lotte, gesturing at the horrible mess I'd made, but bless her, she smiled, a brief friendship.

Another girl whined they were all taking too long and they began to pack up, chugging vodka and chasing it with Pepsi. Ebba offered me a shot, but I shook my head, my hands were sweating.

"Do you think I'm a cunt? Really? Like, if I get hit by a car and then decide to save kids or something, what's bad about that?"

"I think you could save children without getting hit by a car."

"Oh my god, girlie! There's not really the car! You're not getting this."

She angrily threw up her hands and took back her makeup, luckily she didn't check herself out in the mirror as she crossed the room. I hoped I hadn't offended Ebba, but she yelled back at me from the doorway, dropping down into a squat and giving me the peace sign, "Hey! You're still a cool Canadian girl!"

"I really regret not hiring a realtor," said the tall brunette in front of me in line.

I'd woken up early, earlier than I'd needed to for this particular viewing. I didn't want Lotte to think I was a liar. The apartment was slightly more expensive than I wanted, but it looked so beautiful in the photos, and if I ate fewer meals and walked everywhere and never went out, surely I could make it work. Thomas didn't want to come to this apartment, but he promised he would see me tomorrow for a cheaper one.

"For sure, but don't they kinda like, take a cut?"

"I guess, but honestly when I sublet my place last year to travel I went through a service and it was so much simpler. You really can't put a price on sanity, right?"

I thought of the waitlist to get into rehab on the government's dime, and of those who wouldn't make it until their name was called. Before I could disagree with her she went on to tell me that even though she had a condo, she really wanted it to be a calm space where she could relax and entertain, so she was looking for an apartment to be a studio where she could work, she was an artist, her name was Kenzie. She worked with acrylic paint on glass, sometimes, sometimes oil on canvas, she didn't want to be a niche artist.

"I won't get a bed, but I want a fridge and my own bathroom. I don't just want a room and have to use a Starbucks."

"Yeah . . . It's crazy though 'cause your phone has more bacteria than a toilet seat." Fuck me.

"Well, I have the blue light thing, so, it kills everything, right?"

"Right."

"Do you?"

"No." I looked at my phone, the germ-ridden device, why hadn't I lied?

"Some germs are okay though, like probiotics, gut flora."

Of course she was trying to be kind to me by saying this. I reached for another fact I knew, I liked telling people facts, mostly about animals, but I had one about probiotics.

"Yeah, they're really good for yeast infections, probiotics."

We did not talk after that. It was an uncomfortable ninety minutes. I texted Len to see if she could hang out, the sooner I spoke to another human being, the sooner I could redeem myself in the arena of social interactions.

I waited, I couldn't remember if she was at work, she'd started up a home cleaning business with an ex-girlfriend, and I hadn't paid enough attention to her pointed Facebook quotes to glean which one of them had kept the business after their third breakup.

"Hey gurl! D can drop me of downton shees hedding west! I can be in ur hood in lyykkk 10/15? Jack Astor's y/d?"

She was already seated when I arrived, she had a large slushy drink in front of her, bright blue, with a fruit garnish sweating beside it on the paper tablecloth. She didn't get up to hug me, she didn't even wave, just acknowledged me with her eyes before going back to her phone. She was wearing sweats (she always wore very tight sweatpants, which she meticulously lint rolled) and a thin white muscle tee with a bright pink bra underneath. She was incredibly tanned, had a new nose piercing, and two new tattoos, AA slogans across her collarbone.

"It's a drink, some tropical thing. I'm just gonna tell you, I fucking fail at sober shit. I'm going back to this new place in, like, a month, so I'm just, like, getting it in before I go."

"Totally, it's hot out too . . . gotta beat the heat."

"Yeah, are you getting one?"

"Um, no, I think just an iced tea, I need some caffeine."

"That's good, you're doing good."

I shrugged, it was all a fucking game. She was failing, I was winning, whether I wanted to join her or not wasn't the point. I had to be sober in this moment to maintain the narrative that I was doing well. This was my stage, my chance to physically play the part.

The waitress came by, she had used makeup to contour her breasts and I couldn't help but stare, not at the breasts but at the thick brown lines outlining them. I ordered my iced tea, Len took the opportunity to go back to her phone, slamming it down after the waitress left.

"So you're back with Dee?"

"Ugh, I dunno like, she's trying. I think she knows what she's got, right? Like, in my group, I'm like, the girly one, not like lipstick or that kinda thing, but like, I wear tight jeans. Dee's like, a stud, but she wants a girl girl so she better act right."

"Yeah, as long as she's nice to you. Obviously other things too, but she was trying pretty hard before."

"She was just tryna get laid."

I nodded, sipping my iced tea, which had been brought to me by a different waitress. I wondered if I had creeped out the previous one. I certainly didn't mean to, though I found myself staring at women much more than men, I was always fascinated by how they functioned, how they passed as normal girls.

"Maci Ann is pregnant, eh?" Len said.

"That's good, right? She has a son already."

"Yeah, but she doesn't fucking see him, his dad died, so I think he's with her aunt or something."

"I thought I saw she was engaged."

Len shrugged.

"I think this baby daddy is in jail, 'cause she was talking about being a prison wife. He's a Nazi though."

"A real one?"

"I dunno. What's a real one? He has that thing tattooed on him, the square bits."

"A swastika?"

"If that's what they call it. And a white power tattoo."

"I guess he's a Nazi then."

She nodded. We looked at our drinks, she was quickly draining hers to the bottom of her cheery glass.

"So you and Dee, are you still doing the cleaning thing?"

"Nah. People are fucking disgusting. She's just gotta get off the oxys and then she's gonna go back to Police Foundations."

"I guess they drug-test for that kinda thing?"

"Only for the fucking school, not the actual academy. It's bullshit."

She didn't ask me any questions about myself. She looked at her phone a bit more, I took mine out too, as though I was also involved in multiple dialogues. She swung her leg out and I saw she had a large cast on her foot, something she had failed to mention.

"How'd that happen?"

She rubbed her face and sipped more of her drink, I felt myself blushing. I hated this part of talking with other addicts, going toe to toe with who got more fucked up, who had the craziest arrest, the biggest scar, the most outrageous record. My brother once told me we're not defined by the worst things we've done, or by all the hurt we've caused, but in rehab, few of us had done great things, so often we reverted back to who could top whom in moments of desperation and hopelessness. It stopped being fun pretty quick.

"Like, I went to the sober house right after, right? It was supposed to be a transition. Man, never do those, you thought rehab was bad, no. Shit no. Anyways, they were doing room checks which, yeah like, we're used to, but like, I had a bit of shit on me, and I was renting out my condo till the third so I didn't wanna get kicked out, so I threw the gear out the window—"

"You ladies doing okay?"

"I just want the check, separate."

I was taken aback by Len's request, I wondered if asking her about her cast had pissed her off, but she continued her story after the waitress left.

"Anyways, you can't go out after like, I dunno, ten, it's fucked. And it's so boring, you get your phone at least but really like, really what am I gonna do with this? So they're done room checks, my gear's outside, and I just thought like, second floors aren't that high, right?"

"Yeah, I guess they are."

"Fuck yeah."

"Were you kicked out?"

"No! That was the best part, they thought I was suicidal so they gave me this special room for like, three nights, didn't have mirrors, which was annoying, but I had my phone, and it had air conditioning. Plus I got the gear, and they gave me T3s for the leg."

"That's awesome. Did you go to the same place as Steph?"

"Nah, I was up in Orillia, plus Steph got kicked out of hers after, like, two days."

"Oh, you didn't tell me."

"Found out when I got out."

She stretched, almost taking out our waitress, who was dropping off the check. I watched Len count out exact change for her bill, no tip, then stand up.

"Am I bleeding?" She turned around to show me her ass. I shook my head.

"You're good."

"I don't even need a freaking period." She checked her seat just to make sure. "Kay, well, Dee's outside, I'll text you when I'm out again, gonna need some fucking sober friends."

"Yeah, I hope the new place is better. No weirdos."

"Watch Tammy show up, fuck. But I'm good?" She turned for me once more, wiped the rear of her sweatpants with her hand.

"All good."

I didn't watch her walk away. I looked back at my phone, lying to my mother that I couldn't answer her call because I was with a friend. My stomach growled as I sipped the last of my iced tea. I doubted I would ever see Len again, I wouldn't see any of the girls from rehab ever again, the moments we shared meant nothing the moment we left.

Yonge and Dundas was a terrible place to be at the best of times, a fake Times Square. Through the windows, I watched the billboards change from one vibrant technicolor advertisement to another, then realized how shitty I was for taking up table space just to sit around wallowing in my own self-pity. So I moved on.

I was starving and exhausted. It was all a fucking test, this stupid game where the prize was be alone and sober. I came upon the Keg on my way back to the hostel. The idea of having a steak lunch seemed so ridiculous and luxurious.

I stepped inside the restaurant. A woman in a tight black dress stood behind a shiny black kiosk. Her eyes were lined with thick eyeliner and her face seemed darker and older than the rest of her body. I kept my eyes locked on hers, though she intimidated me. I wondered if the crease between my legs and crotch could sweat through my denim.

"Are you here for the open interviews?"

I thought about it, I did need a job, badly, probably more than I needed to buy a thirty-dollar lunch.

"Um, yes, I have a resumé."

I slid out a single piece of paper from my bag and handed it to her. I always kept resumés on me in case the landlords wanted proof that I was working, I wasn't, but the search was tough enough.

"Have you filled out our online application?"

"No, sorry . . ."

I was ready to give up at that point, which should've tipped her off about my work ethic, but instead she held up her hand and passed me a black clipboard with an application secured on top.

"You can have a seat, I'll be with you in a moment. My name is Mei."

She kept smiling but turned away to face the open door, ready for the next applicant. I took a seat on a hard red leather bench and looked over the sheet. I had forgotten what I'd written on my resumé, the dates of my last employment. I didn't think I would have any chance of getting employed if I had a large gap in my working history, it just made sense to say that I had worked continuously, even if lying made me nervous. I wrote that I'd worked up until the beginning of summer, worse came to worse I'd default to my whole Morocco storyline to explain the gap.

"All done?"

"Yeah, thanks."

"You can follow me."

She picked up a small radio and requested a replacement. Then she led me further into the shiny black building, until we were in the back corner of the lounge, next to a wall of fake books and an electric fireplace. Mei and I sat down across from one another in thick red-leather armchairs, a shiny black table between us, and she didn't speak as she looked over my two documents.

"Why do you want to work here?"

"Well, I feel like I would be a strong asset to the team, I work well independently and in a group dynamic, and I really enjoy customer service." I had rehearsed this line many times before, though it never came out perfectly.

"Do you like steak?"

"Yes, very much, I like steak very much."

"What are your weaknesses?"

"Um, I feel any weaknesses I have I'm great at addressing and learning from, in the past I know I've taken more time creating a relationship with my guests, but I think that my time management has only gotten better, and the relationships I have created are still intact." I had no idea what I was saying, she continued to smile.

"If I offered you a job today, when would you be available to start?"

"Oh wow, I'd like to start as soon as possible, if that . . . works?"

"We would need you to start tomorrow evening."

"That would be great."

"You are a size small, we'll have a dress for you, you need black heels, not too high, one to two inches, your hair must be styled and worn down, and your legs shaved, we don't approve of tights."

"I might be a medium—"

"Small. Everyone wears a small. Or extra small."

I didn't argue with her.

"Tomorrow be here at four p.m., do not talk to the guests, you are not trained, ask for me, I'm Mei. You will work full-time, five shifts a week, openers come in at four p.m. and closers leave at four a.m., you must be available for any type of shift, open, mid and close. You get one five-dollar steak every night you work, if you want something else it will be docked from your paycheque for the full amount."

"Perfect, okay. Thank you."

She wasn't smiling anymore. "We are professionals. If you can't be professional, you will be let go."

She picked up the documents and walked away, the opposite direction of where we'd come from. I tried to stand up professionally, not acknowledging that my jean shorts had ridden up over the fatty bit of my inner thighs, and walk out confidently. The new woman at the front gave me a professional nod as I exited, still hungry.

Job sorted. Apartment next. It's a good day. Celebrate.

No, I didn't trust it yet, it was too easy. I didn't know how to enjoy ease. Luckily I would be seeing my father for dinner that night. He was back in town. The counsellors always told us not to have gaps in our days, empty hours to while away that we weren't fit to safely spend on our own. In the past I had pre-gamed for dinners at my father's, knowing there would be more alcohol to come. One time I even took ecstasy, and although he wasn't pleased at first, he later told it like a funny story, how silly I'd been, how he'd played guitar while I'd danced, high and happy.

I killed some time shopping for a new pair of shoes for my professional job. I wore them out of the store, hoping to break them in. I kept stopping to admire them in shop windows, trying to let myself feel good and hopeful. That's the problem with good days. The win is just a reminder of the very real possibility of loss. The better it feels, the harder it gets. Bad days, shitty moments, they make sense, reinforce the narrative that we must not let up the fight, we must continue to grind, suffer, sweat, keep our heads down, move forward towards the good days. And then you get there, to the good—it's like walking out of your apartment, sun shining, everyone out on the street, and they're happy! Walking around, talking, drinking coffee, laughing. It's like being deaf at a disco. You see all the people dancing, and maybe you could too, you could fake it a little bit, pick up the rhythm, but you'll never be a part of it. You know the whole time that if you could just hear the music, you could buy into it. But your world is silent, and slowly you start to see the cracks. All you want to do is turn up the volume to blur every fucking sense and make it fun again. But you're sober. You're on mute. And then you think, This is what the fuck I'm fighting for? This is your good day. This is your win. And it's so much harder than your worst day.

I stood in the elevator of my dad's condo building, trying to ignore the blisters that had already formed on my heels.

"There she is! And with some fancy shoes?" His wife, Pam, greeted me at the door, she was trying very hard to be happy.

"Yeah, I got this job where heels are mandatory—"

"That's bullshit."

She was a feminist who often interrupted me. It seemed like she was always cooking multiple dishes and meal-prepping soups and smoothies, she was a slave to her egg timer. I watched her run into the kitchen to check on the oven. My father exited their bedroom, he looked tired and sad.

"The job's not bullshit," said Pam. "It's the heels, though they make your legs look great. Did you hear that? A new job!"

"That's great, kiddo."

He moved slowly to hug me, he must have been smoking on the bedroom patio, his clothes smelled of tobacco and bourbon.

"Welcome back. And I'm so sorry, you know, it's . . ."

He turned away from me and my condolences, joining his wife to check on the oven. "Yeah, it's . . . it's pretty fucking sad. Can I get you something, water or sparkling water?"

"Just water."

He didn't move, his wife just walked around him, passing me the glass, motioning for me to sit at the table.

"So what's the job?"

"It's the Keg. Like, steaks. So, that's pretty chill."

She pushed my dad to go sit down and handed him a glass of water as well. Finally she arrived with a platter of roast chicken, and she sat down, my father at the head of the table.

"And you're serving?"

"Yeah, back to the ol' grind. But it's good like, I'm still gonna look for stuff outside of the industry, it's just—"

"Well, you're back on your feet, it's a start."

"Mmhmm."

We ate in silence for a bit. I complimented her cooking. I watched my father push his food around. I tried to think of what to say, what would be helpful, or distracting.

"Everyone in Winnipeg is good? Or like, just, everything else is . . . good?"

He sighed, staring at his water glass. "Everyone is taking it in stride. I do have a box, oh fuck I meant to get it out, she left you a few things that the uncles didn't snatch up, this, this here is her dish actually—"

"Yeah, I remem—"

"I'll get it next time you come. The stuff for you, it's just some embroideries and a pin, I think."

"Yeah, whenever. Must kinda suck going through—"

Pam interrupted me again, this time it seemed purposeful. "So when do you start? Or have you started?"

"Tomorrow actually—"

My father pushed his chair from the table. "I'm gonna have a beer. Would that be okay? I don't want to be insensitive, but I also . . . would like a beer."

"Oh it's fine, I'm not like, it's not like I see it and am like, Ugh no, it's—"

"Could I have a glass of wine then? You're okay?" Pam was smiling hopefully.

"Totally fine, please, it'd be weird if you didn't!"

We were silent again as my dad poured a glass of wine and a tall glass of bourbon, I guess the mention of beer was just an ice-breaker. Pam gratefully accepted her drink, then turned back to me.

"Should we watch a show?"

Before I could answer, she stood up and then rolled their TV out in front of the table, searched through Continue Watching. She put on *The Big Bang Theory*.

"I'm just gonna have a quick smoke." My father went towards the bedroom and Pam quickly followed him, closing the door behind them. I stared at their glasses, at the bar behind the dining room table with large bottles of liquor on top and wine below. The laugh track never seemed to die down, I counted maybe five or six words between each roar of joy from the invisible audience.

I hate these fucking nerds. It's inaccessible, they shouldn't make shows like this.

I tried to shift my body away from the TV. I didn't want to look at the dish that belonged to my grandmother or the booze, so I started stuffing my face with chicken and chugging my luke-warm water. Finally the bedroom door opened.

My father stood in the doorway. "It's a funny show."

I tried to nod and smile but began coughing up bits of dry chicken. Dad stayed in the doorway.

They put me in a cab home, my father was drunk enough to hug me very tightly before I left, his eyes welling up with tears, telling me to be good.

Hyle smiled at me when I walked in the hostel, then he followed me up to my room, talking at my back as I climbed the stairs.

"You just missed everyone, they all went to the pub."

"Oh, that's all good. Just gonna get to bed early, keep up the old apartment hunt."

"You don't go out much."

"No, really just trying to save money, um, Africa was expensive."

"You don't get lonely?"

"No, I mean, I'm never really alone, right? I like being alone though like, reading, stuff."

"There are more private rooms, you know, I have one, I did the dorms for a bit when I first camped out here, but there are privileges when you're the boss."

Jesus Christ, was I the new Hyle? Naive in thinking this would be a temporary landing spot, I would become attached to this place, eventually get a private room and wink at all the young travellers, hoping I could threaten them just enough to be my friend.

"That would conflict with the saving money part."

He smiled, inviting himself to take a seat on the bed next to mine. His legs splayed wide, despite being a thin man the thighs of his blue jeans were worn white and looked moments away from tearing.

"You know if you're gonna be here awhile we could work something out, you wanna come take a look? There's a few rooms upstairs, gets a bit hotter, but it's private."

"I really can't afford it."

"Come take a look, real quick."

I followed him, the temptation of privacy was enough to override my disdain for him, or maybe I just felt I couldn't say no. I didn't like saying no to people.

We made it to the top of the stairs, he stopped me with his hand, he would've grazed my breast if I hadn't had my purse firmly pressed against my chest.

"I'm on the left, there's an Australian guy in the middle. We don't see him much at all either."

My first thought was that the Australian guy was dead. Why did I always jump to the worst conclusion? I couldn't smell anything though, only Hyle's bad cologne.

"You could be on the right, you know? Let's take a look."

He flipped through a small key ring until he landed on the only red-capped key. He jiggled the door for a moment, opened it, and motioned for me to look in. It was a small room, with two beds on either side and two small desks with stools tucked underneath. There was a small sink as well, a mirror above it.

"There's a bathroom with a shower on this floor that the Aussie and I share, it could be co-ed, there's two stalls, and there's rarely a time when the second bed gets rented, most travellers want to cohabitate, and there's a window there."

I went to the window, it looked onto an alley and a burger joint with a massage parlour on top, but there was a curtain.

"Yeah, it's great, I just don't think I can spend the money right now, but yeah, it's nice."

He leaned against the doorway, his face cracking into a smile again. "I could charge you five bucks more a week, starting Monday."

You're going to have to fuck him. That's what he wants, that's the fucking give and take, isn't it?

I nodded and smiled my dumb polite smile.

"We'll be neighbours, I'll make sure to make the changes to the system. You want help moving your stuff up?"

"That's okay, it's not much, I could use the exercise."

"I don't think so." He never stopped smiling. I noticed him thumbing his key ring again, and he pulled off a pink-capped key.

"This is yours."

"Thank you."

"Hey, you know, happy to help. Really, it'll be nice having a girl around."

A girl. A polite, smiling, dumb girl. He came closer to me, grinning, looking around the room as if he himself had built it just for me. I felt his dry hand on the back of my neck.

"I'm gonna make sure those monkeys didn't leave the kitchen a mess. You just knock if you need anything, you know? I'm here. Or on the roof," he said in a low voice.

He dropped his hand, letting it skim down my back. He turned to me before heading out, he bit his bottom lip, knocked on the doorframe three times, and left. Any joy I had in my newly upgraded living situation was gone. I stood still for a few minutes, out of fear that if I moved, I'd throw up roast chicken everywhere.

I didn't sleep well that night, every time I heard a noise I thought it might be Hyle the lion man, pacing outside my door. Or the creature I had created, trying to get in, it was always coming, even if it sounded far away, it was like a siren's call. I watched the space beneath the door, debating what was worse—Hyle slipping into my bed, or my strange nameless foe infesting my mind?

When morning finally came, I was exhausted, and angry at being exhausted because I had agreed to meet Thomas for an early viewing before my new job. I was still angry by the time I saw him, pounding my cheap coffee, trying to ignore my hunger, glancing over my shoulder again and again.

"Hiya, stranger! Can't believe I beat you here, I could've walked faster than my bus, but my thighs are chafing like a marathoner's nipples."

I couldn't not groan at his shitty simile, he was a kid, and I was a kid when I was with him. He was the friend who made bad puns while I played the straight man.

"You could try a balm, or baby powder?"

"Could try it, I've always wanted thighs smooth as a baby's bald spot."

"Have you really?"

"I spent all night politely dealing with a woman who yelled at me saying I sold her a haunted telescope, I've got nothing normal left to say."

I had a flash of Agatha calling Thomas so she could yell at him about telescopes. He *was* easy to talk to. She seemed a bit too matter-of-fact though, to yell at anyone regarding supernatural phenomena and especially all night, but it made me happy to picture the two of them crossing paths.

"You worked all night? Why didn't you sleep in?"

"I told you I'd be here."

"Is Becca coming?"

"Nope."

"She find a place?"

"Honestly she texts me one-word answers only, so I asked her how she was, she said fine, asked her if she got the other place, she said no, and I asked her how the job was going and she said uninspiring."

"Huh."

"Yeah, I don't think she's into it."

"Well, she's uninspiring. She's much more like a potato than you."

"Not looks-wise. She's a real tall cup of tea."

"She's more like a plain white potato, you're a whole poutine."

I hadn't complimented anyone in a while, but he seemed really happy about being called a poutine, and we had a good time thinking of insane art installations we could pitch to Becca to make a quick buck.

"What about a dark room where a voice just tells you you're dying for five minutes, then at the end you walk through a giant bouncy castle that looks like a birth canal?" I offered.

"Or how about a room filled with black and red circles, and you touch one and it lights up and says either 'shame' or 'triumph,' and at the end one person at random is given a hundred bucks."

"Maybe one person is executed. Like one of the triumphs is a trick and it's like, 'Oh you're triumphant so you're gonna be a sacrifice to the gods.'"

"I feel that might not be risqué enough for her."

"Needs more nudity?"

"And more animals, preferably nude as well."

It was nice to say the stupidest things that came to mind, and to be met with laughter, or even stupider things. This was my favourite apartment line so far, I was disappointed it moved quickly, soon we were at the front, and we stopped saying dumb fun things in case the landlord was within earshot.

The apartment was beautiful. It had clean white walls and two rooms. One for a bedroom/living space, a small hallway with a bathroom to the side, and a kitchen with a little table and three chairs. The ceilings were high, and the floor was polished hard-wood. I looked out the large window, it faced south onto a busy street, but I could get curtains. And I could put things on the shelves, decorative things, feminine vases and bright-green leafy plants that spilled over the shelves' edges. I could arrange scented candles and shiny bowls filled with lemons. I had only kept a few books, but enclosed by two decorative bookends they would look so posh. I felt I should hide my excitement, maybe even click my teeth, hoping to somehow convey to the others that it was a terrible apartment.

"Jesus Christ, what a shithole," Thomas said. He'd had the same idea.

The other prospective tenants rolled their eyes, Thomas didn't do sarcasm well.

"It's nice, right?" he said.

"Do you think you'll apply?"

"Oh yeah, got an oven and everything, though I kinda like when everything is in one room, that way I can still watch TV while I have something on the stove."

"Maybe it's not for you then?"

I felt like a bad friend, but he was the better applicant, and not as desperate as I was.

"Nah, I'll still apply, I could always use my phone to watch stuff while I cook. You?"

"Yeah, I think so, it's got a lot of light."

"Shit, I didn't think of that, that's gonna be super hard to sleep in."

"Yeah."

"How much are curtains?"

I shrugged, hoping to evoke they would be very expensive.

"I could always put up some towels, I always end up using just the one anyways."

"What about when you want light?"

"Lamps."

"So you don't really want a window at all?"

I was surprised by how annoyed I sounded, even the unflappable Thomas noticed. I just wanted him to realize on his own how much this little apartment meant to me. He smiled at me so warmly, but that only pissed me off more.

"Maybe I shouldn't apply," he said.

"If you want it, you should apply."

I turned away from him. I could feel my cheeks getting hot, I was fighting back tears. I was mad at him for wanting the same apartment as me, standing in line with me despite being exhausted, making jokes, making an effort to lighten shit up, and I felt like a spoiled child. The others were making their way back downstairs, they were my competition as well, why couldn't I get angry at them instead? My new friend, a man who was nice to me just because he was nice, delicately moved around me and followed the group, saying nothing.

We got to the bottom of the landing, the landlord was holding out applications like they were flyers, take one, don't take one, it didn't matter. Thomas bypassed him and stood waiting for me on the opposite side of the line.

"The place was beautiful," I told the landlord, "I could actually fill this out now. I have a resumé . . . and cheques, would that help?"

"You can submit the application at the address listed on top between three and five p.m. You'll hear if you're accepted within six to eight business days. If you don't hear, don't call, it's just an automated line."

"Great, okay, thanks."

I could tell he was tired of repeating the same spiel, he'd probably done it a hundred times already that day. I took the application, my lottery ticket with lottery odds, and walked up to Thomas.

"I hope you get it."

"Yeah, thanks."

"I really want an oven near the living room."

"And blinds?"

"Yeah."

We stood there for a moment, the application waving in my hand. I folded it carefully, just once, and slid it into my bag. I hoped my silence was enough of an apology.

"You hungry?"

"No, I gotta get ready for work soon."

"You got a job, that's awesome! Where at?"

"The Keg."

"Fancy, you get free steak?"

"It's five dollars."

"Your friends get five-dollar steak?"

I shrugged, picturing him in the fancy black building, talking about his thighs chafing in front of my terse professional manager. I didn't want him to be a part of that world.

"I doubt it, they're very stingy."

"Well, I hope so, and I hope it goes well, *and* I hope you get the apartment and . . . win at life."

His kindness made me angry, he was so fucking sincere. He wasn't pitying me, he really wanted those things for me, and I was going to let him down like I let fucking everyone down.

Wouldn't it just be so sweet to watch him choke on his kind-hearted words. This fucking toe of a human being.

"I doubt I will win at life," I whispered, gritting my teeth.

"You miss one hundred percent of the shots you shoot at the stars."

"You do, don't you?"

"Yeah, but you land . . . like a cat?"

"That's what they say."

"Ha, shit . . . but I'll see you soon? I hope you have a good first day!"

"Yeah, I'll, uh, text you like, if I have to, if I don't get this place. I mean I can text you either way . . . sorry. Bleh, my brain. I dunno. Sorry." I was trying, trying to be kind back.

"No apologies necessary! Lemme know how the day goes."

"Yeah. Sure."

I was early to work, I tried the door at 3:45 and it was locked, so I waited outside, wearing my jean shorts and short black heels, trying to look professional. Finally at 3:59 someone came to the door, a small woman in a tight black dress, her long hair in a high ponytail that splashed over her face when she swung the door open.

"Are you waiting to come in here?"

"Yes, I start today?"

She didn't say anything further, just held the door open for me as I hurried in. The woman who had interviewed me, Mei, was waiting. She handed me two black dresses and showed me the locker area, barely saying a word. She handed me a folder full of things I needed to study for a test I would have to pass before I would be paid.

"The test is next week. You can get changed and meet me at the line."

She left, I had already forgotten where the line was, the back of the restaurant was a hazy maze. I could hear men yelling at each other somewhere for more chives. I changed the way I used to back in junior high, stretching the dress over my shirt and jeans, then removing them from under the dress. There was no door to the locker room, just walls conveniently placed to create the illusion of privacy. I put my things in a locker, I didn't have a lock, and hoped my stuff would be there when I got back. The woman with the long ponytail came charging in.

"Shit."

I paused, waiting to see if she was talking to me or herself.

"My fucking ex-boyfriend got some slut knocked up and now they're getting married in Cabo. In a month. Do I look ready for a fucking bikini?"

I looked at her, she was very slim with large breasts and olive skin that looked unnaturally tanned. I thought the real question was why she thought she should attend her ex-boyfriend and his slutty pregnant fiancée's wedding.

"Yes."

"I'm Stacy, aren't you supposed to be on the line?"

"Yeah, to the left?"

"Eventually."

She began spraying herself with some shimmery concoction that smelled like vanilla. I passed through the smog on my way out. When I got to the line, Mei was waiting for me, she looked unhappy.

"Did you have trouble?"

"No, sorry, I didn't have a lock—"

"You should've brought one, you can stay five minutes later."

"Of course."

She showed me the line, where a punky woman in a white chef's coat, with tattoos up and down her forearms, yelled at the men behind the steel grates.

"You'll follow Jane, she's expo, learn all about the dishes, ask questions, and self-motivate."

The woman with tattoos, Jane, didn't greet me, she just kept yelling at the men for Béarnaise sauce. Mei walked away. Once she had disappeared, Jane turned to me and started talking non-stop.

"All right, first day, welcome, this place is a shitshow but try not to get lost, we have a happy hour deal four-ounce cut only fourteen dollars, you always get a side of veggies and potatoes, but if they want their potatoes any way other than mashed, you gotta charge em 'cause we won't make anything extra unless we see the charge, so don't try coming back here to ask for nothing, thinking you'll get in the good books of some steak daddy because the guys here aren't buying it."

She yelled for red peppers and more salt.

"See I garnish here, you look at all these chits, one by one, go through strike 'em off, get hands, girls don't come back here to run food unless it's crazy, which it is, but they hate it, no offence but you're all lazy bitches. Food runners show up, give 'em the plate, look at it, is it garnished, good, send it out, strike the chit, onto the next, always think ahead, otherwise it's gonna go so slow, and that's when you lose money and come back here and bitch at me, even though I'm just the garnish bitch."

I tried to look at the dishes as she flung them out to an array of slender young men dressed in black button-ups and slacks. None of them could be older than eighteen, they loaded the plates onto their arms and took off into the dimly lit restaurant.

"No one's faster than me but my talents are being exploited. I'm quick but I also make puppets for kids 'cause I wanna do children's theatre, you can't be slow with kids they're all assholes they don't like you they boo you so you gotta think ahead. See that one gets a lemon 'cause some asshole wanted to pay twenty-eight bucks for scallops, you should never put lemon on the scallops but seafood gets a lemon so what are you gonna do? Write that down, what do scallops get?"

"Lemon."

"Yeah but don't encourage the guest to put it on the fucking scallops, even though they will 'cause they're all idiots. If I ever pay twenty-eight bucks for three fucking scallops, I want you to stab me with the chef's knife. I need pine nuts! Pine nuts go on the salad, some fucks order this thinking they're being healthy, it's not, all these girls always order salad and then complain that they're fat, there's thirty-eight grams of sugar in the candied oranges alone, don't write that down."

I listened to her talk about the food and puppets and asshole kids and customers and staff. The men cooking the food yelled at her sometimes, mostly telling her to suck their dicks and she'd yell back at them to suck her clit, and I didn't know if I should laugh or if this was a very aggressive way of flirting and I would be better off staying out of it. It seemed to go on for hours, as dishes came out and she yelled facts at me, like how long the meat had been aged versus how long we told the asshole steak daddies it had been aged. I wasn't sure how educational the tutorial was, at one point I realized I was standing against the wall, I had slowly migrated away from her to try to take it all in.

Suddenly Jane went quiet and I realized Mei was standing next to me, she looked upset.

"Can you follow me please?"

We went to her office, she told me to sit down and crossed her arms, looking at me. She then interrogated me about the different dishes, I answered as well as I could. Despite Jane having explained things so fast, I felt I'd understood a lot, but then Mei squinted at me and sighed.

"I'm gonna send you home. You're useless right now."

I'd been called useless before, but not by a woman in such a calm tone.

"You're just standing there, you're not self-motivating."

"Oh, sorry, I was just trying to memorize—"

"You weren't trying anything, you were standing looking scared. Are you scared?"

"No."

"You look scared, it's not professional."

"Right."

"You're going to go home, and come back tomorrow, I expect you'll learn from this, otherwise we will not keep you, understood?"

"Yes."

I walked back to the locker room, there was another thin woman there changing, I felt intrusive and looked away as she climbed into her tight black dress. She grinned at me as she sprayed herself down with a shimmery liquid that smelled like vanilla. I noticed there were a few bottles lined up on a small table, all advertising some sort of luxurious (mostly vanilla) scent.

"First day?" she asked.

"Yeah."

"Great, have fun."

She spritzed herself a few times more before heading into the beef fog. I quickly pulled my jean shorts on under my dress, then struggled to pull the clingy black fabric over my head.

She doesn't know what fucking scared is, how could someone be scared of a side of fucking red peppers and green beans! She should be scared of you, she has no fucking idea.

I walked in the direction of the hostel, running through scenarios that involved me coming into a large amount of cash and never going back to the Keg. I could just quit, find a new job, just like I was finding a new apartment, look how well that was working out for me. I passed a few pubs on my way home, slowly filling up with the after-work crowd taking advantage of the patios and the warm evening air.

Consider today a win. It's extra time off, before the real work starts. Tonight is your last night off before your life begins, where you have to be professional. It's last call for fun, baby.

People dressed in their summer finest, laughing and talking loudly above one another. I wondered if I went in, would it actually all fall apart? I'd heard about relapses like that, two weeks sober and then something breaks, and you're dead, or close to. I wondered how my family would take the call, if they would be confused, the rehab was just *supposed* to take, how could it fail? Or worse, maybe they'd be resigned, already having predicted the morbid outcome, nodding their heads like, "Well, we tried." I didn't want to be sober to spite them, I wanted to be sober to apologize. But in every bar I looked into, I saw myself in the glass, looking back, looking happy.

Don't worry so much! Life is good out here! But if you go back to that fucking hostel, it's over. You'll be in a bed, alone, listening to remixes of old Akon songs.

I walked past the hostel and back, trying to make up my mind, I wanted a part of me back, the brave part. No, I wanted the child back, the one who had friends, who had a safe house and a family that didn't hold their breath around me. I kept going through the scenarios: living, dying, drinking on this beautiful summer evening.

I hate you sometimes. More and more often than not, actually.

I finally made it back to the hostel, my skin was hot on the inside, I wondered if I would see steam if I ripped it open. Hyle was sitting at his desk, smiling as I burst in.

"Hey hun, how ya doing?"

I tried to come up with some combination of words, anything, but every ounce of energy I had was spent and I started to cry. He ran over from behind the desk, cooing at me, his dry hands rubbing my hot arms, I felt my hairs stand on edge and his hands scratched my goosebumps, up and down, friction that made me cry harder. He pushed his body into mine, hugging me, I needed to stop crying, to get away from his smell of dried sweat masked by cheap cologne, but he held onto me tightly and swayed me back and forth. When he did let me go, he kept his face very close to mine, still smiling, telling me it was okay.

"I need to blow my nose."

"Here, come by the kitchen, I have tissue there."

He led me to the empty kitchen. Pots and pans hung from hooks in the ceiling, drip drying. He ripped off some paper towel and handed it to me and we sat down at a table. He folded over and rubbed my legs as I blew my nose, bending his head so it was level with my navel, and then his legs surrounded mine, locking me in.

"You wanna talk about what happened?"

"No, no. Nothing really happened, just a long day, I just am tired and hungry and . . . it's not really anything."

"We can get you some food."

"Oh no, I didn't help, I'll grab something after I clean up upstairs."

"Going out tonight?"

"Pfft no, just gonna take it easy."

"I wouldn't mind some company, might be nice for you too, you know?"

I tried not to look at him. "I'm just tired."

"We could put on a movie behind the desk, I hog the best ones."

He winked and stood up, closed his hand over mine, which held my snotty paper towel, and led me back to the front desk. He pulled up a rigid wicker chair and told me to sit. I imagined he'd woven it from the dry scales of his skin for his few unwilling guests. He sat back into his cushy armchair, rocking back and forth, beaming at me.

"What do you like?"

"I dunno, animal shows."

My stomach growled, he heard it and passed me a plate of muffins, speckled with poppy seeds.

"Animal shows, that's funny."

I stared at the muffins, they looked so perfect with their sugary glaze, did he make them?

"Are you into anime? Go ahead, eat, I made them earlier with some of the Americans."

I picked up the sugary muffin and peeled the paper off, he started some movie on his laptop. I was his prisoner.

"This is *Akira*, if you know nothing, you should know this film, you know, maybe it was based off manga, but it really created a whole new genre, it's better than movies now. *Blade Runner*? Like, this is the fucked-up, you know, real version."

A traveller wandered through the lobby, raised his hand. Hyle waved. I swallowed the muffin quickly, it was not as sweet as I had hoped, almost dusty, and dry, like his skin. The movie started, it was a cartoon, and subtitled, his laptop was too far away and I had to squint to try to read the titles.

"Oh, here." He pulled me closer and took away the plate of muffins. "You gotta really pay attention, it's just layered, you know?"

I tried to focus on the movie, but there were so many distracting things around the office, and every time the door opened and a traveller saw me sitting behind the desk, I felt more self-conscious. Around the laptop there were various papers with guests' info, I tried to read a few from afar. I shuddered to think what Hyle might have written about me. Lonely? Vulnerable? I tried to focus back on the movie, but my mind felt heavy. I was always tired after crying, the beams of anxiety that held me up caved in on themselves and I needed time to build them back up. But this felt like a new kind of exhaustion. My body felt as if it was glued to the wicker chair, frozen. My muscles were replaced by wheels, turning and turning inside a heavy concrete shell.

"You feeling better?"

His voice was faraway, had he asked me that before? Maybe earlier, but what was earlier, if I blinked, would it be ten minutes later? The sky outside the hostel was so dark now, but the movie was still on, maybe it was endless, I couldn't follow the plot so I would never know.

"It's good, right?"

I couldn't answer, my face felt like clay, I tried to push the wet mud to form a smile, tried to nod, though I found once I started nodding, I couldn't stop, there was such comfort and rhythm in nodding. I felt his hand on my leg, his rough hand, was he scraping me? No, I mean I didn't think so, I was too afraid to look down, maybe I was bleeding, or sweating, or peeing, was I? I tried to remember this feeling, it was the same one I had when I smoked too much weed, had we smoked earlier, in the kitchen?

"Those muffins are a trip, you know?"

Jesus fucking Christ. It felt like a carnival was starting in my head, an old-fashioned one, somewhere out in the Ozarks, all the lights slowly turning on, powered by outdated generators. My brain was delayed, I wanted it to stop, I felt his hand on my leg, felt him squeeze, and saw him smile at me, his other hand reaching out for my chin, stroking it.

"It's hitting you pretty hard, right?"

I felt as if I was being attacked in slow motion, his hand moving on my chin as if he was trying to pull my skin away, more material for his uncomfortable chairs.

"You okay? Watch the movie."

I tried to turn my head back to the film, but the colours were so bright I thought I might be sick. I closed my eyes, focusing on breathing, worried I'd forget how.

"You want some water?"

I did but I didn't trust him anymore, wouldn't drink anything he gave me. I shook my head, trying to brace myself, trying to feel my hands gripping the chair, and slowly stood.

"I need to go to bed."

"Okay, hold on, those stairs can be tricky, you know?"

He helped steady me while he paused the movie and put a small sign on the desk that said he'd be right back. He guided me out from behind the desk and up the stairs. I was so grateful for my feet, somehow they remembered how to lift and press and carry my body up each step. I tried leaning on the wall but he kept pulling me back to lean on him, his hand firmly wrapped around my waist. We climbed a hundred floors, maybe more, before we finally reached my little room, he took out his red key and opened the door, no problem, why did he have a key to my room, he ushered me in and onto my bed. I watched as he gently placed my bag on the other bed. He pulled my legs up onto his lap and took off my shoes.

"You're a lightweight, huh, girly?"

"I don't do that."

"Jeez, my bad, thought you wanted to relax, you know?"

I wished my foot actually weighed as much as it felt like it did, that I could push him off with such force he would go flying into the hallway, my door would slam shut, his red key would break in the lock and I'd be safe.

"Oh hey, here we go."

He got up and pushed me hard onto the bed. "You wanna sleep in jeans?"

"Yes."

"You're sure?"

"Yeah."

He sighed and smiled at me, then he reached down and undid my jean shorts, I put a hand up to stop him but it was limp.

"That's okay, hold on to your panties. Let's just get these off."

"No."

"Listen, I've had girls and guys way more fucked up than you, you know? Haven't touched one of 'em." He pulled off my shorts and threw them on the floor, much less delicately than he had handled my bag. "Unless they want me to, you know?"

He was standing over me, I couldn't make eye contact, I was frozen, weakly clenching at the blanket around me.

"I'm tired."

"Yeah, of course, if you're hungry later, come find me, I've got more food." He leaned over, stroked my hair. "We're all friends, right? We gotta be good to each other, you know?"

He watched me for a moment more and then turned to leave. "You feel better, sweetheart."

With that, he left, closing the door, I didn't hear him lock it. My first instinct was to run up and lock it, but what good would that do if he had a key? So I stayed, motionless. I should pack, I thought, leave and never come back. I thought it over and over again, but I couldn't move. I tried not to cry, worrying about what might happen when I had to leave my room to use the bathroom.

I tried to feel the places on my skin where he had touched me. I did this a lot before rehab, when I had my own apartment. I'd start with places that were safer, places only someone who might love me would touch. Behind my ears, the soles of my feet, these were easier to redeem as my own. I would slowly, through small encroachments, start to reclaim pieces of myself. I did it now, trying to touch the small of my back, my legs, below my stomach where the waistband of my jeans had dug in. I pushed my fingertips into the skin and then, after moving them, tried to remember every detail of how it felt. Every nerve, how the small hairs felt being weighed down by my fingerpads. If I waited just a minute, it would be impossible to recall. That comforted me.

These hands are safe, I told myself, lifting my palms, pressing them to my cheeks, my nose. It was hard to focus, memories I had buried kept surfacing. An older man, who had found me staggering home one evening, driving me far out to his home, outside of Toronto, making me stand naked in his bathroom while he crushed up pills for me and shaved my body, told me about his daughter, my age. He didn't touch me until later. These hands are safe, I repeated to myself. The older man wanted to have sex, and when I told him about a boy I had a crush on, a Jewish guy who wanted to be a rapper, he hit me, broke my nose, and threw me out of his house.

These hands are my hands, and they're safe. These hands are safe. These hands are my hands . . .

I woke up early. It felt like there was someone watching me, not in the room, just beyond the door. I could hear a purring of machinery in the alley below, maybe the air conditioner in the neighbouring burger joint. Or massive mechanical cats mocking me. I pictured them arching their backs, every vertebra popping out one by one, then cracking back into place, so terrifically satisfied. I didn't move, not for a long time. The sky through the window gave me no motivation, a matte soft grey, and my body felt heavy.

I heard my phone vibrating and tried, finally, to lift my extremities. My feet tingled when they touched the cold floor, but I was grateful that once more they caught me, held me in place. It was Thomas calling, I stared at it, watching his name vibrate in my hand, he was too close, his voice just inches away. My heart pounded while the vibrations moved through my body, then they stopped. I sat back, staring at the phone, now lit up in red, a warning, I had missed my call. I curled myself into bed, staring at the screen, feeling the warmth of my own body from where it had lain on the mattress.

I tried to curl tighter into myself, ignoring my screaming stomach. I needed coffee, the only vice I had left. I never smoked tobacco, I had tried really hard to like it, all my friends smoked and I wanted to join them outside and commiserate with them about the expense and the smell. Back in Winnipeg, when I was seventeen, I was at a friend's cottage in the summer, I took a pack of her smokes and sat in her screened-in porch, staring at the dying lake covered in algae and riddled with E. coli and I smoked cigarette after cigarette trying to let them soothe me. Trying to conjure up every stress I had and attach it to each cigarette. But I kept coughing and then I thought I was choking, and I read too much into the label about tar filling up your throat, so I drank a litre of orange juice, hoping the vitamin C and acidity would somehow counteract all the shit I'd smoked, but instead I just vomited eleven times. It was a personal best. And I never smoked cigarettes again.

I was at a loss for how I would approach Hyle later, I didn't want to see him, I wished I could spit in his face and scream at him, but on some level I also felt like I owed him. And for what? For not taking advantage of me when he'd created my vulnerable situation in the first place? I didn't know many men who wouldn't have taken advantage of the situation last night, I didn't know many kind men. Hyle must have sensed my fucked-up history in some way, sensed I had scars that were deeper and uglier than the ones on my thighs. Maybe he did it on purpose, hoping I'd shrink down small enough so he could just pick me up and place me where he wanted. I worried I might give up and just let that happen. I slapped the side of my head twice, trying to get my brain to generate something other than fucked-up logic, to generate something that made sense.

I had to get out of the hostel, so I found a reason to, another showing. I hadn't heard from the beautiful apartment. I was lucky to slip past Hyle as he welcomed a new guest, not without briefly hating myself for momentarily acknowledging his presence with a quick nod and smile, while I felt my heart pounding in my throat. I power-walked to the lobby door before I could see if he'd reciprocated my greeting. I hoped that would be it, and we would never mention the night in question again, either that or he would drop dead before I got back.

In line I stood between two women, both very striking in their apparel choices. The one in front wore camel-coloured everything: high-waisted silk shorts, leather loafers, boxy suede tank top, and watch. All camel. Her bag too. Only her thick sunglasses were black, tucked beneath camel-coloured hair framing her camel lipstick. The woman behind me had multicoloured hair, grown out and fading but still clinging to hues of pink and green and orange. She wore yellow sandals with red buckles, a long green skirt, and a paisley blue-and-red oversized button-up shirt. The woman behind me spoke first.

"Fucking hell, is it like this at every place?"

The camel woman and I shook our heads in solidarity. I thought that might make her feel better, but she just groaned.

"I told my boyfriend he'd have to go down on me for like, a fucking week if I did the lines for us."

I didn't know how to respond to that, neither did camel woman, she continued shaking her head in disapproval at the line, or maybe she just shook her head uncontrollably all the time, just a permanent *no* to the world.

She looked back at us, angrily. "They should have magazines like in waiting rooms."

"Yeah, I could go for a crossword." I said it like a crossword was a universal good time, like going for a beer. Camel shook her head and the woman behind her smiled.

"I'm Quartz by the way."

"Oh cool, like the crystal?"

"I guess, fucking hippie parents, right? Fucked-up thing is quartz is like, the least valuable type of crystal, like, how the fuck does that set a kid up for success?"

"I thought it was for healing?" Camel offered.

"Bullshit, I sure as shit ain't a healer."

"Sandrine, it's French, it's derived from Alexandra, which means protector of men."

"Are you?"

"What?"

"A protector of men?"

I couldn't tell if Quartz was trying to be hostile towards Sandrine specifically or if she was just hostile towards everything.

"I mean, do they need protection?"

"My boyfriend has a poetry blog linked to his Facebook and like, every fucking day someone calls him a faggot. Seriously, it's fucking nuts, 'cause we're supposed to be so evolved, right? I don't even get poetry, if it's good or bad, but I'd never call him a faggot. Obviously 'cause I'm fucking him, but still."

"Yeah, it's never nice to bully, your boyfriend should report them."

"I'm not gonna tell him how to live his fucking life."

The line, despite seeming endless, moved quite quickly, which could mean something great or horrible. Middle-ground apartments took more time because most of us went through the same lengthy thought processes: It's not great but I could make it work, maybe some paint, maybe a rug . . . and so on. I hoped for the best.

"What about you?" I realized Quartz was directing her question at me.

"What?"

"Do you have a boyfriend?"

"Oh, no."

"Or girlfriend?" Sandrine interjected.

"Yeah, fuck, sorry, girlfriend?" said Quartz.

"Um, nope. I mean, it would just be a boyfriend, but no . . . but I have friends."

"Fuck buddies?"

"No, I meant, like . . . I have friends. Just to, like, hang with . . ." I trailed off. I wanted to laugh at myself, it was so tragic, lying to these strangers about friendship.

Sandrine shook her head again. "There's a couple great dating sites out there, I met two of the guys I'm seeing through there, the other was through work. It's great for casual dating."

"Fuck, don't miss that. All the fucking games dudes play." Quartz shook her head.

"I just try to be upfront, keep it simple."

"Yeah, but it's never fucking simple, right?"

They smiled at each other, some common ground.

"So you gonna get on the internet?" Sandrine asked me.

I shrugged. "Ah, I'm not good at those things, I don't like writing the bios."

"Why? It's easy. Just go on the web, they have like, fucking stock ones." Quartz spoke to me as if we were close enough that she could be this annoyed with me.

"Or just be honest about your expectations, if you're not looking for anything serious, just say it."

"Yeah, but then dudes think you're just down to fuck like mad," Quartz said.

I thought of Matt, and wondered if that's what I was to him, just a girl that liked to fuck like mad. He hadn't reached out since the warehouse, but I wasn't offended, I would never be the girlfriend in his father's basement, and for that, I was actually grateful.

The apartment itself was dark, windowless, grey-walled, and cheaply carpeted in mustard shag. There was a sectioned-off tiled corner, framed by black grout, that must have been intended as a cooking area. The ceiling was low and sloped, even though it wasn't the top floor. Sandrine shook her head emphatically and quickly turned on her heel without a word.

"I think I'd fucking kill my boyfriend and then myself if I lived here," Quartz said aloud to no one in particular, then she followed Sandrine back down the stairs.

I lingered for a moment, thinking that it could actually be a decent place for Thomas. Everything was in one room like he wanted, he could put a desk under the part of the ceiling that was highest, and pull a string to the mini fridge, maybe even design some sort of contraption to have cans of Coke roll up to his heels. And it had two burners, he could boil potatoes and eat them mashed or fried, storing packets of ketchup in the mini fridge. I messaged him to tell him I was sorry for missing his call earlier, that I had to work and maybe we could do a viewing together tomorrow. He didn't reply right way, he always replied right away. I told myself he was probably working, or maybe even on a date with the impervious Becca. I spent the walk home hoping Thomas would call just as I approached the hostel doors, giving me an excuse to fully ignore Hyle, but practising in my head what I would do if I found myself alone with the lion man in the lobby upon my return.

I braced myself, I knew Thomas would not call and save me, and I felt angry with myself for wanting to be saved. I tried to look relaxed as I pulled at the doors, going through the rehearsed act in my head. If Hyle stopped me to talk, I would say firmly that I needed to get ready for work and run up the stairs. I didn't want to leave him space to apologize for last night, because I knew I'd feel obligated to accept.

As I entered, he was once again busy checking in a new traveller. A woman, alone, she had an English accent, or Scottish. He was trying to be charming, I could tell, and I could hear her politely laughing as he talked her through the hostel's guidelines about dinners and friendships. As I climbed the staircase, I could hear his chair sighing as he got up, they were off to the roof.

I arrived early at the Keg, the heavy black door was locked again but I knocked this time. Knocking showed self-motivation, I was pretty sure. A different beautiful young woman in a tight black dress opened the door for me.

In the locker room, I realized I'd forgotten a lock for the second time. After changing quickly I walked to the manager's office, where Mei sat staring at a computer screen, from what I could tell she was looking at four identical photos of the same steak, and she was peering closely at the monitor trying to spot the differences.

"Yes?" she said without averting her gaze.

"Hey, sorry, I don't know if I should be here this early, I just thought I could catch up on some of the things I may have missed yesterday."

"When I sent you home?"

"Right."

"How could you catch up on four hours of training in twenty minutes?"

"Ha, yeah, I could always stay late, sorry, or come in earlier, like, tomorrow."

"Well, we're just going to have to move on, you're going to shadow Mallory on the open, follow, smile, don't talk, take notes, you have your pen and pad?"

"Yes."

"Make sure you punch in all the orders, but double-check them, you're not technically an employee, so if there are mistakes you pay for them, you understand?"

"Yup."

"*Yes.* We're professionals. Yes."

"Yes."

She hadn't looked up from the computer the whole time we were talking, which was a relief. I weaved back through to the front of the restaurant, it looked lighter than it had before, like a movie set, everything was in its place, the leather all shined up, the plants and chrome underlit to create atmosphere. A young woman sat at the bar in front of the bartender, rolling limes one by one.

"You're shadowing me?" she said when she saw me.

"Yes, I think, Mallory?"

"Mmhmm. We're gonna cut these, have you cut fruit before?"

It seemed like an odd question to ask. Did I appear stunted somehow? "Yes."

She patted a leather stool next to her and I sat, she passed me a neon cutting board and knife.

"Careful, it's dull, you're gonna cut yourself probably, but try not to."

She then proceeded to show me how to cut fruit by the Keg standards. She told me she had tried to cut them into squares when she first started 'cause she had thought that was the most universal shape. Slices, she said. I nodded like this was helpful information.

The bartender began to chat with Mallory. I was trying very hard to focus on the slicing, the knife *was* dull and I had nicked myself already, just lightly, and the lime was making it burn.

"Kasey's leaving next week," Mallory said.

"School, right?" the bartender replied.

"Yeah, I had no idea she's like, really smart."

"'Cause she acts dumb."

"Yeah, but if you think about it like, that's smart. To do that. They love it."

"Well, she's going into philosophy, she's not that smart."

"What type of job do you get in philosophy?"

The bartender shrugged. "Shit, sorry if you're into philosophy," she said to me.

I shook my head. "No, no. I'm not."

"Do you go to school?"

"No. I did, I finished, so just kinda working, trying to find . . . work."

During my illustrious creative writing studies, I'd actually taken a philosophy elective. I'd shown up to class on St. Patrick's Day drunk and ended up almost failing out. I wasn't sure what I really knew about philosophy.

I used to tell people for a little while after I graduated that I was going to be a writer, and in certain inebriated states I did take notes, snippets of overheard conversations between drug dealers, barely breathing barflies, and men who thought they were very intelligent. I thought I was onto something, but when I looked at the notes in the morning, they were usually illegible, and made no sense. I stopped telling people what I wanted to be and started letting people come to their own conclusions, for better or worse.

Both girls nodded.

"This is a nice place to work, really, even if you're into philosophy," Mallory said.

"Yeah, everyone seems nice."

"Mmhmm, we all go out a lot together, it's my birthday tomorrow actually, so you're gonna come, like, after work."

I was taken aback by her forwardness. She reminded me of Grace. I didn't think I could tell someone, right after meeting them for the first time, what their social obligations were. Maybe I could actually learn something from Mallory, apart from how to cut fruit.

"Great."

"There's gonna be a lot of girls so don't worry if you can't remember any names like, except mine 'cause it's my birthday and that'd be a bitch move. Girls come and go so often, just call everyone hun."

The bartender piped up. "Please don't call me hun. Girl. I like girl, but only by girls like, Hey girl. By guys it's just creepy."

"Oh, for sure. How come girls come and go?"

The bartender, Girl, smirked and began sorting neon straws and candied garnishes.

"It's just not a forever type of place, you make your money, you take a lot of shit from guests, the ones who are the worst usually pay the most, and then you get out."

"The guests are that bad?"

"Sometimes, but just giggle and stuff. They're just touchy, the men, sometimes the women, it's kinda like we're steak strippers, just without showing as much tits and ass."

"Except if you're Stacey R.," Girl replied.

"Yeah, she was like a double-*double* D wearing an extra-*extra* small. But she made her money and now she's all up on Instagram as a fitness model. I pay three hundred bucks a month just for her tutorials for a better booty and stuff like that. She put in work."

"Yeah, I mean that's awesome."

"Just depends how far you wanna go. You stay back after a shift or two, have a couple drinks, build up a group of regulars, you'll be outta here in a couple months."

I didn't want to seem naive by asking questions. Just how far did they go? For how much? Not that I could ever see myself staying behind with a self-proclaimed steak daddy, but I wanted concrete numbers, even just to figure out if it was worth investing in a push-up bra. I wore a tight old sports bra every day because when I first bought it the woman promised me it would wick away sweat.

The restaurant opened, all the lights went down and we lit small candles for the tables, it reminded me of when my grandfather died. I came home from a friend's house, and all the lights were off in my house, a rarity. My mother, aunt, and grandmother were all sitting around the dining room table, silently crying, with a large red candle in the middle. It looked like a very sad seance.

Once the patrons started filing in, I followed Mallory around dutifully, watching as she smiled and winked at old men with bloody steak juices running down their chins. Watched as their hands slid down her back and she giggled, the plastic women next to them either not noticing or not giving a shit and ordering more expensive neon cocktails. There were younger men too, they all yelled a lot and called us sweetie, one of them insinuated he'd be happy to break me in.

It went on like that for a while, in a haze of vanilla and steak, it didn't really seem like hard work, my feet hurt, but most of the women I worked with seemed friendly enough. Behind the scenes, in the server's lounge, which was a small storage room filled with packages of toilet paper, the girls drank coffee and Red Bull and punched in orders and talked. I tried to take in everything they were saying. A beautiful group of women, like the kind I'd dreamed about being friends with in my younger years, was somehow now in front of me. They asked me a few questions, if I had a boyfriend, was I in school. One girl said coldly that's about all they'd ask as a collective 'cause asking the same questions gets old and girls don't stick around.

Mei came in at one point to check in on me. I punched in a few orders in front of her, Mallory sang my praises, and despite the sliminess of the situation outside of the lounge, I felt content, but apparently I didn't seem that way to Mei.

"You're doing well but you're not smiling. We're selling more than steak, it's an experience, right?"

"Right."

"Yes. We say yes, never no, or yup or sure. Happy girls, happy guests. Big smiles, all of you ladies. Lacey, I don't care if your uterus is exploding, pump yourself full of Motrin and do your job. Unless someone wants to take her tables."

"I'm fine!"

Once Mei was gone, Mallory told me she was a bitch, that everyone loved her but she was by the book and the book was a bitch. That made me smile, I felt a sense of camaraderie with my small-clothed sisters. Another girl started crying as she walked back into the lounge.

"That fucking toupée, he always makes me sit on his lap and take a photo and he tips fucking fifteen percent!"

"Don't sit on his lap," Mallory told her.

"I tried that once and he only tipped ten. I swear if my son ever fucks with a girl like that, I'm gonna slap him."

"How old is he now?"

"Three, he's a good kid." She couldn't have been more than twenty years old. She adjusted her mascara and then her breasts, smiling into her small compact. "Three more days, ladies." She shut her compact and walked back out onto the floor confidently, as if her outburst had never happened.

I looked to Mallory for clarification.

"She's taking some real estate test, I dunno, her kid's dad is an agent, so." She shrugged.

I looked around at these women and was reminded of a story

I had read in some magazine about the strippers who go to small mining communities, put up with or partake in debauchery for a week or two, make enough money to live for a few months, and bus out as soon as they can.

I would've walked out but I knew that it wasn't just here, but most serving jobs, and I would do better to continue silently shadowing Mallory and giggling at the rich men. Later, when I changed as quickly as possible out of my constricting dress, Mallory approached me and handed me a hundred dollars, for my help, she said. I felt better, bought, but better. I told myself these were stronger women than me, they rode above the bullshit, not letting it touch them, collected their money and left it all behind in a cloud of beefy vanilla. I would change my approach, I would be an agent, extracting money from these men, tricking them with giggles and winks, and I would mock them, even just in my head, I would be untouchable too.

I got back to the hostel late, the bars were shutting down and I trickled in with the other travellers. I was going upstairs just as Hyle and the new British guest came swinging in from the kitchen.

He called out to the few of us stumbling up to bed. "Ladies, lad . . . This is Katya, she's our new guest."

A few travellers murmured greetings and continued on their way, but I thought I should say hi properly, assertively, to make it clear to Hyle that I was fine and thrilled about him and Katya bonding and staying far away from me.

"Hey! Welcome!" I said very loudly.

"D'you have any booze?" Hyle was already pretty drunk. I could smell the alcohol seeping out of his pores.

"No . . . sorry."

I couldn't go one fucking day without apologizing to him for something. Hyle shrugged and turned, cockeyed and smiling, to Katya.

"C'mon, I'm sure I have something stowed away in my room."

Katya smiled in a sleepy way and shrugged his hand off her shoulder. "No, no, it's late anyway, I'm just gonna crash, goodnight . . . whoever you are!"

I smiled, it didn't matter if I gave her my name, she wouldn't remember it.

"Goodnight all."

And with that she sauntered up with the rest of the drunken travellers, leaving Hyle drunkenly swaying alone at the side of the desk, confused. He finally looked up at me.

"G'night. You need anything?"

I shook my head, the plan had failed, I was alone with a drunk Hyle and had asserted nothing.

"You sure?"

"Yes. Goodnight."

He shook his head and pawed his stringy mane, and I ran up the two flights before he could put together that he could walk with me to our neighbouring rooms.

I should have closed my eyes and tried to sleep, but there was a bit of neon from across the alley buzzing in my eye. I went to draw the curtains and looked down. It was dark and I couldn't tell if I was seeing a man crouched in the alley or a pile of trash. At 3 a.m. your eyes can play tricks on you. I was hypnotized, trying to figure out if the movements I saw were the wind kneading the folds of a plastic bag, or a twitch of something human, or not human, but very much alive. The thing moved. The neon light flickered as the figure began to expand, and from it a neck and a head looked up towards me, two small red eyes, and a mouth slowly splitting, molars exposed as it laughed. Then the light went out.

I shut the curtains, catching my breath. I couldn't find the air to scream. I knew that figure, those eyes were mine, bloodshot, spitting, laughing, dying on wet pavement. I tried to soothe myself, telling myself it was a rat, it was nothing, I needed sleep, I was fine, I was fine.

I was on the same route I had taken to see Matt a week ago. This time to meet my mother, she'd begged me to come have lunch near the airport during her layover, that she'd pay for my cab, she needed to see me, she wanted to catch up. I wondered if in catching her up on my most recent life events, I should include the mysterious figure in the alley. Probably wouldn't help to convince her there was nothing to worry about. Besides it was just my mind playing tricks on me in the night, not that I looked to make sure nothing was there once morning came, I couldn't chance it. She came to meet me at The Pickle Barrel at Sherway Gardens, a mall not too far from Pearson. She hugged me for a long time while the server watched, waiting for us to sit down.

"Oh my god, it's good to see you!" She had tears in her eyes.

"Yeah, you too, you look taller."

"What? I'm wearing sneakers."

"Oh, it was a joke, 'cause we've only been apart like a week or whatever."

"It feels longer. But how are you? How's the apartment, you got a job, you're just, you're doing it!"

"Uh, the job's good, I'm still, like, training but apparently you can make really good money, so I'm stoked for that."

"And you like your roommate?"

The server came by with our drinks, glasses of water and coffees that smelled burnt. The waiter stood expectantly.

"Oh, I haven't even looked, I'm sorry one minute!" my mom said.

We quickly ordered wings and a burger to share.

"But you like your roommate, what was her name, Shandy?"

"Shanti, uh yeah, it's actually like, messed up, so we got bed bugs, um so . . . we kinda moved out, but I got my money back, so that's all good and fine."

"What? Where are you living?"

"There's this hostel downtown, it's cheap and safe, and—"

"You can't live in a hostel! Aren't they full of hedonistic Europeans partying and—"

"Not in the hostel. They go out to dance, I actually have a private room it's like, it's like an apartment, like, it's chill—"

"It's not chill! You're not some partying backpacker, you're in recovery."

"Yeah I'm just a ticking time bomb really."

She started to cry, which made me cry because I felt so fucking guilty for making my mother cry in a Pickle Barrel.

"I'm sorry, I'm not a ticking time bomb, I'm fine, I swear, it's just a situation, but I'm not . . . Like, I'm sober and it's . . . it's just a place to live for, like, a second, it'll be fine."

"I just feel so responsible, for all of this, I thought . . . I'm sorry I didn't keep your apartment, I thought it would be good for you to start fresh—"

"It is good. Nothing is your fault."

"You don't have to say that, you don't have to protect your mother—"

"I'm not, I'm fine, I just need you to believe that I am."

"I can't."

We were both still crying when the waiter awkwardly dropped off our food. My mother started tearing into her burger, still half crying.

"I'm sorry, I'm just so hungry."

"No, eat, please. Is it good?"

She nodded, mouth and eyes full. We spent the rest of the lunch talking about the other diners arounds us, quietly theorizing about what they were shopping for and why. After lunch she bought me an overpriced Chanel lipstick, a token of good luck for my apartment hunting and new job, something pretty, she said. Then we hugged again for about five minutes before she handed me cash for a cab. I waved her off when she got into hers first, then walked towards the bus stop outside the mall. It was progress.

I was wearing my new lipstick at work, it was an orangey red that reminded me of my great aunt, Tractor Annie. I had no idea why she had that name, or why she had so much expensive makeup in the closet of her house in Steinbach, Manitoba. When I was five, she died and all I can remember is being given a large blue toolbox filled with her old makeup. I used to wear it around the house, along with crinolines my grandmother had bought for me at thrift stores. I would sing songs from old musicals and feel so spectacularly glamorous.

"Birthday girl!"

Everyone shouted this as Mallory walked up to the servers' station, dressed to the nines. She slid into a booth with other beautiful girls, co-workers I hadn't been formally introduced to yet, who were drinking cheap champagne gifted by Mei.

I smiled at Mallory as I dropped off shots the bartender had sent over. "Happy birthday, these are from . . . uh—" I didn't want to say the bartender, and she had instructed me not to call her hun, so I was at a loss, but Mallory filled in the gap.

"From that slut over there! I love you, baby!"

"Do you guys need anything else?"

"Are you coming tonight?"

"I don't know when I'll get off."

"When did you start?"

"Four, I opened—"

"Oh my god, you'll be done by like midnight, come out after, I'll be so fucking mad. We're going to the Emerson, okay, it's like right fuckin' there."

"Yeah, is it fancy?"

"Wear your fucking dress girl, you look hot, tits on fire!"

"Okay yeah, I'll see ya later."

"Be there!"

I tried to avoid her table until she left, she was yelling at other busboys and customers to come to her birthday party, she didn't actually want *me* to come, she just wanted numbers. I was cut at midnight, as she predicted, and had no real excuse for not going. I mean, in theory I could tell her, No, I can't go, I'm a raging alcoholic just new to recovery, and if I relapse I'll probably cause inexplicable damage to you and others, definitely myself, no one's really getting out of it unscathed, so . . . God, they were all just so fucking normal. All the Keg girls. And somehow they thought I was normal too. We were all sexy, professional, normal young women without drinking problems. Shortly after midnight, I found myself outside a busy club, wearing my Keg uniform with my regular clothes stuffed in my backpack, waiting in line.

"You gotta check that backpack," the bouncer said.

"Yeah, you can check it."

"No, you gotta coat check it inside. No large bags."

The music inside was loud and unintelligible, it may have been remixed top 40 rap or pop or it may have been cleverly disguised satanic chanting. I had no idea. Mallory wasn't hard to find, she had reserved a table on the second floor of the club. I waved at her with my cellphone, coat check ticket, and a small wad of cash in hand.

"You look like a fucking drug dealer!"

"What?"

She stepped over drunk co-workers to reach me. "You look like a fucking drug dealer!" she shouted in my ear.

"Thanks!"

She kissed me on the cheek and pulled me to sit down next to her. Despite our proximity we continued to yell at each other.

"What are you drinking, girl, we got it fucking all!"

"Just water—"

"What!"

"Water, or juice or—"

"Tequila!"

By some miracle, another beautiful co-worker walked up to us, tugged Mallory's hand. "We're dancing!"

That meant I was dancing, Mallory pulled me and three other girls along with her. We made our way—not gracefully, all mostly drunk and in heels—to the centre of the sweaty throng. The girls immediately started waving their hands and swaying their hips methodically to the unfamiliar beat. I stood still, watching them, like I was in a trance.

"Dance, girl!"

Mallory grabbed my hips and tried to lead me into a drunken salsa, I took a few steps, she made me spin her, then came back very close.

"Yes, girl!"

Fucking dance, monkey. Or just fucking drink. Make friends, it's not that deep.

I couldn't tell where the words were coming from, it was as if my creature had shape-shifted into a nearby dancer and was screaming in my ear. Crowds were supposed to be safe, stick to busy streets, don't go down dark alleys alone, that's what they always said.

Tell that to Kitty Genovese.

"I have to go!"

"What?"

"I'm sorry I'm just not feeling well—"

"You should drink more!"

I let go of her hands.

She's right.

"I'm sorry, I'll buy you a drink next shift!" I yelled.

"Boo!"

As I waved goodbye, I saw her shake her head, confused, at the other girls, she was probably telling them how weird I was.

I nearly ran back to the hostel. When I arrived, I acknowledged Hyle with a hasty wave and darted up to my room, locked the door. I could breathe, I was alone. Except maybe I wasn't. Beyond the glass pane of my window, a small tornado of trash was whipping around. It was almost beautiful, this strange, urgent dance. It must have been created by the output of the AC units at the burger joint. The neon sign above blinked like a strobe light, and I watched something, something very much alive, I was sure of it, black and shiny as if covered in plastic, shimmy down the alley. I wanted to bang on the window and scream at it to stop, stop fucking dancing!

Is this what you wanted, this fucking sober life? Because I didn't want this, for the fucking record! I didn't want any of this! Is this really better? What are you doing? Honestly what are you fucking doing? This is a nightmare. Do you feel good about yourself? You turned down a drink, you're so fucking strong, right? Do you feel proud?

I didn't know. I didn't know. What *was* keeping me sober? Why did I bother? I didn't know. I fell onto the floor beside my bed, trying to breathe, trying to catch the breath that was being fisted down my throat and expel it back out.

You know you can fucking breathe, you're just being dramatic. Play-acting, hoping it will lead to actual feelings. I'm so fucking bored of you.

My breath returned, and I slowly slid off my tight dress and replaced it with my brother's old high school basketball jersey. My brother had a basketball coach who would yell, "ICE CREAM!" during games. Which meant run the clock. Just pass the ball back and forth. Don't try to shoot, or do anything fancy. Just maintain whatever lead you have, run the clock. It was almost 2 a.m., everything would close soon. Ice cream.

My nights began to fall into a pattern. I'd watch the clock run down to 2 a.m., have panicked dreams of relapsing, of dancing with a wretched beast, its form changing from night to night. Sometimes its skin would be grafted with bits of black plastic between matted clumps of fur and blood. Sometimes it would be so handsome, ten feet tall, wooing a crowd, slithering through dance partners only to return to me, nipping at my ankles to get me to join. I'd see my mother crying, hear myself screaming at her as the creature laughed. Then I'd wake abruptly, as if I'd fallen straight off the bar stool and into my bed.

I felt heavier every morning, exhausted. What if the dreams were more than a grotesque reminder of my past? What if they were a premonition? I tried to hide my anxiety during phone calls with my mother. Things are good, I'm good, I'm happy, I'm safe. I hated the fact that technology made it so apparent when you were trying to keep distance between yourself and the person at the other end. My excuses for sending quick texts in lieu of phone calls were getting more and more ridiculous (I used "at the gym" sometimes twice a day and she would be expecting a much more muscular daughter the next time I saw her), but I couldn't bear the fear masked by fake enthusiasm in my family's voices. I continued to cancel on my father, citing work, because I couldn't handle more shitty TV and him trying not to cry and getting too obviously drunk in front of me.

During the day, away from the hostel, I felt a bit better. Mostly I visited apartments that were weeks or days away from being condemned. I saw shards of glass that had been kicked into dark corners. I saw enormous rats and chewed-up wires, frayed and exposed, and entire bathrooms coated in black mould. I saw blood on doorknobs and clumps of human hair stuck to flypaper. I saw holes in floors straight through to the apartments below, and I saw soiled underwear stashed in a kitchen cupboard next to ancient boxes of Vector and Special K.

Thomas continued to accompany me dutifully. He didn't seem to care if I didn't answer him for a day or two. If I saw him too much, I would get annoyed with his constant joking and blind optimism, and start ignoring his calls. Then I'd feel the guilt rot in my stomach and I'd make up some piss-poor excuse about being busy with work, and he'd reply that it was no big deal.

Sometimes it bothered me how easygoing he was. Shouldn't he force me to work harder, to be a better friend? But I knew he didn't deserve to be burdened with my shit. To show my gratitude, I offered to buy him a poutine once, and he seemed ecstatic, he talked about it for days, promising to reciprocate once he had saved up a bit more money. I tried to tell him it didn't matter to me whether he ever bought me a poutine, but he said it was the principle. He explained he'd been on two dates with Becca and she'd angrily told him that if he ever tried to pay for her, for food or anything, she wouldn't have sex with him. If she had sex with him, it would be because she wanted to and not because he bought her things. He said he wasn't used to so many women paying for him. He tried to use the money he'd saved on Becca to buy her flowers, but she'd laughed at them because apparently they were cliché. I told him he didn't have to keep seeing her, but he said he was learning a lot from her sexually and sometimes she even told him about the photos of boats, which he enjoyed, so he decided he should stick it out.

I kept telling myself, Set yourself up for success! I had heard that before—start your mornings right, build a solid routine—but I couldn't break out of my new morning ritual, greeting the garbage in the alley below, silently willing the creature to stay hidden away beneath it. It felt like paying tribute to a temperamental god, asking for mercy from its wrath.

I had finished my training at the Keg. After Mallory's birthday, the girls were less friendly to me but not obviously cold. They offered quick glances in my direction during their conversations, lifelines that made it seem like I was part of their discussions. I tried to compliment them, like I had with Maci Ann and Grace, hoping that might be enough to salvage friendships in the real world, like it had in rehab. These girls weren't as desperate for validation though, and I stopped after I overheard two of the girls whispering that maybe I was a lesbian.

Mei continued to tell me that I needed to smile more and have more fun. I didn't want to comment on the irony of being threatened to have fun. She seemed particularly short with me after I volunteered to cover an extra shift so the other girls could attend her bachelorette party. I thought I was being helpful, but when the party moved back to the Keg she drunkenly and sternly ordered me to comp their food and drinks and to not expect a tip. She was wearing a brightly coloured plastic penis necklace around her neck.

I tried to pick up shift after shift, to make as much money and stay as busy as possible, run the proverbial clock. But despite my best efforts I had two full days off, empty vortexes that made me nervous. And Thomas had signed a lease, I was sad to lose my viewing partner. He told me he'd realized, the first night he was there, why the apartment was so cheap, it was right above a laneway where sex workers punched in nightly.

I woke up the morning of my first day off, and below my window, in the alley, there was nothing, no garbage. But I didn't feel relieved at the absence. I felt sick. If it wasn't in the alley, where was it? Maybe goodbyes were too hard and it had run away in the middle of the night, and I was free. Was there a lesson in there somewhere? Ignore the mess you've made long enough and eventually someone will clean it up for you. Or it'll decay and rot and be carried away by the breeze. That would be too easy though, my creature was too cunning. If it couldn't disguise itself among festering burger wrappers, it would simply find a new host. It was a reverse *Invasion of the Body Snatchers*. I was the pod person. Grown in rehab, supposed to replace my chaotic self in hopes of creating a more docile daughter. My creature was forced to hide, strategize, and try however it could to destroy me. To take back control of my form, and use it to execute all of its terrible ideas until my body gave out, and then move on to the next mark.

I had almost made it out of the hostel when a familiar voice caught me and I turned back.

"Hey stranger!"

Since Katya had been staying at the hostel, Hyle seemed to have lost interest in me. I often saw them laughing together, watching anime movies behind his desk late at night, or coming back from the roof as I was getting ready for work, empty brown bottles in their hands.

"Oh hey."

"Haven't had a chance to powwow with you for a minute, you know?"

"Yeah, work's been crazy, and still tracking down an apartment."

"You don't like it here anymore?"

"I do, the room is great, I just can't live here forever, right?"

"I do."

"Mmhmm."

"Tell you what, how about after work tonight, we go hang out upstairs."

"I, uh, I have plans, um . . . I promised my dad I would help him unpack some stuff. Sorry, I didn't know, next time email me! Kidding, I'm not trying to be rude or . . ."

"I didn't think you were."

He winked and I was brought back to that night, him telling me to hold onto my underwear as he freed me of my jeans.

"Job's keeping you pretty busy, huh? No free time."

"Yeah, I don't really have time for anything, but it's good, it's a good job."

"You should make time, you know?"

I wished Katya would come downstairs, distract him. He rose and walked around the desk, I shivered, even though I had just been sweating. He came close to me.

"I liked hanging out with you."

He put his hands on my arms, I felt like screaming, out of the corner of my eye I could see the street, people walking past, but it was like a two-way mirror.

BANG.

Something hit the window of the hostel, hard. It was amazing the glass didn't break. We both turned our heads towards the sound. I swore I saw something slink off to the left of the glass, a large figure, just out of eyesight. My heart thudded.

"Must have been a bird. Hey, you love birds, right? So tonight? Grab some binoculars, birdwatch?"

I kept searching out the window, and then between the pedestrians I could see it, a glimpse of a dark shadow. Fully opaque, but flickering between there and gone.

"So that's a yes?"

Shit, what had he asked again? I looked back at him, he seemed so inconsequential, small suddenly.

"What?"

"Do you want to hang out?"

"I just don't really feel like it," I said, staring at him, wondering why I'd ever been afraid of *him*.

"What, ever?"

"Yeah. Thank you, but I just . . . don't want to."

"You don't want to hang out?"

"Right."

"With anyone? Except your daddy?"

Kill him. Shitty, pathetic, miserable piece of excrement you'd need a hazmat suit to touch.

I looked back out the window, searching . . . but the shadow was gone.

"Sorry."

He dropped his hands and walked backwards towards his desk, leathered skin knitting over his eyes as he squinted at me, any facade of kindness vanished.

"Need anything else?" he asked.

I turned and walked out of the hostel. I had actually turned him down. I felt empowered, it was the most progress I'd made so far, progress that actually mattered. It was weird feeling happy, and dangerous to be happy without obligation. I looked at the clock on my phone, it was still early, too early for bars and liquor stores, not that it mattered, just an interesting fact.

I was untouchable, I was in control. The creature was gone, it was goodbye, and I would not be reverse body snatch—

"Fuck!" I screamed. A man had come out of nowhere, creeping up behind me, trying to pass me. I'd startled him with my yell.

I shook it off. It was colder today, the sun was getting weaker and creating strange shadows all over the sidewalks. I saw one looming behind me and I turned to face the threat but there was none, there was nothing there. Just a woman exiting a coffee shop a few doors down. It was quiet.

The apartment had two rooms, it was square, a decent size, and had two windows that faced the street. The yellow kitchen wall had been crudely painted with a cityscape in red. There was a handwritten sign taped onto it saying it would be painted over that evening. I liked it. It was as though the artist had seen the smoggy city in a rare moment, when the sun was setting and the city was on fire, emblazoned in light. The bathroom was small but adequate. I went back down the stairs and stopped in front of the impassive landlord.

"I love it."

"Okay, I have an application form, should make a decision in the next day or so."

He handed me a form, I felt like it was my movie moment, my time to go for broke.

"I could fill this out right now, I have cheques, or cash, and references. I work not too far from here, full-time." It wasn't exactly a monologue to remember, but it was honest.

"That's fine, I can take the application now, but I still have all these applicants."

"I love the cityscape, I don't mind if it stays. Unless you hate it, but I like it."

"My nephew lived here before, he did it."

"He's talented."

The landlord shrugged.

"If there's anything I can do, I like doing repairs, I'm handy. So for paint and stuff, I can do it. And I'm clean, I work so much, I don't have time to make a mess. And I'm quiet. Loud music? It's not for me." I hoped I wasn't verging on being annoying, I could hear my voice getting higher pitched.

"You'll fill it out now?"

"Yes!"

"All these references check out?"

"Yup."

My references were the last remaining figures of authority I hadn't completely burned bridges with. It had been years since I had spoken to most of them, but they would likely say banal, okay things, enough to pass.

"You're working?"

"Full-time. Overtime too. Six days a week. And no parties, I read a lot."

He waved a few more people through. "Fill it out, I'm gonna call a couple references tonight, got a few applicants, so I'll let you know."

"Perfect, yeah, anytime."

He nodded, it wasn't encouraging, or discouraging, my hands shook as I quickly filled out the form, trying to add any extra detail that would make me seem like the perfect candidate. I brought it back to him and shook his hand vigorously, again hoping he would note my professionalism.

It was early afternoon, I was tired but unwilling to go back to the hostel. I was excited for this apartment. It had been a lot of time to waste, but I had done my work. I had seen the home I knew I had to get.

By all accounts I *had* won. I won sobriety and was creating new beginnings and all that bullshit. I had a fucking abortion, alone, in rehab and no one . . . It didn't matter. All those women, Steph, Len, Maci Ann, and Grace, even Tammy, where were they? I had done what the counsellors predicted and what I'd promised my family I would achieve. A new stable, sober life.

I thought if I bought myself something new and glamorous it might help pass the time, but immediately afterwards I felt sick about how much money I'd spent. The blouse was silky and lacey and dry-clean only, so every time I wore it, I would have to somehow make sure I didn't sweat through the delicate fabric, or prepare myself for the additional cost. I promised myself the next day I would return it, and now I was burdened with carrying the bag as I walked through downtown Toronto.

I thought I might put the blouse on, tags attached, and take myself out for dinner, but I didn't trust myself and the social pressure of sitting alone in a fancy restaurant, so I walked to the McDonald's at Dundas and Bathurst and quickly ate a Quarter Pounder with cheese, trying not to get too comfortable. There were a lot of school kids jeering at each other, I felt uncool and still sick, still sweating, I was happy I wasn't wearing the shirt.

I knew there was an AA meeting nearby, it was the same one we had gone to in rehab. I thought maybe I should show up, show everyone how well I was doing, look at me shopping, thriving, yeah, I was thriving. I wasn't going because *I* needed to, I never needed a meeting. I would be the cool kid, the one who'd won.

I had to grab a coffee first, the coffee sucked at the meetings, I could kill time in a coffee shop. There was one next door to the church where the meeting was held, as I approached from a distance I could see people starting to congregate outside. I needed to stake it out anyways.

The guy working behind the counter was friendly, he didn't charge me for my coffee because, he informed me, it was old and the last of the day, they would be closing soon.

"Is it okay if I wait here until then? I've been walking all day."

"All good. Where you headed after this?"

"A movie."

He nodded and continued sweeping around me. I jumped when I thought I saw a rat run under the counter, but when I looked back the guy hadn't seemed to notice anything. I was worried he was going to turn the lights out on me, but I didn't want to go outside yet, make small talk with my fellow alcoholics.

He turned up the music and was softly singing along, I let my eyes blur as I watched people congregate outside the church, preparing themselves to be saved from their addictions, while their own creatures lay in wait. They were joking with each other, laughing hard, revealing their uvula, their tongues outstretched like panting dogs. What would happen after the sun set and the meeting was over? When the church looked haunted and the addicts were told to go home. I imagined it like the scene from *The Lion King*. The one where the hyenas chase Simba out of the jungle into the desert, clawing at his heels as he tries to make it to safety, laughing terrifyingly. Every single fucking night, were they all chased by dark apparitions, running blindly into whatever light was left on the horizon? It wouldn't be me, I was not prey anymore. I was better than that. I was never one of them to begin with. It was a misunderstanding, rehab, all of it, I saw that now. I did not identify as an alcoholic and I was not going to a meeting.

"Hey, what do you think about ditching the movie and going for a drink?"

I stood up, he was holding a large coffee cup and lighting a smoke. Out of his green apron, he was almost handsome, when he smiled he looked like Roberto Benigni.

"Yeah, okay."

"Great, you all set?"

I nodded. He was rail thin, with delicate sinewy arms.

"Then shall we?"

I followed him, watching as he downed his coffee in two sips. We stopped at a bar close enough to the church that I could still see it through the window. We didn't speak as we took our seats, and he ran up to grab us two pints, of what I wasn't sure, but I thanked him nonetheless.

"You can get the next one. What do you do?"

"Uh, serving mostly, like I don't wanna serve forever, obviously, but for now."

"Yeah, I don't wanna fucking serve frappashit to tweentards my whole life, but a job's a job."

"What else would you do?"

"I'm an actor."

"You have a good face for it. That's not sarcastic, it's a weird thing to say, but I meant it."

"I didn't think you were being sarcastic, cheers."

We clinked our glasses and he took a large sip. I took a small sip, the fizz wasn't as aggressive as the beer at the internet café, it tasted flat.

I told myself this is what normal people do. They meet in coffee shops and go out for a drink. They get nervous, they sweat, they feel sick and hopeless, but they ignore that feeling because this is what normal people do.

"Other than serving though?" he asked.

"I'd like to write stories, in a way, I guess."

"Writers are kinda pretentious though, like they'll be all, I had a fucked-up dream and then take, I dunno, a hundred pages to flesh it out into some sort of metaphor with all this bullshit meaning and, it's not even that deep, right? It's actually kinda fucking manipulative."

"Yeah . . . maybe."

"I guess you like words then, right?"

"Yeah, I really like those three-syllable ones, those are always the best words."

He ignored my brutal attempt at a joke and continued, "I like doing crosswords—"

"Me too!" I said much too excitedly. Why was I trying so hard to make this work? I could picture it now, us older, doing crosswords together, drinking coffee together. I would learn to like him. This would be our story, without any asterisks for sickness. My mother would trust this man to keep me safe, even if we drank. I wouldn't be her burden to bear.

"Yeah, but I can never fucking finish 'em. Dude, there's this old Chinese guy that comes in all the time, and it blows my fucking mind 'cause he barely speaks English but he finishes them all the time. Fucking nuts."

"Maybe he can actually speak English and he's just shy," I said.

"Or like, him so horny."

"What?"

"Like that 'Me so horny,' right?" He was putting on a terrible Chinese accent. "Me so horny!"

I stared at him, for a moment I laughed, purely because it was fucking terrible, but then he laughed as if we were sharing a joke, and it made me so angry.

"I think I should actually go," I told him. It sounded so small, so unsure. I wanted to go back in time, to never having met this guy, having gone to the meeting instead.

"Really? Shit."

"I'm sorry, you can have this." I pushed my beer, still full, towards him. I stood up and turned, refusing to look back, my large paper shopping bag making it hard to leave smoothly, it kept getting caught on chairs.

I went to a movie, as if it had been my plan all along. I wasn't a liar. I wasn't some hopeless alcoholic, I had gone to that coffee shop with every intention of getting a coffee before a movie. I drowned my latest slip-up in popcorn slathered in chemically modified butter, repeating my story to myself, making sure it was airtight, in case anyone asked. Some lawyer in some lawyer show once said the truth isn't what's real, it's just what you can make people believe. I would tell my mom I saw a movie with a friend. I found it almost impossible to focus on the giant machines fighting one another, but it was passing the time.

I took a cab home after to avoid walking at night, it was late enough, I told myself, and should be late enough to be able to sleep. I felt a tinge of sadness when I arrived at the hostel. I was exhausted, standing up to Hyle already felt like a distant memory, it was supposed to have been a good day. It just felt long.

As I walked upstairs, I heard voices, laughing and talking over one another. When I reached the landing, I realized the voices, male and female, were coming from inside my room. I heard a familiar titter, British, gravelly from chain-smoking. Why would Katya be in my room? I heard the second voice then, the two upturned words "you know?"

I was rooted to the floor. Why were they in there? I imagined Katya, drugged and tired, Hyle on top of her, delicately undressing her as he had me. I made up my mind, I would just enter forcefully, as if I had no idea they were in there and was simply coming home. I approached and my footsteps gave me away, I heard them shushing each other. I opened the door and a thick waft of cheap marijuana hit me.

"Hey, how was dinner?" Hyle asked, as if we were starring in an episode of *Three's Company*. They were sitting on the other bed, both with glazed eyes and goofy smiles.

"You've met Katya? Your new roomie?"

Katya nodded lazily at me and held out a soggy-looking joint.

"I'm okay, thanks."

"Rough night?"

"Just tired."

"We have cherry wine," Katya said, drooling, swinging a large pink bottle towards me.

"I'm good."

I watched the syrupy wine run from end to end as she waved it hypnotically in front of me.

"It's sweet."

I shook my head at her, not sure what else to do with my body, I thought that maybe I should just get into bed, but then I thought of Hyle scolding me for trying to sleep in my jean shorts. I placed my things on the bed.

"I'm gonna shower."

"Don't have to on our account."

Hyle took the bottle from Katya, they were both staring at me, he took a long swig.

"I'll be back in just a bit."

I gathered up my pyjamas, toothbrush, and towel. It was a good plan, they would understand, my showering gave them time to wrap things up and be on their way. Although it sounded like Katya would be staying, Hyle's newest prospect. Maybe he would kick me out, send me back into a bigger room. They would have their pick of his room or hers to drink and smoke and giggle in. Did they have sex? Had they? In my room? I would leave either way, the bigger room wasn't so bad, and it wouldn't be for much longer . . . But how long had I been telling myself that? At least there was no pretence of privacy in the bigger rooms, I knew where I stood.

I stepped into the bathroom, it was like a horror movie. The tiles glowed in the blinking fluorescent light, a tap dripped. If I were to follow the script, I would happily undress, humming to myself, confident, unaware I was about to be butchered. My mind was racing. I showered, wide-eyed. If I closed them, the movies taught me I would open them only to find a psycho with a switchblade. Getting gutted didn't scare me as much as what my obituary would say. Or the eulogy my family would give at my funeral, "She had promise," something like that. Everyone would assume my death was connected to my seedy past, and I would die an addict in everyone's minds, despite being stone-cold sober.

See that's the saddest part, if you know you're dying, why not go out with a bang?

I closed my eyes, take me then. Nothing. I turned off the shower. Silence. I stood for a moment, naked in the tiny tiled cell, before stepping out very carefully, the bathroom mirror was fogged up, I didn't want to wipe it clean and have some killer suddenly visible in the reflection. Even if I was alone, I'd still be faced with my own naked body. I didn't need any more proof that I was still the woman I had been when I'd entered rehab. The scars on my legs were still pink, my small gut still pale and cut down the middle by a faint trail of blond hair. It was more horrifying to me than the bloody scene I had just lived through in my head. Ten thousand dollars spent and here I was! Sopping wet, my smeared mascara and feathered lipstick surely clinging to the dry patches of my lips, anxiety ridden and barely holding on. I quickly spackled my pyjamas onto my wet body and threw the towel over my head. I stepped into the hall and made my way back to my, and now Katya's, room.

They were still there, giggling, though the bottle of cherry wine had been polished off.

"That was quick," Katya slurred at me.

I didn't answer, stuffing my day clothes into a drawer. I looked to the bed for my purse, instead of lying where I had left it, it was hanging on one of the bedpost knobs. They watched me as I went to it, taking out my cellphone. Why would they move it? Maybe I'd hung it up. I hated when people told me I'd *misremembered*, that wasn't the word. The purse had been on the bed. That's where I'd left it.

"Not that you're trying to be rude, but is there something on your cellphone better than us?" Hyle's question forced me to turn around, to look at him, with his arm around Katya.

"No, sorry, just checking some stuff."

Katya lazily turned over and moved to the side of her bed. Hyle tried to rouse her but she waved him off. I took her cue and got under my covers, still looking at my phone, pretending I had pressing business. Hyle sighed—yes, leave us be. Instead he turned off the light next to Katya's bed, everything went dark except the glow from the window, they hadn't closed the curtain, and my phone. I heard him wiggle out of his threadbare jeans and throw them on the floor, they sounded heavier than they looked. The bed squeaked under him as he got under the covers. Katya started to snore, but I didn't dare look over.

"Goodnight."

I glanced up at Hyle for a split second. In the cheap neon light, I saw him smile at me and wink, his hands tucked under the pillow. This was worse than that couple having sex next to me in the shared room downstairs, I was looking at nothing on my phone again and I could feel his eyes on me. I felt vulnerable, he could slide right out of Katya's bed and latch on behind me, spooning me, the mixture of weed and wine on his breath, panting in my ear, tickling my nose. I slowly shimmied closer to the wall.

Finally I heard him snore, and allowed myself just the quickest peek to see if he was out. He was sleeping, but when would he wake?

I told myself this was the last night, for real. In the morning I would move back to the bigger room, or find the apartment of my dreams that very day, I could even get a hotel, just one night, pay in cash. Just let me sleep. I repeated this to myself for hours, drifting only once into a terrified half sleep where I thought I could feel Hyle's open mouth on my neck, his wiry mane strangling me.

After that I stayed wide awake. I lay very still in my bed, staring at the sky beyond the neon lights, repeating the lyrics to "Tomorrow" from *Annie* in my head. I should be more grateful that my words were contained, inaudible, within my skull. I hadn't gotten to the point of letting them slip from my frontal cortex and out onto my tongue. Maybe I should write that down, if I ever made another gratitude list: I have continued to manage to contain my thoughts, silently. The therapist would be proud. I sang the old show tune in my head until the sun did not come up, but the sky turned to a washed-out shade of grey, light enough that I knew it was morning. I sat up, then made my way down to the kitchen to make coffee, taking my purse with me.

The kitchen was empty and unfamiliar, I had only been there a few times. I felt like I was trespassing, but I also felt like I'd been trespassed on, so fuck it.

I watched the coffee percolate, my phone lit up, a message from Thomas, up earlier than usual, or maybe still awake from the night before. He couldn't wait for me to see his new apartment, he was almost all moved in. I was happy for him. I told him I would gladly buy him a plant, a housewarming gift, and if he didn't want a plant to let me know, because that was the only thing I could think of. He asked for six microwave dinners instead, saying he'd kill the plant immediately but would very much enjoy each frozen dinner. I agreed.

"Always on that phone of yours."

Hyle was behind me, his entrance must have been muffled by the sound of the coffeemaker. He stretched and helped himself to a cup of coffee, then poured a second one.

"Cream?" he offered.

"Yes, please."

"I like cream too, milk's too thin, you know?"

"Yeah."

"And cream is sweeter."

I accepted the coffee, I had watched him pour the cream, I knew he couldn't have magically laced it. He had poured a ton of cream into it, my coffee was lukewarm and almost white.

"Sorry to spring Katya on you, she wanted more privacy, she's not like the other girls."

"It's fine, it's an empty bed."

"She's paying full price, you know?"

I stared at him, watched him blowing on his coffee, still steaming.

"So on Monday we'll just go back to the full rate. I'll put it in your file."

What happened to my deal? But I nodded, playing the fool. "I can go back to the shared rooms, the bigger ones."

"Full up, jazz fest next week. Everywhere's full, 'cept maybe the fancy hotels."

I knew I was making better money these days, but it was all supposed to go towards first and last, and paying my mother back for so many IOUs. I thumbed the remaining bills in my purse, pretending to contemplate what he was telling me. I felt each bill, ten, ten, twenty . . . Wait. There were at least five bills missing, I had counted them only the night before. I thought of my purse, moved from the bed to the post. My cheeks burned, I cleared my throat and started looking through my purse. I was missing at least a hundred dollars.

"You don't have to pay now."

If my coffee had been hot, I would have thrown it in his face.

I glared at him, he smiled, still sipping his coffee. He had taken it to punish me, all of this was to punish me for turning him down. I tried to regain my breath, I couldn't look at him any longer, I just kept trying to clear my throat, I felt as if the cream was curdling inside it, suffocating me.

"Monday then. It's good coffee."

He cheersed me with his cup and walked out, I was holding my breath, speechless, his threats of friendship had evolved into an all-out attack. I poured the coffee down the sink and stared at the mug, contemplating smashing it.

———

I walked down Queen Street, past Yonge and up Sherbourne. On the west side the shops were glossy and hopeful. On the east, there were various niche shops, shops for leather goods, dildos, cheap pipes, and one-dollar slices of pizza. A corner store or two, with faded banners that boasted lotto winners of a few thousand dollars. I walked past darkened tattoo parlours offering two-for-one deals and happy hour piercings. I saw a man walk out of a dive bar and puke in front of the doorway, then light up a smoke. A woman was yelling at God, something about how he had taken her shoes, she was barefoot but holding on to a pair of sneakers, maybe they were the wrong size.

Thomas' apartment was across the street from Moss Park. It faced a pawn shop and a fast-food joint on the south side. I had to cross a small barrier of burger wrappers and empty paper cups that led from the restaurant to the park. The pawn shop had one window boarded up, and someone had spray-painted "WORLD WIDE DREAD" on the plywood. The park was quiet, the grass matted down from tents. I knew the park, it wouldn't be busy until later that evening.

Outside Thomas' building, I saw a security guard with his earphones in, he had one hand on his gun, staring into his phone. Thomas didn't have a buzz code yet, so he came down to meet me, smiling, I held up the frozen entrees I had picked up on the way. He clapped when he saw them.

"Look at you, you're better than delivery!"

"Isn't this exactly how delivery works?"

"Technically, yes. But no matter how many times I ask them, they never come up to hang out."

We stood in front of the elevators for a while, waiting, smiling. How strange to be standing in a building with Thomas and not in a line. He had found an apartment. A miracle had occurred in the city and I felt for a second, almost, that if I were to drop to my knees, hands up, head back, I might see the face of God.

"We could take the stairs," I offered.

"No."

I'd never heard him be that abrupt. His apartment was only on the third floor. Before I could say anything else the elevator doors opened, a tired-looking woman peeled out with her two young kids, both screaming at each other.

"The stairs are actually closed," he said as we stepped in.

"Isn't that a fire code violation?"

"Yeah, they're not closed closed."

"Just, metaphorically?"

"They found a girl chopped up in a suitcase in the eighth-floor stairwell last week. Before I moved in, obviously."

My heart dropped. Steph had told me she used to score at these apartment blocks. I felt an immediate need to contact her, but I didn't know how to find her, she'd gone off social media.

"Who was she?"

He shrugged. "Some junkie. Who knows."

The door opened, Thomas stepped out first, animatedly waving me off the elevator.

"Are you prepared for Casa Toe Man?"

"It wasn't in the paper. Did they arrest anyone?"

"I don't really know. It was the eighth floor, and voila!"

He was so excited. I smiled, tried to feign enthusiasm for his sake, but when I touched the wall of the hallway outside Thomas' apartment, I felt haunted. I would try very hard to remember the feeling of the wall on my fingertips, I promised the girl in the suitcase.

The apartment was nicer than I'd expected, it had a small dining area, a kitchen, and even a small den, on a slightly lower level, two steps down from the entrance. His bedroom was across from the kitchen, the small hall that separated them ending in a sterile-looking bathroom. Thomas led me around the apartment, stopping at many knickknacks, telling me stories about them, their origins, like we were in a gallery. He showed me his little work desk, and how he was able to see all the calls coming in. Then he showed me the small balcony covered in thick mesh that hung over the alley, and his chair where he liked to sit and smoke cigarettes.

"I didn't know you smoked."

"When I drink. I'm obviously not gonna drink tonight, it's actually rare for me. Just love the ganja."

I didn't step out onto the balcony, I could see ants forming lines around a candy wrapper and I didn't want to disturb them.

"What do you think?" he asked.

"It's great."

"There's a pool. I should've told you."

"I'm not a huge swimmer."

"Just a tiny swimmer?"

I smiled, turning away from him, I wasn't ready to fake laugh just yet.

"Well, I love it, I've already been today, wasn't anyone there, it's in the basement."

"That's awesome."

"Yeah, I'm gonna have a pool party soon. You should come. You don't have to swim. Just party."

"Yeah, for sure."

I realized we'd never been alone together, or at least never in a private space. We'd gone to various spuderies for food and had stood in lines, but we'd never been alone. It felt strangely formal, standing across from him now.

"Have you talked to Becca recently?"

"No, it just kinda . . . I dunno. No. She's really great, we just don't talk. Who knows, it's in her ballpark now."

"Yeah, well . . . they come and they go. I mean, that's probably for the best."

"Yeah. Hey, do you like video games?"

"I'm not very good."

"All you gotta do is mash buttons. Come on."

He moved towards his large-screen TV and set up a game I'd heard of years ago but had never bothered to play. It was all bright primary colours, we were made-up animals, like a half hippo and half Italian man, and we jumped from cloud to cloud throwing balloons or coins at each other, or punching each other if we got close enough. I didn't see the appeal, but I wanted to like it for Thomas' sake. The afternoon went on like this for a while, every now and then he would take a break to smoke weed, I would politely decline and insist I was fine. I couldn't help but check my phone frequently, hoping for a call from the impassive landlord. Eventually the afternoon bled into the evening, the sun began to set over the meshed balcony and sharp rays of light made it hard to see the TV. Thomas jumped up, out of his haze.

"Curtains!"

He disappeared for a moment and then came back with three towels, a hammer and nails. As he furiously nailed up the towels, the room grew dark.

"Should I get the lights?"

He shook his head. "I need to get more lamps, I hate the lighting."

We ate a couple of his frozen meals, he made a big deal of presenting mine to me on a plate, rather than in the tiny black plastic container. He poured me a glass of water in a large tumbler and sat very close to me as we ate. I apologized for bumping into him so much, I was left-handed and he was right-handed, and every time our elbows bumped he dug his elbow into my side playfully. We'd barely touched before this, I didn't find it uncomfortable, just confusing. I blamed it on him being high and tried to remind myself that it was normal for friends to give each other a friendly jab every once in a while.

After we finished eating, we decided to watch a movie. *Grandma's Boy*. Thomas chose it, he was a big Nick Swardson fan. Thomas inched closer to me, I could feel the heat radiating from him. I made sure to keep my hands crossed over my chest, I tried to lean back and slightly away from him, slowly, without offending him.

By the time the movie ended it was late, I could hear activity in the alley below, incoherent screeching and bartering. I would either have to pass the alley to get to the bus stop, or pass the park. Thomas turned the TV to an old sitcom, something to fill the silence. He moved to smoke another bowl, I thought about what waited for me back at the hostel. Wondered if Hyle and Katya were smoking too, drinking and rifling through my things. I couldn't bear the thought of having to sleep with Hyle's eyes on me again, grinning at me with his rotted teeth.

"You're welcome to stay here." Thomas' invitation broke through my thoughts.

"That's okay?"

"Yeah, you'd be my first guest, I'd be honoured."

"I just think it's a bit late to try and take the bus."

"Yeah, you don't wanna end up in a suitcase."

"Hmm."

I saw that Thomas had Keith Richards' biography on his shelf, and it made me mad. I hated those glamorous war stories, the autobiographies of rich celebrities, talented yet broken, captivating the world with their tales of falling from grace and of redemption. But the others who have fallen, they're just faceless, nameless pests. Scuttling in between alleys, thriving in the dark, their weary bodies, thin arms, bloated stomachs, raging against tasers and batons as the police try to reign them in when they encroach too far into our clean parks and "safe" neighbourhoods. But man, we do love the stories: "Tell us more about how you stayed up for five days screaming at a house plant convincing yourself it was Satan. Wow, what a trip." And then the story is over, either it ends with a miracle or in a suitcase, but we really don't care either way.

"You won't, I'm pretty sure those guys didn't actually live here."

I nodded, his assurance meant nothing, but I was in no place to argue, it was too dark to wait for a bus by the park.

"Do you want a hit before bed? I'm kinda tired."

He passed me the bong, but I shook my head.

"I'll end up eating all of your frozen dinners."

"That's okay."

"I'm tired too, I didn't sleep very well last night."

"You'll get an apartment soon, then I'll come visit and bring you dinner."

"Perfect. We'll never buy our own dinners, just keep bringing frozen entrees to each other."

"It's not a bad plan."

He reached out a hand to help me up, it was hot and sweaty even though the temperature was dropping. He pulled me up so that I was standing very close to him.

"I'm gonna use the washroom."

I moved past him, hoping I would hear him making up the couch for me. I didn't want to wash my face, or do anything to get ready for bed, I was just crashing on a couch, this wasn't a domestic routine we'd suddenly slipped into. When I came out I went back to the couch, the towels flapped through a hole in the window screen, I heard more screeching from the alley.

"Ready?"

He stood over me, holding pyjamas. He handed them to me and turned off the TV and we were in total darkness. He laughed nervously before turning on a light.

"You can change, I'm gonna use the washroom, it's really loud in the living room."

"Okay."

I understood now that he expected me to sleep in his bed. While he was in the washroom, I quickly changed, the same way I did at work, not letting any part of my body be exposed. I went to the doorway of his room, he had a large bed, we could be at either end of it, not even touching, it would be okay, still I waited for him to enter. He came up behind me.

"Left or right?"

"The left, if that's okay."

"I'm easy."

I went to the left side of the bed, his pillowcases smelled like weed. He got in on the right side wearing only his boxers and a large T-shirt that had the slogan, "Relax."

"You comfy?"

"Yeah, thanks."

"Okay, goodnight."

"Goodnight."

He switched off the light, his back was to me, I could still feel heat coming from him, the space between us was small, if I made the mistake of moving even slightly, our bodies would touch. We lay there for some time, in the dark. I listened to him breathe, waiting to hear signs of sleep. I thought maybe I should pretend to sleep, I tried to hint at snoring, as believably as I could. After a few minutes he turned, not touching me but facing me, I could feel his eyes on my back, I tried to snore a bit more.

I just wanted to sleep. I felt him shimmy closer, then his hand gently touched my shoulder and slowly ran down to my elbow. I could feel the circumference of his stomach spilling into the arch of my spine, I prayed I wouldn't feel his penis, erect or soft, let it end here. He cleared his throat in my ear, he was trying to wake me up, then he moved his lips onto my neck, kissing me gently.

For a moment I thought maybe this was it, maybe real romance was for other people, beautiful people, maybe I had squandered my chance long ago. Maybe this was our love story, maybe I could grow to love Thomas, like a terminal patient slowly accepting death. I imagined telling Thomas this, years from now, during our wedding vows, laughing, and seeing his face twist in hurt or, worse, rage. I wanted to stop hurting people. I wanted people to stop hurting me. I'd never felt massive attraction to the men I'd dated in the past, most of those relationships began after a lot of alcohol, and from a need to be loved. But hadn't I learned? If I was still letting the men that happened to be in my space at the time fuck me, all for the sake of avoiding conflict, wouldn't I have slept with Hyle weeks ago?

I turned towards him, he grabbed my face and kissed me, his hand, red hot, now on the left side of my face, the right side pushed into the pillow, his tongue licked the top of my mouth. He stopped for a moment, looking at me, my eyes were open now, as if his kiss had jolted me from a thousand-year sleep.

"Hey."

"Hey."

He smiled and kissed me again, I tried to find a natural break, to pull away, his hand moved from my face down to my waistline.

"We should sleep," I said.

He didn't look disappointed, he nodded, smiling at me, he removed his hand from my waist and kissed my forehead.

"Okay."

I turned back onto my side, I had meant to say, "Hey, we should just be friends." But I didn't.

"Goodnight."

He turned back over and almost instantly fell asleep, while I remained awake in the darkness for another night, once more fighting back tears. I tried to breathe through my mouth so I wouldn't smell him on the pillow. What was left of our friendship? Did we ever have a friendship?

I continued checking my phone through the night and into the morning, waiting for Thomas to wake, trying to plan what I would say to him. I hoped neither of us would mention it, or that we'd mention it only to dismiss it, nervously laughing it off as a failed experiment to determine whether two friends could share a bed without making it weird.

When Thomas did stir, he farted, then stopped moving, I could feel his embarrassment. I pretended to snore again. Only after he finally got up five minutes later did I "awake," trying to look groggy and confused. I immediately focused on my phone.

"Good morning," Thomas said.

"Good morning."

He stood over the bed, looking at me for some time. After a minute or two, I met his gaze briefly.

"I'm just so antsy waiting for this phone call."

"Do you want breakfast? I don't have anything, but we could go out?"

"I should get home and shower, I wanna walk, and then shower, I work at four."

My timeline didn't make sense, it was only 9 a.m., the walk was maybe forty-five minutes at most, but he understood.

"Okay."

He stood for a moment more, then left me so I could get changed. I dressed quickly and found Thomas in the kitchen making instant coffee.

"You want a cup before you go?"

"No, thanks. I'm gonna get one of those sugary iced coffees for the walk. Try and keep cool."

"I heard hot coffee actually keeps you cooler."

"Yeah, but it's much more difficult to drink as you walk, I always choke."

I got my things together, I put my shoes on as I sat at his small table, he joined me with his mug.

"It was nice having you over."

"Yeah, lemme know about that pool party. Should be fun. Invite the neighbours."

"I don't really know the neighbours."

"I was kidding."

"Oh, 'cause they might be killers."

"Yeah."

His coffee smelled burnt. He stared into his cup, neither one of us acknowledging that he had failed at making instant coffee.

"I'll let you know about the apartment, if I hear anything. You never know."

"Yeah do, I could bring over dinner."

"Mmhmm, I don't have video games though."

"That's okay. Though you could use the practice."

I appreciated the joke, it felt like a retreat, back to our old routine. I stood, ready to leave, and he matched me, rising, but not coming closer. I almost wanted to shake his hand, to drive the nail into the coffin, to establish unwaveringly that we were no more than friends, that last night had been a strange misadventure. He wrapped his arms around me and lingered. I couldn't make eye contact, couldn't bring myself to raise my chin, knowing it would leave me open for another painful kiss. We parted, and I smiled, opened the door to let myself out.

"I like you, you know?" He looked at me as he said it, trying to be cute.

In one swift, violent motion, I turned and pushed Thomas, hard. We looked at each other, just for a fraction of a second, and then I stepped out beyond the frame of the door and he let it close on me, and it was done. I exited the building quickly, my heart pounding as I waited for the elevator, trying to avoid seeing shadows in the hallways, even in daylight I didn't feel safe.

You're not crazy.

I nodded to the shadowy figure standing behind me, I could almost feel its supportive hand on my shoulder. I took off, walking and then half running along Queen Street, laughing now, but I couldn't help myself.

———

Hyle was sitting at the desk when I arrived. I was ready, baby, ready to tell him to go fuck himself.

"Hey, got a second?"

Another non-question question. Of course I had a second, what a stupid way to get my attention. I walked right up to the counter, trying to look annoyed at him for wasting my time.

"You didn't come back last night."

"Yeah?"

"Everything okay?" He asked like he gave a shit.

"Ex-cell-ent."

"So we should go over the new amount for the bed then, I'm going to have to charge retroactively for a week or two, I hate to do it, but management is up my ass, you know?"

I saw my phone light up, an unknown number. This could be the impassive landlord, oh how serendipitous to receive a call for an apartment just in the nick of time, right before being scammed for some ridiculous amount of money to stay in a room occupied by thieves and perverts.

"I'm *deeply* sorry, I really gotta take this."

I answered the phone, it was him, the landlord! He explained he had a lot of applicants, that all my references checked out, but there was a couple who would be willing to pay extra because of the added use of utilities, and that they both had decent jobs. He apologized, he had wanted to call me personally, that was it. I tried to breathe deeply, watching Hyle watch me, not letting my face give me away. I told the landlord that if anything else came up to let me know, and he said sure, without any inflection, just sure. I thanked him again and hung up the phone.

"All good?"

"Yes, everything is all good. I thought Monday we'd figure it out."

"Well, if you wanna reserve for Monday and the next week, yeah, but I'll still need a deposit and the retroactive payments."

"I don't get the whole retroactive payments."

"It's like a payment *plan,* you know?"

At this point I was having too much *fun*! I was having a lot of *fun* so I pretended to be dumb, for *fun's* sake.

"No?" I questioned.

"Sorry?"

"No, I don't know what a plan is."

He sighed, it was beautiful. "If it's a bad time, we don't have to do it right now, but before Monday—"

"But what about the plan?" I shouted.

"The back payments for the extra charges for the room are to be paid before Monday if you want to continue your stay here. That's the plan."

"That's the plan?!"

I knew I would have to pay. Because what else was there? Pay or what? Go back to Thomas, claim a momentary psychotic break, make love to him, and begin our new life together? Or try, somehow before 4 p.m., to scour the city for an empty room in a safe hostel, during the height of summer festivals. Hyle's eyes were narrowed with fake sympathy.

I lowered my voice, whispering at him in the most intimidating voice that I could manage. "See I wouldn't have taken the room if it wasn't cheap like you said, I told you that."

He sighed and shrugged. "My hands are really tied, you know?"

They weren't, they were dry and rough, and took what they wanted.

I continued to stare at the paperwork, not seeing the words on the page, just the numbers. I could barely see anything, I wondered if my coffee was laced, if my heart would explode. I went back to my professional working woman Keg voice.

"I need to review this."

"We just have the one copy."

"Well, you know where I live."

"It's not really up for debate."

"Okay."

"So we need the full amount."

"But first I need to read it!" I was verging on hysterical, of bursting into tears or maniacal laughter, the blood was boiling in my cheeks.

"I don't know if I can take the next deposit without the outstanding payments fulfilled."

"I'm gonna give you the deposit and then tonight I'll talk to you after work. When I have had time to read it. And *that's* the fucking plan." I steadied my shaking hands and pulled out some cash.

"You can pay for the whole week in full then, right now."

I placed the cash on the counter, being sure to count it in front of him. "Do I get a receipt?"

"You've never gotten a receipt."

"I would like one."

"I'll get it to you."

"Now?"

"Monday."

"Monday then . . . sir."

———

Katya was leaving as I got to the room, I scared her a bit coming up the stairs.

"Shit, I'll open it back up. You just getting in now?"

"Yup!"

I had the impression that she wanted to dissect the night, gossip, but I was too tired, I hadn't slept in days. Besides, what was I supposed to say, I stayed at a friend's, he made it weird, I pushed him, we're not friends anymore.

"You didn't miss anything, I actually went to bed around ten, thought I might be getting a cold."

"Oh *no*. You feeling better?"

"Much . . . Thanks."

I saluted her goodbye and I moved around her. She had made her bed to match mine, and carefully put her own things away. I sat down on my bed, it felt cold. It was too bright to try to sleep, the curtains weren't thick enough, and I knew if I fell asleep now, I wouldn't wake up in time for work. Instead I just sat for a very long time. I couldn't bring myself to look for new apartments, it felt futile, besides I still had another week here, and then another one most likely. Eventually Katya would leave for the next stop on her travels and it would be my own room again, or maybe I would go back to the shared rooms. Hyle and I would continue to trade passive-aggressive barbs, playing nice in a few months when the holidays rolled around, trying to keep everyone's spirits high, the ones who couldn't be at home. I didn't want to think that far ahead into the future, I still had a childish hope every holiday would bring my family back together, like in a TV movie. We'd be gathered around a beautiful tree, and under the tree would be glistening presents, because Santa and magic existed and I would finally, at age twenty-two, get the Easy-Bake Oven

I'd wanted so I could bake tiny cakes in tiny pans for all my friends and family.

I decided to get ready, I would really put it on for work today. Enough of the pitying, I would be stunning. I showered and blow-dried my hair, the split ends at the bottom sticking straight and rigid. I dug up an old makeup pallet originally purchased to create a mask for a Halloween party. I tried to jazz up my eyes with the dollar-store grease paint. In the daylight it looked a bit garish, but I hoped that in the dim, foggy Keg light it would somehow become glamorous. I sang more show tunes, silently, because I was not crazy.

I was a fucking professional steak slinger, this was what the job was all about, selling glamour and sex (and steak, but that was an afterthought) at marked-up prices. Who cares if my palette cost two dollars and was meant to create a carnival clown look, I would make them believe I created these cheekbones with gold-infused unicorn shit.

I noticed I had missed two calls, both from work, and a few messages from my mother. Mei had left a voicemail asking me to come in later, I tried not to curse, if I had gotten the message earlier I could've actually slept.

"Well, ain't that some bullshit."

The adrenaline was leaving my body, the weight of so many sleepless nights was catching up, but I was still afraid to nap and miss my shift. I lifted my head and stared intently at the ceiling, hoping that some cosmic energy would drain back into my body. I made the robotic voice on my phone read the messages from my mother, I didn't want to see them.

"Hey sweetheart, I just got back! We should do lunch again, or a ballgame! Call me when you get a chance! Love you!"

"Okaaay, okay," I said to the ceiling.

The robotic voice didn't actually read the exclamation marks. It was such a lousy facsimile of her voice, so broken up. I made the robot read it to me again, and again. I tried to picture my mother as a robot, then maybe I couldn't hurt her. After the robot had finished reading the message for the fifth time, I realized how truly silent it was in my little room.

"In case I don't see ya, good morning, good afternoon, and goodnight."

I tried to pull a Jim Carrey face in the mirror.

Still got it.

"Yes, I fucking do."

I felt glamorous walking down the street, the glimpses I caught of my reflection in dark store windows showed me the woman I wanted to be. I had a larger backpack than usual, it felt light, and I felt light and cold, when was the last time I had eaten? It didn't matter, I was cold, but it made me feel thin, like my legs were just bone, just so glamorous. The shadows were lighting up the side-walk again, creating spotlights, and I was the star.

I stopped in at a liquor store, electricity running through my veins. I had been there so many times before but now I felt lost, paranoid. What if someone I knew saw me through the store window? I felt like I had the word *alcoholic* emblazoned on my backpack. I wanted passersby to think I was just an ordinary young woman getting ready for a night on the town. I couldn't shake the feeling that I would be caught, outed at any moment. I needed to move quickly. I looked at all the syrupy concoctions, pineapple-mandarin ciders, hibiscus–passion fruit wines, it was all like candy, but I couldn't imagine the taste, only acid at the back of my throat.

I tried to walk into work carefully so the bottles wouldn't clank against each other in my backpack. I held it close to me instead of on my back, my treasure. A few of the girls were still setting up, I waved hello confidently, they complimented my straight hair, I made a disparaging joke about it being totally fried, we laughed. Before I made it into the kitchen, I was stopped by Mei. She had another manager with her and they sat me down in one of the back booths, I had never actually sat down in this area before, it was generally reserved for the older clientele, it was quieter and the servers in this section wore white button-ups and ties.

"How are you doing?" Mei began.

"Good, I got a few errands done before work, so that was nice."

"We're opening later because of a fridge issue."

"Oh, sorry."

"It's taken care of."

I imagined her walking into the smell of rotten meat. The air conditioning was set exceptionally high, I noticed, and the room smelled like cheap air freshener. The other manager didn't speak, he just smiled the entire time.

"So we wanted to speak to you about how you're doing."

"Like a review?"

"No. We don't think you fit . . . You don't really seem to be a good fit for the Keg culture we have here."

"Oh, is there something I should do?"

"No. We don't think it's working. But we thank you for your work, and good luck."

The male manager's smile was gone, turned into sympathetic nodding, and Mei held out her hand to shake mine, I took it, even though I was confused about what exactly was happening.

"I'm not working today?"

"Right, you're done here."

They didn't move from their seats. Slowly, I stood up, not saying another word, taking my backpack, the bottles clanked loudly together, I was mortified, and I hugged my bag tight as I walked out. A girl said hi to me as I left, adding she'd see me in there. It was strange to walk out of the Keg when it was still bright outside.

Fuck the Keg culture, and fuck Mei. They have no idea who the fuck they're talking to.

Tears began to roll down my face, slowly at first, creating little canals between the new pimples that were surfacing below the thick makeup. I was smiling like a fool, humming "Tears of a Clown" while trying desperately to stop crying. I was such a piece of shit! The people I passed on the sidewalk couldn't help but glance my way, I was a clown. Here it was finally, my public outburst, my last vestige of dignity, gone.

You're making a fucking scene.

"Okay!" I said, lifting my shoulders towards some unnamed deity in the sky.

You need to stop fucking talking to yourself.

"Yeah, yeah, yeah. It's square one, right? All good. All good."

YOU NEED TO FUCKING KILL YOURSELF.

I was never good at actually killing myself. I had saved up twelve of my grandmother's OxyContin pills before rehab. My get-out-of-life-free plan. I liked the safety net of having them, I guess my dad must have found them when he was cleaning out my apartment, what a guy for never mentioning it. I would never have taken them anyways, because I knew it would work, and I was a fucking coward.

I didn't know where to go. I stopped at a park and sat at a picnic table, wiping away every tear before it could stream down my face and further erode my layers of paint. It was getting dark, and I was alone with half a face of makeup and a backpack full of booze, the counsellors would be so disappointed. I'd been doing so well.

You fucking tried! And this is not, like, a fucking death sentence, chill out, fucking enjoy yourself. Honestly you checked all the boxes. That's a fucking win.

I should call my mother. Or see if my father wanted to have a late dinner and watch TV, but I didn't want them to know that I had lost my job. And for what? Not being a part of the culture? What did that even mean?

"I am just so fucking sad," I whispered.

Every fucking millennial is.

I had to get up, had to move somewhere, backwards or forwards, I heard the bottles in my backpack clanging, ominous bells. I looked towards the centre of the park, the hyenas were waiting. I walked out of the park onto the street, my skin felt raw, I felt as though if a person, any person, came up to me and asked if I was okay, I would collapse into them, my spine would fold a thousand times, and I would need them to carry me, let them take me anywhere. I clung tighter to my backpack, when was the last time I'd hugged someone or something I truly cared about? What a perfect time it would be to blow away, if only I didn't feel so heavy.

I forced myself to walk. And then walk more, far away from the park and then back. My feet were killing me but I didn't want to stop walking, because when I did, that meant I had reached the hostel. My final destination. I had no reason to keep walking. I thought I should sit on the hostel steps a bit, feel the cool concrete before I attempted the stairs to my room. I would faint, I was sure of it. But this night was different, the neon that lit up the streets seemed to be dimmed, could neon expire? Burn out? The street seemed quieter too, except I swore I could hear faint ringing, as if a bomb had gone off. The shadows on the stairs seemed to pulse, exaggerating the outline of my body. And the night was cold, the smog had turned from a sticky heat to a damp, cutting chill. My arm twitched, I moved it impulsively to try to quiet the twitch, but it began to travel from limb to limb, from one joint to the next, a burning sensation, a thirst, a hunger, a deep need to consume something, anything, or I would die. I had to get up, get away, go inside. Was I truly losing my mind?

I wondered what it looked like to others. What does it *look* like when you break?

My body moved. Where was my backpack? I couldn't feel it in my arms, no, there it was, I had slung it across my back, I needed to hold it again. I stood up taller, ignoring the shadows. I walked inside, across the empty lobby, to the third floor. I hugged my backpack, one, two, two bottles just like before, but my purse, did I still have that, yes, let me quickly feel the paper money in it, twenty, forty, it was all there. I had everything, now I was at the door.

The hallway was dark, the light must have burned out, I felt as if the darkness held me in stasis. Maybe if I moved, the lights would come on, all at once, the curtain would be pulled back, revealing the studio audience, and there would sit my family, some sweaty man with thick foundation and a bad purple suit asking them, "For five hundred dollars, can you guess what's in the backpack?"

I stared at the door, fearing Katya was on the other side, she would be out, she must be out, I couldn't hear a thing beyond the door. It seemed to be getting darker and colder, I should open the door. I slowly felt for my keys, shaking my head, just open the fucking door, open the fucking door. I should run, away from the door, back out onto the sidewalk, scream at someone to help me, but that was crazy. It wasn't crazy to open a door and lock it tight behind you.

The door opened but I didn't want to go in. I peeked inside the room. There was no one there. No Katya, just an empty room, a tomb. Everything looked grey, and so still. My entry would be an intrusion, a cannonball into a placid lake. Still, I couldn't just stand there, my evening calendar was booked and it was time to start the fucking show. I let the door close behind me, waiting for calm to take over my body, but it shook instead. I was safe, I was closed in tightly in this room, there would be no witnesses. I should shut the curtains, just in case. I went to the window. All I saw was my reflection. Remind me I'm real, remind me this isn't a fucking game.

Hi baby.

There behind the glass was the creature, teeth bared, sneering, eyes bloodshot, I could see the top of its head, blood in its fur, its hands were the hands of a giant man, and now they were pounding on the glass, he was relentless. I wanted to scream at it to leave, that I wasn't scared anymore.

I need you to stop lying to me. Stop fucking lying to me, my love.

I closed my eyes, pressing my hands into my cheeks, whimpering that they were safe, I was safe, promising myself in vain. I heard heavy footsteps up the stairs, I was begging for it to be Katya, anyone, any human to save me from myself. The door burst open behind me like a gunshot, and before I could turn, I felt the grip of a large hand, tight, around my neck, choking me.

So this is it, huh? This is where it fucking ends?

The hand loosened its grip, only enough for me to take one painful breath, to taste the blood in the back of my throat, it grabbed me again.

You're a fucking coward.

The creature was all over me, licking me, biting me, its hands invading my body, its nails lacerating my skin, it was every man who'd ever fucked me, held me down, stuffing my throat with their genitals and choking me. I was trying to scream but I couldn't breathe, the creature forced me roughly onto the bed, trying to force its way into me.

"You need to leave me alone!"

No, this is what you want. You want to be fucked and tortured, you want to die here, you poor pathetic girl.

I tried to fight it off, my arms were so weak compared to its giant limbs, it was on top of me now, I was wriggling under its weight, trying to free myself, trying to get air. I managed to loop one hand through my backpack strap, I swung and heard the bottles clank on top of my attacker's skull. I grabbed the bag and ran to the sink, I pulled out a bottle and emptied its contents, sobbing as I watched the liquid drain. I tried to drink from the tap but the creature dragged me back, peeling open my eyes and laughing at me, staring at me, whose eyes were those?

The creature was forcing his fingers between my ribs, breaking through skin and tendons and muscle fibre, trying to reach my heart. My mother would be the one to discover the bloody explosion, she would lose her mind again, she would die. My father would follow, drinking himself to an early death, and my brother, my stoic brother, he would suffer slowly, alone.

But this is what you get! This is what you wanted!

The creature was trying to lift me, trying to put its entire head through my stomach and wear my skin like a puppet. I was still clutching my one remaining bottle, it could free me, I tried to use it as a weapon, but I couldn't move my arm. The creature screamed and slammed my body back onto the bed. I was begging it, leave me, leave me here.

There's nowhere for me to go! You're my home, baby!

I was so tired, and bleeding out, I could feel my broken bones, the shock wearing off, I started convulsing, loosened my grip on the bottle, I was too tired to hold on.

"Then stay."

The creature shrunk down, lay on my flattened body, it felt so light now, like silk, slipping through my skin.

I heard a sound, a thud. I waited a second before opening my swollen eyes, wondering if I'd made it to heaven, an outside chance. But it was just my second bottle of wine, unbroken, it had rolled off the bed and onto my purse lying below.

Katya lay in her bed. I was still in my clothes, there was no sign of blood, my white bedsheets unstained. I felt my body, slowly, with my hands, making sure it was all there. Everything seemed in place.

I pushed the unopened bottle of wine aside and fished my cellphone out of my bag. I needed to call my mom, tell her I was coming home. I squinted at my phone, I had missed a call, just three minutes ago. It was the impassive landlord, he had left a message.

"Hey, Bobbi? Is this the woman I talked to about the apartment? Gimme a call when you have a moment, thanks."

———

It turned out a second apartment had opened up, the woman living there had been offered a job in Lethbridge and had jumped at the chance, left in a hurry. He told me I could move in that afternoon. He said it was almost the same as the other apartment, only the kitchen faced a small row of houses, their backyards, instead of the street. The bedroom/living area had no windows, but it did have a large skylight, he promised me it was properly sealed, he'd never had any leaks even in the worst rain, and it provided a lot of sunlight, and I didn't have to worry about people seeing in. Unless they were on the roof, but why would they be. I told him I didn't need to see it, I would arrive that afternoon with my things, and we could sort out the paperwork then, he asked if I was working, and I said no, coincidentally I had the day off.

I packed up my things quietly, careful not to wake up Katya, I left the unopened bottle for her, a present. She slept, or at least pretended to sleep, while I gathered my few things.

I passed reception, ready to face Hyle, but there was no one at the desk. I scribbled a note underneath my key, saying I was checking out, no need to refund me (like he would). I was tempted to write *fuck you*, but I didn't want to take one second longer and risk him appearing from the kitchen or somewhere. I just wanted to leave.

It's been four weeks since I moved into my bachelor apartment. I still don't know if I'm doing recovery correctly. I don't follow any steps. I sit in silence a lot, relearning how to speak into it, even singing sometimes. I saved my pink journal. I don't want to look back on the rehab pages. Even now, all I can write is "fuck this fuck that fuck her." But I don't worry about it. The words stay on the page, and I always feel a little better after writing them. For a few days I had a goal to try to laugh every day, but the one day I failed I was so heartbroken I decided that just trying to laugh ever, not necessarily every day, was good enough. I've been seeing both my mother and father once a week, and continuing to promise them I'm fine.

I've tried to picture it, the road, and the creature in a shitty car driving far away from me. But I still can never make it drive. I can picture myself though, driving alone, singing loudly, on the open road. I'm never sure where I'm going, but I can imagine my hair blowing backwards, my throat burning from screaming along to a bad '90s pop-punk song, the combination of the heat of the sun and the bite of the wind.

My kitchen has a big window, and it faces east, I've put a few plants there, where they catch the morning sun. I'm trying very hard to keep them alive. I've hung up artwork I printed out at the library. Pushing thumbtacks into the corners, smiling at the remaining empty walls, Look at me, decorating!

I got a job at a local neighborhood restaurant eighteen days ago, so far I've worked every one of them. All the dishes and counters are covered in dust and the basement is badly lit and I can never find extra glassware when I need it, but the other girls who work there are very helpful. The manager is an angry man so when he comes around I try to look busy by dusting things and shining surfaces. He wants us to call him by his surname only, King. I quickly learned that he does not want to make small talk, he does not want to talk at all, he told us to only communicate with him via group text, so even when I'm not working my phone constantly pings with terse orders to mop one of the two flooded bathrooms or with questions about why we're out of our cheapest lager again. When the girls reply, he often replies "Unacceptable" and doesn't respond again for hours.

The girls are nice though, I told them I didn't drink for "health reasons" and they accepted it. They like my animal facts. Recently I told them how smaller fish form a large ball, swimming as fast as they can to not only look like one bigger unfuckwithable fish, but also to make it harder for a predator to break their fish wall and eat them. One of the girls said, "Isn't that just being a woman, we all have to stick together so dudes don't mess with us." It almost brought me to tears when she renamed our group chat "Fishball."

I don't get invited to go out with them, but one morning we did a clothing swap, each girl bringing a bag of unwanted clothing. We took a few things from each other, commenting on the things earlier versions of ourselves used to wear. We gently mocked each other, as friends do, about our past sartorial choices, and the stories that surrounded them. My stories made them laugh, their stories made me smile, I would get there, to laughter, they didn't seem to mind. Then two of them dragged the remaining unwanted clothes to a nearby women's shelter.

In the last text I got from Len, she told me Steph was dead. She wasn't the girl in the suitcase, she was the girl who, at age seventeen, after getting kicked out of a halfway house and with no place to go, hitched out to Vancouver and never came back. I found her obituary online, but all it included was her name, date of birth, date of death, and a short write-up saying she was a promising young girl, and that she was with God now. I was at work when Len's text came in, so I told a co-worker I would do stock and went and stood in the walk-in fridge until I started getting messages from King in all-caps yelling about not letting non-paying customers use the washroom. I told Steph that I'd keep her in Vancouver, far away from her father, and I thanked her for holding my hand so many times in rehab.

I asked Len later how rehab went the second time and never heard back from her. Somehow I doubt I will. Recently I saw on her Facebook page that she was at a cottage with a group of women all decked out in T-shirts emblazoned with cheap-beer logos and corny patriotic slogans like "Canadian as Fuck" and "I'm from Canada. Sorry for Partying, Eh!" Len was still in her tight sweatpants and thin white tank top, making obscene gestures in most of the photos.

The last time I saw a woman from rehab was just two days ago, a few blocks from my place. There she was, still eighty pounds, still smoking and arguing with an invisible audience. Tammy. She was coming out of a walk-up with a trash bag as big as her, a lit smoke dangling from her mouth. The bag looked heavy and for a moment I thought I should run to her and help. I wondered what I would say to her, congratulate her for what, being alive? She'd most likely tell me in her slow sarcastic drawl to either grab the bag or fuck off, then make fun of me to the empty spaces on the sidewalk, and that thought made me happy. Tammy was her own beautiful creature, Tammy would tell Tammy to fuck off when Tammy wanted to drink, and Tammy would tell Tammy to get her shit together and clean out her fucking house. Tammy wouldn't be scared of the shadows, because she was logical, shadows will always be there.

Always, baby.

Tammy would know that shadows don't exist without light, and maybe there's something poetic there. But Tammy wouldn't make it that complicated. Tammy would just say something like, "Well, obviously life can be a bit of a fucking problem, okay?" And turn towards her invisible audience.

ACKNOWLEDGEMENTS

A huge thank-you to my husband, Mark, for his unwavering support. He oftentimes filled in for a certain journal and constantly let me unload every anxious and self-doubting thought, only to respond with love or one of his two jokes. They never get old, and I love you. Thank you to my family—my mother, Miriam, holy shit I'd probably be dead and bookless without you. Hope this acknowledgement suffices as thanks enough for that. To my father, Neal, I'm eternally grateful to have your dark sense of humour and freakishly good dance moves. Both lifesavers in their own way. To Erik and M.P., for always being supportive but never making me explain in detail what the book was about. My brother, Owen, my safety net (even all the way in Winnipeg); Bronwyn, a truly amazing sister-in-law; and sister, Ana/Chips, for the right meme in the darkest times, thank you.

To my agents: Alba Ziegler-Bailey, thank you for all your input and for not giving up when I sent you the first draft years ago. I am forever in awe of your patience. To Sarah Chalfant and Jessica Bullock, I am so thrilled to be represented by two incredibly intelligent and skilled women such as yourselves. To my editors Kiara Kent and Melanie Tutino, thank you for making sense of my run-on sentences and so kindly helping me to explain this world. It is an incredible privilege to be able to work with you both.

Finally, to my kids: You did nothing to help—you actually made this process incredibly difficult—but once you learn to read, know that I'm so grateful for the pressure your respective births put on me to finish the first and then final draft. I've never written an acknowledgement before; it's weird and great and thank you.